The Sultan's Wife

The Sultan's Wife

JANE JOHNSON

VIKING
an imprint of
PENGUIN BOOKS

VIKING

Published by the Penguin Group
Penguin Books Ltd, 80 Strand, London WC2R ORL, England
Penguin Group (USA) Inc., 375 Hudson Street, New York, New York 10014, USA
Penguin Group (Canada), 90 Eglinton Avenue East, Suite 700, Toronto, Ontario, Canada M4P 2Y3
(a division of Pearson Penguin Canada Inc.)
Penguin Ireland, 25 St Stephen's Green, Dublin 2, Ireland (a division of Penguin Books Ltd)
Penguin Group (Australia), 250 Camberwell Road,
Camberwell, Victoria 3124, Australia (a division of Pearson Australia Group Pty Ltd)
Penguin Books India Pvt Ltd, 11 Community Centre,
Panchsheel Park, New Delhi – 110 017, India
Penguin Group (NZ), 67 Apollo Drive, Rosedale, Auckland 0632, New Zealand
(a division of Pearson New Zealand Ltd)
Penguin Books (South Africa) (Pty) Ltd, Block D, Rosebank Office Park, 181 Jan Smuts Avenue,
Parktown North, Gauteng 2193, South Africa

Penguin Books Ltd, Registered Offices: 80 Strand, London WC2R ORL, England

www.penguin.com

First published 2012
001

Set in 12 / 14.75 Bembo Book MT Std
Typeset by Palimpsest Book Production Limited, Falkirk, Stirlingshire
Printed in Great Britain by Clays Ltd, St Ives plc

A CIP catalogue record for this book is available from the British Library

ISBN: 978-0-670-91800-3

www.greenpenguin.co.uk

ALWAYS LEARNING   PEARSON

For Abdel

PART ONE

I

First 5th Day of Rabi al-Awwal
Year 1087 Anno Hegirae (1677 in the Christian calendar)
Meknes, Kingdom of Morocco

The rain has been coming down hard since the early hours, turning the ground to a quagmire. It beats on the roof tiles and on the terraces where usually women hang out washing and spy on the comings and goings of the men below. It beats on the green faience of the Chaouia Mosque and on the four golden apples and the crescent moon atop its tall minaret. It streaks the walls surrounding the palace with dark stains like blood.

The artisans stand with their robes plastered to their bodies, staring at the massive slabs of cedar for the main gate, now sodden and mud-spattered. No one thought to protect the wood against rain: this is the time when marigolds should carpet the scarred red hills like drifts of orange snow and figs begin to swell in city gardens.

A continent away, the French king is engaged in extravagant plans for his palace and gardens at Versailles. Sultan Moulay Ismail, Emperor of Morocco, has declared he will construct a palace to dwarf this Versailles: the walls will run from here in Meknes for three hundred miles over the mountains of the Middle Atlas all the way to Marrakech! The first stage – the Dar Kbira, with its twelve towering pavilions, mosques and hammams, courtyards and gardens, kitchens and barracks and koubbas – is nearing completion. The Bab al-Raïs, the main gate to the complex, is to be inaugurated in a day's time. Provincial governors from all parts of the empire have arrived for the dedication, bringing with them presents of slaves, cloth-of-gold, French clocks and silver candlesticks. At midnight Ismail plans to slaughter a wolf with his own hands, set its skull in the wall and bury its body beneath the gateway. But how, if the door itself – symbol of the entire grand enterprise – is not finished? And what will the sultan do if his plans are thwarted?

At least one of the artisans is contemplatively feeling the back of his neck.

Across the compound a group of European slaves toils away on top of the outer walls, repairing a monstrous hole where there has been an overnight collapse. The pisé is waterlogged: the sand and lime were probably not correctly cured in the first place, and now the rain has made it fatally unstable. No doubt the repair will fail too, and then everyone will be flogged for negligence. Or worse.

The workers are meagre of flesh and pale of skin, their faces sharpened by hunger, their tunics ripped and filthy. One of them, heavy-bearded and hollow-eyed, gazes across the desolate scene. 'God's bones, it's cold enough to kill hogs.'

His neighbour nods glumly. 'As grim as Hull in winter.'

'At least there's ale in Hull.'

'Aye, and women.'

A general sigh.

'Even the women of Hull look good to me after five months in this place.'

'And to think you went to sea to get away from women!'

The laughter this remark provokes is brief and bitter. Survivors of months in the stinking underground matamores in which they have been confined by these foreign devils after being seized from merchant vessels and fishing boats from Cork to Cornwall, they have spent their first weeks in Morocco telling their stories to one another, keeping the dream of home alive.

Will Harvey straightens up suddenly, pushing his rain-slick hair out of his face. 'Christ's eyes, will you look at that?'

They all turn. An inner door within the great palace door opens and an odd contraption pokes out, followed by a tall figure that has to bend almost double to exit, then draws itself up to an exaggerated height. It wears a scarlet robe partially covered by a white woollen cloak with gold borders. Above its turbaned head it holds a round testern of cloth on a long handle which shields it from the driving rain.

'What the devil *is* it?' Harvey demands.

'I believe it's a bongrace,' ventures the Reverend Ebslie.

'Not the implement, you dolt: the thing that holds it. Look at how it picks its way like a trained Spanish pony!'

The figure moves gingerly between the pools of standing water. Over its jewelled slippers it wears a pair of high cork pattens at which the mud sucks greedily. The workers watch its progress with growing fascination and soon begin to catcall:

'Clownish fool!'

'Catamite!'

It is a rare pleasure to pass a fraction of their torment on to another, even if their target is a foreigner and does not comprehend the insults.

'Mincing coxcomb!'

'Lily-white quean!'

'Half-and-half!'

As if this last and most innocuous remark has found its mark, the figure suddenly halts and, tilting the ridiculous contraption back, gazes up at them. If its demeanour and clothing have given the appearance of wilting femininity, the face that is turned up to the hecklers gives the lie to that impression. Lily-white it most certainly is not; nor delicate either. It looks as if it has been carved out of obsidian, or some hard wood blackened by age. Like a war-mask, grim and immobile, it gives no sign of the human beneath – except that a warning line of white shows under the black iris of the eye as the man's gaze scorches over them.

'You should be more careful whom you insult.'

A shocked silence falls over the group of slaves.

'One click of my fingers will bring your overseers running.'

In the shelter of a doorway some thirty yards away four men are brewing up a samovar of tea. The vapour from the pot wreaths around them so that they look like wraiths. But the impression of insubstantiality is deceptive: given the opportunity to dole out punishment they would abandon their tea-making in an eye-blink and come storming into the world of men, whips and cudgels at the ready.

The prisoners shuffle awkwardly, too late realizing the gravity of their error. No one else speaks English in this godforsaken country!

The courtier regards them dispassionately. 'Those men have been chosen for their ruthlessness. Not an ounce of common humanity remains to them. They are instructed to punish the lazy and the insubordinate without mercy and will kill you and bury your corpses in the very walls you are rebuilding without any regret. There are always more to take your place. Life is cheap in Meknes.'

The captives know this is no less than the truth. Desperately, they look to Will Harvey as their spokesman (after all it was his fault for drawing their attention to the man in the first place); but his head is bowed as if waiting for a blow. No one says a word. The tension is palpable.

At last Harvey raises his head. His expression is mulish. 'Are you a man? Or a devil? Would you see us die for a few unwise words?'

There is an intake of breath from the others; but for a moment the courtier gives him a bleak smile; then the mask is back in place. 'Am I a man? Ah, that is a good question . . .' He pauses, allowing them a good look at his gold-trimmed cloak, the expensive bracelets on his muscled black forearms, the silver bond on his left ear. 'I am a half-thing, a nobody: a slave, just like you. You should be thankful that when they cut me, they did not take my heart.' The testern swings back to obscure his face.

No one says a word, unsure what is meant. They watch as the courtier continues to pick his way through the mud towards the long stretch of waste ground that lies between the palace and the *medina* beyond. He passes the overseers; pauses. They hold their breath. Clearly, greetings have been exchanged, but no more. At last, chastened, cognizant that they have survived a hair's-breadth escape, they resume their never-ending toil. They live to work – and die – another day. And that, at the final count, is all any of us can ask.

2

'Peace be upon you, sir.'

Sidi Kabour is a slight, elderly man with an immaculate white beard, carefully manicured hands and perfect manners. You would never take him to be the greatest expert in poisons in all Morocco. He tilts his head and smiles up at me, blandly polite, the neutral formality of his greeting designed to give the impression he has never met me before, as if I am just another random customer who has stumbled on his hidden stall at the back of the Henna Souq, drawn by the scent of incense, Taliouine saffron and more illicit substances. In truth he knows me well: my mistress has frequent need of his skills.

At once my court-bred instincts are on the alert. I look down at him, my already considerable height further elevated by the ridiculous pattens. 'And with you, *fkih*.' Giving nothing away.

His left eye twitches and I glance past him. There is a man in the shadows at the rear of the shop. When I look back the storekeeper purses his lips. *Be careful.*

'What rain!' I try for joviality.

'My wife, God watch over her, took all the carpets from the guest salon yesterday at noon and hung them out on the terrace to air.'

'And forgot to bring them in?'

Sidi Kabour gives a helpless shrug. 'Her mother was sick: she spent the night sitting with her and remembered the carpets only after first prayer. They were my grandmother's, woven of good strong wool, but the colours have run.' He grimaces, but I know the conversation is designed only to dull the ears of the lurking client. As he lists the herbs he mixed for his mother-in-law and the effects they have had on her constipation, the man speaks.

'Do you have root of wolf's onion?'

The hairs on the back of my neck rise. Wolf's onion is a rare plant with contradictory properties. Beneficial substances in its tuber can stem bleeding and promote the rapid healing of wounds, as I know only too well. However, the leaves in reduction have the ability to produce a deadly toxin. The scarcity of the plant and its powerful effects render its price extravagantly high. The buyer's accent places him as coming from somewhere between the lower Atlas range and the Great Desert, which is the region in which wolf's onion is most commonly found (and looking down I see he wears slippers with round toes, which you do not commonly find here in the north). He must therefore know that it can be bought in the souq in Tafraout at a far more reasonable price. Which means that to this man, or to the master he serves, money is of no object, and the need for the plant is urgent. But the question remains: is it required for healing or for killing?

Sidi Kabour scurries to the back of the shop. I feel the man's eyes upon me and smile blandly at him, only to be taken aback by the intensity of his stare. Courtiers are often envied; luxury men and blackamoors frequently despised. I put his look down to such prejudice. '*Salaam aleikum*. Peace be with you, sir.'

'And with you.'

On the pretext of removing the wretched pattens, I slip the paper I am holding, which contains a list of the required items, beneath a bottle of the Empress Zidana's preferred brand of musk, where Sidi Kabour will know to find it. We have used this system before, he and I: you can never be too careful when you deal in secrets. I stow the overshoes beneath the stall, where I can retrieve them later, then straighten up, making a great show of brushing rain off my cloak, so that the stranger can see my hands are empty.

His eyes are still upon me: his gaze makes my skin crawl. Have I seen him around the court? The cast of his face is in some way familiar. Under his knitted red skullcap his bones lie close to the surface: he would be considered handsome if it were not for a certain meanness around the mouth. No slave-bond in his ear. A freedman? A merchant in his own right? Anything is possible: Morocco is one of the world's trade crossroads, the entire country a marketplace. But if the man is a mere merchant why did Sidi Kabour flash me a warning? And why is this man attempting to purchase, in plain hearing, a powerful poison? If he knows who I am, he must know I am here on a similar mission. Is it some sort of test? And if so, by whom?

Of course, I have my suspicions. I have my enemies, and so does my mistress.

Sidi Kabour reappears. 'Is this what you're looking for?'

The customer sniffs the tubers as if he can by the sheer power of his nose ascertain whether they meet his standards. Another false note: any true poisoner knows it matters not how old the root is: like its cousin, the lily, the wolf onion preserves its lethal qualities indefinitely.

'How much?'

The herbman names an extortionate price and the man agrees to it with a minimum of haggling. Which decides me that there is something sinister going on. While the southerner is digging in his pouch for the coins, I walk quickly away out into the Henna Souq, almost colliding with a handcart piled high with water vessels, pots and pans, swiftly putting several donkeys, a bustle of veiled women and a gaggle of children between myself and any pursuer. Taking refuge under the awning of a coffee stall, I stare back and watch the people pass by, looking for sharp features under a knitted red skullcap. When it becomes clear that no one is in pursuit, I curse my foolishness. The catcalling of the European slaves has set my nerves on edge. I am not myself.

Besides, there are errands to be run for my master: I have no time to dally here, coddling my paranoia. Best leave Sidi Kabour to get rid of the southerner and set about fulfilling the empress's order: I will return for it later. There are some items on the list that may take him some while to prepare.

The horse-dresser's stall is on the other side of the souq, beyond the cloth-merchants, haberdashers and tailors, the cordwainers and cobblers. The caparisoner is a big man, almost as dark as myself, with large, lugubrious features that, on hearing my request, arrange themselves in an expression of almost comical dismay. 'A shitbag? Embroidered in *gold*?'

I nod. 'It is for a very holy horse. It has made the pilgrimage to Mecca and its droppings cannot be allowed to fall upon the ground.' I explain in precise detail the design Moulay Ismail desires.

The man's eyes bulge. 'And how much will the sultan pay for such intricate work?' But already he looks defeated: he knows the answer.

I spread my hands apologetically. The sultan never parts with a coin if he can help it. The country and everything within it pertain to him: what need to pay? What need for money at all in such a system? But my master hoards it in the Treasury and, if rumour is to be believed, in many secret chambers dug beneath the palace grounds. The day after his brother Sultan Moulay Rachid died, celebrating the Great Feast by riding his horse wildly through the gardens of his palace in Marrakech until fatally crowned by a low-hanging orange branch, Ismail occupied the Treasury at Fez and declared himself emperor. Since he thus controlled their pay, the army at once pledged their support. He is a wily man, my master: he has a nose for power. He makes a good emperor, albeit self-styled.

I remind the poor caparisoner that the royal commission is sure to win him more lucrative work from those who wish to ape my master's example, but, as I leave him, I can see he is not convinced there will be many other takers for gold-embroidered shitbags.

The rest of my important tasks are accomplished with greater ease, since the tradesmen know the score well enough. Besides, it is an honour to supply the emperor, descended as he is directly from the Prophet. It is something to boast of. Some have even made signs which read: *By order of His Majesty, Sultan Moulay Ismail, Emperor of Morocco, God grant him Glory and Long Life.* He'll live longer than any of us, I think as I walk on. Certainly longer than any of those of us within reach of his temper. Or his sword.

My next appointment is the one I am most looking forward to. The Coptic Bookseller visits Meknes seldom. He has made a special visit at this auspicious time with an addition Ismail has requested for his famed collection of holy books. Not that Ismail can read a word of these volumes himself (what need when he can pay scholars to do it for him? Besides, he has the whole of the Qur'an by heart, a skill which he likes to demonstrate frequently). But he loves his books and treats them with great veneration: he has a great deal more respect for his books than he does for human life.

After the usual fulsome greetings and inquiries after his wife, children, mother, cousins, and goats, the Egyptian leaves me to fetch the order from the strongroom he rents when he is in town, and I idle away the time breathing in the scents of old leather and parchment, touching the well-loved covers, poring over the engraved verses. The bookseller is breathless and flushed and the hood of his *djellaba* is wet through when he comes bustling back. When he takes the book out of its linen wrap, I can see why he has not kept it amongst his usual stock, for its beauty steals my breath. Its bindings have been gilded in two tones of gold. Intricate patterns are tooled into a central panel contained within a bold double border. It reminds me of the carpets in the sultan's own chambers, gorgeous things from far-off Herat and Tabriz.

'May I?' I keep my face very still, but my hands are shaking as I reach for it.

'From Shiraz. Made in the time of the early Safavids. See the cutwork on the inner board? It is exquisitely done, but very fragile.'

'Is this silk or paper?' I run my fingertips over the delicate openwork pattern cut into the inside of the cover, revealing jewel-like lozenges of turquoise beneath.

The Coptic Bookseller smiles indulgently. 'Silk, of course.'

I open the volume at random and come upon the 113th Sura, the Al-Falaq. Tracing the swirling calligraphy with a finger, I read aloud: 'I seek shelter with the Lord of the daybreak, from the evil of what He has created, and from the evil of darkness when it falls. And from the evil of witchcrafts when sorceresses blow on the knots, and from the evil of men when they envy me . . .' It could describe my world. I look up. 'It is an edition worthy of the beauty of the words it contains.'

'It is indeed a priceless treasure.'

'If I were to tell the sultan you say this book is without price, he is likely to shrug and say that nothing he can give will be sufficient and that therefore he will give you nothing.' I pause. 'But I am authorized to make you an offer.' I name a very substantial sum. He cites one twice as large, and after some polite haggling we settle somewhere between the two.

'Come to the palace the morning after the inauguration,' I tell him, 'and the grand vizier will honour this agreement.'

'I will bring the book to the sultan tomorrow.'

'I must take the book with me now: Moulay Ismail is impatient to see it. Besides, tomorrow is the day of gathering: he will not see visitors.'

'In this weather? If one drop of rain touches it, it will be ruined. Let me bring it to the palace myself on the sabbath, suitably boxed for presentation.'

'I will lose my head if I do not return with the book, and ugly though my head is I have become oddly attached to it.'

The man gives me a crooked smile, and I remember that despite the vaunted wife and children he is known to have a boy or two whom he pays well for their favours, a practice that may well be acceptable in Egypt but had best be hidden in Ismail's Morocco. 'Ugly it is not; I would not see it parted from the rest of you, Nus-Nus. Take it, then: but guard it with your life. I will come for payment on the morning of the sabbath.' Sighing, he wraps it reverently in the linen and hands it over. 'Remember: it is quite irreplaceable.'

I would be lying if I say I am not anxious about carrying such a treasure, but I have only two more errands to complete: some spices for my friend Malik, and a quick return to the herbman to pick up Zidana's items.

Malik and I are in the habit of trading favours: we have become friends by necessity as much as by inclination, since he is Ismail's chief cook and I the sultan's food-taster, amongst my many other duties. Mutual trust is useful in such circumstances. Malik's needs — *ras al hanout* mixed to his own recipe and an essence of attar to which Ismail is partial in his couscous — take me back to the Spice Quarter, where I make the necessary purchases. Thence it is only a short step to the hidden stall of Sidi Kabour.

I duck beneath the awning and am surprised to find the place unattended. Perhaps Sidi Kabour has slipped out to take tea with a fellow stallholder, or to fetch more charcoal for his brazier. I move the bottle of musk to one side and am gratified to see that Zidana's list is gone. Perhaps the herbman has gone to fetch an item kept in more discreet premises . . .

Another minute passes and still there is no sign of him. The heady scent of the incense burning in its brass container is becoming quite stifling. It is not the usual pleasant fragrance Sidi Kabour favours — a little elemi resin mixed with white benzoin — but a more complex combination out of which

I can detect wood of aloe and the clashing scents of amber and pine resin, one sweet, one acrid, which no one in their right mind would combine.

Come along, I mutter, and feel my gut twist with anxiety. Wait or go? My anxiety begins to mount. Soon the sultan will begin his afternoon rounds and expect me to accompany him as I always do. But if I go back without Zidana's purchases, she will fly into a fury or, worse, into one of those silent musings that tend to precede an act of cruel retribution. Being caught between the two of them is the daily peril of my existence. Sometimes it is difficult to know which of them is the more dangerous: the sultan with his towering rages and sudden outbursts of violence, or his chief wife with her more subtle terrors. I am not sure that I believe in the efficacy of her magic, for, despite being raised in similar traditions (I amongst the Senufo, her with the neighbouring Lobi), I like to think I have acquired a degree of enlightenment on my travels. Of her ability to use all manner of subtle poisons effectively, though, I have no doubt at all. I do not enjoy ferrying poisons for the empress, facilitating her wicked death-dealing, but, as a slave of the court, I have little choice. The Meknes court is a spider's web of connivance and deceit, confusion and intrigue. Making a straight path for yourself in such a place is near impossible: even the most upright man can find himself fatally compromised.

I pace fretfully to the back of the shop. Boxes containing the spines of porcupines and the eyelashes of mice (those belonging to male mice in one box; those to female mice in another), antimony, arsenic and gold dust; dried chameleons, hedgehogs, serpents and salamanders. Charms against the evil eye; love potions; titbits to draw *djinns* as surely as sugar draws wasps. As I make my way along the dusty back wall, I am confronted by an enormous glass jar full of eyeballs. Recoiling, I catch my hip on the shelving and the jar wobbles dangerously, setting its contents jiggling, till they all appear to be staring at me, as if I have woken a host of trapped djinns. Then I realize the angle of the shelf shifted when I banged into it. I set the linen-wrapped Qur'an down carefully beside me and adjust the shelf so that the jar sits more safely, and applaud myself for averting disaster. I wonder how Sidi Kabour has procured so many human eyeballs, but then realize the pupils are vertical slots, like those of the eyes of cats, or goats.

I must make my way straight back to the palace to attend Moulay Ismail, and explain to Zidana that her requests are being fulfilled and that I will return for them later that day and hope that luck is still running with me. It is the only sensible thing to do. I turn decisively; too quickly . . . catch my foot on some obstacle on the floor behind me, and lose my balance.

I am usually agile, but the eyeballs have unsettled me – or possibly even caused my fall, just as I was congratulating myself on evading their evil influence – and the next thing I know I am on my back with my head jammed up against a pile of baskets, which now totter and come tumbling down, covering me in porcupine spines, dried scorpions and – I pick something off and hold it out with distaste – a veritable plague of dead frogs. In some agitation I spring to my feet, brushing the vile things off me. The spines and scorpions' claws caught in the wool of my burnous are hanging on for grim life. I pluck them off one by one, then catch up the back of my cloak to examine it and see that I have also managed to knock over a container of cochineal, which is creeping upwards through the white wool in a greedy red tide.

All composure deserts me: the cloak, a fine piece, finer than any I could ever afford to buy for myself, was one of Ismail's own, and now it is ruined. Usually when you are given a gift you can do with it as you will, but the sultan has an acute memory and an unfortunate way of asking why you are not wearing whichever item he has grandly presented to you: I have seen more than one man lose a limb, or his life, over an unsatisfactory answer.

Snatching up the corner, I begin to wring the red liquid out of it, only to find it thicker and darker than cochineal and sticky on my palms; and now a bitter tang fills my mouth and nose, a smell that has nothing to do with crushed beetles, or incense or anything beautiful or sacred.

Looking down in some dread now, I find that the obstacle over which I stumbled is indeed the corpse of Sidi Kabour. Someone has slit his throat for him as neatly as a sheep's at Eid. His handsome white beard has been severed too and lies on his chest in a great clot of gore. And in the moment of his death his bowels have voided, which is the filthy smell that underlies the iron: the incense brazier must have been laden with whatever came to hand in an attempt to mask the stink.

A great sadness fills me. Muslims teach that death is an obligation upon us, a task to be completed and never shirked; that it is neither a punishment nor a tragedy, and not to be feared. But somehow that gentle philosophy does not encompass the brutality of this death. Sidi Kabour was a fastidious man in life: that he should have been butchered so and left to lie in a sea of his own blood and filth with his eyes gazing unseeing into the gloom is repulsive. I bend to close those poor, staring eyes, and find something protruding from his grey lips. I prise it away.

Even before I examine it I know with a dull certainty what it is. A chewed corner of the list I made of Zidana's demands: clearly the old man tried to prevent its being taken by eating it. That, or someone has forced it into his mouth. The rest is gone, but whether into Sidi Kabour's gullet or the hands of his murderer I do not know. Nor can I stay to find out: for another terrible thought strikes me; then another.

The first is that I am covered in blood and will be clearly marked out as the assassin. The second is the memory of laying the priceless Qur'an down at my feet when righting the shelf on which the jar of eyeballs rests.

Feeling bile rise into my throat, I turn around, only to have my worst fears confirmed. The once-spotless white of the protective linen is now dyed a patchy crimson. I rip the fabric away from the precious object within . . .

Blood upon a holy Qur'an is a terrible sacrilege. But blood upon the Safavid Qur'an for which Ismail has been pining presages a slow and painful death.

For me.

3

I stare at the ruined book, and then at the dead man, trying to take in the enormity of the situation, thought spinning off uselessly in all directions. I should declare the murder, make a statement to the authorities, assure them of my innocence. But who will believe a slave? For that is all I am, whatever my status inside the palace. Within its walls lies a magical, protected realm; but outside, I am nothing but an overdressed black man covered in an honest merchant's blood. And if I am arrested, I do not fool myself into thinking that the sultan will be so concerned as to save me from my fate: he is much more likely to fall into a temper because I am late and lop off my head the moment he sees me again.

I tear off my ruined cloak and bundle the blood-soaked Qur'an inside it. I look around and see Sidi Kabour's ancient burnous hanging on a peg beside the entrance. He does not dress the part of a rich man: but that is the Muslim way, not to proclaim a better fortune than your neighbour. I stalk over to the cloak, only belatedly realizing I am leaving a trail of bloody footprints in my wake. The burnous is too short, but I feel anonymous in it; except of course for my jewelled yellow slippers, which are now a dull crimson. In this country, only women wear red footwear, and, whatever else I might be, I am not a woman. Off they come, into the bundle with the book. Better barefoot than bloodstained; better to be taken as a beggar or a Jew than a murderer. I pull the long, pointed hood up over my turban, hunch my shoulders to disguise my height, sling the bundle over my back and walk quickly out into the souq with my head down.

'Sidi Kabour!'

The voice is curious, inquiring. I do not turn around.

At the first set of gates I am waved in by the palace guards, who are too bored and chilled to be curious about my change of attire. I cross the processional square and pass quickly by the magazines and the vast barracks, where ten thousand of the sultan's Black Guards are stationed; then through a second set of gates leading into the pavilions.

Striding at speed, I dodge piles of building sand and pyramids of lime mortar; vats of *tadelakt* plaster, stacks of timber and tiles. I run past the koubba, where the sultan keeps the gifts he is brought in tribute. (How furious the givers would be to know that the rare items they so carefully selected have been thrown in a great pile to gather dust. Ismail is like his small son Zidan; he grows bored with his gifts minutes after receiving them.) The guards should have challenged me: a running, bloodied, barefoot man carrying who knows what under his arm; but they are inside, sheltering from the weather.

As I draw closer to the sultan's pavilions, the personnel are of necessity more alert. 'Hoi! You there! Show your face and tell us your business.'

It is Hassan, and behind him are three of Ismail's most trusted guards, terrifying-looking men half a head taller than I and massively muscled. I have seen Hassan break a man's neck with his bare hands, and Yaya take a lance through the thigh without so much as blinking. I push back the hood of the burnous. 'It's me, Nus-Nus.'

'You look like a drowned rat caught stealing bread from the granary.'

'Laundry.' Which is at least true in part.

'Well, you'd best get into the dry or it'll be soaked for a second time.'

I walk quickly past them through the vast horseshoe archway and into the great hall, my bare feet slapping and skidding on the marble. I can hear a knot of courtiers coming in my direction. I reach my room, an antechamber to Ismail's pavilion, and slip inside just before they come into view.

In the fountain in the courtyard outside I wash my feet and hands of blood, hoping no one is watching, and then bury the ruined *babouches* in the loose soil beneath the hibiscus. But what to do with the burnous and the Qur'an? My sparse little chamber is still a grand space, with its arched window, cedarwood ceiling and *zellij* walls, but other than my narrow horsehair divan it contains only a prayer mat, a lap-desk for my writing implements, and a wooden chest on top of which sits one incense burner and a candlestick. These, the clothes I stand up in, the contents of the pouch I carry and those in the chest, are the sum of my worldly possessions.

I put aside the incense burner and candlestick and empty the contents of the chest on to my bed and barely have time to stow the bundle inside when I hear the sultan's voice.

'Nus-Nus!'

That voice is unmistakable. No matter how quietly he speaks, no matter the crowd or the chatter that surrounds him, it affects not just my auditory senses but something visceral, deep inside. I throw off the spoiled crimson robe, put on the first thing that comes to hand (a dark blue woollen tunic), kick on my old babouches, dash out and prostrate myself.

'Get up, Nus-Nus! Where is the book?'

My poor dazed wits have not yet created a plausible excuse for the whereabouts of the ruined Qur'an. I lie with my forehead pressed against the cold tiles, imagining people asking: Did he die well, poor Nus-Nus? Was there much blood? What were his last words?

'The book, boy! Get up! Go and get it! How else are we to record my amendments?'

It takes a moment or two for comprehension to seep into my addled brain and the wave of relief when it comes almost renders my legs inoperable. I scramble to my feet, run back into my room and grab up the book and the lap-desk and run back outside.

Ismail watches me steadily. He tugs on his beard, which is very dark and divided into a neat fork. Above it, his eyes are bright and black, the lids heavy and hooded. There appears to be a glint of amusement in his regard, as if he knows something I do not, which may well have to do with the time and manner of my departure from this earthly life. But he is wearing green today, which is a good sign. Green is his favourite (being the Prophet's own colour) and wearing it tends to signify that he does not have bloodshed on his mind. Red, now – or yellow – that is a different matter. We all look to ourselves when he wears red or yellow, or has his page carry a change of clothing.

'Come!'

He turns his back on me and I fall into line along with the foremen of works, a great gaggle of them, followed by the Kaid Mohammed ben Hadou Ottur (known also as Al-Attar, the Tinker) in conversation with three other court luminaries, and lastly the Hajib: the grand vizier himself, Chief Minister Si Abdelaziz ben Hafid. It is the Hajib who now catches me up and walks beside me.

'Are you well, Nus-Nus? You seem a little winded.' His fleshy lips are curved into a smile, but expression does not reach his eyes. We all have our masks in this place.

'Quite well, *sidi*, thank you for asking.'

'*Alhemdulillah.*'

'Thanks be to God,' I echo formally, though how such a man can mention the name of the Compassionate One without being struck dead on the spot amazes me.

'I am glad to hear it. I would be most distressed if anything bad were to happen to you.' He looks down. 'It seems you have cut yourself.'

My heart shudders. 'It's just mud.' I hold his gaze defiantly and watch as the smile fades from his mouth, leaving his face as inhuman as a reptile's. Then he allows his hand to fall so casually it looks accidental, but in such a manner that it brushes my groin. He watches as I try and fail to repress my revulsion.

'So you say, Nus-Nus. So you say.'

His eyes pin me for a moment more, then he turns and powers his way through the entourage to join the sultan, a tangible reminder to me and all others that he regards himself – he alone – as being on a par with our sovereign.

Ben Hadou's pale gaze sweeps over him, and as it does so I can feel the dislike flow off the kaid, a dislike tinged with contempt, though his face remains stony. Then he turns his head and those grey eyes – sharp, watchful – come to rest on me and I feel as if in those seconds he has perceived everything that has passed between my enemy and me.

The creation of the imperial palace complex at Meknes is an act of immense hubris, grand to the point of monomaniacal. We have heard from some of the better-connected French captives that their king is attempting a similar project, on a rather meaner scale, though currently it is not much more than a hunting lodge in the middle of a mosquito-ridden swamp. When

Ismail first heard about it he laughed dismissively. 'Those Europeans, all they create are follies, personal extravagances that can amount to nothing. But when my project is completed it will be a city of magnificent distances: the grandest offering to the grace of God that anyone has ever made. I am taking a waste land and transforming it to the glory of Allah. His holy word shall be writ large upon the ground, upon the walls and in every detail: his eternal and infinite design brought into existence in the corporeal world!'

The waste land today is being recalcitrant: we encounter problem after problem, which I must minute carefully in the records book as we go. My scattered wits have made me a poor scribe, and the rain does its best to compound the problem, blurring the ink and even completely washing away the words in places. As soon as I am dismissed I run back to my chamber. If I do not write down *right away* the precise instructions Ismail dictated and deliver them at once to the chief of works at once his wrath will be swift and sure.

I sit cross-legged on my divan, open the lap-desk and, dipping my reed pen in the ink, write carefully: 'First, the Bab al-Raïs to be reinforced with iron studs and horizontal bands. A new chief craftsman to be found to add a sunburst design and crescent moons, since if the French king is to designate himself Roi Soleil, Ismail will command both day and night. The new design to be achieved before the inauguration.

'Next, the guardhouse to be demolished and rebuilt on the east side.

'Third, the outer wall nearest the *mellah* to be moved back by fifty paces; which will entail razing the houses within that compass in order to allow a proper space to be maintained between our domain and the inhabitants of the city. The occupants to be informed by proclamation and ordered to begin work at once. Dwellings will be found for them in the meantime, but they are to shift the rubble themselves beyond the site.

'Fourth, the carved frieze in the Koubbet al-Khiyatin to be redone. This time it is important to choose a master artisan who is literate.' (Unfortunately for the original carver, the smiling vizier pointed out that the script which should have read 'The majesty of God' over and over in elegant Kufic script had been misspelled in the first instance and now reads 'The chains of God', the error then replicated a dozen times over.)

These are not the only instructions I have to remember, but they are the only ones I need to write down. The wolf will have to wait . . .

I run to the office of the chief of works, pass him the notes, make sure he understands them; then trot the mile and a half to the other end of the palace to the harem.

The harem is in all ways a forbidden place, its name deriving from the word for forbidden, which is *haram*. To enter into a harem is to cross an invisible line, to move from public into private, from profane to sacred; it is like lifting a veil, trespassing into an intimate space. In the outside world, people hold this barrier within their hearts and minds, but in Ismail's palace the transition points are more tangible: four guarded gates of iron. I am forced to explain my unscheduled presence at each one, even though I am one of very few permitted to move between the two worlds – male and female, outward and secret.

It is the chief eunuch of the harem who stares down at me. 'Yes?'

Qarim is one of Ismail's own: men raised to be totally loyal to the sultan. His brother Bilal is a door-guard to Ismail's private apartments, a lad with muscles like cedar, and a brain to match. Most of these guards are no more than nineteen or twenty years old, but they are huge. I am a tall man, but they top me by half a head and are twice as wide. 'You know who I am, Qarim. You see me every day.'

'Not usually on this day, or at this time.'

The high, light timbre of his voice never fails to take me by surprise, it is so at odds with his size. They say this is what happens with those who are cut early in life.

'Do you have a letter of permission?'

'Qarim, you know that if I did, it would be one I had written myself, as the sultan's scribe.'

This logic seems to fox him: he continues to stare at me.

'I have been running errands for the empress,' I add.

He looks down at my empty hands, then back up at me. I hold his gaze and at last he inclines his head and shouts to a wiry, dark-skinned lad of six or seven, 'Go find Amina and tell her that Nus-Nus wishes to see her mistress.'

The boy scampers off. 'Amina, Amina!' echoes down the halls like the cries of a trapped bird.

I make to walk on, but Qarim's massive hand closes on my arm. 'It would be best not to take the empress unawares.'

At last, the boy comes back, and behind him is a hugely endowed woman whose red slippers slap noisily on the marble. Her face drips with sweat, and her headcloth has been tied in haste. She looks thoroughly out of temper. 'Where are Zidana's things?' she demands.

'Alas, I do not have them and that is why I need to speak to her in person.'

Amina curls her lip. 'She's busy. She sent me to fetch the items she ordered from the souq.' She eyes me suspiciously, as if I have hidden them about my person and am refusing to hand them over, then at last sighs and beckons me to follow her.

I walk behind her, watching those enormous hips dip and sway with a sort of dreadful fascination. A man would be crushed beneath her like a dog beneath an elephant's foot. Large women are highly prized for their abundance here, where only a poor man would have a thin wife. The women gain weight deliberately by feeding on *zumeta*, a rich paste of nuts and butter and the crushed seeds of *tifidas*, the bitter melon. I swear you can watch them growing before your very eyes.

It seems to take an eternity to reach the empress's quarters, but on arrival there, for one horrible moment, I think I have walked into a pit of magic, a place into which Zidana has either summoned a gathering of demons or transformed her women into monsters, for the faces that turn towards me in the flickering lamplight are hideous, deformed and dripping. And then I remember that today is fifth day, when the women give themselves up to arcane beauty rituals and that the figures before me are not djinns but court ladies caked in masks of clay and pulped vegetables, their hair piled up in sticky coils and plastered with henna and oil.

The aroma of almonds and myrtle fills the air; incense burns in the niches around the walls. All around the room lies the evidence of their alchemy: low brass tables stacked with dishes of eggs and milk and honey; glass jars of bright oils, pomegranate peel and walnut bark; bowls of coloured clays and heaps of henna leaves.

Even disguised by a mask of red clay streaked with dripping henna, Zidana is unmistakable: her jet skin gleams between the acres of red fabric in which she is draped and the dozens of shining gold bracelets on her legs and arms. She wears a rope of pearls looped many times around her bull-like neck, and huge gold earrings drag her lobes towards her shoulders.

'My lady, forgive me –' I begin.

She waves her hands at the other women. 'Go away, go away now! Have you no shame? Hide yourselves!'

'It is only Nus-Nus,' someone says and the rest titter, watching me playfully over the veils they hold up over the lower parts of their clay-caked faces. They bat their eyelids in a horrible parody of flirtation.

Only Nus-Nus. This is all I am to them. A thing on which to practise their seduction techniques.

'Are we not beautiful, Nus-Nus?' Laila is more comely than most, with pretty ankles and hands that flutter like a lark's wings.

Once upon a time I would have courted pretty Laila; but now I feel the useless ache, and look away. 'Zidana's ladies are as shining stars to the perfect moon that is the empress herself,' I say neutrally.

'Stop tormenting the poor man and get away with you!' Zidana throws a bowl at Laila and it strikes her on the shoulder, a shower of red petals fluttering out like bloody feathers. After that, the women go quickly, leaving the empress and me alone. For any other man to be alone with the empress would warrant the loss of his head: but I am only Nus-Nus.

Nus-Nus is not the name with which I came into the world, and I hope it will not be the name I take with me when I depart this life, but it is the name I have borne ever since being presented to Zidana, five long years ago. I was led into her chamber, head down and trembling, wearing only a loincloth, an iron collar and fetters. She screeched at the guards to remove the collar and fetters. Not out of sympathy, but because the presence of iron will warp a magic spell. Even when the fetters were struck from me I kept my head down. Her feet were as dark as mine, pink along the sole. Her ankles, I noted, were sturdy. I watched the feet circle me and knew she was taking me in from head to toe – the tribal cicatrices patterning my back, the criss-cross scars left by the trader's whip; the silver slave-bond in my ear. With the stick she always carries she lifted my chin and looked me in the face.

You would expect a sultan with the pick of a continent as well as foreign captives brought to him from all corners of the world to have chosen as his Chief Wife the most glorious of women. Zidana, however, has never been pretty. But those eyes strike through flesh and bone to the very essence of a man's soul. When she looks at you, you sense that she has assessed every flaw and weakness in you and the best way to exploit them. Fear is your first reaction, and first reactions are to be trusted.

'Where is your pride?' she said softly, turning my head one way, then another, examining me from every angle. Her voice was as light as her body was heavy. 'You are Senufo: you are a warrior. Remember that.'

Warrior! I could almost have smiled. In my tribe I was much teased for preferring songs and drums to spears and warcraft.

'What is your name?'

I told her, and she smiled; and when she smiled you could see the Lobi girl she had once been. Our tribes were near-neighbours to the south of the once-mighty Songhai Empire in that part of Africa traders traditionally refer to simply as 'Guinea', not bothering to distinguish between all our separate countries with their distinct lineages, kingdoms, religions and peoples, just as they call the lands to the south of Morocco merely 'the Sudan' – the south, or 'the black'. It does not matter to them where we come from, or who we are: they take us and remake us in the image that best suits them: as bodyguards, warriors, concubines and eunuchs.

Then she said in our local dialect, 'We are nothing to these people, no more than a lump of flesh they can control. But our knowledge and our spirits are our own, and we must keep them strong. Information and will: those are the keys to power.' She leaned forward and her eyes glittered at me. 'Do you know what they call this drink, boy?'

I gazed at the bowl steaming on the table and said nothing.

'It is coffee, a drink both bitter and sweet, just like life. I take mine with half milk and half water,' she said. 'Half-and-half, or in Arabic *nus-nus*.

And that's what I shall call you: because until you take power over what has been done to you, you are a half-thing.'

Now, I lean in towards her and am assaulted by her scent of musk and neroli. 'Is there somewhere more private we might speak, my lady?'

'We are alone, Nus-Nus, unless you had not noticed.'

'Spies have long ears.'

She smiles: a flash of gold where the precious metal has replaced her natural teeth. It is said that when she was bought her front teeth were extracted, lest she bite down on a man's private parts, but that may be a vile calumny. Zidana has always had more subtle and dangerous weapons in her armoury than mere teeth.

I follow her into the inner chamber, which she crosses quickly, carefully skirting the rug. This she flips up, revealing an opening through which the top of some dark stairs can be glimpsed. She eases herself down through this opening with a sinuosity that belies her bulk. 'Follow me.'

A light blooms in the dark below and as I descend I see a long, low-ceilinged chamber with a divan pushed up against the farthest wall, a table bearing a large mortar and pestle, a brazier and some glass retorts, lined on all sides by many-drawered cabinets and shelves displaying jars and boxes much like those in Sidi Kabour's shop.

A magician's den, right under Moulay Ismail's nose!

A sneeze escapes me: something about the smell down here, musty and unpleasant. 'I am honoured, majesty. Who else knows about this place?'

'No one . . . living.'

'Apart from the builder.'

Zidana's smile is eloquent. Wonderful: so now I am the only living being with whom she has shared this secret? My position seems ever more perilous.

She turns her luminous eyes upon me. 'So, Nus-Nus, where are the things I ordered?'

I decide to be forthright. 'Sidi Kabour is dead: murdered.' I tell her what has happened, even down to my own idiocy. When I get to the matter of finding part of the missing list crammed in the poor man's mouth she interrupts explosively: 'You wrote down my needs? And then left the list for anyone to find?'

'I left it where only Sidi Kabour would know to look for it.' The excuse sounds unconvincing, even to me.

She walks around and around the chamber, muttering furiously. Is she mumbling charms, summoning Merra ben Harith, the king of the djinns, or Demouch, commander of *afrits*, to drag me to hell? I wonder how fast I can dash up the steps and hoist myself into the salon above; how far I can run before the guards get hold of me. I take a step backward, and eye the stairs covertly; but not covertly enough. Zidana stares at me. 'What's the matter with you? The threat is to me: I have many enemies who would love to lay hands on such a list and accuse me of sorcery.'

'Everyone already calls you "The Witch Zidana",' I point out.

'There is a large distance between suspicion and evidence.'

'The list was in *my* handwriting,' I remind her, but all she does is purse her lips and look at me contemptuously. 'What would such a one need with such items? No one would believe they were for your own use.'

Her eyes bore into me. 'So why are you so down-at-mouth?'

Reluctantly, I tell her about the ruination of the Persian Qur'an; that the Coptic Bookseller will be seeking payment on the sabbath and that Ismail will surely have my head for spoiling his treasure.

'And where is it now, this "holy" book?'

'In my room, wrapped in the bloodstained cloak the sultan gave me.'

She clucks her tongue. 'Ah, Nus-Nus. You see the trouble that comes when you serve two masters? This is what happens, you see: your loyalties are divided and it confuses your thoughts. You should have made separate visits to the souq for the two commissions. Mixing sacred texts and dark magic can never have a good outcome.'

Although she has converted to Islam, taken a Muslim name and participated in the ceremony that made her Ismail's wife before God, Zidana still follows her own beliefs, the ancient religion that comes out of the dark heart of the jungle. When she prays, it is to Thagba and his minions rather than to Allah the All-Merciful. Through her sorcery she can call upon the afrits and djinns of the Muslim world to wreak their own special havoc, but also upon the *thila*, the children of the forest, those anarchic beings who answer only to Thagba. She may wear silver amulets containing verses from the Qur'an pinned to her clothing, but next to her skin lie fetishes made from God knows what horrors.

She continues to walk about, muttering, and again I have the sense that I am eavesdropping on a conversation with someone I cannot see, and the hairs on the back of my neck start to rise. At last she turns back to me. 'I have a plan. I will send a girl to fetch the cloak and the book from you and I will ensure they are restored to pristine condition. And then you will do something for me.'

That night, I accompany the sultan to the mosque for the evening prayers, taste his food and eat a very little of my own. I sit with him then in the company of twenty or so of his women, all of whom are armed with musical instruments and fearsome amounts of kohl, under the watchful eye of Zidana and a dozen of Ismail's beloved cats. Eventually he makes his choice of partner for the night, and at long last those of us who are surplus to requirements are waved away.

I retreat gratefully to the solitude of my room to make the necessary entry in the couching book:

First 5th Day, Rabī al-Awwal
  Aziza, Guinea slave, gold front tooth, long neck. Virgin.

I sit there staring bleakly at this bald notation, before closing the book with a sigh and putting it aside. Only then do I think to open the chest. Where the burnous and the Holy Qur'an were there is now a yawning space. Somehow, Zidana has contrived to have them removed; just as she contrived to have little Aziza deflowered this night. Aziza is no threat; whereas Fatima, sister to the Hajib, must be kept out of the sultan's eye. Abdelaziz has long had designs on the succession. His lineage is noble, though his family were till his own rise impecunious. Ismail entrusts him with all aspects of state, including the keys to the Treasury; even Zidana fears to threaten him directly, though two of his food-tasters have mysteriously perished. When all is said and done, she is a slave, with no lineage and no status, except that which is accorded her by the sultan's own whim. And he is a whimsical man, as all know to their cost. I have with my own ears heard Abdelaziz advise the sultan that his acknowledged heir should be of true Moroccan stock if the kingdom is to be safeguarded after his death (may the Compassionate One be minded to make that terrible day long hence). Only the Hajib could ever risk his wrath by suggesting such a thing and survive; but Ismail indulges his vizier, treats him like a brother. Though by no means does he treat lovely Fatima as a sister, buxom little baggage that she is. Three years ago she gave birth to a boy; unfortunately the child perished: just as well, or he would have outranked Zidana's second son. Last year she gave birth to another boy, but this one has thus far proved more hardy. Of Fatima there was no sign tonight, though; no doubt she was indisposed by some carefully measured dose of aconite.

Lying down on the divan, I suddenly remember an unwelcome detail of this dreadful day.

The damned pattens!

I left them beneath Sidi Kabour's stall, thinking to retrieve them on my return. My heart threatens to batter down the walls of its cage: my groan fills the night. I cannot be seen to go back to the shop. Could I send a page to fetch them? But what if the boy was stopped and questioned? No one would lie for me out of love, and I have no money.

Sweat breaks out in the runnel between the muscles of my back. Vomit rises in my throat.

Pattens. They are only pattens. A lot of people were wearing them in the streets today, not just me, though mine may be better made than most. I fight down the panic and lie there, staring into the darkness.

4

First Gathering Day, Rabī al-Awwul 1087 AH

The muezzin began his first call to prayer before dawn, reminding me that it is better to pray than to sleep. Generally I prefer to sleep than to pray, but I last night I did not sleep at all. Gritty-eyed and with a leaden feeling of doom in my stomach, I roll from my divan, make my ablutions, dress in my Friday best and go quickly to accompany my lord Ismail to the mosque.

I am just exiting my chamber when two of the sultan's body-slaves come flying down the corridor, nearly knocking me over. 'Hoi!' I cry at their retreating backs. 'Watch where you're going!'

Abid turns back. He looks distinctly pale around the gills. 'His majesty is in a fearsome temper,' he warns, then hurtles on as if pursued by demons.

At the magnificent double doors under the great horseshoe arch that marks the entrance to the sultan's private chambers I enter unchallenged and at once cast myself prostrate, forehead pressed to the tiled floor. It is only then that I see I am not alone in making obeisance, for to the left of me I glimpse Bilal, the door-guard, doing the same. Two things strike me at once: the first being that as a door-guard he should have been guarding the door rather than lying here on the tiles; the second that he is staring at me in a very odd fashion. Then I realize the reason for his peculiar squint.

Bilal's body lies at a small distance away from me . . . and away from his head, which, I see now, sits perkily on its stump of neck, lips slightly parted, as if in surprise at this unforeseen separation.

'Ah, Nus-Nus, excellent timing! Come, get up: help me with this turban. I don't know where those wretched boys have gone; they were here a moment ago.'

Despite all evidence to the contrary, Ismail sounds quite normal, cheerful even. I get nervously to my feet, keeping my eyes properly downcast, for I have already glimpsed that his majesty has this morning donned a robe of sunflower gold, which is now spoiled by an ugly splash of crimson. A yellow robe is always a bad sign. A very bad sign, especially in conjunction with a decapitated guard.

Should I mention the stain? Ismail would not wish to go to prayer with his clothing defiled by blood; but who knows how he will react if I point it out to him and thus infer his involvement in the death of poor Bilal? Lesser errors of etiquette have resulted in a nasty death. But if I let him go wearing the stained robe, he is bound to notice at some point and then may well murder me for failing in my duty. Caught on the horns of this dilemma, I concentrate on winding the turban, but can't stop my eyes from straying to the ever-widening scarlet pool and the red gleam of the sultan's favourite curved blade, chased with silver and inscribed with the sacred words of the Prophet: '*The sword is the key of heaven and of hell.*' It certainly has been in Bilal's case.

The turban completed, Ismail inserts a vast ruby pin in the front, pulls his sleeves straight and begins to flick out the creases in the skirt of his robe. For a moment he stands frowning. He touches the stain. 'How did that get there?' He sounds genuinely puzzled. After a time he raises his eyes and stares at me hard.

His lance is propped against his chair, and within two strides there are a dozen swords and daggers and crossed halberds decorating the nearest wall: any one of them could be the implement that brings my death. 'I do not know, my lord,' I whisper.

'Well, what a confounded nuisance,' he says mildly. 'I can't go to the mosque like this. Go fetch one of the green robes, will you, Nus-Nus? From the sandalwood box. Yes, green will do well for today.'

When I come back I find him in exactly the same attitude, gazing into space as if in meditation. I deconstruct the turban, draw off the saffron robe, aid him into the fresh green robe and rewind the turban. Then I wash his hands with rose water, dry them and wash my own hands.

'Excellent.' He sets the ruby pin in place once more, puts a hand on my shoulder and squeezes it with an appearance of affection. 'Come, then, Nus-Nus, let us go to our prayers.' He beams at me and then walks to the door, lifting his feet carefully to step over the corpse, as if it is an inconveniently placed object. At the doorway he looks right and left. 'Where in God's name is Bilal?' He shakes his head sadly at this dereliction of duty and walks on towards the mosque.

When we return an hour later another guard has been posted and all trace of Bilal has been scrupulously removed. The serenity of the chamber is so surreal that it is tempting to wonder if nothing has happened. But details keep slipping into my mind even as I check the safety of my lord's breakfast, and I cannot help thinking of my own bloodstained clothing and the ruined Qur'an. Not to mention the wretched pattens.

As if he can read my mind, Ismail says, 'Make sure you fetch the Safavid masterpiece to me in the library: now that the rain has stopped there can be no further excuse for delay.' I back out with my head bowed low, my thoughts in turmoil.

As soon as I set foot inside my room I have the powerful sense that someone has been in there while I have been away. I look around but nothing obvious seems to have changed. Then my nose twitches: a faint whiff of musk and neroli, Zidana's own perfume, forbidden to any other to wear. Has the empress herself been here? It is hard to believe that the most powerful, and most feared, woman in the kingdom may have visited my plain little room whilst I have been at prayer with her husband. I imagine her poking through my mean possessions with that sly grin upon her face, and shudder. I throw open the lid of my wooden coffer, half expecting to find some atrocity within; but there, neatly folded, is the white woollen burnous. Picking it up, I shake it out. There is no doubting it is the same cloak that I wore the day before, for the gold embroidery along its hem makes it unique, yet where it was stained with the herbman's blood it is now brilliantly unblemished, perhaps better and brighter than it has ever been.

Beneath it is the Safavid Qur'an, its gilded bindings pristine. I draw it out and press it to my breast. 'Thank you, O Merciful One,' I say aloud, then add for good measure, 'and thank you, my Lady Zidana, may the All-Powerful grant you long life and joy.' Never have I believed so fervently in the grace of Allah, in his infinite wisdom and compassion.

I throw the cloak back into the box, tuck the Safavid Qur'an under my arm and run towards the library.

In there a *taleb* is reciting The Moon in a hypnotic sing-song chant, while my lord Ismail sits on his gold-and-pearl-inlaid throne, entranced by the poetic rhythms of the sacred words. As I enter, his eyes fix avidly on the object I carry. He waits until the scholar completes the sura, then waves a hand at the man, dismissing him. I see how the taleb's gaze also falls upon the book and know it must be a torture for him to be sent away without the chance to look upon this priceless treasure; know also that it is Ismail's pleasure that he be denied the opportunity. My lord has an equivocal attitude to scholars: he values their company for the reflected light they cast upon him, but he does not value any opinion that contradicts his own. He runs through talebs at a considerable rate, since a few ill-timed words or unwelcome sermons are likely to land them in a pit of Barbary lions or poisonous serpents, or head first down a well.

Once the scholar has gone, Ismail holds out his hands. He has long, graceful hands, fingers as slim as a woman's. It is hard to believe that they have that morning cleanly struck off the head of a favourite guard, and one of monstrous size at that. 'Give it to me, Nus-Nus. I want to have a good look at the book that is costing my Treasury so dear.'

I place the Qur'an in his hands and watch as his fingers play along the intricately tooled patterns of its double border, how he turns it this way and that to appreciate the gilding. The hard planes of his face soften, as if he were touching the head of a cherished son, or the breast of a beloved courtesan. He is a curious contradiction, our king: at once violent and tender; cruel and indulgent; ascetic and sensual. I have seen him feed an ailing kitten with warm milk from his own fingers, fingers that an hour later put out the eye of a servant who offended him. When I was struck down with a fever, he carried me to his own bed and stayed with me till it broke, wiping the sweat from me with towels dipped in rose water, his concern for me overcoming his great fear of contagion. Two days later, when I was much

32

recovered, he threw a water jug at my head because I was slow bringing a glass. His nature causes his subjects to love and fear him in equal measure.

'Exquisite. Truly exquisite. You have done well to bring this to me, Nus-Nus, and you shall be rewarded. Ah, but they do not make books like this any more.' He opens the cover and I hold my breath. The delicate cutwork of the interior cover had before boasted a silk inlay of turquoise: the colour of sea-washed glass; but now it is a dusky rose, as if the blood that soaked into it has merely been diluted rather than removed. And when he turns the page to what should be the first sura, I think my heart will stop.

'Read The Cow for me, Nus-Nus.' His lips are curved into a benevolent smile that is truly terrifying.

I have to recite from memory, for the text bears no relation to the holy words that Allah dictated to the Prophet, instructing men how to walk the straight path in his name. The Cow is a long sura, one of the longest in the Qur'an. It is the first sura one learns by heart as a Muslim child. But I was not raised as a Muslim and came late in life to Islam, and not altogether by choice. And everyone knows that as you grow older, the more difficult it is to learn by rote. Besides, to remember without distraction is one thing; but to recite the words that Ismail expects to hear while looking in horror upon those inscribed upon the page before me is another entirely. The calligraphy is elegant; but the contents . . . My eyes bulge in disbelief even as I intone carefully, 'In this book there is no doubt, it is a guide to those who guard against evil. Those who believe in the unseen and maintain their prayers . . .' My eyes skip over the next few lines and I almost choke. Something about it being better to take an ugly or a heathen woman from behind so that you will not have to look upon her face . . . I try desperately to stop the image that is now in my head from contaminating the holy words of the Qur'an. 'There is a covering over their eyes, and there is a great punishment for them . . .'

Has she done this deliberately, Zidana? Taken the most profane text she can find to substitute for the ruined pages? Is it her revenge on me for failing in my mission, or on her husband, who prides himself on his religious sensibility; or on the entire culture that has imprisoned her in this luxurious cage? One way or another I am sure that even now she is sitting in her apartments, laughing at the unholy joke she has played upon us all.

Sweating, I stumble on, making error after error, until I reach 'they shall have a painful chas . . . chastisement because they lied' – at which point, Ismail smacks his palms together and brings me to a halt. 'What is the matter with you, Nus-Nus? You usually read so beautifully: your mellifluous voice is one of the few reasons I keep you by me.' He pauses to allow the implications of this threat to sink in. 'It must be the value of the book that is stealing your composure; you should remember it is not you who has to pay for it! Which reminds me: you had better run along and fetch Abdelaziz so that I may discuss with him the sum he should release to the bookseller.'

I find the grand vizier taking his second breakfast in his own private pavilion within the Dar Kbira. Silver trays heaped with cold meats, olives, bread, cheese and fancy pastries cover the low tables, while Abdelaziz reclines amongst a pile of silken cushions, attended by a pair of near-naked slave-boys who can't be older than twelve or thirteen, despite their burgeoning muscles and gleaming ebony skin. The vizier's quarters are more resplendent even than the sultan's own. The walls glitter with powdered gold looted from the palaces of the kings of the Songhai Empire, and gold and lapis glow in the starburst patterns up in the cupola. I wonder how his quarters can be finished to such a lavish standard when the rest of the palace is still a building site. Then I remind myself who holds the keys to the Treasury . . .

'Nus-Nus – how lovely to see you in my humble chambers: come, sit with me. Help yourself – these almond pastries are superb.' He waves a beringed hand at me, then pats the cushions beside him, giving me a basilisk stare.

I bow. 'The sultan requests your presence.'

'Surely it can wait until I have finished my breakfast.'

I say nothing. We both know that Ismail does not 'request'.

Abdelaziz makes a face, then grabs a handful of the pastries and crams them into his mouth. A little avalanche of honeyed crumbs cascades over his beard as he chews untidily. Then he gets grumbling to his feet and slaps away the hands of the Nubian boy as he makes to brush his robes. 'Presumptuous whelp! I shall whip you when I return.' The words are uttered caressingly, but his gaze is flinty.

I see the boy turn puzzled eyes to him and realize he is new, and does not yet have much Arabic. The other lad understands well enough. He looks afraid, as well he might: thin white scars cover his arm and shoulder. He pulls the other boy away, and as we leave I hear him chattering to the other in their native tongue, catching a phrase here and there. 'He is cruel . . . he likes to hurt, to see pain. Don't give him excuse . . .'

Something twists inside me. I remember those blank, dark eyes watching my own pain, revelling in it.

'So, Nus-Nus' – the grand vizier breaks into my thoughts as we make our way down the arcaded corridor – 'have you given any more thought to my offer?'

To survive in this place I have learned to adopt my 'second face', like the kponyungu mask I wore so long ago in the Poro rituals of our tribe. And I tell myself, *I am not myself: I am another.* The mask smiles. 'I am flattered, sidi, but I fear it would not sit well with his sublime majesty.'

'His "sublime" majesty need never know.' His tone mocks me.

'The sultan sees everything.'

Abdelaziz snorts. 'You mean, his spies do. Spies like the Tinker.' He makes a dismissive gesture, as if brushing away a fly.

The Tinker: he means the Kaid ben Hadou, Al-Attar. No love lost there. We are nearing the imperial quarters now and I have no wish for Ismail to overhear any part of this conversation. Neither, it seems, does the grand vizier, for he catches me by the upper arm and digs in his fingers, instinctively finding the most painful pressure points. I stare him down coolly, summoning my second face. *I am not myself.*

'Do not make an enemy of me, Nus-Nus. It really would not be wise.'

He is already my enemy. I make a bow. 'I am your humble servant, my lord; but first of all I am his sublime majesty's servant.'

'Ismail is a dog in a manger.'

There is a saying I have heard amongst slaves: *what happens in the desert stays in the desert.* We try our best to remake our lives and regain our self-respect. But how can I ever forget what Abdelaziz did to me? My hands curl themselves into claws at my sides.

'No one need ever know.' The basilisk smile.

'Know what?'

Ismail walks quietly: he likes to take people unawares and when he is safe within his private quarters he often goes about alone, and shoeless. The Hajib and I swiftly prostrate ourselves. Down there, on the ground, the fragrant scent of freshly cut wood swirls around my nose like incense.

'Oh, get up, man.' Ismail prods the vizier with his bare foot. 'I have something to show you. A rare treasure.'

Oh, great heaven: the book. I almost forgot it. My god, if Abdelaziz sees what lies between its covers he will recognize the deception at once and, being subtle enough to keep the information to himself while it suits him, will hold my fate in his hands to use as he pleases. Death could not come fast enough . . .

Think of something, my brain goads me, *anything to distract him!* But my mind is a perfect blank.

Ismail takes up the book and I see Abdelaziz's eyes gleam as he takes in the rich binding. He holds his hands out avariciously. The sultan stares at them. Then he brings the Safavid Qur'an down with a resounding thud on the vizier's head. I can make out the imprint of the embellished binding pressed as perfectly into the fine cotton of his turban as a seal into hot wax. The Hajib groans and clutches his head.

'You dare to come to me covered in the filth of your feeding!' Ismail rages. 'There is honey all over your fingers and pastry in your beard! Have you no respect, for me or for the Holy Qur'an?' And he thumps the book down again and again and again, until the vizier is a cowering heap on the floor.

'Mercy; have mercy on me, majesty. Nus-Nus told me to come at speed and I thought it a matter of urgency . . .'

The next blow is less violent; and the one after that glances off the vizier's shoulder as if Ismail has lost interest. The sultan steps away, examining the book for damage, but it is a sturdy object, and whoever has repaired it has made a good job of it. 'Go away. Pay the bookseller whatever he asks.' He passes the Qur'an to me. 'Place it on the topmost shelf, Nus-Nus: it is defiled now.'

How truly he speaks, did he but know it!

Fetching the wooden library stairs, I fit the Safavid Qur'an between two other ancient volumes on the highest shelf and hope Ismail will never change his mind and wish to take it down again.

I turn to find Ismail kneeling on the floor with his arm around the Hajib's shoulders. 'Get up, man. What are you doing down there? You need not genuflect to me: we are like brothers, you and I, are we not?'

Abdelaziz staggers to his feet. His eyes look glazed and there is blood on his cheek. I watch in horrified fascination as the sultan takes the end of his sash and wipes it tenderly away. 'There, that is better, is it not?'

'Yes, O Great One.' The vizier manages a wobbly smile.

Ismail turns to me. 'Have you been to look at the wolf yet?'

Damnation. In the midst of my other woes I had forgotten about the wolf. 'I will go now, majesty.'

The wolf looks more dead than alive. There is a large and bloody swelling on the poll of its head. Two children are standing by the cage, the eldest with a stick in its fist. Both have shaven heads but one long braid on the crown, by which the angels may catch them if they fall. No angels are ever likely to attend these children, though. The massive gold ring each wears proclaims him to be one of Ismail's many little emirs who roam unchallenged and undisciplined about the court. And I know all too well which they are: Zidan, the empress's eldest, six years old and rotten to the core; the other barely more than a toddler, Ahmed the Golden, a small monster-in-training.

I sigh. 'Well, now, Zidan, what are you doing here?'

The older child regards me with defiant black eyes. 'Nothing. Anyway, if I want to play with the wolf I can. Father said so.'

'I am sure your father did not give you permission to batter the poor thing to death.'

He sneers. 'I only gave him a little tap.'

Ahmed laughs delightedly. 'A big tap!'

'No need to pretend innocence with me, Zidan: remember how I found you last week.' I give him a meaningful look. Last week I found him by the stables with an older boy, a slave, cutting out a cat's claws by the root. The slave looked sick: the cat had raked Zidan and he had obviously been ordered to hold her down while the little demon wielded his dagger. I had berated them both roundly and whacked the slave-boy over the head, harder than I'd meant, since I'd wished to administer the blow to Zidan, but dared not. Like his mother, he bears a grudge; like his father, he enjoys the power to deprive a man of limb or life. The cat died anyway. I buried it myself.

'If you tell I will have you killed.' He taps the stick against his leg. It leaves bloody smears on his *qamis*. 'I might have you killed anyway, Half-and-Half.'

'Your father prizes his cats, and the Qur'an says that those who torment them will themselves be tormented in Hell,' I remind him.

'It does not say anything about wolves,' he says, baring his teeth at me. They are already rotting, from the sweets he cons out of everyone.

Thankfully, the menagerie keeper comes out now. He looks cowed, as well he might. Able to vent my spleen, I yell at him. 'What the hell happened to it?'

He shrugs. 'It went for Prince Zidan when I was putting it in the cage. It seemed it would tear out his throat, but the little emir was most brave.'

Patently a lie: the wretched creature looks as if it would have had problems even gnawing the throat of a chicken and the child had evidently been battering it through the bars. Zidan crows with laughter and runs off, towing his little brother after him, confident that he is inviolate.

I glare at the menagerie keeper. 'If it is not walking and snarling by midnight you will wish it had ripped *your* throat out.' There is no point scolding him about Zidan: we both know this. I crouch to examine the beast. It really is a sorry-looking specimen, bedraggled and bitten about the legs and haunches by the dogs that brought it down. It regards me with not an iota of interest, neither raising a hackle nor even wrinkling its muzzle, as if all it waits for now is death. My heart contracts in sympathy.

'Can it even walk?' I stand up again.

'It's stronger than it looks,' the keeper says defensively.

'Get it out and let me see it walk.'

He gives me a look. How dare a jumped-up Guinea slave speak to him, a pale-skinned Arab, so? Contempt and loathing go hand in hand: I suspect I know which way it would go if he had to choose between killing me or the wolf.

Grudgingly he does as I ask, entering the cage with his stick at the ready, but the wolf does not even stir as he fastens the chain around its neck, and he has to drag it out like a sack of turnips, as if it has lost the use of its legs. Even so, the four wild asses of which the sultan is so fond take one look at it, bray shrilly and bolt for the far side of the enclosure, where they disturb the ostriches, which in turn set up a raucous noise. Still the wolf crouches, its nose all but touching the ground.

'This is no good. Is it the only one the hunters brought in?'

'It was the sultan himself who ran it down,' the man says sullenly.

'It'll have to be in better fettle than this for the ceremony. You know the sultan will have your head and mine if the beast is not to his satisfaction and he is made to look foolish.'

The keeper looks pensive. Then he says, 'Can't you ask the witch for something that'll do the trick?'

I stare at him. Does the whole palace know my business? I do not credit his question with an answer, but walk quickly away.

It is Zidana to whom I go now, availing myself of a basket of oranges on the way, knowing I require some sort of excuse for entering the harem without prior arrangement. The guards on the gate are not fooled: there are treefuls of oranges everywhere, even in the harem gardens, like mine still green. They search the basket suspiciously and I stand by, shuffling my feet, till they are done. I notice that Qarim's eyes are red and swollen. Word has reached him of Bilal's death, then – whispers racing through the labyrinth of passages. 'I am sorry about your brother,' I offer quietly.

He nods. It is not done to talk about the demise of those who fall foul of Ismail. They simply cease to exist. 'Let the man through, they're only oranges,' he instructs his fellow guards. Qarim puts a hand on my shoulder. 'Watch yourself, Nus-Nus,' he says in that high, light voice that is so at odds with his stature. 'No one is safe in this place.'

As I approach the inner courts of Zidana's palace, the mellow strains of an *oud* reach me. The oud is a beautiful instrument, the forerunner of the European lute, and I love to play it when I can. It has a sighing, plangent quality, particularly apt for love songs and melancholic airs. I learned to play tolerably well: now hearing the oud strummed with such feeling, I feel my fingers itch to join in. Then a voice rises in harmony with the dark melody and I stop where I am, in the shadows of the vine-covered arcade, to listen.

When I was a man, what a man I was
I loved the ladies, and they loved me
Oh, far and wide have I travelled the world
Now I am a prisoner, woe for me.
A captive to your beauty, my dark maid
Your bright black eyes have captured my heart
But all I can do is watch you and sigh
A man I am no more, and so we must part.

I peer out into the courtyard, to see Black John, Zidana's favourite eunuch, hunched over the pretty oud like an ape over a stolen fruit, his huge fingers moving nimbly as he takes the ballad to a minor key. The song is French, I believe, and did not speak of dusky maidens or black eyes in its original. We all have to shift for ourselves in our changed circumstances, to adapt or die, and John has prospered by his skills. When he starts in on the next verse, which tells how the lover must stand aside and watch his beloved wed another, since he has not the wherewithal to marry her himself (a reference in the original to money rather than diminished bodily capability), I find, quite unaccountably given the blandness of the lyrics, that tears are stinging my eyes.

The last time I heard the song I was in the service of a doctor, Scottish by origin, African by choice. In the few years he owned me, I learned to read and scribe in four languages; to tell the difference between mandrake and ginger root; to play a fair tune on the Spanish guitar and the oud. I knew both the Qur'an and the poetry of Rumi by heart (my master being a convert to Islam, saying jokingly that it was a more Christian religion than Christianity). I had conquered hearts from Timbuktu to Cairo, from

Florence to Cadiz; I thought myself a grand fellow. My cousin Ayew would have said I had got above myself . . .

Ah, it is painful to think of Ayew. His fate was worse even than mine.

The doctor was a good master to me, more of a teacher than a master by the end, which came cruelly. We were in Gao, guests of the so-called king there (in truth no more than an ambitious chieftain, seeking to resurrect the great city from its sacked ruins), when half the household came down with some unusual sickness. Doctor Lewis succeeded in saving three of the king's children and two of his wives before succumbing himself to the sweating and shaking, and finally the raving hallucinations. I tried to smuggle him out of the palace; and failed. He died and I was left friendless and prey to the monstrous ingratitude of that so-called king, who packed me off to the slave-market in case I too carried the seeds of the sickness. And there I was sold to a monster.

Black John's song comes to a close and the ladies ululate their approval. I detach myself from the shadows and enter the courtyard. There is Naima and Mina, pretty Khadija and Fouzia; and there is Fatima, the Hajib's sister, toting her boy on her hip. As always, I am taken aback by how features shared by brother and sister can be so repulsive in the one and so seductive in the other. Fatima wears her extra flesh lushly at breast and hip, but despite her childbearing keeps an elegantly narrow waist. Where his mouth seems vast and slug-like, her lips are pillowy. The blackness of his eye seems as dead as that of a shark; but Fatima's eyes are bright and wicked, promising all manner of bed-tricks. When she sees me they go wide with surprise; then she looks away quickly. Interesting, I think, and file away that look for future reference. I bow to Zidana. She gives me a smile that is one part sugar to two parts sheer malice. 'Still alive, then, Nus-Nus? Clever boy.'

I give her back a sharp look that says, *No thanks to you*, but all she does is grin wider. Then she claps her hands. 'Go away, John, all of you. I need to talk to Nus-Nus.'

'I hope you appreciated the skill of the repair,' she says when they are gone, and when I do not reply, she laughs. 'It could have been a lot worse, you know. The other book I considered binding into those pretty covers had *pictures*. Most instructive and inventive pictures.' She pauses. 'Did he make you read to him from it?'

I nod, seething.

'I wish I could have been there to see it. And did he nod wisely, Ismail, and mouth the words as you recited?'

She knows her husband too well. 'You could have had me killed.'

'Oh, Nus-Nus, you underestimate yourself. *I* don't underestimate you: I knew you'd pass my little test. You're a resourceful man. But it was a good joke all the same.'

'I have come to ask your aid in another matter.' I explain the problem with the wolf, though I say nothing about Zidan's torment of the beast. There is no point: she will not hear a word against him.

'If it were me, I'd have chosen a lion, not some mangy old wolf,' she sniffs. 'What does that say about us to outsiders?'

'That its fate will be the fate of any attacker who dares venture near?' I hazard.

'More likely that we are like sheep in a fold.'

'The wolf is his symbol,' I remind her, but she isn't interested in pursuing the discussion, instead taking herself off and coming back a while later with a small phial of purplish liquid. 'Coat some meat in this and give it to the beast just after sundown. It'll liven it up for a while.'

'Not too much, I hope.'

'Then it would be more of a fair struggle, wouldn't it?' Her eyes gleam. 'Quite the spectacle. I do hope I've got the quantities right.' She gives me a sly smile.

I make to leave, then turn back. Should I mention the pattens? She will be furious at me for my stupidity, and anyway what can she do? None of the women are allowed to leave the palace and unless she can command her spirits to manifest themselves in flesh, even Zidana's magic cannot retrieve them.

She watches my indecision with a raised eyebrow. 'Off you go, Nus-Nus, but remember the next favour will be mine.'

I deliver the dose and instructions to the menagerie keeper, with a dire warning so that he is in no doubt that I will come looking for him if the wolf does not behave as expected that night, and head back to the Dar Kbira, running through the rest of my duties in my head, until I reach the dangerous impression that everything is just about under control. But as I stride through the long vine-covered walkway leading to the sultan's pavilions, someone calls my name. I turn: it is Yaya, one of the guards posted on the main gate.

'There were some men here earlier.' Sweat sheens his face: has he run after me just to tell me this? I sigh. There is always someone seeking a bribe, or an audience. 'What did they want?'

Yaya looks solemn. 'They were making inquiries. There was a man murdered in the souq yesterday.'

My heart stutters, and my insides go cold. 'Murdered?' I echo feebly. A drop of sweat bursts out of my hairline beneath my turban, rolls down my forehead, makes a track along my nose.

Yaya watches me, his eyes bulging with curiosity. 'They questioned all the guards about everyone's comings and goings yesterday, and we said there were not many braving the rain . . .'

'But you told him you had seen me,' I finish, feeling sick.

'Well, I had to,' he says, as if lying was not an option.

'And?'

He makes a face. 'They wanted to talk to you. I said you were running errands for the sultan, helping him prepare for the inauguration, so they went away again.'

Pent-up breath escapes me. 'Well, that's all right, then.'

'They're coming back tomorrow.'

I go hot, then cold. 'But I shall also be very busy tomorrow.'

'I'm not on duty tomorrow.' There is a note of selfish relief in his voice as he says this. Seeing my expression, he adds doubtfully, 'But I'll ask Hassan to turn them away.'

'Wonderful.' I walk quickly away, cursing under my breath. The *qadi*'s men are not usually this persistent: they know the qadi's jurisdiction stops short of the palace walls. Did someone see something that implicates me directly? Sidi Kabour must have been better connected than I had thought, so assiduously are they pursuing his murderer.

43

As I perform my duties that evening, anxiety gnaws at my guts. I find myself asking, 'Is this the last time I will lay out the sultan's babouches? Is this the last good food I will taste?'

The wolf goes to its death in a dignified fashion – heralded in by long Fassi trumpets and musicians all in white. It rears up and growls and snarls and gives every impression of being the wild beast it is supposed to signify, and Ismail quells it with less ease than I expected, given the state it was in that morning. I feel a pang of sorrow as he squeezes the life out of it, and when it slumps and he draws the ceremonial blade to cut off its head, I have to look away.

5

First Gathering Day, Rabī al-Awwal Massouda, black Sudanese, daughter
of Abida, slave previously kept in the Tafilalt. Thirteen years old. Virgin.

A name, a date, the briefest of descriptions: such sterile words on a page to represent the enactment of fertility. The couching book is maintained with rigorous care in order to establish the birth and legitimacy of the sultan's children, to keep a schedule that will settle all arguments, and prevent jealousies and disputes. He is but six years older than me, Ismail, and has been sultan for only the last five, and yet he has already engendered hundreds of infants upon his wives and concubines. The sultan lies with a virgin almost every night, although he has a few favourites to whom he returns from time to time. Unlike King Shahriyar in the Arabian tales, he does not have his conquests strangled the following morning to ensure their fidelity. There is little chance of infidelity in this palace – the harem is fiercely guarded by the eunuchs.

Zidana maintains control over the harem, and over the sultan too. Almost every night, after fifth prayer, once Ismail has eaten and bathed, she will arrange a gathering at which a selection of worthy candidates will promenade in the gardens, or play music for him, or sing beneath the orange trees, or in his private quarters, or just lie on the divans looking seductive. For this opportunity, Zidana is well bribed by those seeking advantage: to sway Ismail's judgement, and to seduce him away from her rival Fatima, she will lead him to a certain girl and extol her virtues, indicating a delicately turned ankle or beautifully hennaed hands; even baring a breast to show off its curve and weight. The sultan, who is as headstrong as a charging horse in all other things, is surprisingly happy to be led by his Chief Wife in matters of the bedchamber.

You would think there was an incalculable alchemy to the piquing of desire, but either she knows him too well or he is indiscriminate. Certainly, he has a prodigious appetite. Even the most energetic of men would be surfeited within weeks of such boundless plenty, but not Ismail. It is another of the reasons he is so revered: the women adore him to the point of idolatry. They creep up behind him to touch the hem of his robe for good luck; if he touches them they do not wash the hand or cheek for days; they keep talismans they have gleaned from their time with him – a hair from his head or beard, the seed that has dried on their thighs, or that they have kept all night in their mouths – in little phials or amulets that they wear so that its *baraka*, that mysterious force of blessing and luck the sultan exudes, will ward off illness and the evil eye. Those whom he beds will be carried in procession about the harem the following morning. The greatest baraka of all is to bear his child: though after his initial enthusiasm – accompanied by the firing of cannons, the proclamation and trumpets (for the birth of a boy), or the fireworks or strewing of flowers (for a girl) – he soon loses interest. Zidana makes sure of that too, for always she keeps her firstborn – Zidan – to the forefront, and although the child is both a brute and a dunce, Ismail dotes upon him, carries him around the gardens on his shoulders, spoils him most horribly and has named him his heir, for all that his mother was a slave.

Of course, there is a high natural mortality rate and many do not make it past the first few months, but it is worthy of note that there is a marked preponderance of boy children born to mothers for whom the sultan has shown more than a passing interest dying of various colics, gripes and vomiting disorders. Often their mothers follow them to the grave: dead of grief, I've heard the empress declare, quite impassively, even as the other women weep and wail and tear their clothes. I say no more.

I put the couching book back in my chest and am visited once more by a shudder of horror. The pattens should be standing in their accustomed place to the right of the chest. But they are not there. Dread fills me as I wonder if they are still where I left them, or whether they have as yet escaped notice.

I do not have long to wait to find out. Later that morning I go to inspect the newly inaugurated Bab al-Raïs so that I can report back to Ismail that his orders have been properly carried out. Sure enough, the poor wolf's head has been set above the gate and is grimacing away in a suitably ferocious fashion. On my way back to the inner courts my way is barred by two men wearing the coloured sashes that mark them as officers of the qadi and they are accompanied by a pair of palace guards, who carry the guns they have taken from the qadi's men before guiding them into the palace grounds. No one but the imperial guards may bear arms within the palace walls, a sensible precaution in a kingdom Ismail has himself described as 'a basketful of rats' – always ready to rebel, and bite the hand that feeds.

'Are you the court official known as Nus-Nus?'

Behind them, Hassan shrugs at me. 'Sorry.'

'I am.'

'We wish to question you over a certain matter. A man has been most foully murdered in the souq.'

I try to look shocked. I try to look innocent. I *am* innocent, for heaven's sake: so why do I feel so guilty?

'Where were you between the hours of eleven and two the day before yesterday?'

I look him in the eye. 'Running an errand for his majesty in the bazaar.' And I tell him about my appointment with the Coptic Bookseller.

The second officer steps closer. I do not like the look of him: he is young and well fed and clearly thinks a lot of himself, judging by the care with which he has trimmed his beard into a fancy shape. I suspect he has plucked his eyebrows too. 'We already interviewed the book-trader so we know you were there after noon. At what time did you return to the palace?' He asks me this in a way that suggests he already knows the answer.

'Just before the emperor's daily rounds,' I concede.

'And what time might that be?'

'Around two.'

'There is a large gap of time unaccounted for. While you were in the souq, did you happen to visit the stall of one Hamid ibn M'barek Kabour?'

The mask is firmly in place. 'That name is not familiar to me.'

'We know you were there. You were seen entering his stall at' – he examines the tablet on which he has written his notes – 'just after eleven, wearing a "white burnous richly trimmed with gold".'

My heart starts to thunder. 'Ah, Sidi Kabour. I do apologize: I have never been on first name terms with him. And you say the poor man is dead, murdered? That is terrible news indeed. What will the emperor do now for his incense? He cannot do without his agarwood and frankincense, and he refuses to buy it from anyone else. I don't know what Ismail will say when he hears this news, he will be most upset. Is there a widow to whom he could make a gift?' I think I am doing well in acting the part of concerned factotum, but the younger officer is not taken in by my babbling.

'Not purchasing illegal substances for the Lady Zidana, then?' he says.

'Good heavens, no. And if I were you I would be very careful about repeating such malicious gossip about the emperor's chief wife.'

'She is a witch: everyone knows it.'

I turn away. 'I have things to do: I cannot stand around here listening to your vicious tittle-tattle.'

He catches me by the arm. In a former life he would be laid out cold on the ground, but you soon learn to curb your natural reactions at Ismail's court. 'I have a warrant signed by the qadi to take you into custody if you do not cooperate with us.'

So they really do consider me a suspect. With a sudden lurch of memory I recall the voice shouting after me as I left the herbman's stall. It had called Sidi Kabour's name, but what if someone recognized me despite my disguise?

'The white cloak you were wearing – where is it now?'

Thank God for Zidana. 'In my room. Why do you ask?'

'The man who killed Hamid Kabour would have been covered in his blood: it was a brutal slaying.'

I make a sign to ward off the evil eye, and so does the older officer. He catches my eye. 'Do you have this cloak so that we may see it? Then we can leave you to get on with your day,' he says, rather more gently than his companion.

'Of course: the emperor himself gave it to me. It is one of my most treasured possessions.'

The guards flank us as we walk through all the hammering and scurrying of the ongoing building works. In the second courtyard a great hole has been dug for the mixing of tadelakt, the special plaster that can be polished to a high sheen. It is a delicate and difficult art and can take months to cure. In the early stages it can be very volatile. Even as we walk past there is a cry and one of the workmen staggers backwards, clutching his face. 'Lime burn,' I say, shaking my head. 'He'll probably be blind for life.'

'Good God,' says the older officer. 'The poor man.'

'If he's lucky he'll escape with his life.'

'*Insha'allah*.' He thinks about this, then adds, 'And if he isn't?'

'They'll add him to the mix.' He looks appalled. 'You'll see worse than that if you stick around. On average we lose thirty workmen a day.'

After that, we walk in silence, although, as we make our way towards the inner courts where the buildings become ever more immense and highly decorated, I can see the older man's eyes darting everywhere. Who can blame him? Nothing of such size or scope has ever been undertaken in Morocco before. The younger officer seems unimpressed, and I suspect he has already been inside the palace complex. He seems impatient, his chin thrusting out with every step, as if nothing can swerve him from his duty. I toy with the idea of admitting that I had found the corpse of Sidi Kabour and walked away without reporting it, but something tells me they are set on their course and this will only make matters worse.

At the entrance to my room, I stop. 'I will bring you the burnous to inspect.'

'We will come in with you.' The second man gives me a gimlet stare.

They stand in the doorway taking in the sparse furnishings as I go to the chest and take out the cloak, which they examine minutely. Finding no blood, they hand it back. 'And this is the only white burnous you own?'

'I am not made of money.'

The younger man sneers, then turns to Hassan. 'You said you were on duty yesterday when this man returned?'

Hassan nods. 'Yes, I opened the gate to him. He was running –'

49

'He was *running*?' He turns back to me. 'Why were you running?'

'It was raining.'

'You did not say he was wearing a white cloak when he returned,' the officer says to Hassan, though his eyes remain upon me.

My eyes flick in consternation to the guard: he stares back at me impassively. 'I do not have time to take notice of what everyone wears, but I am sure Nus-Nus was wearing that burnous.'

The younger man's disappointment is palpable. 'And what about your footwear, sir?'

The 'sir' is new, which is a better sign; but I forgot the babouches.

'You were barefoot, I believe,' Hassan supplies helpfully.

'Barefoot?' Both officers stare at me with renewed interest.

'The mud was appalling: I did not want to ruin my babouches.'

The younger man refers to his notes again. 'It says here that you left the palace wearing a pair of high cork pattens.'

Oh, good God. 'Does it?' Have they even interviewed the wretched slaves? The idea is absurd, but even the walls have eyes in this place. 'I was wearing pattens when I went out but they were the devil to walk in, so I took them off, preferring to go barefoot. It is a lot easier to wash mud off one's feet than one's shoes.'

The two officers exchange a look. I wonder what it means.

'May we see the babouches, sir? For the sake of completeness,' the older man says almost apologetically.

Hell and damnation. I point to my feet. 'Here they are: I have them on.'

They look down. These Fassi slippers start life the colour of a new lemon, but with time they mellow to a muddy brown, and the leather spreads and moulds itself to the shape of your feet. Mine are as scuffed as those of the poorest carpenter, hardly warranting the necessity for pattens. The officers look suitably sceptical. 'And these are the only babouches you own?'

'Yes.' It sounds unlikely even to me.

'You won't mind if we have a quick look through your room.' A statement, not a question.

I stood aside. 'Go ahead.'

It does not take them long: there is not much to see. They go through the chest, even flicking through my books, as if I could have hidden incriminating slippers between the pages. They find the wrapped packages I bought for Malik and forgot to give him: the ras el hanout and essence of attar; but these are easily identifiable by smell. Then they have a good look at the lap-desk, sniffing the inks as if they think I have bottled poisons out on display. When they find my *khanjar*, the ceremonial dagger all men (even the cut) carry on special occasions, they become quite animated; but their faces soon fall when they find it blunt and rusty, useless for sawing through an old man's beard and throat. At last, unsatisfied, the young officer takes out of his satchel a roll of cloth and lays it on the floor. On it the shape of a foot has been imprinted in a dark, rusty brown.

'I made this impression at the scene of the crime. Would you be so good as to place your right foot upon it, sir?'

Still so polite. I do as requested. The leather of my old babouches has spilled over the original line of the sole: my foot engulfs the smaller impression.

'Thank you, sir.' The officer's voice is pinched, spiteful. He rolls up the footprint resentfully. But still he isn't finished. 'Rachid,' he says to the older man, 'the pattens, please.'

Oh, Maleeo . . . there they are, the damned things. The second officer removes them from his bag and places them on the ground before me.

'Would you slip these on . . . sir?' His tone is spiteful.

Should I pitch myself to the floor, feign sudden illness? Should I bluster and refuse to comply? I do neither. Balancing carefully, I push my right foot into the corresponding patten. But instead of incriminating me it sticks halfway down, the comfortable old leather babouche a good two sizes bigger than its pretty jewelled counterpart. The officer seeks to force the issue, but it is obvious that slipper and patten do not fit together. With a wrench that almost has me losing my balance, he separates the two and throws the offending patten aside.

A huge smile threatens to light up my face, but I summon my kponyungu mask and quell the urge.

'They must have belonged to the dead gentleman.' I spread my hands apologetically. 'Is that all, sir? I have many duties to attend to.'

The first officer regards me stonily. I return the stare, unblinking. At last his eyes slide past me. 'And do you have the private use of the courtyard?'

'Others use it too,' I say warily, but out they file.

The rain has washed all the traces of blood from the fountain: the marble gleams pristine white. They kick around the enclosed square for a few minutes while I stand propped against the door. Behind me, Hassan and the other guard are discussing a woman one of them has glimpsed in the mellah. As it is the Jewish quarter, the balconies there face out to the world and she wore no veil and was apparently a peach. The guards of the outer courts are not always castrated unless they seek promotion to the inner courts: their banter is bawdy.

'Are these yours, sir?'

In his hands he holds the bloodstained Fassi slippers I buried out there. You can feel the glee boiling off him. Then, like a man performing a piece of theatre, he unrolls the bloody footprint again and places the right babouche upon the stain. It is, of course, a perfect match.

'And what do you have to say about this?'

Calm, Nus-Nus. Calm. I am careful to maintain silence, rather than saying anything that would incriminate me further.

'Remove your babouches,' he orders me, and when I have done so he indicates the ruined slippers. 'Put them on.'

The blood has dried and crusted on them. They were already tight: I pray they will be more so now, but the treacherous things go on, at a pinch.

Cocksure now, the officer retrieves the discarded patten, makes a great show of placing it on the ground before me. 'Now place your foot in the overshoe.'

I do as he says. The fit is perfect, of course. I am lost.

'Court official Nus-Nus,' he announces with pompous triumph, then pauses. 'Do you have no other name?'

I shake my head: none that I will give to such as him.

'Court official Nus-Nus, these guards bear witness to the fact that we are arresting you on suspicion of killing the herbman, Sidi Hamid Kabour.'

'It is not me you should be arresting: there was someone with Sidi Kabour when I arrived, a shifty-looking young man, thin in the face, with a southern accent. He was still there at the stall when I left, when the herb-man was still alive. That's the man who must have killed him, not me!'

The younger officer sneers. 'The defence of the desperate! The man of whom you speak is a gentleman of impeccable character, well known to the qadi. He came forward as soon as he heard of Sidi Kabour's death and has been extremely helpful in our inquiry.'

'He said it was *you* he left with the herbman,' the older officer says, and I can tell by his tone that he no longer believes a word I say. They bind my hands and take me away.

PART TWO

6

2nd May 1677

'My name is Alys Swann and I am twenty-nine years of age.'

'No, I have no children: I have never married.'

'Yes, I am still a maid.'

I answer their questions with my head held high. I am not ashamed of my estate. So I look the foreign picaroon in the eye with all the courage I can muster and speak out clearly. Had our circumstances been different, some of those present would probably have sniggered, but since we are all in fear for our lives they have other more pressing matters to concern them than my spinsterhood and long-preserved virginity.

My captors' scribe takes down these details for his record in a script that reads from right to left. That, in conjunction with his dark skin and cloth-wrapped head, suggests to me that we have been boarded by Turks. Behind me, I can hear Anouk and Marika, my maids, sisters hired to accompany me on the voyage from Scheveningen to England, snuffling and gulping, and feel a brief moment's pity. They are barely more than children, and, although sullen and unbiddable, they do not deserve to meet an early death. Poor dears, they are just starting out, full of the dreams I had at their age – of young men and marriage, of babies and laughter. They have spent most of the voyage giggling and making sheep's eyes at the crew; but now many of those handsome lads lie dead on the deck of our ship, or in chains aboard this one.

'Do you think they will rape us?' Anouk asks me, her eyes huge.

'I hope not,' is all I can honestly say.

And yet a man grasped my breast as they took us off the other vessel. I was so surprised I did not even think to scream, but simply took hold of his hand and pushed it away. An unmistakable expression of shame crossed his face: he bobbed his head and muttered something in his strange language that I believed to be an apology, which did not correspond with the ruthless fashion in which our ship had been taken.

But it does not take us long to realize that we are merchandise, worth far more than the bolts of cloth in the hold of the ship. The two mulatto women who served the dead captain as cooks (and I am sorry to say also more than likely mistresses) roll their eyes. 'Slaves,' one says; and the other replies: 'Again.'

Slavery has always seemed to me a deplorable practice. The idea of owning a person like a stick of furniture seems to me morally wrong and I have refused to buy anyone. Mother berated me for my lack of economic management: Amsterdam is the slave capital of Europe and we could buy slaves for a bargain price. But after Father's death I kept the books and I dug my heels in, though she complained bitterly not to have a parcel of little black boys she could dress up in fancy clothes as an enhancement to her person when her frightful friends visited with their own sorry retinues. But, to my shame, I have never even considered the possibility of a white person being sold as a slave – least of all myself.

I have heard about slave-vessels, of men chained in their own filth and disease below-decks, of more corpses being thrown overboard than arrive alive at the destination; but it seems that is not to be my lot. I am taken to a small cabin, which, although cramped and dirty, affords me some degree of privacy and dignity, and I lie there in the dark contemplating what might have been had our ship reached England. Once married, I would have lived with my husband, Mr Burke, in his newly built house in London's Golden Square – a place that sounds magical, but that I have never seen, and now probably never will see.

I have not met Mr Burke: the union was arranged between our families, though it was not, I fear, the alliance for which my mother hoped. She cherished grand dreams, told me I would marry into the nobility and thus remake the fortune my father lost when he fled from the Parliament men to Holland at the outset of the English War. Why she married him, I do not know, for it was clear to me even as a child that she did not greatly care for him. She too was an émigré, daughter of a family living on the edge of court life, mixing with the rich and famous, without the wherewithal to do so. There was some scandal, I believe; she married Father as a result.

Throughout my youth I was thrown with ever greater urgency at a succession of visiting gentry, but with King Charles restored there were sufficient girls of greater beauty, substantially larger fortunes and better family at home in England to supply the marriage market, and so my mother became an increasingly disappointed woman. Disappointment turned to bitterness; bitterness to a sickness of the spirit that soon became a sickness of the body; and I have been her attendant ever since. It was only because our debts had mounted and she had a 'hankering to see my beloved England before I expire' that she had accepted on my behalf the hand of Mr Andrew Burke.

The closest I had ever come to my fiancé was a small portrait that he sent, but, since I had seen the one made of me for the purpose of the betrothal, I rather doubted its honesty. In my own portrait I was petite and fair, my eyes larger and bluer than they are in life, my skin porcelain white, with no trace of freckle, and a good ten years erased by the lack of detail, as if someone had shone a bright light upon me that washed age and care away. Seeing it made me laugh out loud. 'He'll send me back when he sees what he's actually bought!' Mother was not amused.

Mr Burke's portrait offered a ruddy, black-bearded man of middle age, substantial of belly, dressed in sombre clothing, with a roll of rich fabric spread before him and a yardstick in his hand to indicate his trade as a master draper: a mile lower down the social ladder from my mother's dreams of glory.

However, enlivened by the prospect of being shipped back to England once I was safely married, Mother actually managed to sit up in her sickbed and pronounce him 'a most handsome package'. So it was all weights and measures and merchandise: and now perhaps that system of commodity has found its truest possible expression. Instead of being parcelled off to a fat, ageing draper in London, I will be sold to some other man in another foreign land.

★

We are many days at sea – far more than the three it takes between Scheveningen and the English coast. I have never in my life had so much time to myself. When Father died I was thirteen. Mother took to her rooms on the day they buried him and never stirred from them again, but spent her time dozing, or reading poetry, staring out of the window and sighing for her lost youth; or playing execrably on her *spinetten*.

We had staff while Father was alive: a cook, a housekeeper, a valet, two ladies' maids, a gardener; but upon his death the true state of our finances was revealed, and in short order they left, one by one, as credit ceased and debts were called in and we could no longer pay their wages. At last we were left only with old Judith and her daughter Els. Judith cooked, after a fashion, and Els could just about handle a peeling knife and knead dough. So, young as I was, I stepped into the role of housekeeper. We did not live well, but I was forever occupied with the small things that make a household run – the sweeping and cleaning and sewing and mending, the tending of the garden, which I turned over to the production of legumes and espaliered fruit trees.

One by one, I sold Father's collection of antiques: his Italian glassware and porcelain, his books and curios and his collection of scientific instruments. Then I started on the pretty Turkey carpets, and at last the furniture in all but the reception room, where guests occasionally still came. The rest of the house was stripped to the bare minimum: less to clean, I reasoned, and applied myself to the household accounts. (How I wished I could have sold Mother's wretched *spinetten*: the sound of its misstruck notes echoing through the rapidly emptying house was most jarring on the ears.)

When Mr Burke's proposal arrived, I should have felt relieved that at last we would be taken care of, that I would not have to concern myself with such base matters any more. But, in truth, I enjoyed the practicalities of such a life, the simple logic of knowing that if I did not stir my bones when the sun came up to help Judith and Els in the kitchen, there would be no bread for breakfast; if I did not sow my seeds in May, there would be no beans in September; if I did not mend a torn petticoat as soon as the tear appeared, in no time it would be of no use for anything but cleaning rags. How we managed to maintain the façade of genteel living, I do not know, but I believe no one was aware of the extent of our penury. Every night I went to bed satisfied that all was in good order; only when I slept were my hands still.

So as I lie here in this little cabin my mind wanders greatly. I ponder the identity of our captors and wonder whether we are heading through the Gates of Hercules into the Mediterranean, to the slave-capitals of Algiers or Tunis; or maybe even further east, to the Grand Turk himself in Constantinople.

Barely a week passes before my curiosity is satisfied.

When we finally put into port and the ship is disembarked, I find myself on the shore with tears running down my face – my eyes being now so accustomed to darkness and the light in this new place being so sharp. They take me from the ship by mule through narrow alleyways in which we pass a multitude of brown-skinned men in turbans or point-hooded robes who watch us go by – mainly in silence, though some hurl imprecations, or maybe blessings, in their strange, guttural tongue. We pass rib-thin donkeys and dark-eyed children, and women swathed from head to toe in fabric (a draper's dream). At last we stop at a tall white house without a single window but just a vast, iron-studded door. There I am put into a room with half-a-dozen other women, none of whom speak a word of English, though one, Saar, speaks a little Dutch. She tells me that she and the other women have all been taken from Spanish or Portuguese villages.

All are younger than me by more than a decade, even though the sun has weathered their skin and etched deep lines in their faces. These are girls who sat on wharf sides and sea walls mending nets and packing pilchards into hogsheads of salt. They are tough and pragmatic: there has been no talk of romance or nobility in their families, and so they have no illusions as to what awaits us, and appear resigned to their fate.

'Just think: what do we all have in common?' Saar asks.

'We are all women.'

'Beyond that?'

It does not take long to realize what she means. 'We are all maids.'

'All virgins, yes. That makes us valuable.'

There is only one reason why an entire hymen might make one a valued commodity. I firm my jaw. 'Well, at least that means they will wish to preserve their investment until we are sold.'

'It is worse than that,' the one called Constanza says.

What could be worse?

'They are Mahometans: they will make us turn Turk.'

I stare in disbelief. 'That I shall never do.'

'That is what you say now.'

A dumpy woman in local garb comes in and starts to fuss about us, examining our hands and teeth, as if we are cattle. When she comes to me she grins and pats my hair. Then she says, quite clearly in Dutch, 'What a gem: he'll be pleased with this one.'

I answer her in the same language, which surprises her. She tells me she is called Yasmin, and that her mother 'used to be Dutch', whatever that means. 'You don't look Dutch,' I say, for her skin is a deep olive-brown and her hair dark and wiry.

'I take after my father. My mother worked for Sidi Qasem for many years. She came from Amsterdam with her husband, a renegado sailor who joined the corsair fleet here; but he died in a sea-battle off Gibraltar, and she converted and married a local man, a Berber from the Rif.'

'It seems to be a most cosmopolitan place,' I say wryly.

'Oh, yes!' she exclaims proudly. 'We have captives from all over the world.' She says the town is called Salé and that it lies on the northern coast of Morocco, a word until now I have associated only with the fine tooled leather goods in The Hague's central market. It is, apparently, the chief port for the trading of foreign slaves in all of Barbary. 'The sidi's matamores are full of slaves from Spain and Portugal, from France and Sicily, from Corsica and Malta, and even as far as Ireland and the northern lands beyond.' She tells me that in the time of her mother there was a famous raid on the Arctic city of Reykjavik, when over four hundred captives were taken in a single day. She reaches forward and touches my cheek. 'They were even paler than you, those girls: my mother said they looked as if they had been carved out of ice. Ever since, the aristocracy here have been mad for pale women with yellow hair. They're a status symbol, you see: only a rich man can afford such a rare creature.' She pats my hand again, made familiar by our shared tongue. 'You'll fetch a good price.'

So this is why, despite my age, I have been separated out from the other women on the ship. 'And who is this Sidi Qasem?' I ask.

'He is very venerable.' She murmurs something in her heathen language, runs her hands down her face, kisses her palms and touches them to her heart, as if he is some sort of icon, or saint. 'Sidi Qasem is the leader of the corsair divan. The number of foreign captives his ships have brought in, Allah be praised! You have great good luck to be captured by one of the sidi's captains,' she says, without a hint of irony. 'His wife, Lalla Zahra, was also a captive. She came from England, and was called Catherine there. But here we call her the Rose of the North. She took the name of Zahra when she converted.'

I recoil. 'She became a Mahometan?'

'She is a very great lady, an example to us all. You will meet her shortly: it is a great honour for you.'

I fold my lips and say nothing to that.

Later I am taken downstairs to a large salon lined with low couches. The furnishings are simple, yet rich. My mother is a first-class snob. Raised to appreciate minute calibrations of wealth and taste, I can tell at once that the proprietor of this house has money to spare but uses it wisely, and not for ostentatious show. I am made to leave my shoes at the door of the salon: the carpets I cross are silky underfoot, and in the colours of a muted sunset. There is a carved plaster frieze that runs around the tops of the walls that is as intricately fretted as a honeycomb. The ceiling is of some carved dark wood, the walls are white and the couch coverings of plain cream linen, but the cushions ranged upon them are bright silks and velvets, and the wall-hanging above it is enough to take your breath away. I touch it with wondering fingers, turning up the corner to see the stitching on the back, which is as exquisite as that on the front: the mark of a true craftsman. It is strange to find such beauty in a place that thrives on cruelty.

'I see you have an interest in embroidery.'

The cool English voice makes me start. I turn to find a stately-looking woman of sixty or sixty-five regarding me with a half-smile. Her eyes are a wintry grey-blue, but the inner eyelids have been painted with some dark concoction which makes them leap out at you in a way that is at once very foreign and very direct. I am not used to being scrutinized so; it makes me uncomfortable. I take in the detail of her large silver earrings, and the intricate beaded necklace she wears high on her throat. Her robe is a rich dark blue, its facings and cuffs embroidered with silver wire threaded with seed pearls. She is tall and holds herself straight: she is impressive. But, as she lowers herself on to the cushions, she grimaces as if her joints are stiff, and I realize she is older than I thought.

'Welcome to our house,' she says, gesturing to me to sit, as if I am a Sunday afternoon guest come by for tea and chatter. 'My name is Lalla Zahra, and I am the wife of Sidi Qasem, whose house this is.'

'My name is Alys Swann of The Hague, though my family came originally from England.'

Her lips quirk. 'So did I, once. From a place called Kenegie in west Cornwall. It is not often I have the opportunity to speak my mother tongue these days.'

'Not that many English slave-captives passing through, then?' I ask acidly.

She slaps her hands on her thighs and laughs out loud. 'Well, Alys Swann, what a shame we have to pass you on. It would have been fun to keep you here for a while. It's nice to see someone with a bit of spirit, though I should warn you that it may not be wise to show too much of that where you're going.'

I swallow. 'And where would that be, I wonder? I should like to know my fate. I find it helps in accepting one's lot to have time to assimilate it first.'

She raises an eyebrow. 'You have been earmarked for Meknes.'

Tagged for the marketplace, like a sheep. 'And who or what might "Meknes" be?'

'Can it be that our great sultan's fame has not spread as far as Holland's high society?'

'I do not move in such circles,' I say stonily. She is toying with me, and I do not like her for it.

'You have been set aside as a prize for our most holy majesty, the Emperor Moulay Ismail, who holds court in the imperial city of Meknes, which he is, according to my husband, in the process of reconstructing in a most sublime manner.'

I digest this silently. When Mother spoke of marrying me into the nobility, I do not think this is quite what she had in mind.

'You will be welcomed into the royal harem, if you behave with sense and propriety, and you will never want for anything for the rest of your days. You will be housed in a palace of marble, porphyry and jasper; your meals will be eaten off platters of gold and silver, you will be garbed in the finest silks and in winter the softest wool and perfumed with all the rich scents of Araby. What more could any . . . girl wish for?'

'The Emperor of Morocco wants *me* as a courtesan?' The idea is quite absurd.

'You are pretty enough, with your pale hair and skin, so you will be presented to him as such: what he does with you after that is his own affair.' She smiles sweetly, as if it is quite normal to be sitting here like this, discussing such matters. 'Come now, Alys, it is not so bad. Foreigners may paint the sultan as a monster, but he is a man like any other. As a woman in his harem you will live a comfortable life, and will probably have to lie with him only a handful of times in your life. Maybe even once only.'

I cannot hide my outrage any longer. 'Once is one time too many!'

'It is hard to accept, I know, this loss of choice and will. I was luckier than you, though I too was taken captive by the corsairs.'

'If you were also taken by pirates I would expect a little more charity from you.'

'They are corsairs, Alys, not pirates. There may seem little difference to you, but within this culture these men are heroes, not criminals. They do what they do not for their own personal gain but for the benefit of the community.'

I gesture at the sumptuous room. 'So your beautiful house does not count as "personal gain", then?'

She bridles. 'I understand that it is hard to be robbed of what you think of as your freedom; but answer me truly, Alys, are women ever truly free?

In England, and I imagine in Holland too, we are bought and sold, parcelled off in marriage to consolidate a family business here, political aspirations there, to shore up a failing country estate, or simply to get us off our family's hands. It must have come as something of a shock – I quite understand – to be taken at sea as you were and find yourself amongst people whom you regard as heathen. I know that it can be very frightening. I was taken prisoner during the raid on a church in Penzance in 1625 and sold on the slave blocks here in Salé. I thought my life was ending, but it had only just begun. The man who bought me took me to wife, and it has been the happiest of marriages. You will say that I have been lucky, but I say to you, Alys, that these people are much the same as all other people: some are God-fearing and respectful, even kind; while others are wicked and hateful. All we can do is to hope for the best –'

'And prepare for the worst.' I finish for her, annoyed by her proselytizing.

She spreads her hands. 'It may all turn out far better than you fear. But it is good to be pragmatic and to accept the situation that presents itself with the best grace you can muster; and that way you may preserve yourself and minimize the . . . difficulties.'

'I will not convert.'

'You must make your choices according to your conscience. But, Alys, it is what you keep in your heart that matters. Do not be stubborn, I beg you. For your own sake.'

For a moment, the air hangs heavy with intimations of violence, then there is a rustle of cloth behind me and in an instant the sharp planes of her face are gentled and a blush suffuses her skin, as if someone has lit a lantern inside her. From behind me comes a man's voice, deep and vibrant, and the master of the house comes into view and stands there looking down at me.

He is old and gaunt, with a dark face and close-cropped, snow-white beard. His eyes blaze, shrewd and fierce, under the brim of his intricately wound headcloth as he looks me up and down. I am taken aback when he addresses me in English. 'Good day, Alys Swann. My captain has a tendency to exaggerate, but I see that for once his description has not done the subject justice.'

Made bold by disbelief, I look back steadily. 'Lovely enough to be forced into servitude as a harlot to some monstrous sultan, or so I am told.'

His eyes gleam. 'It strikes me that you are a woman of some conviction. Conviction and beauty are two qualities to be prized, but when combined, it is like harnessing a wild stallion and a mule to the same single carriage: the result can be . . . dangerous.'

'For the coachman or the passengers?'

'For all concerned. But especially for you. Alys Swann, it would be a shame indeed to see such spirit broken and such beauty marred.'

'They would torture me into converting?'

'The emperor will not lie with an infidel.'

'Perhaps it is best to put me on the blocks and sell me to the highest bidder.'

He folds himself with surprising grace and suppleness to sit before me cross-legged so that he can look me in the eye. 'The emperor is always the highest bidder, Alys Swann; even if the price he pays is not monetary. You will not understand this, I know, but believe me when I say that I dare not sell you elsewhere. Moulay Ismail would hear of it and have my head. Young women of such striking appearance are too rare a commodity in our markets not to draw attention.'

'Then keep me here as a servant,' I challenge.

'It is not possible. I am sorry, but we must pass you on. You are a prize fit for an emperor, and for the emperor we shall prepare you.'

7

Three days later, Lalla Zahra comes to my room bearing a bundle of silks. She lays them down on the rug and sorts them into brightly coloured piles. Then she holds up one of the items against me. 'This will suit you.'

It is a plain silk robe in a glowing green-blue, with wide sleeves and frogged buttons running down the front. It is unlike any piece of clothing I have ever worn. Pragmatic concerns, constrained finances and the strictures of a climate that encouraged worsteds and wools have prevented me from ever wearing anything so impractical. I itch to wear it; and yet I fight the urge. 'I doubt it,' I say, folding my arms.

'Try it on.'

We stand there for a long moment, staring at one another. Then she smiles. 'I understand your reluctance, Alys. I am not made of stone. But events have their inevitable path and it is impossible to go back from here. Let us make the best of it, and of you.'

I strip to my chemise and she drops the robe over my head and upraised arms. The silk feels like water against my hot skin, and too flimsy for decency.

'This goes over the top of it.' She offers another filmy garment, a sort of outer coat of embroidery on a ground of gold net. It is extremely finely worked. I find my traitor hands reaching for it as if they have a will of their own.

She shakes out my hair around my shoulders, then leads me to a mirror, and I stare at my unfamiliar reflection. The transformation wakes an almost physical pain. If I had looked like this, would Laurent have walked away as easily as he did?

Laurent was an itinerant artist: Holland is full of them these days. They say it is the easiest country to make a living in, if you have a little skill with paint and brush. After the war with Spain finally came to an end and trade flourished, every Dutch merchant suddenly wanted to show off his wealth, to surround himself not only with the beautiful, real objects that bolstered his faith in the new reality, but with representations of those objects too. Depictions of flowers and fruits, town scenes, portraits: a house was not a home unless its walls boasted a dozen framed images of the world inside and out. Holland hung its soul from a hook for all to see. Laurent had tried to make a living as a painter in his native France, but the French are snobs about such things and Laurent had made no name for himself. Although he had some skill, he was by no means an outstanding draughtsman; but in The Hague he made a good living. He was handsome; that was one reason why. Merchants' wives and daughters encouraged his attentions. Black hair, dark eyes, sculpted bones: he was as unlike the broad, blond, ruddy-complexioned men of the town as could be. I never considered myself a romantic ninny whose head could be turned by a striking face or a flowery compliment, but when I met Laurent it was as if my heart had plunged off a cliff and the rest of me had followed an instant later.

He came to the door, seeking a commission: seeing a solidly built, well-presented merchant's house he no doubt expected a solidly built, well-presented merchant to open the door to him, but when I explained the lack I saw his face fall before he recovered himself and started to make his apologies. It was that moment of perceived disappointment that was my downfall: for in that moment I fell in love. A perverse decision, indeed: to yearn after something you can never have. He had clearly shown me in that unguarded moment his true estimation of me: that I was neither rich enough nor lovely enough to interest him as either subject or object of his skills.

Although we had acres of empty wall on which to display a painting, the last thing we could afford was a commission. But I commissioned him any-way. Judith overheard our conversation. She was right behind me when I turned back into the house after standing there watching the Frenchman loping away down the street with a swagger that made my insides flutter.

'We can't afford it,' she said. 'You know we can't.'

I was her employer and she just a servant, but when you bake bread together at sun-up each morning, these inequalities rather get knuckled in with the dough. I was used to her speaking her mind and rarely rebuked her for it.

'He's dangerous,' she went on. 'You can see it in the way he walks. Go after him: tell him you've changed your mind.'

I knew she was right, but I made her be quiet: having an external conscience is never a comfortable thing.

He came the next day, and the next and the next for three whole blissful weeks, and I sat on a chair in the kitchen garden for him. 'The light will be better there for you,' I said; meaning, there's not a stick of furniture in the house, and you will guess my motives.

He set up his easel amongst the bean-poles and trod on my seedlings, but I never complained. It was intoxicating, having my portrait painted. He was used to dealing with uneasy subjects and had a way of flattering that made me go limp and complaisant. Being inexperienced, I took each compliment at face value. I hugged them to me (in place of him) in my narrow bed each night: to have such a handsome man examining my face minutely, even though I was paying him for the privilege, was a heady experience for an unmarried 24-year-old who had never considered herself worth looking at. Each touch of the brush on the canvas felt like a caress; and with each brushstroke I felt myself grow more beautiful. I dreamed of the life he and I would have together, the children I would bear him. And suddenly I wanted his children with a passion. I had never thought of having a child until that time: but after, the idea gripped me like a sickness.

Did I think I was exerting some sort of silent spell over him during those quiet hours? The more deeply I fell in love with him, the more sure I became that my feelings were reciprocated – by the tilt of his head, the set of his lips, by the way he stayed to take a glass of sugared lemon water or one of the little cakes I took such care to prepare for him each day.

He refused to show me the work while it was in progress, but by the time he completed the commission I had convinced myself of what I would see captured by his clever hands, in the immortal oils he squeezed out so lasciviously on to his palette. So at last when he revealed the finished painting I thought he was playing a trick on me, had substituted for mine another woman's portrait. This woman was plain and dull-looking, in her sensibly high-necked dress and her starched white cap and collar . . . Her eyes, screwed up against the light in the kitchen garden, were lost in folds of white flesh; her nose was beak-like, her lips set in a firm line. She looked a severe Puritan virgin, rather than like the daughter of an English royalist who was dying for a French artist to tear off her clothes and ravish her amongst the broad beans and radishes.

I choked down my disappointment, paid him and bade him farewell. He had spent four hours every day for three weeks in my company: he took the money and was gone within five minutes, not looking back once. I never saw him again.

I took a long, hard look at that portrait. Then I burned it. I carry the painting within me as my image of who I am . . . and it is certainly not the woman staring back at me from Lalla Zahra's mirror. This is the woman Laurent should have painted, this exotic minx, with her glowing skin and bright, loose hair, whose eyes shine with the same turquoise lights as the silk. This woman might have captivated him as I had so longed to do.

I give my reflection a wry smile: just as well, I think, that I did not.

Lalla Zahra misreads my expression for one of self-satisfaction. 'You see, Alys, you will make a fine courtesan. The kaftan becomes you.'

She does not understand at all when I tear it off and throw it back at her and burst into tears. It is the first time I have cried since being taken captive.

The kaftan is only the beginning. I am taken to a place they call a hammam, a type of communal bath. There, I am stripped and marched into a very hot chamber filled with steam. It is hard to see for all the vapour, but when it clears I find large numbers of local women walking about stark naked with no more shame than Eve before she bit the apple. Some sit; others squat, displaying clefts as hairless as a child's. All of them chatter away in their strange language, and their cries and laughter echo off the close stone walls. If I close my eyes, I can believe I have entered a colony of apes.

This easy nakedness shocks me, for in the streets the women cover themselves from head to toe in swathed attire that offers nothing to even the most prurient imagination. I will have to reassess the people I find myself amongst. If the gentler sex can be so brazen, what must the men be like, and how would they treat a woman like me?

The maids wash my hair and scrub my skin and I give up trying to fight them off, until, that is, I am taken into an anteroom and made to lie spread-eagled on a block of stone. The strip of chemise with which I have covered my loins is unceremoniously torn away, and for the next half an hour I have to close my eyes and think myself back in the tranquil courtyard at Lalla Zahra's house, for the indignities I suffer are quite unspeakable.

Later that night, when I examine myself in the privacy of my room, all over my poor red skin is as innocent of hair as any of Raphael's cherubs.

The next day Lalla Zahra tells me to make ready for my journey to Meknes. She hands me a book. 'You are an educated and intelligent woman: I think you will appreciate it. Promise me you will read from it whenever you can.' Then she hugs me briefly and regards me for a long moment, her eyes glittering in the bright light.

It is small and simply bound in dark brown leather. I think, foolishly, it is a Bible and thank her for her kind gesture. But when I open to the flyleaf I find it to be 'The Alcoran of Mahomet, Translated out of *Arabick* into *French*. By the *Sieur du Ryer*, Lord of *Malezair*, and Resident for the French King, at *Alexandria*. And Newly Englished, for the satisfaction of all that desire to look into the *Turkish* Vanities. London Printed, Anno. Dom. 1649.'

The heathens' holy book; and printed in London too! When I lift my head to voice my outrage, I find she has slipped away as silently as she came in. I throw the offensive book away from me; but when I go down into the courtyard there it is, perched on top of the bag of clothing and toiletries I am to take with me on my journey.

8

It is a Friday when we leave the city, the Mahometans' holy day. All over the city the eerie cries of their prayer-callers echo through the warm air like the cries of foreign birds.

Three of us travel inside a curtained box. The two other women are dressed in a similar fashion to me, in cotton kaftans with bright scarves bound around their heads. Like me, they are blue-eyed, but they look as foreign as the Moroccan women, with their dark brows and lashes. We sit in stultified silence as the cart rattles and jolts its way through the narrow city streets. Once I twitch aside the curtain and a shaft of sunlight cuts through the carriage like a knife. The girl next to me flinches and turns her head away. Her hands are never still, her fingers working listlessly against one another in a nervous fashion.

There are men everywhere, flowing in a stream towards the nearest mosque: men in white robes and little skullcaps; men in tunics and wide trousers that stop short of the ankle; men in turbans or beneath hooded robes. Their faces are as brown as polished walnuts and their black eyes are inquisitive. Their stares are frank, piercing: like hunters who have sensed quarry.

After what seems an interminable interval, but may have been only two hours, we come to a halt.

'Are we here already?' asks the girl on the other side of the carriage.

'You're English!' I cry, almost an accusation.

It is the other one who answers me. 'Irish. We're Irish, not English. We're sisters, so we are, Theresa and Cecelia: sisters from Ringaskiddy, though there's not many as knows where that is so I just say Cork.'

Which explains the telling of the phantom rosary beads. My mother was fiercely anti-Catholic, blamed the old king's French wife for his, and therefore our family's, downfall; and when his son married a Portuguese

Catholic, she was incandescent with rage. I peer through the crack in the curtains. 'We're in a forest.'

They relax visibly. 'Mother Mary, thank you. Cecelia and I have sworn to be martyrs like Saint Julia and Saint Eulalia.' Cecelia bursts into noisy tears. Theresa pats her on the arm. 'It's all right: you shall be like Saint Julia: *I* shall be Eulalia.' She turns back to me. 'Saint Eulalia refused to recant her faith; so they cut her breasts off.'

Cecelia's sobs rise to a wail.

'They put her in a barrel full of glass shards and rolled it down a hill, so they did. But even that was not enough to make her turn apostate; so two executioners tore her flesh with iron hooks and held flames to her wounds till the smoke made her swoon. And then at last she was crucified on a cross and after that they decapitated her, and a dove flew right out of her neck. It was a miracle!' Her eyes flash with fanatic fervour. 'She was only twelve years old. Theresa and I have pledged our virginity to the Virgin Mother herself. We'll be Saint Cecelia and Saint Theresa of Ringaskiddy. There will be girls all over Ireland saying their prayers to us in years to come.'

I do not think this is much of a consolation for such a violent death, but the desire for martyrdom is not enshrined in the Protestant religion. 'I envy you your certitude,' I say gently; and I do. Will my own faith bear me safely through the trials to come?

Suddenly the door to the carriage creaks open and a man peers inside. Cecelia stifles a shriek.

'Sidi Qasem.' I incline my head.

'Miss Swann. We will make a brief stop here.'

While the two Irish girls are availing themselves of a thick stand of vegetation, I spy in the distance, heading towards us, a long line of men, prisoners, making their way along the forest track. The man leading them rides forward to meet Sidi Qasem. Leaning from his horse, he takes the old man's outstretched hand and raises it to his lips. It seems there are hierarchies even amongst slavers.

Cecelia and Theresa stomp noisily through the undergrowth and stand beside me brushing burrs and grass seeds off their robes, their eyes trained on the group of men approaching. 'Holy Mother.' Cecelia crosses herself. 'They look half starved.'

The sisters make for the safety of the carriage, but I cannot tear my eyes away. The men's hands are bound with rope, and heavy weights have been secured to their ankles to impede any attempt at escape. Where the iron moves with the movement of their legs, the weights have rubbed raw, red patches into the skin, and so they shuffle to minimize the chafing. Many wear no shirts and have been burned across the shoulders by the sun; their ribs show as clearly as the staves in a wrecked boat, and when they pass I see that a number of them bear livid weals across their backs.

I feel ashamed to be watching them with good food in my belly and silk against my skin. Their faces are bleak and hopeless, each man trapped in his own private hell – except for one. He turns his head towards me as the line passes the carriage. He is tall and his skin is fair, his beard showing through in little tufts of yellow. I realize with a shock that he is barely more than a boy. 'Pray for us, lady!' he says in one language after another; then the overseer spurs his horse back and lashes at him with his whip so hard that the boy cries out and stumbles.

I turn away, my eyes swimming. What hope is there for any of us, that these men can be treated as little more than beasts?

Sidi Qasem appears beside me. 'Why the tears, lady?'

'Must they walk all the way to Meknes?'

'They will walk, or they will die.'

'And what will happen to them when they get there?'

'They will help to build Moulay Ismail's new city. If they do not die on the march, they will certainly do so at Meknes. In a week; a month; a year if they are hardy. Ismail is a hard taskmaster: he makes no allowance for illness or frailty.'

'Such a waste of human life, just to build a city.'

'It is not "just a city", Alys. It is a devotion to God. Our religion is a civilization-building religion: it came out of the desert and within a century it had created the greatest civilization in the world. Allah commanded us not to let a desert remain a desert, or a mountain to remain a mountain. The world must be transformed to the divine pattern; and it is in that transformation that we find our connection to the divine. Meknes is a prayer to God, a single song of praise, and Ismail is both architect and praise-singer. We all play our part in the grand design.'

I shiver as I sit back down in the carriage, beside two girls determined to die for the Catholic cause, while Sidi Qasem speaks of murder as part of a divine pattern. I am surrounded by fanatics. The question remains, am I one too?

9

Third Sabbath, Rabī al-Thūnī 1087 AH

Three weeks I have been rotting away in this dark cell, surrounded by mad-men and criminals. Three weeks is not very long in the greater scheme of things, I know: but time in the pitch darkness drags like perdition itself.

The qadi had me fetched to him in the first week, very pleased with him-self: another foul crime solved, another criminal to be dispatched. The punishment for murder is to have a nail driven through the top of my skull with hammer blows. He told me this with relish. A short, squat man, he had that softness to him that comes only from a good living had from receiving plenty of *baksheesh* up the sleeve. Unfortunately, I had nothing with which to bribe him. I am a slave, no matter how elevated, and slaves do not get paid.

I asked him if the sultan was aware of my plight and he laughed in my face. 'Why should the sultan give a fig's pip for one more black felon in this town? We have executed thirty already this month, and like rats there are always more.'

The very fact that I am still languishing in the gaol after three weeks away from my duties tells me everything I need to know: that I am expend-able, forgotten. I wonder who is attending Ismail at his prayers, checking his babouches for scorpions or his food for poison, delivering messages, keeping the couching book. I torture myself at the thought of my replace-ment being given my room, throwing out my few possessions: the little my life has been reduced to. I wonder if even now he is taking a few minutes between his duties to sit in the courtyard where I so foolishly hid the spoiled babouches, enjoying the warm caress of the sun on his upturned face and the scent of the jasmine tumbling from the catwalk. All I can smell here is shit and piss and sweat made sour by terror, and I can assure you none of it smells much like jasmine.

When the muezzin calls I turn to pray along with the other unfortunates. But who knows the direction of Mecca in this place, in such darkness? I think of Ismail making his rounds with his army of astronomers armed with their astrolabes and calculations, fiddling with their rules and angles, aligning the alidade with the degree of the sun to tell them precisely in which direction the Holy City lies, before the sultan can kneel and pray. All I can do is turn away from the bucket of shit and hope for the best.

One morning I run a hand across my jaw and find bristles there. Can it be that a spell in gaol is turning me back into a man? I allow myself a mirthless smile, then put my head in my hands. God loves a joke.

Suddenly the viewing window shuttles open and a voice calls, 'Nus-Nus? Which one of you is the court official known as Nus-Nus?'

There are a few titters; but they stop when I stand up. 'I am he.'

The guard opens the door and beckons me out. 'And don't try anything or I'll take your leg off.'

Seated at a table in a side-room, sipping tea and swathed from head to foot in black, is a woman. I know who it is at once, despite the veil, by the thickness of her wrist and the colour of her skin, even though she is not wearing her usual jewellery. I am alert enough to say nothing. The guard shows no curiosity, and shuts the door behind him. I wonder how often women come to this noisome place for their last conjugal visits, and shudder.

'So, Nus-Nus, this is where you are,' she says in Lobi.

'So it would seem,' I reply in Senufo.

'No one took the trouble to tell me until yesterday,' Zidana says. 'I thought you were ill.'

I do not believe her: Zidana's spies are everywhere. 'Why are you here?' She is taking a risk, and I doubt it is for my good. If Ismail discovers she has flouted his will by slipping outside the palace walls, even being his chief wife is unlikely to save her. I have seen him strangle one so-called favourite with his own hands for the heinous crime of picking up a fallen orange from the ground to eat. 'We are not paupers, to stoop to such behaviour!' he chastised as he choked the life out of her. 'Have you no dignity? If you would shame your sultan by doing such a thing, what more would you do?' He had nightmares the following night, calling her name over and over again in his sleep – *Aicha, Aicha* – and the next morning his pillow was wet.

'I needed to ask you about the list,' Zidana says simply. 'Have they mentioned it? Do they have it as evidence?'

I sigh. 'No one has spoken of it.'

'Good. Well, that is something, at least.' She sips her tea and we sit in silence. 'How is the sultan?' I ask after a long while.

'Ismail is Ismail, but in a worse temper than usual. He sent Zina away last night without touching her. That's a first.'

'He has not asked for me?'

'He has not mentioned you to *me*.'

'But who is keeping the couching book for him? Who is tasting his food?'

'Do not torment yourself so,' she says, and rises to go.

'Will no one intercede for me? You know I am innocent of the charge.'

'When did innocence save anyone? Knowledge is far more useful.'

'Indeed. I would not wish to be tortured,' I say suddenly, made bold by desperation. 'For fear of what I might say, about my reasons for visiting Sidi Kabour.'

She laughs then. 'Oh, Nus-Nus, show a little fortitude, a little Senufo spirit.'

And then she taps the door and the guard lets her out into the light and takes me back to the darkness. I am so caught up in my own thoughts that I eat mindlessly, like an animal, when they bring food. Forgetting that there may be stones in the barley bread, I bite down hard and crack a grinding tooth, and thus have a new woe to think upon.

The next day the guard comes for me again. 'You're suddenly very popular,' he leers. I know something is up when he brings me a bucket of cold water, a handful of olive paste for soap and a knotted rag with which to clean myself in the corridor outside. I turn away, trying for some degree of modesty, but he just laughs. 'I've seen all sorts in here: nothing shocks me.'

Even so, his eyes fix themselves curiously on my crotch as I strip, but when I straighten and stare him in the eye he looks away. I wash and put on the clean linen breeches and long grey tunic he gives me.

As soon as I see the rich silk of the back of his turban, I know my visitor. He turns and looks me up and down. 'Ah, Nus-Nus, it pains my heart to see you so reduced. Obscurity comes quickly, does it not? One moment you are at the centre of all things with the blessed light of the sultan shining upon you; the next you find yourself in the outer darkness. It is chill there, is it not?'

'Have you come to taunt me?'

The grand vizier smiles. 'Come, come, Nus-Nus. Won't you beg for your life? You know I have the power to save you.'

I fold my arms. 'I doubt my life is worth the bargain you would strike.'

'You value yourself too low.' He puts out a hand and touches my thigh, his fingers kneading the big muscle there as if he will make bread with it.

I school myself to ignore it. What was it Zidana had said? *A little Senufo spirit*. I gather my resources and attempt to summon the lost warrior within.

His hand creeps closer to my groin, shielded by the long tunic and I know at once he chose the garment carefully and for this purpose. His fingers close on me through the thin fabric of the breeches, caressing. *I shall see you dead, I promise* – if by some miracle I should survive.

'I would rather take my punishment than be your plaything.'

He smiles unpleasantly. 'An innocent man prepared to die horribly for a crime he did not commit?'

'What do you know of it?'

'Enough to save your ungrateful black hide. Think about it, Nus-Nus. A place in my household, the best of everything: a life of luxury. That or a nail driven through the top of your head. It doesn't seem like much of a choice to me. But take your time. I shall ensure the qadi doesn't carry out the execution for a few days, to give you the space to consider your decision.'

'What about my trial?'

'What trial? The qadi has all he needs by way of proof of your guilt. Unless he decides to torture you for a fuller account of your visit to the herbman, of course. That would be most unpleasant, to go through the bastinado, the pincers and the rack, before ending up with a nail in the skull.'

'As a member of the palace staff I can't be executed without a warrant signed by the sultan,' I say stiffly.

Abdelaziz snorts. 'Did you not know, Nus-Nus, that I am in charge of such warrants?'

I hang my head, defeated.

'Ismail has not even noticed your absence, my dear boy. Well, no, that is something of an exaggeration: he noticed when you were late appearing the first day you went missing and went roaring around, demanding your head. He beat his two body-slaves almost unconscious when they said they did not know where you were, and after that he never mentioned you again, no doubt thinking that in one of his fits of madness he had lopped off your head. Have you noticed this strange habit of his? Killing someone one day and pretending the next that nothing has happened? I remember when he beat Kaid Mehdi black and blue over his failure to quell some small rebellion in the Rif: the man lost an eye. The next time Ismail saw him he was wearing a patch over it, and Ismail took him by the arm and asked him most solicitously what had caused the loss of the eye. The poor man stammered out some lie about falling from a horse and the sultan heaped gifts upon him, no doubt to assuage his conscience. But guilt will out. They say he has bad dreams after such bouts, from time to time. Is it true?'

It is, but I don't answer.

'No matter. My nephew Samir Rafik is taking care of him now.'

And with that dagger to my heart he leaves. When the guard comes to take me back to the cell, he winks at me, and, though I washed thoroughly a bare half hour ago, I feel dirty to the depths of my soul.

Early the next afternoon the guard calls me out again. What now? The grand vizier must think me feeble-minded indeed that a single night of reflection should sway me to his will.

'They say the third time's the charm,' the guard mutters cryptically and, unlocking the door to the side-room, pushes me in.

I stare at Kaid Mohammed ben Hadou Ottur and he looks back, faintly amused. 'You were expecting someone else?'

'You are my third visitor in as many days, sidi.'

He barks out a laugh. 'Zidana and Abdelaziz, I believe?' He has a reputation as an astute man and I suspect that he runs a battery of spies. 'Get undressed.'

I have not heard he is a sodomite, but clever men learn to hide their vices in Ismail's palace. But when I start to undress, instead of staring frankly, he tosses me a bundle of clothes: a pair of cotton trousers and a plain wool djellaba. 'Put the hood up,' he advises. 'I'll explain as we walk.'

Walk?

Two minutes later, just like that, we are outside. I stand there with my head tipped back, blinking in the hot ochre light, suddenly overwhelmed by the blue of the sky; the eye-hurting green of the new fig leaves in a nearby courtyard. The last time I saw the tree, the leaves were in bud, their silken undersides barely visible against the silver bark.

'What happened?' I ask, running to catch up with my liberator, who is moving away at speed towards the medina with his long, loping stride.

'We have need of you. The sultan and I.'

My heart soars: not forgotten, after all! 'I shall be for ever grateful to you for restoring me to the service of my lord . . .'

'Do not be too quick to thank me, Nus-Nus. You will not like the reason for your release. There is a task for you to perform. It is, shall we say, unpleasant.'

I cannot imagine what can be so onerous. We pass a group of women comparing braids and beads at the haberdasher's stall. They watch us with interest, batting their eyelids over their veils.

'And what of the . . . matter . . . of Sidi Kabour?'

The Tinker puts a finger to his mouth. 'If you achieve this task, Sidi Kabour will never have existed.'

I frown. 'But . . . but, his family —'

'Everyone necessary will be paid. Reports will be burned. Learn some discretion, Nus-Nus. If I tell you it is night while the sun shines, don your night robe and light a candle. Do as you are bid and no one will ever speak of this matter again.' He says something else, and I think I hear the name of the grand vizier, but now we are passing through the metal quarter, where men are sitting in the sunshine beating out giant copper bowls and couscous vessels so vast they must be destined for the palace kitchens, and the noise of their hammers drowns out his words.

Sometime later we emerge from the warren of alleyways into the Sahat al-Hedim – 'The Place of Rubble', for all the building detritus that has been dumped here outside the palace walls. The first thing my lord Ismail did when he decided to make Meknes his capital – rather than nearby Fez (which, apart from being cramped and dank and stinking, is rife with dissidents, *marabouts* and Qur'anic scholars too ready to voice an unwanted opinion) or Marrakech (which is held by his rebel brother, and is always an untrustworthy place) – was to send in thousands of slaves to raze the old town to make way for his grand new design. That was five years ago, and although the first stage is nearing completion, chaos still reigns. He is a great man, Moulay Ismail, Emperor of Morocco, Father of the People, Emir of the Faithful, Overcoming of God. Yes, a great man; but he is no architect.

A mule train is being unladen on one side of the square, the animals tended to as they are disencumbered of their packs. Traders sit around them, dickering with their tally sticks and weights. A swallow dips and twists over their heads, as if flies were released when the goods-packs were opened. I see the flash of a red as dark as old blood on its throat as it swoops past, the forked plume of its tail, and then it is gone.

I do not recognize the guards on the gate, but they yield quickly enough at the sight of the man with me, and it strikes me how quickly the world has changed since I was incarcerated. As we walk at a fast clip through the marble corridors, I work up the courage to ask about my room. 'In that place, the quiet and comfort of it was much on my mind. I know it is a small thing, below your notice, sidi . . .' I trail off, hopelessly.

'Your quarters are your own again, Nus-Nus: your things I have restored as best I was able. If I have overlooked something, forgive me. If you find anything missing, let me know and I will do my best to replace it for you.'

Such kindness is unexpected. Gratitude warms my heart; then I remember the onerous task. 'So what is it you want me to do?'

He gives me a flat-lidded, enigmatic look. 'I am led to believe you can converse most persuasively in this heathen tongue,' he says to me in perfect English.

I am unable to hide my surprise. 'A previous master educated me in many things, amongst which was a passable fluency in English.' I pause. 'But, sidi, how is it you speak it so well?'

'English was the mother tongue of my mother,' he replies shortly, and looks aside.

That explains those curiously light eyes. I remember it is whispered that he had a European slave for a mother, but thought it malicious slander. If it is true, he must have had to work hard for Ismail's favour.

'Is there something in English you wish translated?'

'You could put it like that.'

As we approach the harem gates, he stops. 'You may take your hood down now. Announce yourself to the guards. They know what to do.'

Strange. I watch him walk quickly away and wonder what linguistic problem can be so important as to have prompted him to rescue me from gaol and risk the wrath of the grand vizier. The guards on the gate usher me through, the boy sent to guide me drags me by the hand, past Zidana's pavilion to a building I have never visited – or even seen – before. 'Wait here,' he tells me, and runs inside.

Leaning back against the sun-warmed plaster, I close my eyes and turn my face up to the sun. Somewhere, a peacock sounds its melancholy cry, but all I can think is: I am free! Every night, amid the stench and babble of that foul cell, I imagined the cold iron nail entering my skull, and now here I am with the sun on my face, and the backs of my eyelids glowing vermilion, breathing in the scents of neroli and musk.

My nose twitches. I know that scent . . . I open my eyes, but the sun's after-images confuse my vision. I blink, and find Zidana bearing down upon me. A little black slave-girl runs panting alongside her, fanning her wildly with a fistful of ostrich feathers. I sneeze loudly, the fan having wafted dust into my nostrils.

'Why, Nus-Nus, is this how you greet your sovereign? Down you go like the dog you are!'

I prostrate myself, since it seems expected. Why so formal? Zidana does not usually stand on such ceremony with me.

There is a cat in front of me: a sleek blue-grey thing with slanted amber eyes. It lowers its wedged-shaped head to regard me curiously. Then it turns and winds its body sinuously around a pair of legs behind it and I see that the fur on its back is spotted dark red, as if paint has been dripped on it. When it moves behind the legs I see a pair of feet clad in slippers embroidered with gold wire and studded with gems. I know the style: I buried the last pair he cast off in a plant pot in my courtyard, covered in Sidi Kabour's blood. I press my forehead into the tiles.

'Has she capitulated?' Zidana's voice.

'She is most wretchedly stubborn.'

'I did warn you: she has a look in her eye.'

'Perhaps it was that quality in her that drew me.'

'I am surprised she has not yet said the *shahada* —'

The shahada — those few words an infidel must utter to renounce their own faith and become a Muslim in the sight of God. And suddenly I realize what it is the Tinker freed me to do. Something for which he had not the stomach . . .

'I fear she may not have properly understood the situation.'

'Clearly she has not understood the honour you do her.'

'The honour I intend to do her.' I can hear the desire in his voice: it comes off him in waves.

'Dear one, hold still —'

A pause.

'Child, run and fetch me a cloth and rose water.'

I hear the little girl's feet slapping away on the tiles. No one bids me rise, so I stay where I am with my forehead pressing against the ground. The girl returns. A bowl is set down beside me. Medici porcelain, soft blue flowers on a white ground. In the water it contains I see the reflection of Zidana reaching up tenderly to wipe her husband's face.

'She has soiled you, the little infidel. There, that's better. Ah, a moment, there's some on your precious Afaf too.'

The cloth that is dipped in the bowl stains the water. I watch as the blood flowers like a red tide to the edge of the porcelain, the precise rusty hue of the stain on the swallow's breast.

'What a foolish creature she is to make such a fuss over a few words,' Zidana is saying. 'I am surprised that Sidi Qasem had not schooled her better.' She sounds complacent, as if to change one's faith is as simple as putting off an old robe. Easy enough for you, I think: you said the shahada and gave up your slave-name, but you never relinquished the old religion, just went on practising it under everyone's nose.

Suddenly I feel the weight of the sultan's gaze on me. Then a sharp tap on my shoulder releases me from the prostration. I scramble to my feet. 'Majesty.'

Ismail stands there with the cat, Afaf, cradled in his arms. It sits placidly, perfectly relaxed. I do not *think* the sultan has ever tried to force the shahada on any of his beloved animals. 'Ah, Nus-Nus, good.' A pause, as if he is seeking and failing to find a missing piece of information. 'Good. I have been waiting for you.'

For three weeks, I think, but do not say.

Ismail looks me up and down. 'Excellent choice of robe, black to hide any unpleasant stains, and to ward off the evil eye: good thinking, boy. She has remarkable eyes, this one; but I fear demons lurk within her.' He turns back towards the doorway and gestures for me to follow him.

'Good luck, Nus-Nus,' says Zidana, her lips curved into a malicious smile. 'You'll need it.'

A slight figure sits upright with its back to us on a gilded chair in the middle of the chamber below, one of a set donated by the French ambassador on behalf of his monarch. As a gift, they did not win favour: Ismail recoiled at the sight of them, with their immodestly curved legs, and banished them from his sight. I always wondered what had become of them.

86

Beyond the figure two men come sharply to attention as the sultan enters. I know the first to be Faroukh, one of Ismail's favourite torturers; a shaven-headed Egyptian with the cold, black eyes of a dead shark; the other is a minor lordling, a cousin or distant by-blow, no doubt pressed into this gruesome service by more ambitious members of his family. Certainly, he looks sickened, pale and clammy, as if he may throw up, or faint, at any moment. Woe betide him if he does: Ismail has no mercy for the weak of stomach. Which the Tinker knows well enough, and so has smartly side stepped and brought me here to do his dirty work for him. And to think I was grateful. Small wonder he told me not to thank him yet . . .

'What is her name?' I ask of no one in particular.

Ismail gives a dismissive snort. 'When she goes into the couching book, only then will you need to know her name. She is an obstinate heathen and must be chastised and persuaded to the right path. Tell her to cease her foolish resistance and embrace the true faith. If she does not relent, she will lose her life. If it is her virginity she seeks to preserve, tell her she shall be given to' he looks to the lordling, then away, clearly unable to summon up the lad's name – 'to that one first, and then to Faroukh; then to any guard who wants her and finally to the dogs; and only when all are satisfied will her soul be released into the arms of Jesus the Pretender.' He fixes me with his burning black regard. 'Do whatever it takes to convert her; then have her cleaned up and brought to my rooms. I shall expect her there, submissive to the will of Allah, after fifth prayer. Do this for me, Nus-Nus, and you will be well rewarded. Fail, and I shall give you to Faroukh, who is working on a special new technique for me. An exquisite flaying of the extremities that delivers excruciation, but keeps the victim alive for the longest time. You are just what he needs: a brawny, well-muscled man with some fighting spirit in him. The others have been too feeble to waste words on, let alone Faroukh's best knives.'

10

As the sultan's footsteps ascend the stairs towards the light, I almost wish myself back in my prison cell. Almost. I hope the woman will succumb to reason, but my first sight of her is not promising.

Her fists are clenched in her lap so that the tendons stand out on her forearms. Every line of her body is taut with defiance, even though her face is hidden behind curtains of yellow hair. But then I see how she has drawn her feet up, as if the turquoise silk of her stained and tattered robe might protect them. Her feet are bloated and bruised, glistening with blood and curled in towards one another: she has been bastinadoed.

I look accusingly at Faroukh and he holds my gaze, impassive. In his hands he grasps a long, thick Brazil stick. It is fearfully painful, to be beaten on the soles of the feet. Some men never walk again afterwards. Abruptly I remember the distant peacock-screech, and feel ashamed that, even as I was congratulating myself on my freedom, this poor woman was being battered in the name of God.

'Go fetch cold drinking water and another bowl for washing; clean towels too,' I tell the lordling and he runs for the door.

Contempt for my compassion deepens the lines around the torturer's mouth. Suddenly I cannot bear to be in the same room as him. 'Go outside, Faroukh,' I tell him. 'Wait at the top of the stairs.'

'The sultan told me to stay.'

'Do you think she is likely to escape?'

He gives a barely perceptible twitch of the shoulders. 'They try. You would not believe what I have seen prisoners try.'

I do not want to know what he has seen, but I do know what I would have liked to do to Abdelaziz when he held me captive. 'Just go,' I repeat firmly. 'Guard the damn stairs if it makes you feel better.'

He holds my gaze for two insolent beats, then strides towards the door, tapping the Brazil stick nonchalantly against his thigh.

The effect his absence has is tangible: the woman's shoulders slump as if it is only sheer will that keeps her upright, and her hands open like pale flowers unfurling. I go down on one knee beside her and take one of her hands in mine and turn it over. Crescent moons of blood have been carved by her nails into her palm.

'Such a little hand,' I say, and close her fingers gently over the wounds. 'They call me Nus-Nus, which means "half-and-half". What is your name?'

Her head comes up. In the instant in which our eyes meet I see that hers are a startling colour, a wild flare of twilight blue around the black dilated pupils. Her lashes and eyebrows are golden. I have never seen such a thing. The women of the harem are black of eye and brow and make much use of artifice to heighten the dark drama of their regard. It makes her eyes seem naked, open and vulnerable. In the second before she looks away I know she could not have had a greater effect on my heart had I stared unblinking at her for an hour, or an eon.

I watch a pink wash tinge her white face, rising up to darken the bruise across her cheekbone, almost but not quite obscuring the smear of blood that runs from her nose. Then she says in a clear voice: 'My name is Alys Swann.'

It is as well that the young courtier returns then; for in that moment I am lost. I get up and take from him the pitcher of water, pour myself a cup and drain it down in a single gulp, then refill the cup for the prisoner. She tries to sip it daintily, but, as the desert people say, *aman iman* – 'water is life' – and she cannot help but drink it greedily.

The servant who follows the courtier brings folded white cloths and a bowl of water with rose petals floating in it, which seems a ludicrous courtesy in the circumstances: I tell him to set them down beside the gilded chair, thank them both and send them away. Carefully, I bathe her feet, though she bites her lip so that blood wells up over her teeth. 'You are lucky, Alys,' I say after a while, when my hands have stopped trembling. 'No broken bones.'

She makes a mirthless sound. Then she raises her extraordinary eyes and pins me with them. 'My bones aren't yet broken, and neither is my spirit –' She stops. 'Why do they call you Nus-Nus? It sounds insulting.'

'I am what they call a cut man. A eunuch.'

She gazes at me, unblinking. 'You must forgive me if I do not properly understand exactly what you mean by that.'

I summon a crooked smile. 'Only those who share my sorry estate can truly comprehend it.'

I see her thinking, putting together the cruel name with the implication. She gives a little nod. Then she asks, 'What is your real name?'

For a moment there is just a blankness in my mind. What *is* my name? It is so long since I have used it. From the depths it surfaces and I tell her, and she repeats it twice till the intonation is correct. In her low, melodious foreign voice my name sounds exotic and honeyed. I feel my stomach swoop and fall.

'Does it mean something, in your language, your name?'

'It means "Dead, Yet Awake". I was so slight at birth my mother thought me stillborn; then I opened my eyes. But I'd prefer that you call me Nus-Nus: the boy who was called that is long gone, and much changed.'

A small smile. 'And you have been sent to effect *my* change?'

Her wits are still sharp, for all the pain of her beating. 'I am here to persuade you to accept Islam and save yourself from further . . . unpleasantness.'

She laughs. 'Unpleasantness! Are you some sort of diplomat, Nus-Nus? You are mealy-mouthed enough for one.'

I bow my head. 'I am just a slave, a eunuch to the court; a servant to the emperor. I am sorry. This is not a task I would have wished to undertake. But I have known suffering and witnessed much and would not wish to see you cruelly used.'

'No one would consider me a brave woman, Nus-Nus. I've never had to endure physical pain. Until now, no one has laid a hand on me in all my life. But in these past hours I have discovered there is a strength in me I had not expected, a hard seam that lies beneath the surface. Some might call it obstinacy. I don't know what it is, and I don't seem to be in control of it: I fear it may drive me to behave in a way that will threaten my own life.'

'Then why not master that dangerous trait, cede now and save yourself?'

She pushes the cup back at me. 'My mother was an expert in cajoling, wheedling and conniving. Your words may be gentle, but your aims are the same as theirs, whether delivered with a kind mouth or a stick.'

I change tack. 'Let us talk about conversion, then. The change of one form of religion for another. We all serve one God. He is one and the same no matter what we call him – whether Deus, or Allah or Yahweh. He is the same one who hears our prayers. What does it signify to change the name of the religion that reaches out to him, if your faith remains true in your heart?'

Her lips firm into a flat line.

I press on. 'We are all just people, Alys. I have travelled widely and know enough to tell you that there are good Muslims and wicked Christians just as there are wicked Muslims and good Christians. It is not the form of their religion that makes them so, but their essential nature.'

'I have met plenty of bad Christians, it is true. And I dare say there is kindness and charity to be found amongst the people here. But they are not my people and their religion is not my religion.'

'I should not say this, for I am counted a good Muslim, but in my heart I know that God is God and the rest is only words, and words are just noises we use to communicate with one another.' She does not cry out in horror at this heresy, and so I continue. 'Plato said that the assignment of names to things was arbitrary, that any name might be given to any object, so long as enough people understood what it signified and agreed to use it to define that object. He also argued that existing names for things could be changed without any loss to the nature of the thing itself. So I ask you again, Alys: what does it signify that you say the words required of you, change the name of your religion and speak of Allah?'

'Is it not hypocrisy to accept the outward form and believe another thing in one's heart? Of what value to your religion is such a convert if they do not truly believe?'

I shrug. 'There is much hypocrisy involved in surviving from day to day in the world, especially in this world. I do not think God would sanction you for preserving your life in the face of such alternatives.'

'I will not make myself apostate. The case is not as simple as you suggest. How can I knowingly reject every truth I have been taught regarding the

Holy Trinity and man's salvation through Christ? Just to save my own skin. Jesus hung for three days and nights on the cross to save our souls; I may be only a feeble woman, but I think one beating that has not broken even the bones of my feet does not suffice as excuse to revolt against God.'

I sigh. I am surrounded by those who believe fiercely in the oneness of God, people who will torture and murder without compunction anyone who avers otherwise. My own people believe that every tree and pool in the forest contains a spirit; that ancestors speak to us in our dreams and have themselves become divine. I am hardly the man to turn to in matters of theological debate. And yet I have said the shahada and embraced Islam . . . 'Alys, I would not seek to change the nature of your beliefs: I just ask that you accept the outward form that is offered to you. Say the words and save yourself. They will not stop until you are completely broken, in every terrible way. I speak from experience.'

'You do not look completely broken, to me. But then I do not know what you were before coming here today, a courtier sent to convert me. Tell me your experience. I want to know what has made you the person who would do such a thing.' She tilts her head back and gives me a long, challenging look.

'We are not here to talk about me.'

She folds her arms. 'Then we shall talk about nothing and you will fail in your attempt. And then no doubt I shall not be the only one to suffer.'

Of course, she is right in this assumption. If I fail to convert her, I shall surely be given to Faroukh. I swallow. Must it really come down to this? To the removal of my mask and the showing of my true face? I look at her, at the determination, will and pride holding together this fragile woman, and know I owe her as much truth as I can give to her.

'I was born in a village of the Senufo people. Far from here, beyond the mountains and the Great Desert. My father was a chieftain of a small tribe. I had two brothers and three sisters, but I was the eldest and my mother's favourite. I was a disappointment to my father: he wanted me to be like my cousin Ayew, a warrior and a hunter, but I preferred to make music and dance. I wish I had paid more attention to the art of lance and sword: I might have saved the lives of my mother, my youngest brother . . . but when our enemies came and sacked our village I was in the woods, making a drum. By the time I realized what had happened it was too late. They caught me and sold me to slavers, but I had more luck than I deserved. My first master was a decent man, a doctor. Rather than treating me like a slave, or even like a servant, he made me something of a companion. Taught me to read and write, about medicine and anatomy; he bought me instruments and encouraged my love of music; he took me all over Europe with him and dressed me well. I thought myself a grand fellow. My cousin Ayow would have said I had got above myself.'

She gives a little smile at that. 'A slave who thought himself a gentleman?'

'Something like that.'

'Not so bad so far. He does not sound the sort of master who beat you to accept his religion.'

'He did not need to. He was himself a convert to Islam, finding it a kinder and more charitable religion than Christianity. I elected to accept it for his sake, then came to love it for itself.'

She firms her lips. 'So, you were well treated, educated and pampered into apostasy. You are not doing well in persuading me you are any sort of expert in the matter of suffering.'

It is a fair remark. 'What comes next I have never told another living soul. It is' – I close my eyes – 'painful even to remember.'

She says nothing, just looks at me. Expectant, determined; unwilling to be deflected.

I take a breath. 'My master the doctor died . . . suddenly. I was sold again, but this time my new master was not so kind. He had a scheme, of which I was a small part. And a small part of me was to be sacrificed to that plan. Must I explain in any detail?'

'You must.'

'When they led me into the hut on the edge of town, I thought they were going to kill me, and started to fight them. When I realized what they had in mind, I wished they had. At one and twenty I was tall and strong; but profit made them determined. They dragged me inside. When I saw the table, stained black from the spilled blood of those who had been gelded before me, and the wicked knives laid out in a gleaming row on the cloth beside it, my knees gave way and I staggered like an ox hit between the eyes with a mallet.'

Her eyes are upon me, wide and shocked. One of her hands flies to her mouth.

'What happened after that, well, it passed in a kind of daze. The body cannot comprehend such pain: it sends the spirit elsewhere. Like a bird roosting in the eaves, I looked down on myself, spreadeagled and bleeding, and felt nothing. I am told that for the three hours after the operation they walked me around to keep the blood circulating; then they buried me up to my neck in the desert sand and left me there for the wound to heal. I was given nothing to eat or drink for three days, though they placed a wide-brimmed hat over me to keep the sun off and paid a boy to keep the ants and prey-birds away. But he could do nothing about the young nobles of the town, who came each day to jeer. I was unaware of them the first day; the second day their voices were indistinguishable from the noise of the crows and vultures. But on the third day I regained consciousness and I saw them lounging against a wall, the sunlight glinting on their gold jewellery. They ate dates and tossed the stones at me. When I cried out they laughed.

'"Hear him roar!"

' "A mangy-looking lion, indeed."

'"Whoever saw a black lion? He is a hyena, a feral dog."

' "Not much of a luxury man!"

' "Man? He is no man, not any more!"

'They all laughed at that. I threatened them with death and dismemberment, in Senufo, then in English, Italian and finally Arabic, until one of them came and stood over me and hauled up his robe and shook his male parts at me. "This is what a real man looks like, you stinking pander!" He was about to piss on me when the man who had paid for my mutilation came out and drove him and his companions away and gave orders that I be dug up. Remarkably, I healed. I knew I was healing, for I was aware of the cost of every ingredient in every poultice and liniment they applied to my mutilation and could calculate the return on their investment. By the time they took to using wolf's onion, which is a very expensive herb, I knew I was going to survive and I took a perverse pleasure in the expense.'

Her eyes are shining – with tears? I have been so caught up in the telling I have not been watching her face.

'Did you not want to die?'

'I did want to die. For a long time I wanted to die. I lay there full of grief and hatred and fury and shame. I denied God; then I prayed to him. I suffered nightmares and flashes of memory – of my former life, of the mutilation. But little by little there came a time when I found I noticed other things than my own misery. The small bliss of clean cotton against the skin. Losing my terror of pissing. The flicker of sunlight between rushes. The song of birds. The taste of bread. The sound of children's laughter . . .'

A tear that had swelled in her eye now overflows the lid and spills slowly down her cheek. I find my hand, of its own accord, reaches out to brush it away.

She shifts backwards away from me like a startled animal.

'I am sorry.'

'No. No. You took me by surprise, that's all.' She gives me a steady look. 'I had not expected kindness.'

Kindness. Is that what it was, that gesture? Perhaps, in part: but there was self-interest there too. For now I feel a bond with this woman, a connection, a slow-burning fire: somehow I must save her from herself. I must persuade her to convert so that she will live and I may see her, just occasionally, in the gardens of the harem, with the sun in that yellow hair, meet her eyes across the fountain as Black John sings his melancholy songs . . .

I summon every iota of persuasion I can dredge from my soul. 'My life now is not so bad. I take what small pleasures there are to be taken by simply being alive. Of which there are many, even here, even in my reduced state.'

'Life persists, I suppose, the urge to survive. What stubborn beings we are, holding tight to what little delight is left to us.' She shakes her head wonderingly.

'I ask myself if there is some mystical vessel in the soul in which such pleasures accumulate like water in a glass? Finally the emptiness is replaced with life and suddenly one day, in a great surge, you want to live more than you want to die. I have come to accept that I shall never be a free man, nor marry nor father children, yet I eat, I sleep, I laugh, and think and watch and *feel*. I am myself. I persist.'

She casts her gaze down and I see her hands knot in her lap. 'Children. Ah, yes, there we are: the weak spot. And yet I would be a fruitless tree, twice dead,' she says softly at last.

'I do not understand.'

'In the Book of Jude it is the description of an apostate: one who is spiritually dead, and will go to the Lake of Fire. But it means more than that, to me.' She looks up from her interlocked fingers. 'It's what I am. A virgin woman, untouched and without issue. Yet I have always wanted children.'

Something knots inside me.

'I was on my way from Holland to be wed to an Englishman when they captured me. Just think, I might be there now, in my great house in London, a married woman of estate, maybe even, a month and more into my marriage, a woman with child.'

Is this my chance to press my case? 'If you want the chance to bring new life into the world, Alys Swann, then just say the shahada. You will be gently treated; you will be fêted. The sultan is good to the women of his harem; their lives are far from onerous. You are more like to die of boredom and too much comfort, than of fear or pain.'

'And the children that are born of such a union?'

'They are his own, and acknowledged. Bear him a son and you will be accorded great status, maybe even taken as an official wife.'

'A high honour to which to aspire.' Her tone is clipped. 'And the children stay with their mothers?'

'Children here are greatly cherished. They stay in the harem until they are of an age to be trained in their duties.' I pause, but conscience drives me on. 'Sons are greatly cherished,' I amend. 'Sons buy you status within the harem; but they may also buy you jealousy and enmity from the other women, and that can be . . . dangerous.'

The amazing eyes flicker over my face, then she drops her gaze and sits there contemplating her hands, until I feel sure I have destroyed every chance of persuasion by my honesty. Fool! I chastise myself. For a moment there I sensed the tide turning in my favour, but now there is a terrible still-ness to her that suggests some degree of acceptance. Of her martyrdom? If she goes to her death, she will take me with her. The memory of the bliss I experienced on stepping outside the gaol earlier that afternoon returns to me, poignant and mocking. Ben Hadou is an arch-manipulator, I think. A diplomat, an ambassador, a negotiator. And yet he appears to have decided that the task of turning this woman would defeat him, and offered me up in his place. I can imagine his words now: 'Nus-Nus will make a more favour-able impression on her, majesty, than your humble servant. Such a big, black man, speaking in eloquent English? A low jungle-dweller, raised to the heights of court servant and educated enough to pour poetic phrases in her ears? How could she not trust the word of such a fellow? Perhaps he will even tell her his own story: how could she fail to be moved by that?' And Ismail, forgetting that he has not seen me for three weeks while I fes-tered in a cell, says, 'Yes, he has a gentle manner for an *abid*: you are a wise man, Al-Attar: go fetch the boy at once.'

I am expendable; already facing a death sentence. Who would miss me? No one. I see Zidana's lips curled into that malicious smile. 'Good luck . . . you will need it.'

Will I have to beg this fragile woman for my own life, I wonder? It is a last resort, and ignoble. I feel a tremor of intent run through me as I prepare to cast myself down and beg Alys for my sake, if not for her own, to submit herself to the sultan's will. Outside, the mournful wail of the muezzin calls the faithful to prayer: fourth prayer, appositely the maghrib – 'The Wester-ing', the setting of the sun. I wonder if it will be my last.

'I have known all the time it would come down to this,' she says quietly. 'To whether the hardness of my will and the strength of my faith can over-come the tenderness of my heart.' Pause. 'It seems to me there is much to fear, whichever prevails.' Her eyes seek mine. I do not know what she sees there, but the smile she gives me is sweet indeed. 'If I resist, they will kill not only me but you also, won't they?'

Suddenly I cannot speak. Instead, I nod dumbly.

She looks away.

II

My little room has been restored, just as ben Hadou promised. My old blan-ket is spread smooth across the narrow divan; the prayer mat sits square in the middle of the chamber, and my lap-desk has been placed on the wooden chest, beside my incense burner. A new candle has been inserted into the candlestick. I move these items and open the chest, to find my clothing neatly folded within; but of the couching book there is no sign. Abdelaziz's nephew must have taken it elsewhere. I wonder why; and whom I will have to go to ask to have it returned to me. I hope I will not have to go to the vizier himself.

I walk out to the courtyard and stare around in the twilight. Nothing has changed out here except that with the warm weather after the rain the veg-etation has grown more lush and there are more flowers out on the hibiscus, cheery scarlet trumpets proclaiming their indifference to the strife of the world of men. Usually the sight of them would lift my heart, but today they depress me.

'Nus-Nus?'

I turn, to find Abid, one of the sultan's body-slaves, regarding me with a wide grin. 'You're back! We thought you were dead. Samir gave us to believe as much.'

'Did he now? I wonder why.'

The lad looks awkward. He knows more than he is saying, I suspect. Then I look down and see that he is carrying the couching book.

'Well, that's a relief: I wondered where it had gone.' It seems that things are returning to normal, little by little. I take the book from him. Its old leather feels warm and comforting in my hands; its proportions and weight are as familiar to me as my own. As I turn to cross the room with it hugged to my chest, Abid says, 'You're to come now. The sultan is asking for you.'

I bend and stow the precious book back in the chest where it belongs.

'What are you doing?'

'Putting it away for safe keeping.'

'Well, don't! Bring it with you.'

'Now?' I say stupidly.

'Now!'

'Are there corrections to be made?' I imagine that Samir Rafik has filled it with errors and that this has been contributory to his removal . . .

'His majesty has a woman with him now.'

Fifth prayer is imminent. The sultan would never ignore the 'Isha' salah' in favour of a couching: he is a devout and fervent man, meticulous in observing the correct forms of worship. Perhaps Abid has misunderstood.

'It's too early.'

'And to translate for him. He can't make the white woman understand his orders. He needs you to translate for him so that she does as she is told, and then record the couching in the book.'

My heart stalls, then kicks wildly. But what had I expected?

Arriving at the sultan's private quarters, I find him stripped to his long cotton undertunic, stalking the room stiff with fury and frustration; but at least his hands are empty of weapons.

'Majesty!' Placing the couching book down carefully, I prostrate myself upon the silk rugs.

'Get up, Nus-Nus,' he says impatiently, hauling me by the arm. 'Tell the stupid woman to take her damned clothes off!'

I scramble to my feet. Alys sits hunched on the corner of the sultan's divan with her hands crossed over her chest. Tatters of a silk kaftan – a clean rose-pink that has replaced the soiled turquoise – hang from her shoulders like strips of flayed skin. She does not look up as I approach.

I have seen so much random violence in this place, witnessed sudden deaths, mutilations and woundings; I have been privy to hundreds of deflowerings, seductions and – not to put too fine a point on it – rapes, that I should be immune to one more incidence of the same; but it seems I am not.

'Alys.'

She lifts her gaze to me. 'I'm so sorry to cause such a fuss,' she says.

'Alys, you must not anger him any more. Let him do what he must and it will be over all the sooner.' The words seem terrible to me even as I speak them. 'Take your gown off, Alys.'

For a long moment she holds my gaze. I do not know what I read in those blue depths. Accusation? Disappointment? Anger? She keeps her eyes fixed firmly on me as she shrugs the remnants of the kaftan down from her shoulders. Beneath it she wears nothing at all. Even pinned by her regard, my peripheral vision takes in every inch of her bare skin, the delicacy of her clavicles, the narrowness of her upper arms, the full swell of her breasts.

Ismail pushes me aside. 'Stop gawping, boy. Not that I blame you: she's a peach, is she not? A little thin for my liking, but a peach nonetheless.' I swear he is salivating.

The sound of the muezzin calling the faithful to fifth prayer shivers through the candlelit air and the sultan hesitates. He closes his eyes for a long moment and I see his lips move as he whispers, 'Forgive me, Merciful One.' Then in a single swift movement he tears his tunic up over his head and stands there stark naked. I avert my eyes; too late, and see more than I intended.

It's not that I haven't seen his august majesty naked before: I have attended him a thousand times at the hammam. I have scrubbed his back and rubbed liniment into his limbs after the hunt. He is wiry, this king, wiry and well knit. His muscles look like knotted wood: in a man-to-man fight, I should be able to break him in two. But power radiates from him, from his smallest movement, as if he were born to kingship, though he came to power but five years ago. That sensation is compelling, even when he is in his most relaxed state; but rampant it is overwhelming.

'Get behind the screen, Nus-Nus, and tell her to get on the bed.'

I feel Alys's gaze on me as I cross the room, retrieve the couching book and take my place behind the carved cedarwood. Her eyes remain locked on my face even through the fretwork. My voice shakes as I say, 'Please get on the bed, Alys.'

Wordlessly she gets to her feet, letting the torn kaftan pool around her ankles. She should look vulnerable, defeated; but her dignity is like armour.

She turns towards me as if offering herself and I find I cannot take my eyes from her, or even blink. Time feels suspended so that my heart feels caught between one beat and the next.

'Tell her to get on the bed, damn it!' Ismail barks, breaking the spell. 'On her knees.'

Particularly with the Christian apostates, he does this: makes them present their hindquarters to him like an animal to be mounted, allowing for no human contact but the sexual act itself. It is his way of reducing them; making them know that he values those who convert under duress or out of self-interest less highly than those born Muslim. It is another of those strange contradictions in him, that he should be the one forcing the apostasy, yet prizing the strength of their conviction. I have seen him shed genuine tears for women who have chosen martyrdom rather than apostasy.

I pass on his order in faltering terms and see her shudder. 'I am sorry, Alys,' I start; but she stays me with a look. 'It will pass. I shall pray for a son, a good strong healthy boy.'

She arranges herself on the white sheet that has been spread across the great bed, face towards me. When he enters her, without niceties, I see her grimace, but she masters herself and as I relay his instructions she makes the mechanical adjustments required, as if asked to move a chair or open a drawer.

I hope the coupling will be swift, for all our sakes, and before long Ismail is growling, his head thrown back, every muscle tense with lust. All the time her eyes remain locked on mine and I know I am her refuge, the still point into which her spirit flows even as her body is abused. It is as if a red-hot wire has been stretched between us: I feel her pain like a fire in my own abdomen, every nerve in me alive with empathy.

And then suddenly, even more disconcertingly, I feel myself swell and harden. The phenomenon is so shocking that I break eye contact and look down. There can be no mistaking the tenting of my djellaba. What unholy magic is this? Have I been possessed by a demon? Is the sultan's potency so singular that it has infected me? But I have witnessed a hundred – a thousand! – of his couchings and experienced nothing before but distaste and detached boredom. It must be a miracle! I feel like crowing in triumph; but then a profound shame falls upon me. Am I so perverse that I should come alive only at the cost of another human being's humiliation and pain? The erection wilts as quickly as it rose and when I force myself to look up again, the sultan has finished his business and Alys is turned away from us both, the bloodied sheet clutched against her.

His business concluded, Ismail shrugs into a heavily embroidered robe and, striding quickly to the door, shouts for the women to take her away. They bustle in, coo over the bloodied sheet – as of course is their purpose (for now they will rush back to the harem and proclaim the purity of the Englishwoman and the potency of the sultan so that whatever offspring may result will be unquestionably his own), cover Alys in the extravagant gown reserved for those deflowered by the sovereign, and whisk her away.

My eyes follow her; but she does not look back.

She has survived the worst of it; what matters now will be endurance. But there is no comfort to be had from that cold fact. I feel bereft, emptied out – appalled. I feel, I realize, much as I did after sleeping with one of the whores in Venice. I did not admit it to myself at the time, or revisit it since, but those loveless encounters have left me with a good dose of shame, and I feel now as if it were I, rather than the sultan, who has used Alys, and then cast her away.

'Nus-Nus!'

The voice of command shatters my reverie. I shoot to my feet in such panic that I drop the couching book and, in bending to retrieve it, bring the fretted screen crashing down between us. For a long moment we stare at each other, just two men revealed to one another as men; no more. Then the moment passes and the fear returns and I find myself wondering whether he will sense my lapse, but he simply smiles. His expression is unfocused, dreamy.

'Magnificent, the Englishwoman.'

'Alys.'

'Was that her name?'

'Yes, sire. Alys. Alys Swann.' And suddenly, as if plucking the memory out of the air, I remember where last I came upon this English word. *I will play the swan, / And die in music.* I recall the words, though not their context. Doctor Lewis taught me English by reading with me from his much prized folio, fifty years old and battered by love and use. The words come from the play about the Moorish king and the white woman he had taken to wife: my lips curl.

'Why do you smile?'

It will hardly do to explain the source: I try instead to essay an explanation of the word but I cannot remember the name of the bird in Arabic. I resort to mime: my hand makes a flowing line in the air and his hand follows the arc of the creature's graceful neck.

'*Al ouez abiad*. The White Swan. That is what I shall call her.'

Samir is no scribe, that much is certain. His entries in the couching book are in a poor hand, and include many crossings-out and ink smudges. On a clean page untouched by his uncouth hand I write:

Third Gathering Day, Rabī al-Thānī
  Alys Swann. Converted English captive, twenty-nine years old. Virgin. A gift to his majesty from Sidi Qasem ben Hamed ben Moussa Dib.

My hand shakes as I make the entry, there is such turmoil in my mind. It is a savage irony that the task of maintaining this chronicle of lust and potency should fall to a eunuch, is it not? More painful still, to a eunuch who was entire till recently, and had already tasted the glories to be found between a woman's legs. Did I ever make any children of my own? I fear I was never around for long enough to make serious attachments: my master rarely stayed in one place for more than a month or two, but was always on a quest for knowledge that took us all over North Africa, to Spain, and once even as far as Venice. Those Venetian courtesans, with their soft white arms, those provocative dresses that all but bared their breasts, their rare perfumes, knowing eyes and surprising tricks. Ever since my cutting I have veered my thoughts away from such things: but surely nothing can be so useless as desire to a eunuch.

And then there came Alys Swann . . .

Even the sound of her name in my mind stirs that part of me I thought long dead, and I have to quell the surge of blood that beats in my groin. It is surely unnatural; and yet, and yet, I cannot help but wonder if I have somehow been singled out, the recipient of some kind of miracle . . .

To divert my rioting thoughts, I riffle through the book that has been my pride to keep both accurate and elegant. Most of the couchings listed took place in Fez, before the court moved here to Meknes. I remember the old palace chambers, so grand and sumptuous, but somehow gloomy despite their soaring arches and rich ornamentation. That was a place that had seen too much: it was as if a miasma of suffering imbued the very plaster on its walls. I flick through the entries and remember the women one by one: Naima and Habiba, Fatima, Jamilla and Yasmin, Ouarda, Aicha, Eptisam, Maria and Chama – some of them little more than girls. One or two wept when he took them, not understanding what was expected of them. There is even one very early entry in which the ink was blotched where I cried in sympathy for one child. I look for it now. I will never forget the look on her face after the event: her pupils more like holes than eyes, as if her spirit had been pushed out of her by the force of the coupling.

Back I go, to the start, then forward again, towards the present, my life and the life of the women here mapped out in daily stark entries. I frown. Where is that page? Before Samir laid his hands on the book it was the only one that was not pristine.

I locate the Emira Zoubida, who knew exactly what she was about: a proper little temptress with skin the colour of an aubergine. She bore the sultan twin boys; there were noisy celebrations. Of course, they did not last long, sickly to begin with and probably helped on their way by Zidana. Nearly all the rest around that time produced girl children; of the boys, none appear to have survived. Save Zidan, of course, the apple of his father's eye. I turn the page, and find . . . not the page blotched by sentiment, which should have followed, but an unfamiliar page. I stare at it, confused, for a time. On closer examination I realize the writing on it is not my own, though it is a very fair copy: such a fair copy, in fact, that probably only I would ever know the difference. There is a faint line down the gutter, and near the foot of the page a little mark. I carry the book out into the fading light of the courtyard, but I do not need its confirmation. I know . . . I just know.

A page, very cleverly altered, has been moved from its original place. No untruth told in it, except for the date: a son, leapfrogging a number of other sons, placing him higher in the succession, a pawn for a game-player to move into position. You can barely see the join, it has been so carefully done: torn, rather than cut, the warp and weft of the linen meshing almost seamlessly. A very time-consuming process. Perhaps three weeks' worth of work, to practise my hand, revise the entry and make the switch . . .

Did they really think I would not notice the forgery? But of course if everything had gone to plan I would be dead of a nail through the skull by now, or, having accepted his unholy offer, been tucked away in a safe house, prisoner to the grand vizier's every depraved whim.

I had guessed my enemy already: what I did not understand was his motivation. But at least now I know the game and the stakes, which are high. His investment in the scheme to remove me from my duties has cost him dear: he will not be happy that I have escaped his clutches and am back in charge of the couching book again. I wonder how long it will be before the next attempt on my life comes.

12

The next day my usual duties resume as if there has been no lacuna. It is as if the whole affair of Sidi Kabour has, as ben Hadou promised, never existed. And yet the world has changed shape: am I the only one who can see this?

But, as we tour the building works that afternoon, Abdelaziz watches me out of the corner of his eye, when he thinks me engaged in the taking down of notes. There has been an explosion of lime and four workers dead in it; and one of the huge vats of tadelakt – the plaster made from marble dust and albumen – has mysteriously been ruined: three months' work and twenty thousand eggs wasted. Ismail is much exercised over the matter, rattling off instructions and making dire pronouncements; but, despite my apparent attention to my scribing, I can feel the vizier's eyes, like an insect's, on me.

When I look up and catch him, he looks away and engages in deep conversation with the chief astronomer. But he seems perplexed, as if he has perceived the change in me. He must, I remind myself, be alarmed at my sudden reinstatement. I wonder what has become of his nephew. I wonder too about Alys. Is she well? Has she been kindly treated by the sultan's women? Does she blame me for her decision to convert and hate me for my part in her ordeal?

We are heading back to Ismail's quarters when a functionary comes running to announce that one of our generals has come riding into the palace complex, covered in dust, requesting an urgent audience. We find him in a receiving room, still filthy, attended by a group of his men, equally unkempt, bearing a dozen huge sacks. They have been putting down a Berber rebellion in the Rif, and meeting stiff resistance.

Until recently the campaign has not been going well, for they are a wild and woolly people, these people of the mountains, and well known for their independence of thought. It took more than two hundred years to persuade the Berbers to submit themselves to Islam, and some say they've never fully given up their old animism and goddess worship on the quiet, and have even been known to eat the wild pigs that run in their mountains, though the only Berbers I have encountered have been tough, honourable men, astute and intelligent, though superstitious and prone to magic and curses, and far too proud and too partisan to bow the neck to any not of their own tribe. Ismail loathes them with a fervour and is personally affronted by their refusal to accept his rule. He is, after all, God's own representative on earth, directly descended from the Prophet himself. How dare they not submit to God's holy will?

Usually Ismail would not countenance such lack of ceremony or propriety as to stand in the same room as unwashed men, but he is avid to know their news; his eyes light up. 'Show me what you've got for me!' he demands even while the men are on the ground in prostration. 'Quick: jump to it!'

I expected captured booty: gold and silver, fine cloths, treasures taken from the fallen chieftains of the Rif. Well, I suppose that was exactly what he'd brought: their most precious possessions of all. There is a collective gasp as the heads roll out of the first sack and trundle, ghastly, across the marble floor. That'll take some clearing up, I think. The heads are so fresh they are still leaking blood and fluids. They must have marched the prisoners most of the way here and butchered them this morning. I wonder what the sultan will make of that, if he realizes it: he would have, I am sure, preferred to have dispatched them himself, and not quickly either. But it does not seem to matter: he is down on his hands and knees amongst them, oblivious to the ooze and muck, turning each one over and regarding it with satisfaction as the general reels off names and tribal affiliations. 'Excellent,' Ismail keeps saying; 'excellent. Another of God's enemies dead.' When last I heard, the Berbers were Muslims like the rest of us; but apparently you can't be a good Muslim and oppose the sultan.

I am dispatched with a contingent of slaves to gather up the grisly specimens and carry them to the Jews, while Ismail inspects the horses and other chattels his soldiers have brought to him. The mellah, the Jewish quarter of the city, derives its name from the Arabic al-mallah – 'the place of salt', and that is why we are here, for it is only the rich Jews of the quarter who have sufficient salt with which to preserve these tokens of triumph, so that when Ismail has them impaled on the city walls they will last a sufficient time and not drop bits of their traitorous flesh on the heads of the good citizens of Meknes.

The Jewry of Meknes is easily distinguished: inside the city, the men must by law wear red caps and black cloaks and nothing on their feet; but in their own sector (which is close to the palace, for ease of access for the sultan to their money) they dress as they please. The women walk about bare-faced, and are handsome and bold; the men are clever in trade, which is why they are here, and mix easily enough for the most part with the Moroccans. There are a number of them at court, for they are more respected and less reviled here than in other parts, though the sultan taxes them mercilessly. It's said that without them he would be like a man with no hands: they pay for his army and his renovations. In return they are left to pursue their business interests and their religion in some degree of peace.

I take the heads to Daniel al-Ribati, a well-respected merchant who runs a dozen Saharan caravans the size of small villages, and a fleet of ships to sell the wares he brings out of the desert – ivory and salt; indigo, ostrich feathers, gold and slaves, amber and cotton – to Europe, the Levant and Constantinople. He is a man in his later years, perhaps his late fifties, dark and foursquare, with a neatly cropped beard and bright blue eyes. He has contacts everywhere and a reputation for being both shrewd and fair, which is a rare thing in business. It is also said that his fortune is buried in caves beneath the mellah, that he pays barely a hundredth of what he earns as tax, that he is as rich as Croesus, or Sheba.

He takes a head out of one sack and regards it solemnly. It is a ghastly object, ragged at the neck, with a great sword-slash bisecting the face. Al-Ribati clucks his tongue: it's going to be an expensive business (for him, obviously; never for the sultan), but he does not quibble at the work; his continued existence here depends on give and take, though it probably seems to him it's more give and give. 'Two weeks,' he says succinctly. 'Come back in two weeks and they'll be perfect.'

I express my doubts that Ismail will wait so long for his trophies and he laughs. 'Even the sultan cannot hurry salt.'

That night Ismail takes one of the fallen chieftain's daughters to his bed, a pretty girl of fifteen with unruly eyebrows and a bush of black hair. She seems docile enough when she is brought in and I am dismissed from the royal presence, but am only few paces towards my chamber when a great roar issues from my lord's apartment and I run back in to find the door-guard wrestling a knife off her. How she managed to smuggle that in, I cannot imagine. Or, rather, I can. Good heaven, she must be a determined creature. Ismail sees me and waves me away with a laugh. 'No damage done, Nus-Nus, off you go.'

I slope off, feeling some relief, first at not having to witness the coupling, which I am sure will not be pleasant; second, that she is not Alys. I leave a gap for the Berber princess's name, which I did not catch, in the couching book and go to bed, where I sleep like a baby, right through the night. Until, that is, I am rudely awoken.

As soon as I open my eyes, even without the lad shaking my arm, I know something is amiss: the light, it's the light that's wrong. Too bright, even for these summer months: first prayer must have been and gone by an hour or more.

I sit bolt upright. 'The sultan?'

Abid nods, hardly able to find his words. 'Not well. Asking for you.'

I throw on a robe and run. He is lying on his divan, looking pale. Beads of sweat stand out on his forehead. I am alarmed: Ismail is rarely sick, though he complains frequently about imagined ills. And he never, ever, misses first prayer.

'Fetch Doctor Salgado,' he all but whispers.

The doctor – a Spanish renegade – is asleep when I find him, and wakes slowly, red-faced and bleary. His breath stinks of garlic and hippocras. When I tell him the sultan requires his services urgently, his eyes bulge in panic. I dash out into the nearest courtyard and pick a handful of mint leaves for him while he dresses. He chews them like an animal, mouth open, breath rasping, as we make our way back to the sultan's apartments.

Ismail is not fooled by our ruse: he recoils from the man and sends me to fetch Zidana instead. It is as well he is feeling weak, or Salgado's head might be on its way to joining the Berbers'.

I find the empress squatting in her inner courtyard, poring over a pile of chicken entrails, watched over warily by a group of women. She looks up. 'There will be a death,' she proclaims cheerfully. She places her hands on her vast thighs and pushes herself upright: at once the flies swarm in to settle on the hot meat.

It does not take chicken entrails to tell me this: there are deaths every day here.

'The sultan is asking for you: he is unwell.'

She does not ask me what is wrong with him: it is as if she already knows. As she gathers her things, my eyes dart everywhere, but there is no sign of Alys. I am not sure whether to be relieved or disappointed; my nerves seem as alert as a cat's, too close to the surface. I do not know what I would say to her even if I found her. But she is not here, and now I begin to worry that something has happened to her. Gripped by sudden terror, I turn to Laila and ask after her health and she simpers prettily and says she is well, 'but a little lonely'. It is not unknown for eunuchs to pleasure the ladies of the harem: people are inventive in their quest for rapture – fingers and tongues and male parts made from wax, from stone, from gold, even the occasional well-formed vegetable. If the sultan knew what went on beneath his nose, he would be apoplectic; it is in everyone's interest to ensure such things remain discreet.

Laila has been trying to lure me to play with her for the best part of a year. I think it is more the pursuit of the unattainable that thrills her than any genuine fondness for me, but I smile and say I am sorry for her plight and then ask about various other favourites of the harem and the health of the various children whose names I can remember, and only then, after listening dutifully to the catalogue of small ailments and aggravations, do I ask after Alys – or the English convert, as I call her.

Laila rolls her eyes. 'She avoids company. Anyone would think she was a nun, the way she behaves.'

Two nuns were presented to Ismail in the last raiding season and had been so steadfast in their repudiation of Islam and the sultan that, strangled, they had died with smiles on their faces, as if achieving everlasting bliss. Two Irish girls who were presented at the same time as Alys collapsed in such hysterics at the first threat that they were sent to the palace in Fez to serve as skivvies. I could almost wish the same fate for the White Swan, but at least she is still alive. There is no time to ask more, for Zidana returns now, properly dressed and with an armful of potions and unidentifiable items.

Back in Ismail's chamber the cause of his malady becomes clear: stripped to the waist, the bite marks stand out livid against his skin. They are no mere scratches either, but deep and torn, the skin around them puffy and infected. I cannot help but feel respect for the Berber girl: first the knife, then teeth and claws.

'Love bites?' Zidana asks playfully and Ismail growls at her. 'Poor lamb,' she coos, 'has he been mauled by the little wolf cub, then?'

They have a curious relationship, the imperial couple: she treats him like a child and he rarely bridles. They still share nights, even after all these years, and the rest of the time she helps him choose his bed partners, selecting them for qualities that will pique his jaded palate; it is another form of power. But perhaps the Berber princess was a step too far into the wild.

'She is a savage! A barbarian! I shall strangle her with my own hands.'

'Hush, you will inflame the wounds further. I shall do it myself.' She fusses over him, muttering chants and waving her hands around in a mystical fashion. Incense is lit in braziers to cleanse the air of whatever contagions still linger here. He is made to drink infusions from the potion bottles. Zidana sorts through her simples, her bangles clashing, then curses. 'Nus-Nus?'

'Yes, sublime majesty?'

'Run and fetch me two wolf onion tubers and some comfrey; oh, and some thyme honey – you know where to find them.'

Down in the secret chamber it is hard to see a thing. I search for a candle, for a flint; then for the items I have been sent to fetch. There is so much down here, and no apparent order to any of it. Everything seems to take an age. I find the honey first – so dense and dark it is almost black: not for eating, this stuff. It has a powerful, rank smell, worse than Doctor Salgado's breath. Then the wolf onions, and I am still searching grimly for the comfrey when someone says, 'What are you doing here?'

I turn, to find little Zidan standing behind me. His eyes glitter like a djinn's in the semi-darkness. 'Your mother sent me to fetch some things.'

'You lie! This is her secret place. Only I know about it.'

I spread my hands. 'Not strictly true, as you can see.'

'Call me "emir" or "sir"!'

'Sir.'

'I shall tell her I found you here.'

'You go ahead and do that.'

A pause as he digests this. 'What did she send you for?'

I show him the honey and the onions. Of course, he has no idea what the latter are: he is only six, almost seven, but he makes a great play of assessing them, holding them to his nose and sniffing them.

'Are they poisonous?'

'I don't believe so.'

'Do you know a lot about poisons?'

'I know a little. Why do you ask . . . sir?'

He shrugs. 'What's the most powerful one?'

'Your mother is a greater expert than I: ask her.'

This does not please him. He dogs my steps as I continue my search for the comfrey and eventually locate it in a basket of dried herbs. 'Who is it for?'

'Your father.'

'Is he ill?' His eyes gleam. Before I can answer he says, 'If he dies I will be king: then everyone will have to do what I say or I can have their heads cut off. Is he going to die?'

'No, he is not going to die.'

'Give him poison and he will.'

I stare at him, aghast. 'Zidan, that's treason! If I were to tell him what you said you would be beaten, or worse.'

'You won't tell,' he says confidently.

'And why is that?'

'Because if you do, I will kill you.' He smiles till his eyes are little slitted half-moons. 'Or Mama will. If I ask Mama, she will kill you for me, just like that.' He snaps his fingers.

I refuse to answer that: there is no answer. For fear of what else I might do, I brush past him and run up the stairs and out into the sunshine. I have left the candle alight down there: not very responsible to leave a candle alight in an enclosed place stuffed with dried tinder along with a six-year-old child; but I cannot help wishing for the whole palace to go up in flames and take him with it: poisons, plants, magical dealings and all. The world would be a better place.

All this talk of death and poisonings is unsettling: I walk fast with my head down, straight into a group of women pulling an unwilling participant in their game by the hands. I see there Laila, Naima, Fatima; Massouda, Salka. They flow around me, giggling, till the victim and I are practically nose to nose. Even then I do not recognize her at first, for her face has been made unfamiliar with dark cosmetics. Kohl and henna have darkened her pale brows and lashes and lips, and given her Egyptian eyes.

'Alys!'

She has been crying: the kohl is streaked down one side.

'They treat me like a doll!'

I am so relieved to see that loss of dignity is the worst of her concerns that I burst out laughing. Abruptly her face crumples and she turns her back on me and walks quickly away, into the arms of her tormentors, and I am left standing there, gazing after her in mortification.

By the time I arrive at Ismail's apartments he already seems better, less pale and sweaty. Zidana chastises me for my tardiness, but I can tell that she has enjoyed an excuse to have her husband to herself for a little while: it reinforces the power she holds over him, being trusted to tend him with magic and kind words. Sex, magic and kindness: the most powerful weapons in any woman's armoury, and no one uses them better than Zidana. She has already given him three strong sons: Zidan, the acknowledged heir, three-year-old Ahmed the Golden and earlier this year baby Abdel Malik (no one even realized she was pregnant till the birth, she is so fat: it seemed he popped into the world like a little djinn, out of thin air). Because she is First Wife, all three will have to die for any others to succeed. Until a few days ago I would have said this was an impossibility; but now I am beginning to wonder.

I wait until Zidana has applied the last salve, smeared the healing honey over it and bound a cloth criss-cross over his bitten ribs and shoulder (how determined had the girl been to press her head hard into those bony parts, hard enough to get some flesh between her teeth?) and then follow her out into the hallway. There, out of earshot of the guards, I tell her what I have found in the couching book.

'I knew something was afoot when he had his nephew gelded.'

'Samir Rafik? Who took my place?'

'Of course. You think Abdelaziz has a superfluity of ball-less nephews?'

The man is a monster. Even his own family signifies nothing more to him than a means to power.

She sighs at my innocence. 'Why come to me with this information?'

'We both hate him. I thought you might make use of it.'

'You mean, you thought I might tell the emperor.'

I wait expectantly; but all she does is sigh. 'Do you not think I would leap at the chance to bring my enemy down? It would take much more than mere words scribbled in a book presented to a man who does not read. Bring me tangible evidence of the Hajib's plotting if you would see him brought low.' She laughs at my expression of dismay. 'Foolish boy. Leave the book in your chest while he is at prayers tonight and it will be restored.'

I remember the Safavid Qur'an, and shudder.

Before last prayer I make the entry:

Third 1st Day, Rabī al-Thānī. Illi, Berber princess. Vicious.

13

Alys

Over a week has passed and I have not been recalled to the sultan's bed. For a time I feel relieved that I will not have to repeat the vile encounter. But have I quickened? That is the question that plagues me. Indeed, is it even possible to fall pregnant from such a peculiar coupling?

After his violation of me I was swaddled up like a baby by two dark-skinned girls who chattered like jackdaws, so as not to disturb the seed he might have implanted; the next day when they unwrapped me they touched my skin with wondering hands and poked their fingers into my arm, pinched to see how easily the flesh turned pink. Washed, dried and dressed, I was hoisted shoulder-high on a bier and carried through the courtyards of the harem, while the rest of the women made high-pitched warbling howls, their tongues shuttling from one side of their mouths to the other, like creatures in a madhouse.

For them, it seemed some sort of celebration, but it made me feel ill just to look at them. And so I looked away. Above their heads, arched colonnades and tumbles of flowers; little birds; deep blue sky. Somewhere beyond that the god I spurned was gazing down, judging, judging . . .

I have wept for my sins until I have no more tears.

'Alys!'

My name is pronounced oddly, the syllables widely separated. I look up and see that it is the queen (or whatever she is) who has come to visit me. Vastly fat, she is garnished all over with gaudy jewels and cloths: ropes of thick gold and pearls are looped around her bull-like neck; heavy earrings drag her lobes low; a headband encrusted with sequins and jewels sits upon her brow and disappears into the thicket of her hair; bangles sit from wrist to elbow (it is a wonder she can raise her arms, except that she is as well muscled as any man). Her skin is as black as jet, as black as that of the eunuch Nus-Nus, he with the face like a mask. She lays her forearm against mine and laughs at the contrast. It does not seem like a friendly laugh, more as if she is making fun of me, pointing out that in contrast with her – dark and glowing, lush and abundant – I am a pale, thin, feeble creature. She grins so widely that I can see her gold teeth and the gaps where others are missing, but her eyes glitter at me like lumps of *steenkool*, hard and cold and mineral.

Then she turns and takes something from one of her attendants and holds it out to me. It is a cup, as gold as the Grail, and inside it some dark liquid gives off a little vapour with a curious odour. All the while she keeps speaking in a soothing tone, patting me on the arm, as if the very touch will convey her meaning.

Whatever is in the vessel, I do not wish to drink it. I shake my head and push her hand away as politely as I am able, but she persists, even lifting it to my lips and cupping my head with her other huge hand to force me towards it. The contents of the cup smell rank and bitter; I twist my head away. She tries again, more insistently, becoming angry at my evasions. Then she pinches my arm with undisguised malice.

I cry out and dash the cup from her hand and the liquid spills out of it over the carpet and steams in the air and she stamps around me, arms raised in frustration, no doubt inveighing against me to her heathen god. Her bracelets rattle and clash.

I am frightened of her, but I will not show it, though my legs are trembling, and I hope it does not show. She takes one more furious look at me, then strides off, screeching for her women to follow her, and I am left in blessed peace.

The next thing I know, she is back and there is a man with her. He is so tall he fills the doorway and for a moment I have the irrational sense that between them they have sucked all the light in the place into themselves, leaving none for me. Then he comes closer and I see that it is Nus-Nus.

'Good day, Alys,' he says, unsmiling.

I cannot speak, for his eyes are on me and the weight of his regard makes it impossible.

'Alys, are you well? You look pale.'

'I am so light-skinned I wonder that you can tell the difference.'

He dips his head. 'I must apologize for my behaviour the last time we met. I pray I did not offend you.'

I remember how he laughed at me, and square my shoulders. 'Not at all, sir. It is quite forgotten.'

Our words are careful, but a dark gulf stretches between us. He has seen me stripped naked and used like an animal.

The queen jabbers at Nus-Nus and I see his eyes widen. Then he says to me, 'Alys, listen carefully. Nod and smile when I tell you to do so. Show no outrage: appearances are crucial to survival in this place. You must learn to wear a second face, one with which you hide your own. Do you understand me?'

I nod, but my heart begins to jump. What can be worse than what has already been?

'She has something for you to drink. Take the cup from her and thank her. Take it and kiss her hand in gratitude. I will explain to her that you did not understand the honour she did you before. But, and this is very important, Alys: do not drink it. Make it appear that you are taking a sip from the cup, then I will find some excuse to take her away with me. Drain the liquid from it into the ground out of sight of everyone and be ready to give the empty cup back to me in a few minutes.'

I feel myself go hot, then cold. 'Is she trying to poison me?'

'Smile,' he urges me, and I comply. 'Not exactly. I will explain when I can.'

The queen clicks her fingers and a slave appears with a refilled cup. I find I cannot take my eyes from it. What is in it? *Not exactly* poison. Something that will make me ill but not quite kill me? How, in such a short time, can she have conceived of such a hatred of me? What threat can I be to her?

'Take the cup and thank her profusely,' Nus-Nus prompts and I can see his concern. Is this the face beneath his 'second face'? There are lines there I had not noticed before, strain showing around his eyes and jaw. He is a very well-looking man, I shock myself by thinking; dignified; impressive. At once I can imagine my mother's outraged voice in my head: He is a savage, a slave – as black as tar! Actually he is not quite black: his skin is a very dark brown, the colour of my grandmother's well-loved oak settle, the wood polished and blackened by time and a thousand backsides. It looks warm, his skin, where mine is cold. I find that I am shivering again, my knees trembling under the cover of my foreign robe.

'The cup,' he says again, hoarsely, and I snap my eyes away from him and take the thing and then, remembering, kiss her hand. 'Thank you, my lady, you are most kind,' I babble. 'It is good of you to think of me.'

She watches me intently. I feel like a fly struggling in the sticky silk of a web with the spider looking on, biding its time before moving in to eat its prey.

'Pretend to sup from it,' Nus-Nus tells me, and I put my lips over the edge of the gold until the liquid touches my skin. It is warm, and it smells rancid. It is all I can do to go through with the pretence of sipping and swallowing.

'Tell her the taste is foreign to me, but that I am very grateful for her care and I shall be sure to drink every drop,' I say to the eunuch, and I watch as he translates. The queen nods, but does not move. I take another pretend swallow, and this time the liquid gets in between my lips and touches my tongue. Despite the sweet smell it is as bitter as wormwood. Perhaps it *is* wormwood. It makes me splutter, and that makes the woman smile. Nus-Nus looks alarmed, but he talks urgently to the queen to catch her attention and they move away, out of my chamber. A moment later the rest follow, more curious to find out what they are talking about than to watch me drink my bitter draught.

I turn up the corner of the rug and upend the cup. Then I sit on the divan and wait for them to return, the empty vessel held dutifully in my lap. When they come back, the queen strides swiftly to my side and inspects the cup, then the area around me. She is suspicious; but the liquid has drained away into the untiled ground. We smile insincerely at one another, and she leaves.

Nus-Nus steps forward. 'The sultan has requested your presence again tonight.'

I feel as if I have been hit in the stomach. I think I may vomit; but I master the urge, knowing that more of the bitter liquid is sure to be administered if I do.

'Bear up, Alys,' he says. 'It is a good sign: you have his favour.' He turns away.

'What was in the cup?' I call after him; but he does not answer. Instead, he goes out into the courtyard and returns a moment later with a green sprig in his hand.

'If ever you have need of me, send your servant to me bearing a piece of coriander,' he tells me, 'and I shall come at once.'

14

Alys has become the sultan's favourite: three times in the past week he has asked for her. I suspect he would request her presence every night if it did not provoke Zidana's wrath so.

As it is, the empress fulminates about Alys. She refers to her as the White Worm, the Serpent, the English Stick and other such unflattering names. In this, as in other matters, I have become Zidana's confidant. She complains constantly to me about Ismail's neglect of her, for since Alys entered the harem the sultan has not spent a single night with his Chief Wife. She demands information from me as to every detail of Ismail's state of mind, his temper, his eating habits and bowel movements. She wants reports on everything I hear him say about the Englishwoman. Of course, I do not fully comply: Zidana does not recognize the logic that separates message from messenger. And so I report back to her what I deem to be safe, committing many sins of omission; and, in an uncomfortable twist of fate, find myself acting as her mouthpiece and go-between with her rival.

Zidana encourages me to spend time with Alys Swann – under the cover of teaching her Arabic (which she is learning with greater ease than I had expected) – to win her trust sufficiently so that she will drink without question the noxious concoctions she brews up to prevent her from conceiving Ismail's child; or to kill it in the womb. Such apparent complicity appals me, but I cannot help but look forward to each visit, and reason that only by keeping close can I keep Alys safe. But in my heart I know myself fatally compromised.

The stallholder who has now taken over Sidi Kabour's business in the souq, a small, dark man from Imchil, is both subtle and circumspect. We both pretend that he does not know for whom I work; and I pretend I know nothing about herbs, which enables me to ask questions. When I am sent to procure dried tansy flowers and the leaves of pennywort, which will stimulate miscarriage and poison the womb, I bring away with me red clover, dried raspberry leaves and an elixir of agnus castus, which will promote fertility. Sometimes I manage to switch the concoctions; at other times, it is necessary that Alys discards or conceals those that Zidana has sent her. There is a powerful emetic I have had the herbman make up, if worse comes to worst.

It is a risky venture: if Alys falls pregnant, Zidana will know I have been playing her false and will surely attempt to kill her rival, the unborn child and me as well; but it will consolidate Alys's place at court and make Ismail more attentive to her welfare. Perhaps he will even allow her to be removed to another pavilion, away from Zidana's direct influence.

Today she asks me, 'Has she bewitched him? Does she have knowledge of some form of European magic that is stronger than my own?'

I am not used to Zidana showing any vulnerability. 'Not to my knowledge,' I say carefully. Maybe if she believes Alys has some witch-powers it will make her more circumspect.

'It's those eyes,' she declares, walking around and around. 'Blue: it's unnatural. Normal people don't have blue eyes: it's an abomination.'

I assure her that Ismail pays little attention to the Englishwoman's eyes, and it's the truest thing I've said all today.

'It cannot be that sickly white skin. I know Ismail too well for that. It is black women he loves.' She thrusts her huge chest out. 'He was raised by a black woman: his mother had skin as dark as mine, or yours. He likes women with some meat on them too: he values sturdiness and strength. She is like a ghost, a wraith, a drifting spirit. Why would he want to mate himself to a dead person?'

There is a lot more of this: privately I think Alys looks like one of the angels in the paintings I saw in the great houses of Venice, but wisely decide to hold my tongue.

'Even if she manages to produce an infant, can you imagine what it would look like? I've blended walnut cankers with arsenic paste: I know what happens when black and white are mixed! Does Ismail want a grey worm as a child?' Zidana raises her hands to the skies and her bangles rattle deafeningly. 'Ah, Thagba, take her from this life!'

★

I am soon to be brought to full understanding of the root of Ismail's fascination with Alys. Finished with his coupling that very night, he calls me out from behind the screen before she even has time to dress herself. I watch as he lays a hand upon her bare haunch and moves it caressingly; they exchange a look no witness was ever meant to see and for the first time jealousy washes through me like lava.

'Is it not remarkable with what fortitude this fragile creature bears my attentions, Nus-Nus? She has such a force of will: she reins in her passions! She is clever: she understands the true nature of survival and takes a long view: instead of flying at a man with teeth and claws like the little Berber bitch, she masters herself, keeps her emotions in check, like a master horseman forcing his will upon a wild stallion. Imagine the strength such reserve requires. She is magnificent! She will give me such children: sturdy of body, powerful of mind.' He turns to me, his eyes lit with triumph. 'I have a plan, Nus-Nus, and it too is magnificent. I shall fortify my army, increase it a hundredfold, and with that army I shall expel the foreign invaders, every one of them: the Portuguese from Mehdiya, the Spanish from Mamora, Larache and Asilah, the English from Tangier. I shall purify my kingdom of the infidel and dedicate it to the glory of Allah. The only foreigners who will be permitted to stay shall be yoked to my command. My corsairs shall scour the seas and coasts for ever more white women and I shall breed them with my *bukhari* and create such an army as the world has never seen, an army which will combine the best of all races, the black and the white.'

He strides about the chamber, his arms outflung, his voice filling even the vault of the high ceiling. He talks of spreading Islam once more throughout Iberia; taking it to the very door of the Catholic Sun King in France, a new caliphate, greater even than the reign of the Almohad Dynasty. His rhetoric is sweeping; persuasive, theatrical. Doctor Lewis took me to the playhouses of Italy, and there I saw such grand gestures as these, gestures designed to reach out to an audience. Here, there are only two of us for him to play to: I look across to Alys to see how she fares in the face of such wild drama, but her face is turned towards Ismail like a flower towards the sun. She cannot understand more than a word here or there of his oratory, but she is captivated by his energy. The sultan has a near-magical charisma: he draws others into his orbit. It is what makes him so powerful, and so dangerous.

The bukhari he speaks of are the elite force of Black Guards he has brought from the lands to the south, captured in Saharan raids, traded for salt and iron. He captures or buys them, converts them to Islam and makes them take an oath of allegiance on a copy of the Salih al-Bukhari, the holy sayings of the Prophet, after which he presents them with a copy of said volume – a precious object indeed – and thus ensures their undying loyalty. He has been breeding them with black slave-women for some time now, marrying them at an early age and encouraging frequent congress so that they produce many offspring. There are thousands of these children being raised in the provinces where he stations his troops while the barracks here are completed: when they reach ten years of age the boys will be trained in the arts of war, the girls in domestic duties; and as soon as they reach puberty they too will be married and encouraged to breed. For years Ismail has been proclaiming that the troops thus produced will be the best in the world. But this is a new twist on his old idea.

He turns back to me now, thrilled by his own invention. 'Imagine, Nus-Nus: just imagine what children you would make – were you entire – with one such as Alys!'

The surge of hatred I feel for him when he says this takes me by surprise. Even when terrified by the sultan – especially when terrified by him – my loyalty has been unquestioning. But something has changed in me, and the catalyst of that change is Alys.

I nod and smile, composing my expression to some semblance of admiration; as soon as I am dismissed I go quickly, the couching book tucked under my arm. I walk with my head down, paying no attention to my surroundings. Once inside my chamber, I lay the book down on my divan and turn around. The cool air of the courtyard, its floral perfumes and pristine night sky beckon me. Wrestling with my churning emotions, I am quite unprepared for the attack.

They are upon me in an instant, four at once. The first blow catches me on the shoulder, which flares with sudden heat. Some devil has hit me with a club! Pain awakes a demon in me. With a scream, I rush at them, lashing out with wild, ecstatic abandon. It is a bliss to hit someone, hit him so hard he flies backwards and crashes into the wall. 'Get the book!' someone else shouts, and one of them tries to land a blow to my head: he is shorter than me and it glances off, merely serving to enrage me further. My arm is a club, a weapon fuelled by fury: my fist connects with some soft part of his face that gives beneath the knuckles, then renders up bone to the force of my blow. There is a crunch, then a bubbling sound, and down he goes and I kick and kick and kick, oblivious to the fact that I am probably doing more damage to my feet, unprotected in their soft babouches, than to his ribs. The third man stares at me. His face is white beneath the moon and I recognize him as a bruiser I have seen around the court on occasion. I cannot recall his name – Hamid or Hamza or something. We lock eyes and he sneers at me, but there is fear as well as contempt there, and as I make a step forward, he makes a shrug of his shoulder, as if to say 'This is not my fight', and walks away; and I am left staring at the fourth man.

'You!'

I am so startled to see him that I am hardly aware of the knife he suddenly produces. Perhaps, I think, even as I duck away from his first strike, it is the same knife with which he slit poor Sidi Kabour's throat. It looks sharp enough: its wicked blade gleams in the semi-dark.

'You fucker. You black bastard,' he hisses, advancing again. 'Who would have thought a slave would have the balls to stand his ground?' His southern accent is pronounced. His thin face breaks into a reptilian grin and I see that his teeth are small and pointed, like a dog's.

I know him. 'I know you!' I cry, and the realization is so immense it fills me from head to toe. I quiver with the knowledge. 'I know who you are; your uncle took my balls, just as he took yours!'

He lunges at me then, a murderous lunge. For some reason, instead of backing away and ceding him the advantage, I take a great stride towards him, and as the knife comes at me, I grab his wrist with both hands, turn and pivot my back into him, using the arm as a lever. The limb cannot withstand such torsion: I have helped dissect enough corpses in my time to know the workings of the human anatomy. Besides, he is smaller than me, and suddenly (for the first time in my life) I want to hurt someone: hurt him badly. Because of this man – pawn though he may be – I have suffered all sorts of hell. With grim satisfaction I hear the shoulder socket give way with a wrench of gristle. The knife clatters from a hand unable to grip any more, and now I have him backed up against the wall (there is very little room in my small cabinet for such brawling), my other hand across his throat till his eyes bulge. There is loathing there, not fear: you have to give him that. He really hates me, it seems, for the loss of his testicles. That much I can understand: but there is no fellow feeling in the understanding. I take in the pointed features, the fancily cut beard. 'I know who you are,' I say again.

'It took you long enough.' Beads of sweat are standing out on his forehead, popping one by one out of his pores.

'You killed an old man who never hurt another soul, and left him lying in a pool of his own blood.'

'Never hurt another soul? Not with his own hands, maybe, but think of all those other hands, which purchased his evil merchandise; think of those countless victims. That she-devil poisons all who stand in the way of her precious brat – and you, you help her! But one day she'll poison you too – she's a sorceress, a witch –'

I can hardly disagree, but suddenly I feel very weary. I lean on the arm barring his throat, stopping his words. 'All this I know. You can tell me nothing. I know your uncle had you cut so that he could manoeuvre you into position at court; he had you kill the herbman to implicate me, so that you could replace me and he could lay hands on the couching book and make the amendment. He had Fatima's entry moved forward, so that her child moves up the order of succession –' It pleases me no end to see his eyes widen. 'So' – I am thinking out loud now – 'Abdelaziz's next step must be to do away with Ahmed, a child of only three . . .'

'The child is a monster and the child of a monster.'

Does he mean Zidana, or Ismail, I wonder? I am sure the world would be a far better place without the little horror in it, but, even so, my duty is to uphold the true succession. I am, after all, the Keeper of the Book. 'I could call the guards, it would take no more than a moment. I could call them and have you taken to the sultan. I could show him the book, show him the forgery . . .' (Of course, I cannot: Zidana's book-binder has already restored the book to its original state, but he is not to know that.) 'I would hardly need to explain its significance to the emperor: he is an astute man, and cruel. He would have you all executed, and no doubt tortured first. But for my own reasons I have decided not to do this. Go to your uncle and tell him that I know everything, and that he is to keep away from me or I will tell the emperor all.'

He curls his lip at me. 'The Hajib and the emperor are like brothers. Ismail will not hear a word against Abdelaziz. He will never believe you.' But despite the bravado of his words, there is uncertainty in his eyes.

I tighten my grip, and at last he nods. I release him. He massages his throat with his one good hand, then bends to retrieve his knife, but I place my foot on it. 'Just go,' I say again, and he does, taking the other two men with him.

As I lie abed later that night I replay the fight in my head, relishing the unchecked violence of it, the unleashing of the warrior within me who till that moment I had not known existed. I do not regret my bruises: I cherish them. The grand vizier will surely kill me now, object of his desire or no, but I shall no longer be a witless pawn in this game of nobles: I shall safeguard myself. I think of all the ways he will try to do away with me and decide that poison is bound to be his preferred method. The next day I go to the market and buy a monkey – a well-set-up Barbary ape – from a trader of livestock. A tailor runs up a robe for it like my own and a little red *tarboush* that it wears on its head, secured with a ribbon under the chin. The ape makes no complaint at this frippery, happy to be out of its cage and given fruits. I lead it back to the palace by a cord, and when it pulls on the cord and chatters at me I stop and it squats in the gutter to relieve itself. Already it has some training, which makes my task easier.

Ismail is charmed by it (he prefers animals to people); the harem ladies love to feed it nuts and dates. It comes with me wherever I go. I am teaching it little tricks and mannerisms, which make Ismail laugh, especially when it takes on my role of food-tasting and I in turn pretend to be the sultan (a dangerous conceit, but he takes it in good part). I have named him Amadou, 'little beloved'.

Thus far, Amadou and I are both still alive.

15

Rajab 1088 AH

Summer comes on like a wave, submerging us all beneath its stifling heat. The women in the harem lie around half clothed, half asleep, their silks staining where they touch the skin; but the building works continue apace. Workers die like flies: they are not used to these temperatures, to sweating their lives away, driven and scourged by their overseers, given little or nothing to eat or drink. The matamores, the prisons where the slaves are kept, stink to high heaven since water is scarce: there is none to spare for cleaning such low quarters. The lions in the menagerie try to burrow their way into the nearest matamore. Who knew that lions could dig? They must have developed an avid taste for human flesh from the poor wretches who are tossed into their enclosure for punishment and the sultan's entertainment. The hole they make – more of a tunnel – is the length of two big lions: they manage to drag one man into it (a Frenchman: he cried *Mon dieu, m'aidez!*, then lost his legs to a lioness's jaws and fell into unconsciousness) before the other slaves beat off the attackers, with stones and fists, and no doubt their rock-like bread. No one decides to risk the tunnel to the lions' pit in an attempt to escape their prison; instead they scream for the guards, who throw down sufficient mortar and rubble to fill the hole. The menagerie is fortified. The sultan is much amused by the incident.

The corsairs bring new captives all the time, men and women; but none of the women capture Ismail's imagination. It seems that Alys has satisfied what appetite he has for Europeans: the rest are farmed out to his bukhari. He keeps her busier than ever, but still there is no tangible outcome of their meetings. She complains of the heat, which is extreme. She is not used to such temperatures, she says; she feels faint much of the time, heavy the rest. During the days she sleeps; she is listless, and bored. About the only thing that brings her to life is the sight of Amadou trailing around after me in his perfect copy of my robes. She coos over him, goes soft in the eyes as she watches his antics.

One day I go out to the souq and purchase her an ape of her own. It is an inspired gift. She names it Hercules, though it is a tiny thing: a vervet monkey as small and soft as a baby, and she carries it everywhere with her. To see her cradling the little creature, stroking its head, letting it grip her fingers with its tiny claws, pierces my heart: I have to look away. The beast is not just for mothering, though, for I still fear Zidana's hatred of her rival. I instruct Alys to allow Hercules to taste a little of her food first and then wait some minutes to watch for any change in his demeanour before she partakes of the food herself. But I fear the gentleness of her heart: I think she had rather taste the food herself to ensure its safety for the monkey.

Soon, however, monkeys are all the rage in the harem: everyone wants one. The place is alive with their chattering and screeching and the smell of their shit. I am not popular with the servants, who have to clean up after them; or with the harem guards, who must put up with the noise of the beasts all day and night. Now that the women are not bickering and fighting amongst themselves, the monkeys have taken over. Every day there is a vicious fight; those who intervene risk being bitten. In the end Zidana has them all rounded up and slaughtered. With her own hands she harvests their brains and internal organs for her magic. Alys is inconsolable.

After that, I keep Amadou in my courtyard.

Months pass. Ismail takes Abdelaziz with him on a visit to his armies in the Rif and along the north coast as far as the English encroachment at Tangier to assess their needs and the taxes he must therefore extract from the Jews and the corsairs. Alys is curiously unnerved by his absence. She takes me by the arm one day, oblivious to the stares of the courtyard women. My nerves sing at her touch, even through the thin cotton of my sleeve.

She turns her heart-shaped face up to me and my head suddenly feels immensely weighty; it is all I can do to master myself and resist the urge to bend and kiss her. 'He will come back, won't he? Ismail? It's not so dangerous in the north, is it?'

Disappointment kicks me in the gut. Stiffly, I assure her that the sultan is both blade- and bullet-proof. Who would dare to kill the Sun and Moon of Morocco? God would strike a man dead at the very thought. This is said only half in jest; half of me believes it. For the rest of the week I stay away from the harem, going about my duties mechanically, making my reports to ben Hadou and the other functionaries who have been left in charge in the sultan's absence. The Tinker is a hard taskmaster: he keeps the palace running like French clockwork. The court is calmer without the presence of the sultan and grand vizier; even the harem spats and rivalries dissipate.

But I cannot stay away for long: Zidana summons me to entertain her entourage since Black John is indisposed. But, as I strum my oud and punctuate the songs with poetry, I direct Rumi's undying words to one pair of ears only:

> *My heart is like a lute*
> *Each note cries with yearning*
> *My Beloved watches me*
> *Wrapped in silence.*
>
> *When you reveal your face*
> *Even the stones dance for joy*
> *When you lift your veil*
> *Even sages lose their wits.*
>
> *The reflection of your face gives*
> *The water a shimmer of gold*
> *And turns the heat of flames*
> *To a gentle glow.*
>
> *When I see your face*
> *The Moon and Stars lose all their glory.*
> *The Moon is too ancient and too dull*
> *To be compared with such a mirror.*

Alys watches me intently; even when I do not look back I can feel her eyes on me. I wonder, is she thinking of me? I think so often of her it feels almost a reality. Almost, I can imagine lying with her, skin to skin. But then my mind shies away from the charade that would follow and I chide myself for my stupidity.

At night I take my beloved leather-bound volume of Rumi to my bed and seek solace in the long dead poet's words.

> I am the black night that hates the Moon
> I am the wretched beggar who is angry with the King . . .
> I have no peace but I will not sigh
> I am angry at sighing! . . .
>
> I run away from the Magnet
> I am a straw resisting the draw of the Amber.
> We are just tiny particles helpless in this world
> I am angry with God!
>
> You don't know how it feels to drown
> You are not swimming in the sea of love
> You are just a shadow of the Sun and
> I am angry with the shadows!

I *am* angry – with the devil who took my manhood from me; with the sultan, who fills his palace with eunuchs for fear his collection of women will breed indiscriminately; with the harem women, who see me as no more than a sexless servant; with Alys, who has made me burn with an ambition that can never be fulfilled. But, most of all, I am angry with myself. Night after night I lie in the darkness questioning who I am, what I have become; what I may be. Must the loss of my testicles define me? Is there so little to me that the cutting away of two small balls of flesh should make such a difference to my identity, reduce me to a being that is less than a man? What *is* a man, after all? More, surely, than a beast that fertilizes a female. I think about the men I have known: my father, a once-proud man laid low by battle wounds and sickness, who ended his life lying on a rush mat issuing petulant orders to anyone within earshot, a king whose kingdom had been reduced to the confines of a tiny, stinking hut; my uncle, who, having fathered a dozen children, found himself unable or unwilling to feed his ever-growing family and one day simply disappeared, taking only his spears and his *calabash* with him. The doctor: a man fully endowed, but who never showed any interest in women at all, of which I was aware; or in boys either, to my relief. All that drove him was his quest for an understanding of the world: it was a hunger in him, an appetite that could never be assuaged, the only thing that ever made him happy. There are the guards on the outer gates — entire men still, whose treating with women has little of romance to it, serving largely to satisfy an urge and thereby to produce more children to replenish the palace staff.

The sultan? He is far more than just a man, nearing the divine: there is no profit in examining such an example.

As for the other palace eunuchs: well, there is an odd spectrum of humanity . . .

There are those who have embraced their new state of life so thoroughly they have practically turned into women: whose breasts and bellies have grown pendulous, whose skin is as soft as a pillow; who rub powdered butterfly wings on their faces each morning to prevent any unsightly growth of stubble. For the most part they seem content with their lot, happy to sit all day gossiping with their charges, eating and eating, waiting for the next thing to happen about which they may talk. Then there are those like Qarim and Mohammadou, who take what pleasure they may find together as tenderly as man and woman, as if the cutting has changed not only their bodies but their very nature. Seeing them with their heads bent close together, the smiles they secretively exchange, I almost envy them: they have found a certain peace here with their new estate that would be hard to do in sight of the wider world. Is it wrong to say that seeing them happy makes me feel emptier still?

I am like none of these men. I shall never be a father, nor a man who abandons his family; I shall never, if I can help it, be a soft man with breasts and a belly like bags, nor one who takes his pleasure with other men; nor a brute, nor a sultan. So I must make of myself what I can. I may be a slave, and a gelding at that, but I still have some pride and spirit left to me.

I am Nus-Nus. I am myself. I must, as Zidana charged me, find the iron in my soul; the warrior within. And perhaps that will suffice.

Well, something seems to have changed. A few days later Zidana says to me, 'My, Nus-Nus: I must say you are looking very fine recently. Like a minor king. Something about your carriage, perhaps?' She walks around me, giving voice to her big, deep-throated laugh. 'A little straighter in the spine, if my eyes do not deceive me; a little freer of movement. Have you been rattling your shackles, my boy, feeling your liberty a little too much while your master is away?'

I look at her askance, and she just grins wider. 'You can tell me, you know: I shall not betray your confidence. Is there a girl?' She leans closer. 'Or perhaps a boy?'

I can feel the shutters come down behind my eyes. I cannot afford to be so transparent. She shrugs, annoyed by my lack of response. 'I'll be watching you, Nus-Nus,' she threatens.

So: it seems I am a book full of clear calligraphy, easily read by scholars of human foibles. This will not do: I must be careful to encode my feelings, especially from Zidana. For she is right, of course: the discovery of my new-found strength, which makes me walk taller and hold my head higher, is not fuelled by resentment or vengeance, but by love.

For it is love, this feeling: I may as well admit it.

PART THREE

16

Safar 1088 AH

Ismail returns in the early spring, not in the best of tempers: plague has descended on the north, sweeping in from the ships in Algiers and Tetouan, and he has barely outrun it.

Plague. The word spreads like running fire through the court until everyone is whispering about it. They have heard rumours of the European sickness that some call the Black Death, which comes on with shivering headaches, intolerable thirst, vomiting and stabbing pains, followed by great glandular swellings in the groin and beneath the arms. Drought grips the land: everyone is already thirsty and hot and headache-ridden. Add the usual panoply of stomach complaints into the mix and you can imagine the panic that grips us. In the harem the women (who never have enough to do) inspect one another's bodies constantly for signs of the black roses they have heard appear on the skin of the afflicted, presaging death. Bruises and insect bites provoke hysteria.

Even Ismail is not immune to the paranoia. What am I saying? He is the worst of them all, despite the fact that the name of every man destined to die is already recorded in the Book of Fate, and no medicine or precaution can therefore cure or prevent his inevitable fate. Yet every day I am sent to fetch Doctor Salgado, who, for the sake of his own health, has avoided strong spirits since his last near-death experience with our lord, to inspect the sultan: to judge his temperature and his tongue, the colour and scent of his urine; the consistency of his stools. Every day, despite being declared healthy by the doctor, Ismail calls for his astrologers and numerologists, who cast his omens and calculate his luck (which is remarkably, uniformly favourable). Salt is strewn at the cardinal points around the palace to dissuade djinns from entering and bringing the plague in with them, mischief-makers as they are. Hyacinths are planted in all the courtyards: their scent is well known to cleanse the air. Ismail orders the talebs to write verses of the Qur'an on scrips of paper, which he then ingests. He has Zidana make up tisanes and potions for him. She sends me to the souq almost daily for ever more items, and over the passing weeks as the plague comes closer the list of requirements grows ever more bizarre – chameleons, porcupine spines, crows' feet, crystals and stones from the Himalaya, lapis from the pharaoh tombs, hyena skins and spiderwebs. But when she sends me to fetch her back the corpse of a newly buried child, I refuse.

She laughs at me. 'If you don't do this for me I will just find another way.'

I incline my head to this piece of blackmail, but say nothing and she does not press the point, so I go away, feeling as if I have escaped her evil influence. But the next day there is a great wailing in the harem: a child of one of the black slave-women has gone missing. My eyes meet Zidana's. She has that blank, brazen look that I recognize only too well, and I know exactly what it means. I do not sleep that night.

The plague passes through Tangier, taking with it many of the hated English, who are currently occupying this strategic port, key to the Mediterranean trade routes, gifted to their king in the marriage portion of his Portuguese bride. It reaches Larache and Asilah, sends its tendrils down the coast to Salé and Rabat. Traders bring it inland with them: every week it creeps closer and appalling stories reach us of entire families succumbing, of farms where the livestock starve to death; stray sheep wander untended in the hills; merchant caravans plod the trade routes without the benefit of their overseers. It reaches Khemisset and Sidi Kacem, barely a few dozen leagues away.

We wait in the airless heat, hardly able to breathe, praying that by a curious twist of fate it will pass us by and fall instead upon Marrakech. Surrounded by hysteria, I cannot help but feel some dread. I have not seen this disease at first hand, but I have heard about it from my old master, Doctor Lewis, and with him I saw its aftermath, the great outpouring of superstitious horror that still infested the city of Venice thirty-odd years after the last outbreak. He was much fascinated by the pestilence, and by the fervent belief of the Venetian population that they had been delivered from its worst ravages by the power of prayer. 'These people are no more civilized than your own,' he told me more than once as we went about the city. 'They put their faith in grand gestures – but rather than sacrificing animals and enemies to secure the favour of their idols, they sacrifice vast sums of money in commissioning towering buildings and religious paintings, thinking it will buy them indemnity.'

In a little backstreet the doctor went into an apothecary's shop and bought a pair of the curious bird-beaked masks that Venetian doctors had worn to go about the city in safety. He put one on when I was not looking and took me greatly by surprise, so much so that I fell down in the street. When I had recovered myself, he showed me how they had stuffed the beaks with herbs to cleanse the air they breathed, and then tutted. 'I am sure, however, that the pestilence is not airborne. We'll have to hope for another outbreak so that I can test my theories.' I shivered, and sincerely hoped such an occurrence would be avoided: to be trapped in that city – so beautiful to the eye at first sight but so full of narrow, dark passageways, dank corners and foul-smelling basins that must surely harbour every disease – was my nightmare.

We made our way out to San Giobbe in the north-west of the city, close to the Jewish ghetto, where we had business, then visited the Church of the Santissimo Redentore and finally the Scuola San Rocco to satisfy the doctor's curiosity about the city's plague-churches. For the most part the images we saw in them were far distant from reality, full of big white angels, glowing madonnas and corpulent babies; but in a studio close to the Scuola we found the young artist Antonio Zanchi completing a monumental painting that showed in graphic detail the barely clothed corpses of plague victims being handed down from bridges and out of windows to brawny men who stacked them in their into newly black gondolas; bodies thrown down into the canals; the afflicted displaying their horrible buboes and boils. I was transfixed as the man worked. To lay paint on to canvas, to create shape and perspective on something flat and plain, seemed to me a quite magical process, and also disturbing in a way I could not explain. I felt almost as if he were bringing the plague back into the world by depicting its effects so graphically.

As he worked Zanchi told us about San Rocco, the Italians' patron saint of the plague. We had seen images of him all over the city: attending the plague-stricken in the hospital, where of course he too had succumbed to the disease; lifting his robe to show the plague-mark on his thigh. According to Zanchi, the saint then crawled into a wood and lay there awaiting death, attended only by his little dog, which brought him daily loaves stealthily robbed from the city's bakers; but in reward for his goodness in tending the sick, an angel came down to tend him, and so, miraculously, he was saved.

I could see that my master was sceptical, though he waited until we were outside before declaring, 'More superstition. People do recover from the plague: make it through to the fifth day and your body's humours have won the battle. Nothing to do with prayer or goodness: I've seen more sinners than saints fight their way back to health! But it's not called the Great Mortality for nothing – they say it carried off one in three in this place in 1630.'

One in three. I remember this dire pronouncement now.

Alys. Zidana. Ismail.

Alys. Zidana. Me.

Alys, Ismail. Me.

Night after night I torment myself with dread.

Messenger birds arrive from Fez bearing terrible reports day after day. People are dying in the souq, in the street, falling off their mules stone dead on their way to market. At the tannery, where it is thought the noxious smells of the guano and urine used to cure the hides must surely keep the pestilence at bay, a man keels over into one of the dyeing pits unseen by his fellow workers. His corpse comes to light dyed such a virulent yellow that at first it is thought to be a demon from a lower hell. The pest is no respecter of status or goodness: *sherifs*, nobles and marabouts are amongst the reported dead; imams and muezzins too. Ismail returns messages ordering a census, instructing the Fassi kaids to divide the city into sectors and count the number of dead in representative streets to suggest a mean. By this method it is soon calculated that over six thousand have already perished; the number is doubling and redoubling week by week. The Tinker seeks an audience with the sultan. 'Sire,' he says solemnly, 'this pestilence is deadly and out of control. We should decamp from Meknes into the mountains.'

Of course, Abdelaziz, positioned at the sultan's right hand, opposes him. 'Meknes is perfectly safe, my lord: no one is infected here and we can make sure it does not enter our gates.' He takes Ismail by the arm – the only man who could ever dare to touch the sultan without his permission – and leads him away. Ben Hadou watches them go, then turns and catches my eye. 'Still alive, then, Nus-Nus?' he asks softly. 'I thought you might like to know that Abdelaziz's nephew has gone away. I've had him sent to Fez.' His eye twitches: a wink or a tic? Hard to tell with the Tinker.

Ismail has the gates of the palace locked and issues orders that Meknes is to be completely isolated and that all travellers arriving from infected towns are to be put to death on sight. He is vehement: he will not leave his new capital, though he frets constantly about the omens and makes us check his body night and day for any sinister signs of the disease. He even spends two consecutive nights sleeping alone, for the first time in the five years I have served him, and when he chooses a girl after this the coupling is perfunctory, as if he has his mind on other things.

Some days later comes the first fatality in Meknes. Is it coincidence that it should be the wife of the keeper of the messenger-birds who succumbs? Ismail has all the birds slaughtered: he believes them to have flown through infected air. We wait. Perhaps it was some other malady that carried her off, some sickness that mimicked the signs of pestilence. We are all still speculating when three more suddenly die, quite unconnected with the dead woman.

When Ismail hears this he turns pale. He makes me tell him all I know of the plague in Europe, all I learned from my former master, saw on my travels. He has bird masks made for the court and insists we all wear them in his presence. Masks over masks. Food is prepared for him only by Zidana's hand. She sits with her head bent over her cooking pot while he sits opposite her, telling his prayer beads. This would make for a homely sight were it not for the fact that Zidana has a big white beak strapped to her face, while the emperor sits there, watching her every move like a gigantic bird of prey. He eats away from the court, which means that Amadou and I are accorded the same privilege, and though the diet is monotonous (chickpea couscous day after day) we do not sicken.

Just as it seems the epidemic will not take hold in Meknes, the plague claims its first victim in the harem: Fatima. It is the headache first, then pain in the joints, and no one thinks much of it to start with, since Fatima is always complaining about something or other, seeking attention. But when the sweats come and the buboes swell, her screams can be heard from one end of the palace to the other. Ismail is distraught: she has given him two sons, though one is dead. He sends for Doctor Salgado to attend her.

What can the poor physician do? The pestilence has its claws deep into her vitals by the time he arrives. He cools her, he bleeds her, he wraps her in cold towels. When this fails to have any useful effect, he consults with Zidana, who makes up poultices to draw the evil humours out of the boils. The pus that spurts out is so foul-smelling that even the doctor must go out into the courtyard and vomit. An hour later she is dead, and so, by curious coincidence, is her boy. And so, in one fell swoop, the Hajib's succession plans come to naught.

When word reaches the sultan, he storms to the harem, meets Salgado hurrying away and, in a moment of madness, or grief, takes his sword and runs him through, there and then, for failing to save her.

So here we are, trapped inside the world's most magnificent palace, stalked by death and ruin and with no one to tend to us in our peril. I am sent into the medina to find, by whatever means possible, another European doctor. Wearing my bird mask stuffed with herbs, I leave the palace and go out into the city. It is a strangely changed place. The central square is deserted, by people at least. Thin cats skulk in the shadows and mew plaintively as I pass; feral dogs lie boneless and exhausted in heaps, there being no one to chase them off. I find a mule wandering in the abandoned spice quarter: all the stalls and *funduqs* are closed up. In the alleys of the medina there are just blank walls and locked doors. Although all family life in Moroccan houses goes on behind these closed façades, it is eerily quiet; even the pigeons seem to have flown. As I near the mellah, a piercing shriek sets my heart racing and suddenly a woman comes running around the corner of the street, stark naked. To see a woman unclothed in a public place is so unprecedented that I simply stand transfixed. She runs right at me, her long black hair snaking around her head, her mouth open in a wail. Blood runs from her cheeks: she has torn them with her nails. The signs of plague are upon her: dark roses on her thighs and chest. Terrified, I flatten myself against a wall, and she runs past me, unseeing.

Maleeo. Ancient Mother, preserve me!

I walk on quickly towards the mellah. At the house of Daniel al-Ribati I knock loudly on the door. The sound echoes down the narrow street, an intrusion into the silence. It is so still I can hear my own breathing, made stertorous by the mask. For a long time I stand there, waiting, and hear nothing within. Then a shutter opens on the window above, and I see, indistinctly, a figure. Impossible to tell whether it is Daniel himself or one of his household, until a voice says, 'Who is it?'

I pull the bird mask up for a moment to show my face, and a moment later a set of heavy iron keys come clattering at my feet. I let myself in to the cool, dark interior.

'You look like a demon from a Hieronymus Bosch painting.' Daniel appears at the turn in the stairs. He looks amused and alarmed in the same degree.

Feeling faintly ridiculous, I remove the mask, and the merchant comes running down the steps and embraces me warmly. It is an odd feeling, to be enveloped so by another human being. I cannot remember the last time I was so embraced. For a long moment I stand there, unable to respond, not knowing what to do, then I hug him back.

'I am very glad to see you, my boy. These are terrible times.'

I ask after his household and he tells me he has released the servants so that they can be with their own families. His wife is upstairs, asleep, having been up all night tending to the birthing of a cousin's child. 'Some would say it was an evil omen to be born in a time of pestilence, but I say God has given us a sign that nothing is stronger than love, not even death.'

To this, I can only nod. We take tea, which the merchant makes himself with the careful deliberation of one who has to concentrate hard over an unfamiliar task, and I explain my mission. Daniel's regard is hooded, unreadable, as I tell him that Ismail requires a European doctor, one well versed in treating the afflicted in Rome, Paris or London.

'The sultan wants what the sultan wants.'

'And I must find it for him. Or face the consequences.'

The merchant purses his lips, considering. After a long while he says, 'Why do you do this, Nus-Nus?'

'Do what?'

'Continue to work for Moulay Ismail. The man is, not to put too fine a point on it, mad.' The back of my neck prickles with heat as if there may be spies in the wall behind me. When he sees I am unable to frame a response, Daniel smiles sadly. 'It is treason to speak the truth, is that it?' He leans forward, touches me lightly on the knee. Have I misjudged his interest in me all these years? There are men all over the city with wives and children and the outward show of respectability who keep a boy in the medina. 'Nus-Nus, listen to me. I have seen plague cities before: I grew up in the Levant. Everyone fears it, and rightly so: but plague is like war – it creates many opportunities. Where there is plague, there is also greater freedom of movement, fluidity – even chaos. A man can disappear without much fear of pursuit.' His blue eyes are intense. 'Get out while you can. Leave Meknes, leave the mad sultan. You may be a eunuch, but you don't have to be a slave. You're an intelligent man, cultured, educated. You could easily find work elsewhere: I could help – I have contacts in Algiers, Venice, London, Cairo, Safed, Hebron: merchants like myself, traders and businessmen who would appreciate a man of your talents – you could make your way to any of these cities and make a new life for yourself. Ismail has far too much to concern him than the whereabouts of one runaway slave. Get out while you can, or you'll regret it for ever.'

All I can do is stare at him like an idiot. He is right, of course. And I have seen enough of the world of which he speaks, the fluid world of international trade in which questions about origin are seldom asked. I have often dreamed of escape from Ismail's yoke, from Abdelaziz, Zidana, the horrid intrigues and vendettas of the court: but with a slave-bond in my ear and this colour of skin, without money, influence or friends, I knew I would not get far before someone took their opportunity to return me to my master and claim his favour. But now: now, in this time of chaos, perhaps I *could* make my escape, set myself up as an amanuensis, a translator, a go-between . . . I feel suddenly weightless, buoyant with possibility. And then my heart reminds me: I cannot go anywhere, without Alys.

He reads my answer in my unguarded face. 'You are too loyal.'

'It is not loyalty, precisely, that keeps me here.'

'Fear, then?'

'Not that, either.'

'Ah, then it is love.'

I feel the heat rise in my face and struggle against it. 'It is love,' I concede at last.

Daniel al-Ribati looks wistful. 'Whoever it is who keeps you here should think themselves lucky to have such a stalwart heart at their command.'

'She knows nothing of it: I have not spoken.'

'Ah, Nus-Nus, love one-sided is a pathetic thing. At least speak your heart and see how she answers you. Maybe she will leave with you: and, if she will not, then you have your answer and should leave on your own.'

'I wish it were so simple,' I say fervently.

'Love is always simple. It is the simplest thing in the world. It sweeps all before it, makes a straight, clear path.'

I give him a wry smile. 'How well I know it. It has made a straight, clear path through my heart.'

'I hope she is worth it, Nus-Nus. You're a good man.'

'Am I good? Sometimes I am so filled with rage and fear, I think I am the world's greatest sinner. As for being a man, well –'

'It takes more than the cutting away of two small pieces of flesh to change that state.' He presses his palms against his thighs, pushes himself to his feet. 'Come, then, let us see if Doctor Friedrich is at home.'

We walk the maze of deserted streets. The merchant moves with determined vigour, arms pumping, robe swinging, his leather shoes slapping the cobbles. He keeps them on even when we pass the Great Mosque, which is illegal and would earn him a beating, were there guards around to punish him. But the city has been taken back by its true inhabitants, the feral animals and the populace: everyone else has either fled or perished. I follow Daniel, one loping stride to his two, the bird mask swinging from my hand, feeling a freer man than before, if only in my own head.

In the back streets behind the central market, Daniel takes a right, then a left, and stops at a dusty, iron-studded door, its paint flaked away to a ghost of its original blue. He raps loudly and we wait. Silence stretches out and no one comes. My newfound optimism begins to ebb.

The sound of footsteps approaching, noisy in the resounding quiet, makes us turn as one. A solitary figure rounds the corner. It is a tall man wearing a flat, round, black hat: no hood, tarboush or turban, thus no Moroccan.

The merchant steps forward. 'Friedrich?'

The figure stops, then comes towards us quickly. 'Daniel?'

They grip arms, laugh and speak together for a while in German, not a language in which I can converse. At last they turn to me. 'And this is Nus-Nus, court eunuch to Sultan Moulay Ismail.'

I find myself eye to eye with the physician, a rare experience. Bear-like, he grips my hand and shakes it briskly, then nods towards the beaked mask. 'That won't do you any good,' he laughs contemptuously.

He unlocks the studded door and ushers us inside. Beyond dark corridors I glimpse a sunlit garden rampant with vegetation, and my heart yearns towards its light and birdsong, but the doctor leads us up to his study, a room stacked with books, scrolls, papers and all manner of paraphernalia. Doctor Friedrich subsides weakly into a big wooden chair and gestures for us to sit on two of the large crates in the centre of the room.

'You are packing up?' Daniel asks.

'Time to move on. There's no profit to be had from staying here: those who aren't yet dead or dying are leaving in droves.'

'Where are you going?'

'I hear the plague has yet to reach Marrakech.'

'It can only be a matter of weeks away from the Red-Walled City,' the merchant says. 'And what lies beyond Marrakech? Only the mountain tribes, and then the wild men of the desert. Nus-Nus here has a proposal for you.'

I explain my mission. Friedrich looks sceptical, and I cannot blame him. 'Why the sudden need for a new physician? Has Salgado finally drunk himself into oblivion? Or has the plague claimed him?'

Without elaborating on the cause, I say that Salgado has indeed expired.

He shrugs. 'It surprises me he's lasted this long, to be honest: he was little more than a charlatan.'

'Would you count yourself a better physician than Doctor Salgado?' I ask.

'That wouldn't be too hard. His medicine stems from another age. There are extraordinary advances taking place elsewhere in the world: I try to keep up with them as best I can. In London there are remarkable discoveries afoot. I should like to go to see for myself what the members of their Royal Society are capable of. But at the moment buying passage out of Morocco's plague ports comes at a prohibitive price, and I fear I lack the means to make my escape.'

'The sultan would pay you very well for your services,' I press.

He steeples his fingers, rests his chin on them, and at last sighs. 'I suppose I may as well die by the sword as by the plague.'

He packs a small bag: I will arrange for the rest of his things to be brought to the palace. Daniel walks as far as the Sahat al-Hedim with us and embraces us both warmly. He steps away from the physician to say to me, 'Remember what I said, Nus-Nus. Come and see me if you change your mind and I will do what I can to help you. But do not leave it too long. If Sarah decides to join her sister in Tetouan, then I shall go with her.'

'Go with God, Daniel.'

'And you, Nus-Nus.'

We watch him leave, then make our way across the deserted square towards the palace. My heart is pounding as if it has got ahead of itself, as if I am already on the run. Suddenly there seem to be possibilities, other roads my life may take. As we walk I say to the doctor, with attempted nonchalance, 'In your life you must have amassed a great deal of medical knowledge of the human body . . .' I hesitate, trying to frame the question.

He stops and looks at me. His expression is unreadable. 'Go on,' he says slowly.

I cannot meet his eyes. Suddenly, my shame at my own condition overwhelms me and I am unable to speak. We walk on in silence to the Bab al-Raïs. It is now or never: I steel myself and manage to get out, quite hoarsely, before we are within earshot of the guards, 'Doctor, you know of remedies for every malady. Tell me, do you believe there is any cure for a eunuch?'

He stops and gazes at me steadily, and there is such a depth of warmth and understanding in his regard that abruptly my eyes swim with tears. 'You are asking for miracles, Nus-Nus,' he says gently.

Ismail is delighted with the doctor, who tells everyone to dispense with the bird-beaked masks, and who has tales to tell from the world over. His reading of philosophers old and new gives the pair of them much to discuss and argue over, which provides ample distraction from the immediate horrors of the plague.

While the sultan is thus distracted, I steel myself while the resolution is strong in me and stride towards the harem. At the gate Qarim stares at me hollow-eyed. He looks as if he has not slept in days, but I am in too great a hurry to stop and ask after his well-being, and when he makes to engage me in conversation, I nod impatiently and give him short answers and he waves me through in some resignation.

It is fifth day, which I have quite forgotten. The women are beautifying themselves: even the plague cannot impede such a priority, though perhaps the atmosphere is a little more hectic than usual, their chatter louder, their cosmetic experiments bolder and more bizarre. I am relieved to find Alys alone, except for a servant, in her own apartments. When she sees me in the doorway her eyes shine: she beckons me in.

Now is the time to ask her to come away with me, to hazard an escape. I cross the room, my question burning in my mouth: is this the moment when my life will branch into a new and wonderful future? But it is Alys who speaks first.

'I think I may be with child.'

My heart stops, then plummets, pierced by sudden pain, like a bird that has been flying in a serene blue sky and without warning is shot through by an arrow.

'Are you sure?'

Her smile, downcast, is secret, smug. She is sure.

'How long?'

She splays three fingers against the rich blue silk of her robe. I stare at them, at the whiteness of her skin stark against the vivid fabric. Three months. For three months she has been carrying the seed of Ismail's child within her and I did not know it. A succubus; the harbinger of the sultan's New Model Army. I feel – what? Numbness, followed by a chill that spreads through me, as if my vitals are dying, inch by inch.

Her hand rests protectively on her still-flat belly, and as she glances down I see her lips curve and she looks just like one of those prim Italian madonnas. For a moment I almost hate her. She is . . . happy. And I?

With the greatest effort, I master myself. 'Congratulations. The emperor will be delighted,' I say, my tone formal. 'I hope it will be a boy.'

17

The sultan is indeed delighted. He sends Alys extravagant gifts: a chiming clock for her apartments, a ewer of Egyptian rock crystal, a Syrian incense burner, a set of Iznik plates, silk robes, an antique comb inlaid with silver and mother-of-pearl. He pats her belly and kisses it: he abstains from mounting her. I have never seen this behaviour before with any of his other women, which makes it all the more painful to witness.

I do not pass any of these intimate details back to Zidana, but still she quizzes me relentlessly. 'How can she be pregnant?'

I pretend I do not understand what lies behind the question.

'If she has been drinking the tonics I send her, it would be impossible.' She fixes me with a glare.

'I am sure, Beneficent One, that she would never spurn any . . . tonic you sent her.'

She tries a different tack. Places a hand on my arm. 'You spend a good deal of time with the little Englishwoman: tell me, Nus-Nus, is the child truly Ismail's?'

I feel the heat of guilty thought rise in me. 'You know as well as I that the sultan's women are kept pristine at all times and that all blessed events are uniquely in the gift of the Sun and Moon of Morocco himself.'

Her fingers tighten on my arm. 'Are you quite sure of that, Nus-Nus? You've been looking very pleased with yourself lately. Have you found a sorcerer to reverse your condition?' Leaning in closer. 'Are you sure you have not had congress with her, a little love-play when she is lonely? You can tell me: I am discreet. I know it happens from time to time.' She pauses. 'Though there was that one Egyptian, do you remember, took her slave-boy to her bed when Ismail did not choose her, and suffered a hysterical swelling of her belly? She convinced herself she was with child; in the end I stuck a skewer in her belly and air rushed out till she was quite flat, do you remember? She died not long after, if I recall.' She laughs uproariously.

'The lady is entirely proper. She is proud to be carrying the emperor's child,' I say, feeling ill.

There is a light in Zidana's eye now, a light of conviction. She starts to pace, never letting go of my arm. 'The woman is a sorceress. She has magicked up a djinn and offered it a home in her belly. It is sitting in there, biding its time. I know about these things: I have studied them. In my village a woman had a brood of ten stashed away in her cunt. They love blood, the djinns, especially the blood of a woman's womb. They feed on it and grow strong, and it bewitches them, ties them to the giver, till they want no other sustenance. She had them all doing her bidding: making other women barren, men impotent; tying knots in the clothing of newly-weds so that they'd brawl with one another; killing asses, poisoning rivers. There was nothing she couldn't do. That one had light eyes too, I tell you. It is a sign of their power.' She lowers her voice. 'I know what she is: you can tell her that. I am watching her every second of the day.' She turns away, looks down, turns back to me. 'You see?' She points to the ground.

I look where she is pointing. The stones may not have been swept and there is dust where her shadow lies, reddened by the falling sun. 'What?'

'There, there!' She stabs the air with a finger. 'My shadow: see how thin it is! She has bewitched it. She is not pregnant at all: she is stealing my size to augment her own! She is trying to ruin my beauty, she wants to destroy me. She knows Ismail cannot abide a thin woman!'

All I can do is gape. Do I point out that all shadows run thin at this hour, elongated by the angle of the sun? Or would that be unwise? I have never seen her so crazed. For a moment (a moment only) I feel sorry for her: a fellow feeling almost, both of us thwarted in our affections.

The sultan's delight in Alys is short-lived as other concerns overtake him. The kaids report ever greater numbers of deaths in the city: they have devised a method for calculating such things using tally sticks and averages that delivers alarming results, and after the latest report he suddenly declares that he and a select number of his household will take up temporary residence in the mountains until the pestilence has abated.

Initially, the idea sounds charming, an outing merely: an extended picnic – though his picnics can be elaborate affairs, involving a battalion of staff, gold and silver platters, tea samovars; herds of mules bringing chosen companions from the harem, hordes of musicians and baskets of Ismail's beloved cats to share in the delights. Ismail himself prefers to arrive in a gilded carriage drawn by eight of his favourite courtesans. I remember when one of the cats was so bold as to chase and kill one of the royal rabbits; it then had the temerity to settle down to eat it, nose first, in front of the sultan, as if it were simply joining in the picnic. Ismail had the cat collared, whipped and dragged through the streets of the city for destroying royal property.

It is announced that the sultan will require the attendance not only of his personal household, but also of two hundred chosen women from the harem, seven hundred guards and his standing army. Which means that the best part of thirty thousand men, women, children and eunuchs will be heading into the mountains between here and Marrakech.

Making provision for so many stretches the resources of even the grand vizier. I swear in the last week he has lost the equivalent of a sheep in weight running here and there about the palace to meet with this supplier or that, organizing transportation and habitation, and making bargains with the tribal chiefs, whose support will be required as we make our progress. I hear that the sultan's gold in itself will require a dozen wagons and four dozen oxen to transport it (the rest, I believe, is buried in secret chambers guarded by ghosts and curses). And Zidana's demands are even more exigent. I have already been back and forth to the souq for sacks of henna, olive soap, herbal remedies – and a hundred other ingredients, largely poisonous. Then there are bales of silk and stacks of haberdashery and finding thirty seamstresses to accompany us into the mountains, which, given the plague, proves more problematic than you might expect.

At night I cannot help but turn Daniel al-Ribati's words over and over. If I am to escape my servitude, this will be my best opportunity. Already the court is in chaos. Strangers come and go; functionaries are sending their families away to stay with relatives in the south, where the plague has yet to strike, and my errands take me in and out of the palace at all hours of the day, unchallenged. I could walk right out of here. Find Daniel, accept his help. Leave Meknes, and never come back. Make a new life somewhere else. Anywhere else. As a free man.

One morning, when Ismail's frustration with his perceived laziness of the builders boils over and he bodily drags one away from his task and throws him to the hungry lions, who make short and bloody work of his body, I find my thoughts returning inexorably to the idea of escape.

All morning the idea nags at me, until I can stand it no more. As soon as I am dismissed, I run back to my room, open up my wooden chest, sort through my things in a kind of blind fury and a moment later find myself striding purposefully along the colonnaded walkway towards the Bab al-Raïs with a makeshift sack over my shoulder. I wear a djellaba whose hood will disguise me once I make it into the medina. Beyond which lies the rest of my life. Wrapped in a length of turban cotton: my copy of Rumi, my Qur'an, a clean tunic, a pair of long qamis, my best pen; a small bottle of ink. If worse comes to worst, I shall offer my services as a scrivener or a public letter-writer. On a belt against my skin, a small pouch holds every coin I possess. Enough, maybe, to purchase a mule. How much does a mule cost? I have no idea. More than it did since the plague struck Meknes, no doubt, with so many desperate to escape the city. Well, I think, if a mule is too dear, I shall make good use of my own two feet . . .

'Nus-Nus!'

The words are barely audible, she is so out of breath. She bends out of breath, hands on thighs, chest heaving. Straightens up, laughs a little embarrassedly. 'I've been looking everywhere for you.'

It is Makarim, the slave-girl assigned to Alys.

She holds something out to me and I stare at the coriander, its pretty leaves wilting from the warmth of the girl's hand.

Coriander.

People stream past us as if we are twin boulders in a river. Trying to stop my voice from trembling, I ask, 'Your mistress, is she well?'

'I don't know. She's anxious. Jumpy. Paler than usual.'

We go via my room, where I leave my things. At the harem gate I am surprised to find no sign of Qarim but an older guard whose name is, I think, Ibrahim.

'Where is Qarim?'

Ibrahim grimaces, runs a finger across his throat.

'Dead?'

The guard gives me an open-mouthed grin so that I can see the stubby root where his tongue has been cut out. I shiver, not at the mutilation, which is common enough, but at the memory of how ill Qarim looked when last I saw him; how he made to speak to me, how I hurried by. As I pass through the gate I say a small prayer for his soul; and hope he will forgive me for being a poor friend.

Alys is as white as a jasmine flower. When I bow, formally, she bursts into tears, which is not like her. I frown. 'Why have you summoned me?' Suddenly, I feel as aggrieved as the djinn in the lamp, disturbed from its rest for no good reason.

With a shaking hand she indicates on the carpet at the other side of the room a square of lace upon which sit four or five dark patches. 'The woman is a monster! Not content with trying to poison me with her potions, now she sends me this . . .'

I stride over to the piece of lace and stare down, uncomprehending. What are these things? Slices of dried fig? Fragments of tree resin?

'"Wear it next to your heart," she said. "It will bring you luck." She did not say, of course, what order of luck she meant!'

I bend to examine the items more closely.

'Do not touch it!' Alys cries in anguish.

They are scabs: I see it now. Dried pus and blood, crusted solid. Instinct tells me these are the leavings of poor Fatima's plague-boils, and recoil violently. 'Maleeo, Ancient Mother, protect me!' The words escape me before I know it.

When I turn, Alys is smiling at me through her tears. 'Old habits die hard.' So saying, she crosses herself.

'Alys –' I say warningly, and she drops her hand.

'We are not so different, you and I, despite every appearance to the contrary: we both pray to our own gods in extremis.'

'In extremis, and in secret, if you value your life.'

I send the girl, Makarim, for tongs from the kitchen and when she comes back I make a fire in the courtyard and burn the kerchief and its contents and we watch till it is nothing more than ash; even that, I bury.

'I thought you had gone away and left me,' she says in a low voice.

I hesitate, then concede, 'I very nearly did.' How nearly she must never know. While I was packing my few things and planning my escape, she was opening a kerchief full of plague-poison. The thought brings bile into my throat.

'I could not blame you for doing so. We must all look to ourselves in these times. You should go, Nus-Nus. Leave now: it may be your only chance of freedom.'

When your heart and your conscience are in chains, what freedom is there? I just shake my head. 'I cannot go.'

'I would be lying if I said I was not glad.' She gazes at me steadily, and though her blue eyes are endlessly expressive, I do not know what I read there, only that I cannot look away. At last, she extends her hand, an English gesture, and I take it, lightly, between my own. It feels hot with life, with two lives. I bend my head and press it to my forehead; and then I have to leave quickly, for my eyes are wet.

The transport stretches for miles: dozens upon dozens of carts and wagons for Ismail and his personal clothes and jewels and gold and weapons; his bed, carpets, covers and favourite items of furniture; his travelling hammam; his incenses and perfumes, braziers and flagons, his Qur'an, his prayer mats; his favourite cats. Abdelaziz, Doctor Friedrich and ben Hadou travel with Ismail, surrounded by the elite bukhari troops and the cavalry. I travel with the household slaves and our pitifully small needs: clothing, bedding, our few personal possessions. Behind us come the women and children and the palace guards of the inner court, some five hundred of them, all eunuchs. Behind them, the astronomers, the court lords and higher functionaries; their families and households. Next are the store-wagons; Malik and his kitchen staff; the seamstresses, tailors, grooms, smiths and other artisans. The baggage train winds over the hills behind us and far out of sight. Somewhere at the back I know there is an army of slaves on foot, mostly Africans; the Christians remain in the city to continue work under the supervision of the most trusted (thus cruel) overseers. Ismail has left with his master builders a long list of tasks he expects to see accomplished on his return, and woe betide them if they are not carried out to his full satisfaction.

After five days riding south we reach the cooler foothills of the Atlas Mountains, and there, by the limpid green waters of the Melwiya River, we make camp. Stripped to the waist in the hot sun, I labour with the other slaves to set up the sultan's tents, a matter that is complicated by the fact that the ground is not perfectly flat and so the pavilions – black and white on the outside, green and red and gold inside – are more crowded together than is ideal, and everyone is getting in everyone else's way. Already a scuffle has broken out because someone got accidentally clouted on the backswing of a mallet and the victim has taken exception to the blow; and the astronomers, finding it hard to set their instruments to their satisfaction in unfamiliar territory, have split into two factions and are arguing amongst themselves about the precise direction of the *qibla*: a vital detail, since the sultan must at all times lie down with his head towards Mecca. It is at this point that Ismail bears down upon us with Alys at his right hand and Zidana at his left.

We all make the prostration on to the grass and keep our gazes down.

'What is the meaning of this?' Ismail has ears like a bat's: he has picked up on the altercations.

I see the stargazers exchange panicked glances and immediately heal their rifts. 'The slaves will not listen to instruction: they have taken it upon themselves to pitch the tents in quite the wrong alignment. The Qaaba is precisely in this direction –' The chief astronomer shows the sultan his qibla indicator, and Ismail bends to pore over the complex markings on the etched brass discs. When he straightens up, his face is purple with fury. I should not, after all these years, be surprised by how quickly his mood can change, but even I am not prepared for the violence of his temper.

'Shoot them all!' He screams to the attendant guards. He sweeps an arm to indicate every man of the tent-pitching team, forty or more of us. 'I want them all dead. They insult the Prophet! They insult *me*! Shoot them all!'

I am desperate to propel myself to my feet and run. But, as if some sorcery pins me there, I am unable to move. All I can do is shift my head minutely to watch my doom come upon me.

The guard closest to the sultan hesitates: fatally. In an instant, Ismail is upon him, wresting his gun away. The poor fool holds on to it for a moment too long and it will be the last thing he does, for now he looks down in some surprise to find the jewel-studded hilt of an imperial dagger standing proud from his chest. His mouth drops open, revealing a stub of tongue. Then, silent, he crumples, relinquishing the weapon. Ismail takes the gun and cocks the hammer and, barely aiming, discharges it into the prone body of the man next to me, who cries out in shock and bounces a foot off the ground, pouring blood, much of which splashes hotly on to me. As if this is their signal, other guards begin shooting wildly. At once, all is mayhem.

I hear a woman scream, and though I have never heard her scream before, I know it is Alys.

'My lord, no!' A man's voice: the Tinker: the Kaid Mohammed ben Hadou Ottur. 'We need the ammunition, sire. The hills are full of Berbers.'

He is a clever man, the Tinker; brave too. There is never any point in appealing to Ismail's gentler side: he does not have one. Ben Hadou takes it upon himself to gesture for the guards to stand down. There ensues a short exchange between the sultan and his kaid, and then Ismail comes amongst us, violence emanating from him like a volcanic cloud. I see his gold-embroidered babouches flash past me, and then, a little space away, there is a wet crunching sound and a man howls like an animal. I cannot help but turn, to see Ismail laying violently about him, arms swinging in a whirlwind of brutality, a tent mallet in each hand, crushing skulls to the left and right.

I am going to die. The certainty is lead in my stomach. Here, ignominiously on my belly on a scrappy bit of grass in a land not my own, for no good reason, I am going to die.

I have been close to death many times. Every day in the imperial palace someone dies, often at Ismail's own hand. Some regard it as an honour, to be dispatched by the sultan himself: he is, after all, a sherifian, of the line of the Prophet and thus as near to God as any of us is likely to get. They say that anyone whose life is taken by the sultan will surely be rewarded in paradise with shady gardens full of roses in which run rivers of milk, honey and wine, and fountains scented with ginger and camphor, surrounded by virgins perfumed with frankincense. The trouble is, in times of panic it is Maleeo and Kolotyolo who command me, and sadly they do not offer such inducements.

I try to prepare myself to meet my ancestors, but all I can think of is the crushing blow, the subsidence of my fragile skull, the rushing out of blood and brains, and that I will die here on the ground, mashed by a tent mallet, right in front of the woman I love.

That is the thought that shocks me to action. I look around. Ismail is ten feet away from me, his frenzy unabated. He is coming closer. I see him kick the body of the next slave; the man is unresponsive, clearly dead, and he moves on. The man lying beside me is the victim of the shooting, half his head exploded over the grass. Covertly, I reach out and cup a handful of the poor soul's blood and matter. I plaster it swiftly over my head and neck, adopt a tortured pose, neck awry, and lie there, waiting for the end.

I lie there till the warmth goes out of the day, till the darkness falls and the moon rises.

'You can get up now, Nus-Nus.'

I blink and turn my head and my face feels odd: cold and stiff. Abdelaziz is standing over me, hands on his hips. Moonlight illumines the jewels in his turban. His face is in shadow, but I can feel his smile hovering in the dark air between us.

'Clever boy. I saw what you did.'

'Is he gone?' I try to move but my body is unwilling. With great effort I manage to haul myself upright. Still my face feels strange, as if it is not my own, and then I remember. 'Oh.' Revulsion washes through me.

The next thing I know, hands have closed around my arms and I am hauled to my feet. A piece of cloth is wound about my face, and it is cold and damp and smells of some strong chemical, and then suddenly the world is upside-down and I am being carried like a slaughtered sheep. They take me to a tent on the edge of the encampment. It looks like any other soldier's tent from the outside; but within . . .

Someone has equipped this place for one purpose alone. It is piled with mattresses and cushions, ringed around by French mirrors, and it stinks of strong smoke, sweet incense and spilled seed. A stake has been driven into the ground amongst the cushions. I start to struggle, but my limbs lie slack and useless, overcome by whatever I have inhaled through the cloth, and I think then what a devil he is, to have found some concoction that leaves the mind alert while the body is put to sleep.

They throw me on a mattress and bind my hands to the stake, and all the while I tell my feet to scrabble on the ground so that I can lever the stake out of the ground and use it to club my enemy to death; but every muscle in my body seems deaf to my bidding. I hear one of the slaves being ordered to fetch water and soap and a washcloth, and a few moments later a lad comes back and cleans the blood and matter off me. I have seen the boy about the camp, but I do not know his name, and couldn't speak it even if I did. Instead, I widen my eyes at him, trying to communicate my lack of assent to this vile indignity, the wish that he run to fetch help, but he keeps his gaze down-turned, closed off: it is no doubt not the first time he has seen such a thing. Probably, poor child, he has been subjected to worse himself.

The grand vizier goes about the tent lighting candle-lanterns and sing-ing softly to himself – 'The Hunter and the Dove', that tender, pretty song beloved by the harem women – and I feel my guts clench in disgust. That is how he sees me, is it: as helpless prey, about to be skewered by his arrow?

At last, he is finished with his preparations. He squats beside me. 'So now, Nus-Nus, this is pleasant, is it not? Just the two of us. He thinks you are dead, Ismail – if he thinks of you at all. So now you are mine to do with as I wish.' He pushes up my robe, exposing me, and gazes at what is left of my genitals. Then he takes my penis in his hand and begins to fondle it gloatingly. 'It is a fine, neat job, is it not? And so it should be: I paid for the best man in the busi-ness, having seen the butchery carried out on others, the botched excisions, the infections, the poisoning of the blood. There were choices to be made.'

His eyes flick lazily over me: he is enjoying this exertion of power over one who in other circumstances would kill him in an instant. '*Spadones*, the dragging off of the testicles; or *thlibaie*, the simple crushing of them; or *sandali*, removing both the member and the testes, which is the usual course with blacks. Many die from that sort of castration, and of those who do survive many are left with so little they find it hard to make water.' He leans in closer. 'Black John wears a great silver pin with an emerald set atop it in his turban: you may have seen it?'

I have, but I just stare into space over his shoulder as though he is not there. I hear the sly smile in his voice as he says, 'It's not a pin, you know: it's a hollow tube. He uses it to piss through.' The squeeze he gives me makes me wince. 'You were lucky: I decided against taking everything – I saw your potential as an investment for the future.'

Dead! I shall see you dead, with your head caved in and maggots in your eye sockets.

'Xenophon tells us that vicious horses, when gelded, have their worst tendencies curbed and will no longer bite or buck, but are still fit for service in war; and that dogs, when castrated, lose none of their strength or capacity for hunting, but no longer run away from their masters. I believe the same and more can be said for men. The removal of their balls alone will render them more placid. More grateful too, I hope. I have also heard that the procedure may actually enhance rather than hinder the sexual performance; and that if the cutting is done after puberty, there may be no diminishment of desire. And I am sure, Nus-Nus, that with the right degree of encouragement, it will prove to be thus with you.

'It's not exactly the way I would have wished for us to come together, but you can't blame me for taking the opportunity when it is so neatly presented. A passage of sweet love-play, and then we shall take you back to where we found you and smash your skull in for real. And no one will know that you survived the massacre for a few short hours. It really is such a shame it should come to this, Nus-Nus. It could all have been so different had you been less . . . obstinate. All I have ever wanted to do was to instruct you in the art of pleasure. You are such an accomplished boy in so many other ways: it would have rounded out your education beautifully. Such a waste of this glorious body.'

He beckons to the slave, and together they turn me over and arrange me so that my rump is presented. As the boy is dismissed, I remember with horror Alys so arranged on Ismail's bed that first night. And then I feel his hands on me, and all at once I am back in the desert, suffering my first violation, and it is like being in a nightmare in which you are pursued by a monster but are unable to run . . .

The vomit rises out of my gullet, comes spewing out all over the gaudy silks, ejected with such force that it even spatters the glass of the French mirrors.

'For shame!' the grand vizier cries with revulsion. He springs to his feet and kicks me in the ribs. More ejecta erupts, and now he has it on his shoes, which are no doubt expensive. He howls like a dog, kicks me again, lower in the gut. This time I can feel the pain of it and it is good: it surges through me like cleansing fire. I can feel the effect of the drug wearing off, a little. I flex my toes, and feel them move against the ground, feebly at first, then with more intent. Come on, I urge my useless body. I focus on my hands, bound to the iron stake, drive my thoughts into my fingers, one by one; and one by one I watch them move. I catch hold of the stake and start to twist and pull . . .

'What? What?' Abdelaziz's voice rises to a screech. He fumbles for his dagger.

The stake comes loose and I catch him with it, a blow that connects sumptuously, triumphantly, with the middle of his turbaned head. But of course the grand vizier wears a turban that is even larger than that of the sultan. It contains acres of fabric, wound in incessant, intricate folds, so that his head resembles a vast onion. The blow stuns him for a moment only, then he comes at me with the dagger, all his thwarted desire in his eyes. I sidestep the first attack, try to barge him on the second, but he is like a rock. The dagger punctures me below the ribs. I feel it not as pain but as a heat that fuels my fury. I swing the stake around my head, allowing its full length to carry the momentum into the blow, which lands crushingly across his chest and sweeps him off his feet: an airborne hippopotamus, he lands on his back and all the wind goes out of him with a great huffing noise. He is not getting up from this: I will not let him. I stand with one foot amongst the cushions, the other on his belly, and take his dagger out of his limp hand.

'That's enough, Nus-Nus.'

At the door, ben Hadou, with Abdelaziz's silent slave-boy at his side. The child looks in alarm at the dagger, then at his recumbent master, and runs away.

'Come away. Much as we both dislike him, this will do no good.'

Life resumes as if nothing out of the ordinary has happened. When I reappear, in a change of clothing, and with my flesh wound dressed with calm practicality by the Tinker, Ismail simply orders me about my tasks as if he has not come within seconds of caving in my skull with a mallet. At dinner, once Amadou and I have carried out our tasting duties, he is in melancholic mood, as he often is after the spilling of blood.

We are seated on a carpet outside his main pavilion and he is gazing skywards. 'My astronomers tell me that the same stars that shine on us now are those that shone on the Prophet as he sat in the entrance of the cave of Hira. See there Ash Shaulah, the raised tail of the scorpion.' He gestures towards the myriad indistinguishable points of light in the night sky. 'At-Tinnin, the serpent; Sa'ad al-Malik, the star of the great king.' He lingers over this last spark of light for a long time, silent, thoughtful, the moonlight limning his fine profile, lending a silver sheen to his eyes. At last he says, 'How will I be remembered, Nus-Nus?'

Was there ever a more perilous question to answer honestly? Over the years we have discussed many things, but they were in the main practical concerns: the merits of wool in winter and cotton in summer; the quality of salt from different sources – sea, or desert; the nature of cats and camels. He had asked me about Venice but I saw his eyes glaze as I told him about its watery streets: he could not imagine such a thing as a canal, nor did it interest him. But when I spoke of the architecture and the wealth on display, he listened attentively and asked many questions. He has asked me about matters of language and translation, especially in relation to business terminology; we have even discussed Aristotle, Homer and Pliny – writers who, because they pre-dated the birth of Islam, offered safer ground than

my beloved Rumi, with his flights of ecstatic imagination and his dangerously heretical views. But Ismail has never once shown me a glimmer of
vulnerability or doubt, and I do not know how to respond. 'As a great
king?' I venture.

He nods slowly. 'But what makes a great king? What will history say of
me?'

'I know little of such things, sire.'

His dark eyes are upon me, glittering. 'Abdelaziz told me you are yourself the son of a king.'

I could deny it, and aver that the grand vizier had lied, but it would be a
lie, although my poor father's kingdom by the end was barely bigger than
one of Ismail's pavilions, and I had never considered myself a prince. I
incline my head. 'A very minor king, sire: there is little comparison to be
made.'

'Come now, lad, don't be coy.'

Is there anything so nerve-racking as to have the cold gaze of the execu-
tioner upon you as he asks you to condemn yourself? I trawl desperately
through my brains for all I know of kings, from the words of the *griots*, the
storytellers, spinning their songs and tales by firelight. The names tangle in
my head: Akhenaton the pharaoh, Askia Toure, King of the Songhai, Cae-
sar of Rome, Hannibal, Cyrus, Alexander and Suleiman, who sawed a child
in two and gave a half to each of its mothers, or some such thing. My brothers and I were much taken by the bloody details of tales of these great ones
– the prisoners whose skulls were crushed beneath elephants' feet; the enemies interred alive; the babies burned in sacrifice to pagan gods, the
massacres at Jenné and Babylon . . . It occurs to me that maybe cruelty is a
necessary quality for a king; or perhaps kingship forces such behaviour
upon a man. Does the propensity to be a monster propel a man towards a
crown? It is said that Ismail worked his way through a dozen or so more
deserving claimants to Morocco's throne, though I do not know how much
of that is true. Or does power twist a man's soul so that he believes himself
to be above all others? If all bowed down to me, treated me like a god on
earth, indulged my every whim, cast themselves terrified at my feet and
looked away if I spilled blood, would I also be like Ismail? The thought is

treasonous, and I fear it may be written on my face. Already, I have taken too long. Quickly now, Nus-Nus, say something. Say anything!

'I think, sire, that you will be remembered as the Champion of Morocco.'

The glittering eyes narrow into half-moons – suspicion? No, delight. 'The Champion, yes, I like that. I shall be remembered as the Defender of the Faith, the Scourge of the Infidel, the Bringer of the Crescent Moon. And also as the Architect, the king who raised Meknes from a peasant village to a great imperial city. And as the founder of a glorious dynasty.' He is up on his feet now, striding about as if determined, right now, to propel this image of himself into the world. He is, of course, already part of a dynasty: the Alaouites, the sherifs descended from the Prophet through the line of his daughter Fatima. I do not say this. Neither do I mention his appalling beast-children, found only this morning in one of the store-wagons gorging themselves on an unholy mixture of dates and sugar and *smen*, the aged fermented butter worth near its weight in gold. I swear his sons have crammed their faces with it because it is so valuable. There are old women in villages who eke out a jar of smen spoon by judicious spoon, to glaze a sauce, add depth to a special-occasion couscous, a marriage tajine. But the rich and the spoiled understand the true value of nothing. They eat till they spew; then eat some more. The royal emirs were tracked by the trail of vomit they left behind them: but of course they were not punished. They are of Ismail's glorious line, carriers of his wondrous dynasty. The theft was blamed on two poor slaves; and they were beheaded for it. Greed drives the powerful to excess. They live to consume: food, drink, men, women. The world. Their appetite cannot be quelled; the avid, vicious void within them cannot be filled.

I think of my father lying, embittered, in the dark. Sometimes it is better not to be king.

18

Alys

For days now I have been in shock, sitting in the women's pavilion like a big wax doll, barely taking in my surroundings, the constant magpie chatter, the comings and goings of servants and children and food, barely daring to breathe. I knew already that the man whose child I carry was fearsome, but now I have seen his true nature and I feel as if I have stared into the abyss. The hands that caressed me I have seen dealing out shocking murder. When I close my eyes I see those long hammers coming down, left and right, caving in heads, smashing backs, legs, ribs, without mercy, without reason. The elemental brutality, the insatiable bloodlust of the man who got a child upon me has become my definition of the Devil himself.

Worst of all, there was Nus-Nus, lying face down on the ground simply waiting for the killing blow to fall. What level of terror must grip a man that he would just lie there and wait to die? I looked to Zidana, as if she might put an end to her husband's rampage, one force of nature to counter another, but a single glance was enough to show me her eyes shining and her hands flexing and clenching as if she would like nothing better than to wade in amongst the carnage and crush a few skulls herself.

I was so sure I would see my friend die that, I am ashamed to say, I almost ran away in his stead. But then I saw his hand reach out. He scooped up the blood of the poor man next to him, smeared it about his head and neck and then lay still again. My eyes darted to where the sultan was dispatching another victim. His back was turned, but he was moving towards Nus-Nus, his bloodlust still unsated, and I could not believe that this simple ruse could possibly work. The sultan went to him at last and stood staring down at what appeared to be his handiwork and at that moment something seemed to go out of him, as if an evil spirit was exorcized from his body, and he let the mallets fall from his hands, took the grand vizier by the arm and walked off with him in easy conversation, as if discussing the morrow's weather.

I had no idea until that moment that he was capable of such monstrosities. And I? I am carrying his child. It sits there within, growing moment by moment into some tiny replica of its father. Is this not a terrible thought? I wished for a child so hard that I chose apostasy over death, and thus am I punished for my sin. I have been trying to pray, but it seems I have forgotten the words of every prayer I ever knew. They say shock will do strange things to a person's mind, but this seems the cruellest blow of all.

Life goes on, and I begin to seek acceptance within myself of the people on whom my existence now depends. I tell myself that the sultan must have been sorely provoked, insulted; betrayed. That the violence of the punishment must reflect the heinous nature of the crime committed against his name or person or estate, that his response was in some way justified, made all the more honest by its directness. The personal touch . . .

Sometimes I catch myself thinking in this way, using phrases like those I so despised when my mother used them to explain the profligacy of her husband. 'He is a man of generous heart,' she would say, after he racked up another gambling debt, leaving us short on the housekeeping. 'He is spontaneous. He gets carried away by the spirit of the moment. He does not like to spoil the enjoyment of his friends, when abstention would shame them . . .' And so on.

But what one cannot change, one must accept. Somehow I must school my thoughts to quietness, my emotions to gentleness, else the turmoil I feel will transmit itself to the baby and encourage monstrosity to take hold.

I find, after some weeks in this place, once the torrid heat of summer passes, that I am beginning to enjoy the peace of the life here, away from the hectic competition of the harem. The other women grumble and complain about the homogeneity of the food, the basic furnishings, the insects, the enclosed space offered by the tents; but they rarely go outside. Whereas I, once the evening meal has been eaten, have taken to walking a little way away from the pavilions (although still within the designated area for the women: I am not so foolish as to try to stray beyond) and sitting upon a rock where I can see the river spooling past, and the mountains rising above it.

It is the first time in my life that I have seen such a landscape. There is barely a hill in Holland, barely even a prominence. From the top of our house in The Hague I could see all the way out to the coast at Scheveningen, across miles of park and farmland, polders and dunes, to the flat grey sea beyond. It was, if I may speak plainly, not the most inspiring view; though it was open and honest and serene, much like the Hollanders themselves. I begin to wonder, sitting here beside this turbulent river, whose waters roar brown and muddy after downfalls of rain, beneath the giant hills whose jagged peaks jut into the clouds and scratch the sky, whether the temperament of the people of this place may not also reflect the landscape that engendered them, making their humours more extreme, their passions more pronounced. Perhaps this goes towards making the sultan the man he is. I place my hand on my belly and pray to all the gods that the child within me will combine the best elements of both worlds. I pray that I will not bring another monster into existence.

19

Sha'aban 1088 AH

As winter draws on word reaches us that there has been an uprising in the Tafilalt, where Ismail installed his elder brother Moulay al-Harrani as governor after showing him unprecedented mercy following the Marrakech rebellion. Al-Harrani has, it is reported, joined forces with his younger brother Moulay al-Saghir, and a tribe of particularly troublesome Berbers, the Ait Atta, and together they are preparing to march on Meknes to take the undefended capital.

As soon as the sultan hears this, his face fills with blood till it is almost black. He blows around the pavilions like a storm cloud, issuing furious orders, walking so fast that beads of sweat pop out on the face of Abdelaziz as he struggles to keep up with him. 'Damn my brother! Does he want to destroy everything I have achieved? Does he hate me so much? I should have killed him the first time, instead of pardoning his insurrection. I thought it was the good angel on my shoulder I listened to that day when it spoke of clemency; but it was the black demon after all. I should have put his head on a spike on the walls of Marrakech when I had the chance. This time I'll take it and put it over the main gate of Meknes!'

Abdelaziz concurs effusively. When the sultan is in this mood, to do otherwise is suicidal. But when Ismail talks of taking the army south through the mountains to deal death to the rebels, I see the grand vizier blanch. At night a freezing fog lifts off the river like the ghostly breath of a thousand djinns and envelops the tents so that they are stiff with ice in the morning. Camping in the foothills is bad enough, away from his accustomed luxuries, but a forced march through fierce terrain in the depths of winter? Our vizier has not grown slack and fat by going on forced marches: already he is volunteering to return to Meknes to oversee the building works.

There is a glint in Ismail's eye as he turns and I realize he is well aware of all this, that he is in fact baiting the Hajib, a man who would be of little practical use to him in battle. After allowing him to stew for a while longer, Ismail puts an arm around his shoulder. 'Do not worry, Abdou. I shall not be forcing you to ride into battle with me: I doubt we have a horse strong enough to carry you! No, I need someone I trust to remain here to supervise my court while I am gone.'

Abdelaziz's shoulders slump in relief. Then something else occurs to him and he slides a glance at me, sharp and calculating. We have largely managed to avoid one another during these past weeks, the vizier and I; or, rather, I have avoided him; but with Ismail and the Tinker gone, there will be no one who can shield me from his intents.

Suddenly I find myself saying, 'Do not leave your faithful servant behind, O Sun and Moon of Morocco: take me with you. I would dearly love to prove myself in battle!'

Abdelaziz shoots me a killing glance. 'Nonsense, Nus-Nus! The mountains are no place for eunuchs: they have not the fortitude to withstand such conditions, let alone the wherewithal to survive a battle. Besides, the emperor will have no need of a Keeper of the Book or Servant of the Slippers on his campaign!' He invests my two poor titles with such scathing sarcasm that they sound ridiculous even to my ears.

'I do not think Amadou would be very happy in the mountains,' Ismail says gently. He bends to stroke the monkey under its silken chin and it chitters delightedly. If Ismail ruled over a kingdom of animals both he and his subjects would be happy indeed.

'I will place him in the care of the White Swan.' Thinking of her gives me a pang. By going with the army I will be leaving Alys to the mercies of Abdelaziz and Zidana, either of whom would gladly see her and her child dead. 'But, sire, I am at your command to stay or go.' As if it needed saying.

He looks thoughtful. 'I shall make you a bukhari, Nus-Nus. You will look the part.' Then he takes the vizier by the arm and away they go, talking logistics.

A bukhari: the idea is so preposterous that a laugh escapes me. It seems the warrior within will have the chance to reveal himself after all.

On the day before we are due to march, a nomad approaches the camp, coming down out of the hills with her little herd of goats, each of which wears a silver amulet around its neck, which causes much amusement and conjecture. 'She is not a woman; she is a sorceress and those her children, travelling in disguise.'

'No, they are the souls of bewitched men trapped in the bodies of goats,' declares another, and makes the sign against the evil eye. I smile, remembering Homer's Circe.

Ismail, who would usually be appalled at the idea of a woman travelling alone, and with her face brazenly uncovered, is greatly intrigued. Nomad women converse with spirits and have the ability to tell the future, and he likes to consult omens before a campaign. He is charming with her, for all that she is elderly and sun-worn, and complimentary of her charges. She names them all for him, one by one, and he recalls each name even though there are dozens of the little beasts, all looking identical – black and scraggy bundles of energy. She throws bones and declares he will see an easy victory, and then makes him a gift of one of the amulets she wears pinned to her clothing: a large square of silver with foreign symbols etched all over it, to ward off evil influences. In return, he kisses her hands (a gesture I have never seen him make before) and generously gives her a pouch of gold that he takes from Abdelaziz, since he himself never carries anything so vulgar as money.

As I escort her away, I ask her who she is and whence she has come and she says to me that she is Amzir, a Tuareg out of the *tinariwen*, the deserts. She has blue-black staining on her lips and around her eyes, and is adorned with heavy silver jewellery at ears, neck and wrists, proclaiming that she has no fear of brigands. I begin to wonder if she does have sorcerous powers. And then an idea strikes me. When I have outlined it and bargained a price with her, she grins widely, showing strong white teeth.

We leave her goats in the ambassadors' tent and I take her to Zidana. 'This lady is Amzir. She has come out of the Great Desert, and like you she is a mistress of the spirits. I thought you might like to consult with her.'

The empress looks the nomad woman up and down, clearly unimpressed. 'You are very thin,' she says dismissively.

The Targui smiles: a thin smile sharp enough to cut bone. 'You are very fat.'

Zidana preens, delighted. As if this exchange has somehow sealed the social order between them, she gestures generously for the visitor to sit, and rings for tea. They spend some time comparing the names they have for different spirits, and the desert woman shows enough knowledge that soon Zidana is drawing symbols in the soil and Amzir responds with her own curious combination of circles and lines.

'That will protect your boys,' the older woman proclaims at last. 'From fire and flood and pest.'

'And poison?'

A nod.

'And the blade?'

The Targui adds another symbol.

Zidana thinks hard. 'There is death by water too; and the rope . . .'

'Your sons will be safe . . .' Amzir pauses, interrogates the symbols, then makes a small sound of disapproval.

'What? What is it?'

'There is a white woman, foreign.'

Zidana sits back, her eyes slitted. 'Go on.'

'She is with child.'

The eyes widen, just a fraction. 'I know the woman. Will it be a boy?'

The Targui wags a finger. 'Not so you'd know. Her only child will turn out to be a girl. Even if at first it appears to be a boy.'

This pleases Zidana mightily: she chuckles. 'A boy that is really a girl! Ha! I like that. So my sons will survive to succeed their father?'

'For as long as the white woman lives.'

This pleases her less. I hold my breath. To my ears it seems an obvious confection, but at last Zidana nods thoughtfully; then she loads the woman up with gifts: jewellery and rocks of sweet-smelling amber, almond pastries, fruit for her goats. They both seem well satisfied with the encounter. When I take my leave of the Targui, she looks me full in the eye, and then addresses me by my name: not Nus-Nus but my tribal name. This takes me so much aback that I hardly hear what she says next, and have to ask her to repeat it.

'Be steadfast, you who are both dead and alive. You have seas to cross.'

Then she calls her goats to her and they come tumbling out of the ambassadors' tent, and away she goes, downriver where the sweet pastures have not yet been blighted by the frost, and I am left staring after her, frowning.

That afternoon I am tricked out to Ismail's satisfaction (and I must admit, in my small vanity, to my own) in the garb of the elite Black Guard, that is to say, a long scarlet tunic belted over a white shirt and wide trousers with a long sash of green cotton. Over one shoulder goes a leather baldric, and into this a small, curved dagger worn close against the chest. No turban, for Ismail professes that to cover the head makes his bukhari weak in battle; besides, how will the angel sweep them up to Paradise if he cannot catch hold of their topknots? I have no topknot: without a turban my naked head feels vulnerable, and cold. If I fall in battle, I shall slip swiftly down to Hell.

When I take Amadou to entrust him to Alys, she does not at first recognize me, but starts to her feet. It is the first time I have seen her standing for some time. Her belly is as pronounced as a ripe watermelon and I realize with sudden misgiving that she will surely give birth while we are gone to war.

The monkey sets off on a foraging mission around the tent, seeking treats beneath the cushions, which makes me yet more melancholy – it is easy to think animals value you for yourself, rather than as a source of food. It is probably the sight of Amadou that spurs Alys's recognition. 'Oh, Nus-Nus, I thought you some stern-faced guard!'

'I am sorry to have alarmed you. I came to say farewell. And to leave Amadou with you; I do not think he is ready to go into battle.'

'Are you?'

With an attempt at a bravado I do not feel I indicate my uniform and the long sword that lies against my hip, given me by Ismail himself. 'Do I not look the part?'

For a long moment she assesses me in silence, her mouth down-turned. Then she takes a step towards me and places a hand on my arm. When she gazes up at me, I am struck forcibly anew by the huge blue ocean of her regard. 'Please do not be a hero, Nus-Nus. Do not be foolhardy.'

'Tonight I must swear an oath to lay down my life for our sultan.'

The emphasis on the word 'our' does not pass her by. Her eyes begin to well up. 'Even so,' she whispers. 'I had rather you come back a coward and alive than only as a brave memory.'

'Berber women tell their husbands never to return in defeat. Plutarch tells that the women of Sparta exhorted their sons to come back with their shields, or on them. The Ashante say it is the woman who puts the iron in a man's sword. Are Englishwomen so different?'

'You know too much.' She smiles wanly.

'It is never enough. Knowledge. A man cannot live all the time in his head.'

'You are no dry old scholar, of that I am sure.'

'I, my lady, am sure of nothing. Actually, that is not true. There is one thing of which I am quite certain.'

'And what would that be?' Her grip on my arm intensifies. I feel each touch of her fingertips separately, my skin alive with the sensation. How can I say what is in my heart to a woman who is about to give birth to another man's child, and that man my lord?

'It is treason to speak it aloud.'

'I think,' she says softly, 'that it is sacrilege not to. But I would not have you risk yourself.' She places a finger on my lips to keep the words in.

I take her hand by the wrist to move the finger away, bend my head to her and kiss her firmly, every nerve alive with desire.

The world is spinning: or maybe I am? I would swear that for a fleeting moment I feel the gentle pressure of her hand on the back of my head, pulling me to her; but then it is gone and she steps away and we stand there, staring at one another. The enormity of what has just happened swells between us as if a planet has dropped suddenly out of the skies and into the tent. I could be executed for what I have just done – thoughtlessly, stupidly; and Alys could be too.

Then Amadou, frustrated in his search for food, comes chittering out from under the cover on the divan and the tension between us is broken.

With immense effort, I put on my second face and make a bow. 'Be well, Alys. I hope the baby will come easily.' And quickly I walk away, my heart beating against the cage of my ribs as if it would fly out to be with her.

That evening I take the oath of allegiance on the Salih al-Bukhari, an exquisitely bound volume some centuries old that had been an accession gift from the Governor of Hejaz, Barakat ben Mohammed, protector of the holy city of Mecca. For this reason, Ismail treasures it greatly and it accompanies him always when he travels, housed in its own perfectly aligned tent, and transported by a gorgeously caparisoned horse (the very animal, in fact, for whom I had sought the gold-embroidered shitbag on that fateful day in the Meknes souq).

It is telling that it is with his First Wife that he passes his last night in camp. I enter the details in the couching book before first prayer the next day.

Before the sun is fully risen, Ismail takes his leave of a bleary-eyed Abdelaziz. 'My dearest friend, take good care of the women of my harem, of my wives and sons. If anything evil befalls them I shall have you dragged behind mules!'

The grand vizier's eyes become round with horror; then the emperor roars with laughter.

'You are so easy to tease, Abdou.'

We ride out after breaking our fast: seven thousand cavalry and fifteen thousand foot, and cross the Melwiya at the ford, the horses' hot breath creating a fog that wreaths around us, so that when I look back towards the camp, I can see nothing but what appears to be an army of phantoms, moving between worlds.

20

Ramadān 1088 AH

I did not sleep that first night for thinking of that kiss, soaring at one moment to the heights of elation, the next to the depths of anguish. Torment endlessly succeeded delight; days later, I am none the wiser for all the thought I have given the subject, though unfamiliarity with keeping my seat on a horse has trained my mind to more practical concerns. Now, exhausted by a long day in the saddle, I sleep better than I have in years, despite the freezing temperatures and hard ground on which I lie. Conditions in the mountains are challenging: I have never experienced such cold. It freezes the hairs in my nostrils, the tears in my eyes, the urine I piss into gullies. I learn to breathe shallowly, to avoid the sensation of knives inside my chest. The sultan forces us on mercilessly, driven by his overriding desire to crush the uprising. When it becomes clear that the baggage-wagons are slowing us down, he ruthlessly jettisons beds, tables, braziers – anything that cannot easily be packed and carried on a mule. He tolerates the same conditions, sleeps on a cloak on the ground and eats the same dull fare as the rest of us. I am beginning to learn a grudging respect for Ismail as a man who bears hardship more easily than the toughest of his soldiers. Until now I have thought of him as a despot, a voluptuary, a divine madman who merely exercised his power in order to indulge his pleasures and obsessions. Now I begin to see glimpses of the man behind the title, the man who started his life as the younger son of a minor warlord a long way from the centre of power and plotted, schemed and fought his way to a throne that he has defended with grit and determination against all claimants and enemies; the man who is determined to unite the kingdom, extend its boundaries, found a dynasty and leave a magnificent legacy behind him. I also see ever more clearly the religious fervour that drives him: even when Ramadān begins he observes the fast and enforces it on the whole of his army. Although by sundown our unfed bodies shiver as if afflicted with ague, and many fall rather than dismount from their horses, Ismail shows no sign of discomfort or distress, and always ensures the mounts are well tended before he allows himself to rest.

When one of the kaids foolishly suggests that since we are *musaafir*, travellers, which legitimately entitles us to postpone our fast until after the campaign, Ismail masters his great desire to behead the man and merely demotes him to mule-tender at the rear of the column. 'We are on a holy mission to defend God's kingdom!' he storms. 'Who needs bread when his will fortifies us?'

No one dares to remind him that jihadists are also spared the fast.

And so we march on with empty stomachs through crystal-bright days, the horses picking their way through snow so white it blinds the eyes. At night, a million stars wheel overhead and the cries of jackals shiver through the air, haunting our dreams.

We come down out of the mountains just after sunset, having seen no living soul but a couple of ragged herders in all the weeks of journey, and approach a small settlement nestling in the hollow of a valley. Smoke is rising from an open fire: an entire sheep is turning on a spit. As we approach, an elderly man in tattered robes and a grubby head-wrap throws himself on the ground in prostration before the sultan's horse.

'*Marhaban*, my lord! Heaven's gates are opened, Hell's gates are closed, Shaitan is safely chained and the djinns are locked away. I beg you, break your fast with your poor subjects.'

This pleases Ismail mightily and he happily hunkers down in an unkingly manner on the shabby rush mats that have been set around the fire, shares a meal with the villagers and avails himself of the virgin they offer for his bed that night. I do not have the couching book with me, as a result of the grand vizier's sarcasm, and no one can tell me how to spell the girl's name: for none of these people read or write. They repeat the sounds for me until I can make a fair approximation, and I inscribe it with a sharpened reed and ink I mix from ash and water on a piece of linen. That night all I can think of is Alys. I pray that she is well, and wonder if I will survive the battle to come when we ride into the Tafilalt tomorrow.

21

Alys

What have I done? I try not to think of it, but some devil is in me: memories of that lewd kiss I bestowed upon my poor friend, which drove him from me in shame and confusion, keep returning, hotter than ever. I remember too the sight of his naked torso on that terrible day when the sultan went mad, a sculpture in obsidian. I must be possessed by some evil spirit, a spirit that is growing fatter and stronger by the day in my belly. Surely I will give birth to a monster.

I try to pray, but feel a hypocrite to offer up Christian prayers when I am an apostate. My turmoil drives me to seek out the *ma'alema*, who comes to offer religious instruction to the women of the harem, alongside her more practical duties of overseeing their embroidery skills. We left Meknes in such a hurry that this latter has not overtasked her, for, ousted by sacks of henna, paints, jewellery, sweetmeats and bales of satin, our embroidery frames and silks were left behind at court and no one has felt the loss sufficiently to send slaves back to fetch them.

I have a little Arabic now, but still it is not easy to make myself understood. When I show her the translated Qur'an given me by the English renegade Catherine Tregenna and try to explain what it is I would like – some instruction in their holy book – she throws it away from her as if it were poisonous, spits on her hands and then wipes them on the skirt of her robe. After this, she goes bustling off, muttering to herself, and I feel sure I have offended her beyond repair, but a while later she is back with a little volume most beautifully bound in green and gold morocco. This she opens, from the back, and, moving her finger from right to left, traces the symbols inscribed therein while she chants. The sound is rhythmic, repetitive, hypnotic; even the monkey is soothed by it. He lies quietly, curled up at my feet, watching us with unblinking eyes. Nus-Nus has taught me some Arabic, and I recognize words from the women's prayers. I follow the sounds and learn them by heart and repeat them over and over like a talking bird, and sometimes the ma'alema makes a little gesture with her hands to help my understanding. Thus I discover that Al-Fatiha means 'opening', which she mimes by placing her hands together, then letting them fall open at the hinge; and that in their faith there are many names for God. The ma'alema is delighted with me. She pats my hands and chatters at me and struts around with newfound pride. It seems I have become her best pupil, a testament to her skill and powers of persuasion.

Zidana comes stamping past swathed in blankets and furs and, seeing the ma'alema sitting with me and a Qur'an open on my knees, bestows black looks upon both of us. Amadou takes one look at her and creeps beneath my skirts.

One of the other courtesans is, like me, nearing her time, her pregnancy perhaps a week or two in advance of my own. She is a young black woman with protuberant eyes as soft and watery as those of my mother's pug-dogs. On the day that her labour pains begin the other women lave her solicitously and renew the henna on her nails, and the palms and soles of her hands and feet. After this, she is toted about like a gigantic baby, fed by hand, carried to the latrine and back, and finally to the makeshift hammam, where the paste is washed away, leaving behind a violent orange design, with which she seems inordinately pleased. Kohl is applied around her eyes; even her lips are coloured. These are, I have ascertained, superstitious gestures designed to keep evil influences at bay. Apparently the spirits they call djinns are apt to take advantage at times of weakness and may assay entry into the body. I find myself wondering where else the henna has been applied.

Well, it seems that the henna has not worked its protective magic and that the djinns have had a feast day, for the poor girl's child was stillborn.

Lamentations fill the day, the women all wailing and shuttling their tongues. The bereaved mother tears her clothing and rends her face with her nails and will not let the child be taken for burial, even holding on to its tiny ankles as they try to drag it away. It is a most heart-rending sight. Afterwards, I sit with her a little while, stroking her hands and murmuring consolations, but the sight of my ripe belly brings yet more tears, and at last I take my leave, feeling dread settle upon me at the thought of my own imminent ordeal.

This is no place for birthing children. Even with the braziers burning you can feel the cold outside. It seeps in between the warp and weft of the fabric of the tents, through door flaps that never quite close, up through the ground, the reed mats and oriental carpets that overlay them. And yet sometimes I imagine slipping out into the night, crossing the river at the ford and heaving myself up into the mountains to give birth all alone in a cave, like a wild animal.

22

Shawwāl 1088 AH

The taking of the Tafilalt was achieved without even a blade drawn. It appears the villagers who feasted us so well for the two days we spent with them were well paid to delay us, allowing Al-Harrani and Moulay al-Saghir to flee north towards Tlemcen. We enter the city of Sijilmassa to a great show of celebration by the inhabitants, who no doubt only days before had supported the rebel cause. Every householder brings the carpets out of their homes and lays them down on the streets for the sultan to ride over. Of course, we do not have the luxury of shitbags (gold-embroidered or otherwise) with us on this campaign; I fear the good wives of Sijilmassa are liable to have much work to do before their carpets can be rehabilitated.

The rebels have created their own barbaric, magpie splendour in this place. Evidently they have been receiving foreign backing for their insurrection, for amongst the items they have left behind in their haste are rich carpets from Turkey and Isfahan, new French furniture gaudily dressed in gold leaf and English cannon that make Ismail's eyes gleam. A succession of local chieftains comes grovelling, laden with tribute and outpourings of loyalty, pledging their lives, their swords, their sons and daughters, most of whom are exceedingly unattractive. Ismail is delighted. As Ramadān comes to an end and we celebrate with a great feast, he indulges his weeks of abstinence by taking two or three of the girls to his bed each night, as if determined to repopulate his homeland single-handed.

The 'courtiers' who have stayed in Sijilmassa are a motley group: ruffians and ne'er-do-wells, chancers and speculators from a dozen different tribes and nationalities. There are two men who claim to be princes of the Asante; renegades from Portugal and Holland; and merchants from Egypt and Ethiopia who immediately start trying to peddle their wares to the new arrivals. Ismail has their goods confiscated and paws through them dismissively. 'Here,' he says, throwing to ben Hadou a little gold casket of frankincense. Any other man would be well pleased with such a rich trinket, but the Tinker's smile is wry: he is not a great user of perfumes. The doctor gets their odd collection of dried beetles and scorpions, used in some charlatanry or other: I learn later than he has cast them in the privy and, from the cry that issues from the little room, given the next user quite a fright. Ismail gives to me a silver box, ornately decorated, for which I thank him profusely. When I open it, I find it contains some sort of fragrant dried leaf that smells woody and sweet and peppery, a little like nutmeg. Later that night, whilst the sultan is sleeping off his latest conquest, the Asante princes befriend me, bringing with them clay pipes and a pouch of dried leaves they call tobacco, which my master the doctor used to smoke. They suggest we mix some of the herb, which they refer to as *kif*, with the tobacco, to make it 'sweeter'. I shrug. 'If you like.' I tried a pipe of tobacco once and did not much care for it. But it is true: the herb does improve the experience, and soon the three of us are chattering away like old companions, swathed in clouds of sweet-smelling smoke, laughing at each other's stories, which become progressively disconnected and bizarre. After a while, a fierce hunger overtakes me and I go off to the kitchens to find something for us to eat.

I am just on my way back with a trayful of cakes and almond biscuits (which are delicious: I could not resist a handful even as I loaded the tray) when I am accosted in the corridor by a girl with heavily kohled eyes and a startling smile. An unveiled Ait Khabbashi nomad. She runs the tip of her tongue over her lips as she stands in my path, like a cat about to eat a bird.

'Hello.'

She is exotic in her heavy triangular silver earrings and collars of cowrie-shell that glitter in the light of the sconces. She puts a hand on my arm and, looking at me rather than at the tray, says, 'That looks good enough to eat.'

I remember my manners and offer her a cake. She laughs. 'I did not mean *that.*' Her hand brushes deliberately against my robe and comes to rest on my groin. Instead of being shocked, I find myself laughing. I am still laughing when she pulls my head down towards her and kisses me languorously. When we separate she says, 'I have been watching you all day. Have you not noticed me?'

I have to admit, apologetically, that I have not. How so? She is extremely striking. But, she is not Alys.

'You are a very beautiful man.'

This sets me laughing again. 'Women are beautiful; not men.'

'Let us go somewhere more private and examine that proposition at our leisure.' She takes the tray from me and leads me, as compliant as a lamb to the Eid slaughter, to a little room carpeted with deep-pile rugs of sheep's skins.

I am so light-headed it is as if I am witnessing some other pair of lovers in hallucinatory flashes. Her pale fingers trace my scars. She murmurs, 'Well, you certainly are a rare one,' before climbing on top of me. In my dream-state I am not surprised to find myself hard. My two hands, balancing her on the fulcrum of my cock, almost entirely encircle her waist, around which she wears a silver chain hung with magic charms. Whatever magic she possesses is powerful: on we strive, and on. She is long-limbed and flexible, high-breasted and narrow at the hip. Her skin is luminous and her dark eyes are wickedly knowing. A change of position, and I see that her buttocks are as round as the moon in her fullest phase. There are inked patterns on her hands and feet; the pale soles of the latter are presented to me as I kneel above her, like a gift.

When daylight fills the chamber, I find I am alone. But the long pile of the sheepskin beside me bears the unmistakable imprint of a woman's haunch.

Images present themselves one after another, crude pictures too vibrant and strange to be long-held memories. My God, what djinn has possessed me? I am a eunuch, a cut man: none of this is possible. I lie there, parched and exhausted, havering between disbelief and certainty, elation and shame. It must have been the kif; or the woman's exotic magic. But now, like a lodestone, my heart yearns towards Alys, and a small, triumphant voice whispers that, although I may not be able to give a woman children, it seems I can still give pleasure, and is that not a gift in itself?

Our time in Sijilmassa is only a brief respite, for word reaches us that the rebels' allies, the Ait Atta Berbers, rather than swear fealty to the emperor, have abandoned their great castles in the Draa Valley and retreated into the Atlas Mountains. And shortly after this defiant messages arrive from these renegade chieftains, goading Ismail to attack them. Spies are sent out into the mountains; days later one wounded man returns, and before expiring reports that they have taken refuge in a series of caves high up in the steep limestone cliffs of the Djebel Saghro.

We march again, even though it is the depth of winter and the High Atlas is perilous territory. But Ismail is determined to bring these troublesome tribes-men to heel, or to destroy them for ever. The vistas are spectacular; but the cold is paralysing and many of the passes are snow-blocked. Even the toughest of the bukhari are suffering: raised in tropical regions, we are not used to such desperate conditions. One by one we fall, or are crippled by numbness, then gangrene of the hands and feet. Still Ismail is undeterred and drives us on.

At our approach three chieftains come down out of the mountains to make parley. They are gnarly-looking men, hard of face and eye, and, though they smile and offer gifts and extravagant compliments, their smil-ing does not reach their eyes, especially when Ismail offers them a gift of cotton tunics, useless for winter wear and of poor quality, as if suggesting they are no better than beggars.

'I do not trust them,' I say quietly to ben Hadou, who is standing beside me, watching this charade.

He does not move a muscle, and his eyes do not waver from the sultan. 'It hardly matters if you or I mistrust them. They will do what they will do, and Ismail will do what he will do. They are the players in this game, and we are mere onlookers.'

'Onlookers who may die at a whim.'

He turns to me then, impassive. 'Life and death both turn on a whim, Nus-Nus. Surprised you've survived this long at court without learning that lesson.'

The chieftains take their leave, their stated intent to return shortly with the rest of the Ait Atta tribe to lay down their arms before their emperor. And so we wait in the freezing cold, eating through our already meagre supplies.

When a month has passed and they have still not surrendered, it becomes clear that they never intended to, and have instead spent the time they won shoring up their defences and mustering their forces. Ismail is furious. Ignoring all advice to the contrary, he orders us to attack. 'The Prophet tells us that a drop of blood shed in the cause of God, a night spent in arms, is of more avail than two months of fasting or prayer! Whosoever falls in battle, his sins are forgiven: at the Day of Judgement his wounds shall be resplendent as vermilion and odoriferous as musk; and the loss of his limbs shall be supplied by the wings of angels and cherubim! For the glory of Allah, and our great kingdom, charge!'

It is fine oratory, but even now the cavalry general continues to remonstrate. He is swiftly silenced: his tongue is still wagging even as his head hits the ground.

That puts an end to all hesitation: up the scree slopes we charge, brandishing weapons, yelling our defiance. But of course the dead cavalryman had the right of it: horses are worse than useless in such a place. They cannot negotiate the narrow goat-tracks or the treacherous rolling rubble these mountains produce; all around us horses are stumbling and falling, becoming as much a hazard as the Berber arrows that arc down from the skies. There is a renegade European soldier next to me who swears mightily when an arrow whistles past him. 'Christ's eyes! Who are these fucking people? Fucking savages! No one uses fucking arrows any more!'

The sound a wounded horse makes is horrible to hear: it shakes even the most battle-hardened. I, who am as far from battle-hardened as it is possible to be, can feel my knees grow weak and my grip on my scimitar slacken. Poor beasts, I think. Will I also scream like that, at the end?

Encouraged by the hellish noises below, the Berbers have come out on to ledges and, now that we are moving into range, are taking shots at us with their muskets. A bullet pings off a boulder a little distance away from me and a chip of rock strikes me on the shin. The pain is so sharp and unexpected that I cannot help but cry out, and am at once ashamed even though the sound is lost in the general din: the cut is oozing, but it is barely a wound. Keep climbing, Nus-Nus, I tell myself, though your lungs burn and you barely know how to shoot the pistol at your hip. Take no notice of the dead and dying. Don't look up. For God's sake, whatever you do, don't look *down* . . .

As the ground steepens sharply, the cavalry must give way. Those horses that have survived are led off by their riders down the side of the mountain that is out of the sultan's line of sight. As for the rest of us, as the muskets take their toll, the kaids marshal us into a more sheltered gully, and we keep on climbing, weapons sheathed now, since we need both hands to grab for holds. No point in waving a weapon around here in any case: the enemy are far above and the emperor, who loves to see the show of swords shining as his army attacks, far below. Our feet, unsure on this chancy terrain, dislodge rocks and stones that shower down on the fellows below us: I think we are more dangerous to them even than the enemy. I risk a look behind me and wish I had not: the ground falls away precipitously on one side. It is like climbing over an abyss. My heart thuds so hard I cannot breathe; for a moment my head spins and I think I may vomit.

And I have only myself to blame! I could have stayed in some comfort with the harem in the low green valleys of the Melwiya and had only the grand vizier to hold at bay, rather than doing battle with a thousand wily tribesmen on their crumbling mountainside. Though, thank the Lord, it must be said they are poor shots! Hardly a man amongst us has thus far been cleanly taken down by a bullet, though many have been winged and lost their footing. Barely have I consoled myself with this thought than I look up and see the ledges above us are bristling with Berbers, the long barrels of their guns pointing down, as if the mountain is spawning them, moment by moment.

With certain death above and below, I freeze, my forehead pressed against the cold rock, the blood beating in my ears.

God help me. My whole body is shaking now, the muscles gone into an automatic tremor that is worsening by the second. Even my teeth are chattering. Much more of this and I will shake myself off the mountain without the help of any other soul.

'Move on!'

The voice is familiar, but right now it could belong to God himself and I wouldn't care.

A face appears beside me: thin, dark, intent, the eyes filled with some burning inner light. Teeth grin at me. It is ben Hadou. 'Courage, Nus-Nus! Onward to glory. Or Paradise, depending on how your page has been written.'

I had not thought the man a zealot, but it really looks as if he is enjoying this. For a moment I hate him more even than the mad sultan who sent me up here.

'Come on, lad, get on. And stop thinking: thinking is a fighting man's undoing.'

On with my warrior face, on with the kponyungu. I force my traitor limbs to some form of obedience and keep on climbing, blindly, idiotically, towards my doom.

An hour later I find myself amongst the survivors. We have prevailed; or at least the Berbers have withdrawn, leaving us in charge of the first line of their defences, supplies, and a lot of livestock. Those who made the direct assault fared less well: a trail of broken bodies testifies to the recklessness of the attack. Hundreds of men dead, and for what? To gain an inaccessible rocky peak, a few sacks of grain and a herd of mangy sheep. Even so, those of us who have made it this far are filled with fiery energy, an elation that consumes all our doubts and fears. We make our victorious way down a wide col, driving the sheep before us, propelled by visions of roast mutton.

No one is prepared for what happens next. The Berbers come at us from all sides, howling like djinns. The air is thick with musket smoke and the cries of the dying – both men and sheep. I do what ben Hadou bade me: I stop thinking. That is, I let my body think for me, for it seems to have a far greater understanding of what is required than my mind. The first man I kill is armed with a long knife – but my reach is longer. The second comes at me with a club: I stumble and his blow comes whooshing past and, failing to compensate, he overbalances and my sword (more by accident than intention) catches him in the neck. Abruptly, I am drenched in his blood. I remember the body my master the doctor dissected, and, even as I parry blows from a man in a stained turban, the words *carotid artery* come and go like a pulse beating in my head. The next man I stick in the ribs as he is struggling to reload, and after that I lose count, but simply hack and scream as if possessed by demons, or terror; and am not even aware of the knife that scorches across my back and leaves a wound from shoulder blade to shoulder blade.

At some point our adversaries must have melted away again, retreating swiftly into the fastness of the mountains, for mayhem and slaughter are gradually replaced by an eerie quiet, broken only by the moans of the wounded and the cries of carrion birds that suddenly appear, circling overhead to survey the feast to come.

We lost four thousand men that day, the flower of the Meknassi troops, the best of the bukhari. Fighting in unfamiliar terrain against seasoned mountain-men: what chance did they have?

When he sees me, the sultan thinks I am a dead man walking. 'Ah, Nus-Nus, am I to lose you too?' When he realizes the blood is (largely) not my own, he escorts me to a stream and helps me to wash it off with his own hands, and when I am clean he embraces me like a father. I do not know what to say or do: I fear his mind is disturbed. Later, it occurs to me that maybe I represent for him all the poor, faithful bukhari he has lost that day, all those loyal soldiers from the plains and jungles of my own region, and that this is his way of seeking some form of atonement for sending them to their deaths.

Ismail is forced to sue for peace: even he can see we cannot beat the Ait Atta on their own ground. Some of their chieftains come down out of the hills, and the sultan slaughters a camel with his own hands to honour the pledge that henceforth the Berbers shall live independent, and free of taxation. In exchange, the tribal chiefs swear allegiance against the common enemy: the Christians. It is an empty exchange, as we all know, one designed for the saving of face, since the Berbers are already wily enough to avoid their taxes, and no Christian army is ever likely to threaten this remote part of the kingdom. However, with the agreement comes a promise of safe conduct through the Atlas valleys. It is a bitter thing to the sultan – a sharp humiliation. I am quite sure we all know he will never forget or forgive it.

23

Alys

I have a son! It is hard to believe that such a perfect little being could come from such a union, let alone the bloody business of birthing him. I spend hours every day just staring at him, as if he might at any moment disappear like a figment from a dream. I gaze at his wide eyes and floss of curls, his tiny feet, each toe a toe in miniature, complete with joint and nail. His skin is a colour I cannot adequately describe: it is a rich cream touched with coffee; the delicate interior of an almond nut; the hue of a hen's egg, or the down of her under-feathers – all, and none of these things. And in this pale olive-brown, eyes of the most striking cornflower-blue. He has a cry on him like a banshee, and the appetite of a lion. What a miracle of nature he is, my magical hybrid child! Has any woman ever produced such a remarkable baby?

I know even as these feelings gush out of me that this is what motherhood must do to all women and that I have lost all objectivity. But I do not care. He is a miracle, this baby, and I adore him with such intensity it is as if my heart lies there before me, curled in sleep. And then, sometimes, those hot waves turn chill, and fear engulfs me that any bad thing should overtake my boy. I hardly dare to sleep when such terror has me in its grip.

The boy is named Mohammed, which is not my choice, but a common custom here for the eldest firstborn. I call him Momo.

Zidana visits me every day on some pretext or other; and every day she must unswaddle Momo and inspect him closely. She picks him up and regards his tiny body with the most curious expression and then she chuckles and goes away again without a word. She sends little gifts often – roasted nuts and sweetmeats, candies and once, memorably, a dish of sugared locusts – but I know better than to eat anything she sends me, and will not even let Amadou try them, despite Nus-Nus's instructions.

It is not only Zidana who looks upon my child strangely: the monkey often sits beside me when my son is in my lap sleeping and gazes at his tiny form with such bleak menace that I fear he will do him some severe mischief if ever I leave the two of them untended. Sometimes when I feed the child Amadou will clamber into my lap and try to set his teeth to my other bosom. Repelled, he sets up such a chatter you would think I had tried to murder him. Such behaviour mars my days and peace of mind, for I know that if it continues, I will have to make a hard decision.

It seems that the absence of the sultan has led to some relaxation in the strict rules surrounding the harem, for today I am visited by the grand vizier himself, Abdelaziz ben Hafid. I am, I must admit, most perplexed by the sight of him here: I was given to believe it was death for an entire man to look upon the harem wives, but he tells me he is paying the sultan's respects in proxy, and wishes to inspect the child. When he sees Momo, he seems much puzzled and asks if he may see him unclothed: I am afraid I demur. He has hands like a woman, Abdelaziz; the palms soft and padded with fat, but there is muscle behind the fat, and he has a determined, cool look in his black eyes. I do not trust him and feel sure he has come to do us mischief; even Amadou dislikes him, baring his gums at him and shrieking from a distance.

But my resistance does not deter him; he keeps coming back, each time bringing some fine gift: pots of perfume rich with musk and frankincense, blocks of sweet-smelling amber with which to fragrance my clothes, a French-made cot for the baby, covered all over in gold leaf. Laughing at the absurd extravagance of such an item, I try to refuse it. '*La, bezef, bezef, sidi!*' (I have learned a little Arabic now.) '*Ja mil* . . . It is lovely, but no.'

But he insists. 'The child is Ismail's and must be honoured.' He pauses. 'It *is* Ismail's, is it not?'

'Of course.'

'There can be no doubt of that? Only' – he spreads his hands apologetically – 'there has been talk.'

'Talk?'

'Of another interested party?'

I do not understand, and say so.

'Forgive me such blunt speech, but I have heard the Lady Zidana saying that the slave Nus-Nus has a fondness for you.' He watches me intently and must perceive my shock. I cannot help but colour: I feel the heat rise, like guilt writ plain upon me.

'Nus-Nus is a perfect gentleman, and the emperor's good servant.'

'This is not the word that has been put around the court. It is said he lies with you and that the child is his.'

'The child is the emperor's, and no other's. Besides, the gentleman you cite is, I believe, a "cut man" and so not capable of such a feat.'

An unreadable expression passes over his face. Then he says, 'I believe you, my dear. But Zidana is an implacable enemy, and dabbles in sorcery. If you were to bring me evidence of her wicked dealings, I will be your shield and your strength against her. If you want to keep yourself and your child safe, that is.'

He leaves it a week before making his next visit. The ma'alema's arrival coincides with his, and she brings armfuls of rosemary with which to perfume my tent, shrieks and veils herself, then bustles in and sits between us, as if to shield me from his presence.

When he makes his excuses and leaves us, she says, 'Powerful man. Dangerous.'

'Yes, I know: he is Ismail's right hand.'

She shakes her head vehemently. 'Only my lord Ismail's right hand is his right hand. Abdelaziz ben Hafid is something else altogether, and he should not be here.'

Powerful. And dangerous. I should have remembered her words. Perhaps my English upbringing prevented me from upbraiding him, or running from his presence. It is true that I am afraid of Zidana and would welcome an ally. For some reason, Momo is entranced by the grand vizier. It does not take too long to realize why. The man is covered with jewels. There are pearls in his turban, and gold thread glitters in the hems and facings of his robe; gold wraps his forearms and fingers, and he wears many chains of office bearing precious stones the size of ducks' eggs. Jewels flash on the hilt of the dagger he wears (which does not look as if it has ever done more than peel an apple), even on the toes of his slippers. There is a particular emerald that the boy has taken a huge fancy to and one day he grabs hold of it and simply will not let go, no matter how we cajole, or pull, or try to draw his attention with something else. Detached from the stone at last, he lets out such a wail you'd think that Hell had opened and was issuing forth from his mouth. Abdelaziz takes a step back. 'He has considerable lungs: and quite a temper too. Truly, he must be his father's son.' His black eyes bore into me until I look away.

When next he visits he brings a gift for Momo: a gold ring bearing the seal of the sultan, a single huge pearl set at the centre. 'Ismail would give the boy this himself were he here.' He has threaded the ring on a gold chain, since it is far too large for a boy to wear, and places it around the baby's neck. Momo latches on to his new plaything with the utmost glee. 'He gives one of these to all his trueborn sons.' Abdelaziz leans in closer and pats me on the hand. 'Best not let Zidana see it, eh?' And he winks at me most familiarly.

I sit away from him and stash each hand in the opposite sleeve. 'It is very kind of you, sir – *mezian, mezian* – but perhaps it would be better to wait until the emperor returns from his campaign so that he may bestow it himself?'

The grand vizier smiles indulgently. 'Dear lady. Ismail may not return from this war with his brothers for a very long time.' He pauses significantly. 'If ever . . . You should remember that, and my offer to you.'

'But who could withstand such a huge army? I do not think the King of England himself could muster such a number.'

'The King of England!' Abdelaziz scoffs. He waves his hand dismissively, as if shooing a fly. 'A minor principality. His father had his head cut off by his own people. What sort of a king is that? And his son was an exile who ran from pillar to post without a coin to his name, throwing himself on the charity of the French court, then the Dutch . . .'

'Indeed,' I say smoothly, 'he once lodged with my own family in The Hague.'

That surprises him. 'If the King of England is a friend to your family, why is it you have not sued for ransom?'

'It was a long time ago,' I say shortly. I do not add: besides, my mother is so poor she sold me to a draper.

This exchange alters in some degree his manner towards me. But instead of becoming more respectful, as you might expect, it seems to make him even more intent on my company. Sometimes he visits me two or three days running. I keep the gold chain hidden beneath the divan.

'It is not right,' the ma'alema says one afternoon, folding her lips. 'It is not my place to say so, *lalla*, but you should have a greater care for your reputation. He is a great enemy of Zidana. But she is far more dangerous than he. And if she takes his visits and turns them into something more than they are, well . . . The sultan is not a forgiving man, *charaf*.'

The next time the grand vizier comes to see me, I make sure I am in the company of other women and like them pull my veil over my face; though I note that one or two of the bolder ones make eyes at him over their veils.

One night Makarim brings me tea for a headache. 'It will take away the pain,' she says gently, pouring the tea from its little silver pot into the glass from a great height. The scent is fragrant and complex: sweetened tea and garden herbs. I wait until she has tasted it, then take a mouthful and hold it for several long moments, assessing. A deeper taste than the usual mint tea; less sweet. I swallow, and feel the liquid go down my gullet and into my stomach, warming everything in its path.

When I awake my head is heavy and pounding; I cannot think straight. I blink and try to focus, but it is dark in the tent, and unnaturally quiet. I lie there on the divan, knowing that something has changed. I look around, through the gloom. At first glance everything looks as it should; but I sense a void, an absence. I sit up, too fast: the world swims. When the world settles, I light the lantern beside me with a trembling hand, suddenly full of dread, and hold it aloft. Its golden bloom illuminates the gilt-decorated cot in which my angel sleeps. As the light falls across it, the quiet is broken by a raucous chatter that makes me cry out. There is no child in the cot, but only the ape, Amadou, with the gold chain draped around his neck, the ring catching the light as it swings. His eyes glitter triumphantly in the gloom.

'Momo?' The keen of my voice is reedy and tremulous, but it gains power as panic enfolds me. 'Momo?' It rises to a wail.

On unsteady feet I run out of the tent. 'My baby! *Waladi!*' I scream. 'They have taken my baby!'

Women come running, but Makarim, my maid, is nowhere to be seen.

'Perhaps she has taken him to be with the other babies,' says one.

'Perhaps he would not sleep and she is walking with him.'

'Perhaps they are in the hammam. We will go and see.'

But others exchange wary glances when they think I am not looking.

I run wildly from tent to tent, barging past furniture, throwing covers aside, howling like an animal. Tears and mucus run down my face. I run out into the darkness again. From somewhere I have got a knife, a little decorative thing. I wave it around, drunk with terror. It is the ma'alema who comes at last and takes me by the arm. 'Hush now, *lalla*. Shhh, calm yourself.'

Relieved that someone has taken control of the madwoman, the other courtesans drift away.

'Do you know what they have done with him? Do you know where he is?'

She flinches as the little knife glints past her. 'Come with me, but quietly, and put that thing away.'

She leads me around the back of the tents. For a big woman she is agile and her eyesight is excellent, for never once does she stumble. As we go I listen for the cry of my child, and the cries of other children do not distract me, for each baby's noise is as distinctive to a mother as its look. And yet all the time I am listening out for him I picture him in my mind's eye lying motionless in a tumble of cloth, discarded and lifeless. Or bundled up and dug into the midden. Or left somewhere on a mountainside for the wolves and jackals. And whenever I think these terrible things, little moans escape me. I cannot help it; even when I press my lips tight shut, they tremble so much that the sounds slip out.

At last we creep around a tent loud with music, a tent that is decked out in rich velvets and silks, richer even than the sultan's own, and by this, and the fact that we have passed no harem guards, I know it must be Zidana's. Candlelight within throws silhouettes of dancing figures with their hands in the air and it seems suddenly obscene to me that others should be light-hearted and rejoicing when my child is missing. The ma'alema puts a finger to her lips, then points to a smaller tent a little way from that of the empress. When she sees I have marked it, she nods once and walks quickly away.

I walk to the tent, listen for a moment, then take my little knife, cut a slit in its wall and peer through. Inside, it is full of stores: sacks and jars of flour and butter and honey, cones of sugar and salt. Near the entrance, two women are sitting on stools, bent over some glass contraption over a little burner. The light it gives off is eerie, for whatever is inside the glass is emitting a coloured smoke; but, even so, I can see that the women are my maid, Makarim, and Taroob, one of Zidana's servants. And what is that in the darkness behind them? In a space between the bags and jars, something pale, wrapped in dark fabric. One of the women bends forward and the light picks out white-gold curls of hair poking through the sacking. Momo . . . He is not moving, and my heart falls dead inside me. I have to stuff my hand into my mouth to prevent a cry of despair and fury bursting out of me. Makarim and Taroob are just sitting there, surrounded by the smoke that spirals up from some vessel that sits beside them: they pass the gaudy mouthpiece one to another, and laugh.

I move to the side where the sacks are piled highest and with gargantuan effort heave out some of the pegs that pin the tent's wall to the ground. Going down on my belly, I crawl inside. But all the time I hear a voice in my head telling me my son is dead: he is dead, and they are guarding his corpse for Zidana to use in some magic rite . . .

And then the bundle moves. I freeze in mid-crawl: have I imagined it? For long seconds I hold my breath and wait, and watch. A hand appears, a tiny fist, waving. It is Momo's pre-waking habit, this small challenge to the world: in a moment he will wake fully and demand food with a scream. The thrill jolts my blood back to life, and it pounds jerkily through me. Another few inches on elbows and belly and I have hold of the sacking that swaddles him; a pull, and I have his foot in my hand. I can see his face now, screwed up in almost-sleep, his mouth opening, sucking in air for a howl. A third pull and . . . the sacking snags on an unseen obstacle. Desperate, I tug harder and there is the sound of tearing. To me, it sounds deafening, as if I have just pulled a hole in the fabric of the night itself, but the women are so intent on their smoke and gossip that they do not even turn around. A moment later, my boy is in my arms, seeming so surprised by the sight of me that he forgets to cry; and then we are outside the tent once more, swallowed by the velvet darkness.

Back in my own tent with Momo feeding contentedly, watched on by a wary Amadou, who has squirrelled the gold chain away in some secret cache of his own, I sit weighed down by a deep black dread that has now replaced the soaring relief of finding my child. For what shall we do now, just the two of us, with enemies all around? I do not think I shall ever sleep again.

24

Barely a fortnight after the accord with the Berbers was made, the weather turned against us and terrible snowstorms swept in across the mountains. The English brass cannons we brought all the way from the Tafilalt with us had to be abandoned: we ate the oxen that drew them. Then we ate the few Berber sheep we had rounded up. Now all that remain are the pack animals, but they are, as the imams explain to us, haram: forbidden by the Prophet, for every creature has its designated purpose, and beasts of burden are born to bear, not to be eaten. But we have eaten everything else, except for the harnesses and leather tack, so perhaps that comes next.

At last, when we are weak from starvation, the holy men declare that conditions are sufficiently critical for the prohibition on the eating of the mules and donkeys to be put aside and great celebrations break out. But Ismail would rather starve to death than contravene one word of the Qur'an: he declares that he and his immediate staff (which unfortunately includes me) will go without until halal foodstuffs are somehow miraculously made available to us. I am afraid there are some of us who curse our master in our hearts, though no one would do so aloud: there are djinns everywhere in these mountains who would carry the word to him. You catch them out of the corner of your eye at twilight and in the height of a snowstorm: a twist of light where there should be no light; a dull flame in the darkness.

Some of the body-slaves slip into the soldiers' camp after last prayer and beg a bit of mule: I catch Abid sucking the last scraps of meat out of a hoof and he all but weeps in relief when I promise I will say nothing of it. In truth, I do not have the energy. There are times when I think all I want to do is to go out into the snow and lie down and let its feathery white wings sweep over me, like the White Swan herself, and carry me into oblivion.

Just when dark memories of rumours about neighbouring tribes' cannibalism begin to haunt me, the longed-for miracle occurs and a hunter staggers in with a mountain sheep he has stalked out on the perilous peaks draped across his shoulders. The sultan heralds his arrival with great praise and prayers. He marvels over its extravagantly curled horns and rewards the hunter with a bag of gold, which the poor man takes with proper gratitude but then looks at mournfully. Ismail, seeing that the man would trade each coin for a mouthful of mutton, graciously presents him with part of one of the beast's roasted legs, at which the hunter bursts into tears and prostrates himself and declares the sultan the most magnificent, munificent, godly and beloved leader Morocco has ever been so lucky to have. Ismail is so delighted by this that he raises the man up with his own hands and declares he is now a kaid and shall have equal shares of all the booty we have brought out of Sijilmassa. The man cannot believe his ears, and all that night goes from one to another of us, asking for the sultan's promise to be repeated, in case he was dreaming.

The weather worsens. For three days we cannot move. Snow engulfs us, covering everything. Guards are posted to keep the snow from collapsing the imperial tents and suffocating the occupants. One morning we find two of Ismail's door-guards frozen solid in place, grey shadows of their former selves.

When at last the snowstorms clear, a lookout reports that a horde of Berber tribesmen has gathered at the head of the valley below us, preventing our descent from the mountains. 'They intend to starve us out,' ben Hadou says grimly.

It will not take long. The mountain sheep is a distant memory. 'Go take them gifts and find out who they are,' Ismail tells the Tinker, who, even in his worn, emaciated state, is the best diplomat amongst us.

We wait, exhausted and frozen. Surely the barbaric Berbers will kill the Tinker and send back his head as a taunt? Perhaps he will simply expire in the snow. Or in a moment of weakness he will be tempted to their side by a fine dish of spicy *mechoui* (we are sure it would take less to win us over). No one expects a great deal from his envoy: the tribesmen have much to gain from the annihilation of their enemies, and nothing to lose. But the sultan, wily as ever, had other plans than mere diplomacy. When ben Hadou returns, he is not alone. With him are two of the Berbers, well bribed with imperial gold to guide us to the Telwet Pass and thence to the Plains of Marrakech, circumventing the Berber army in the dead of night.

With the calm pragmatism of the truly desperate, we leave behind three thousand tents, all the costly treasures looted from the palace at Sijilmassa, and the bodies of the two hundred slaves who refused to walk another step, and make a silent retreat by the light of the full moon.

A full day's march later, we are in sight of the Red-Walled City. Since plague still rages within, Ismail returns to the hills, where we sack a Berber village and eat our way through every sheep and goat that the villagers have cosseted through this hard winter. The mood is one of elation. We are alive! The Defender of the Faithful has yet again proved worthy of his title.

By the time we reach Dila, where the court has relocated, more than half a year has passed. With every step, I find myself gripped, not by anticipation but by dread. Has Alys survived the birth, and, if so, has she then survived the predations of Zidana?

It is a torment not to be able to storm straight into the harem and seek her out, and there is no one left behind of whom I may safely ask news. Instead, as the sultan avails himself of the luxury of a long-awaited steam bath, I find myself wandering between the soldiers' camp and the court, a full member of neither one nor the other. There are celebrations all around as friends and families are reunited; wails of mourning as news of the fallen is received. But no one cares whether I am alive or dead, and I feel like a ghost as I drift around the compound.

'You look forlorn, Nus-Nus.'

I turn. It is the cook, Malik. We clasp arms like old friends. We *are* old friends. From being cast down in the depths of melancholy, suddenly I am raised up on high. We grin and grin at one another.

'Come,' he says. 'There's lamb roasting for the emperor's supper, and his highness's favourite sweet pumpkin and chickpea couscous. You look as if you could do with some feeding up.' He holds me at arm's length, regards me with his head cocked. 'You've changed, you know. Lost weight, not that you had much to lose; you look older.'

'Thanks.'

'Not in a bad way. Anyway, war will do that to a man. Toughens you up, I suppose. The High Atlas in winter certainly isn't my idea of fun.' He leads me to the long tent that functions as his kitchen. It is hot and bustling, full of pungent vapours that make my mouth water so hard I have to keep swallowing rather than drool like a dog. I take my place on a stool while he chops and shouts and stirs, and at last he brings me a dish of couscous ladled over with fresh, bright vegetables – vegetables! for the first time in weeks – and then anoints it with a magnificent scarlet gravy and for moments on end I just sit there with the dish cradled between my hands, gazing at it. Ruby tomatoes, emerald peas, opal chickpeas, golden squash. After our winter fare in the monotone mountains, it is a feast for the eyes, a treasure-trove of colour. I can hardly bring myself to spoil its perfection by eating it; but then Malik drops into the middle of the dish a steaming shank of lamb fragrant with garlic and cumin and I cannot help but fall upon it like the dog I am.

As I eat he tells me the news of the court, most of which streams in a meaningless babble past my ears as I apply myself to my food, until I catch the word 'swan', at which my head shoots up. 'Say that again,' I mumble through a full mouth.

'The White Swan was delivered of a child, though there has been a lot of discussion as to its nature.'

My heart soars and dips like a dragonfly over a pond. 'And are they both in good health, mother and child?' I ask, trying to sound nonchalant.

Malik shrugs. 'There were rumours . . . It is not for me to say. I am sure she is well enough, but –' He has loose, mobile features, ridges of soft skin on his brow that furrow when he concentrates. He turns his steady brown gaze upon me. 'Take care, Nus-Nus: there are malicious gossips who like to whisper that the child is yours.'

I stare at him. 'Mine? That would be quite a feat!'

The frown becomes a half-smile, lopsided, ironic. '*I* know, Nus-Nus; and *you* know. But, even so, be aware. Your tenderness towards her hasn't gone unnoticed.'

I force out a laugh and bend my head to my food again so that he will not see the truth of it, and eat my way to the base of the dish, long past the point at which I am no longer hungry.

'So, Nus-Nus, How is your first taste of real food in all these weeks?'

Ismail is being uncharacteristically solicitous as we go through the daily rigmarole of my tasting his dinner for poison. I had completely forgot myself earlier. My belly feels as if it may give birth at any moment to a child made of pumpkin and couscous, with beady white chickpeas for eyes. It is all I can do not to belch as I force another spoonful in. I swallow and smile, swallow and smile. I force myself to rapture, making suitably appreciative noises, and as soon as the meal is declared safe for the sultan to eat, I am dismissed and waste all of Malik's artistry by heaving it up into a bucket.

The next day the sultan visits his harem. First he pays his respects to Zidana, who exclaims dolefully over his lost weight.

'Djinns have taken your flesh! Someone has cursed you!'

Ismail has little patience with talk of djinns. 'I think you have stolen it yourself,' he tells her, slapping her ever-more capacious rump. The empress is so surprised by this breach of protocol that she says nothing, but lets him lead her away to his quarters, to be the first in this new chapter of the couching book.

This gives me the chance I have been waiting for. I tell the harem door-guard that I have come to take back my monkey, and he waves me through with a knowing smile that I do not like the look of. Once inside the harem, another problem: Alys is nowhere to be found. I accost a harem servant. 'I don't know, she keeps moving,' one girl tells me in exasperation. 'Don't waste your time with her.'

Another says, 'The White Swan? Don't make me laugh!' and walks on, as if I had asked the whereabouts of a unicorn or a phoenix.

And then I spy Makarim, Alys's body-slave. She sees me coming and makes to dodge me, but I stand in her way. 'Where is the Englishwoman?'

The smile she gives me is mocking. 'The djinns took her.'

I catch her by the arm. 'What do you mean? Where is she?'

She tries to pull free, but I am desperate now. I shake her, not gently.

Makarim squeals. 'Take your hands off me! I will scream and have the guards cut your head off!'

'Where is Alys? I know you know!'

'What if I do? She is just a crazy woman and you are just a cut-man. She has no wits and you have no balls: be damned to both of you!'

This is not the compliant little body-slave in whose charge I left Alys: something has changed in the balance of harem power. My fingers dig into the tender flesh of her upper arm: suddenly I want to hurt her. As if she knows this, she makes a sudden, jerky effort and wrenches free of me. But, instead of running away, she steps out of my reach and just looks at me. There is something in her expression that reinforces the sense I have that she knows too much, something bold and gleeful and exultant. She examines the reddening marks on her arms, then stares back at me, her eyes hard and glittering.

'I will pay you back for that, eunuch,' she spits like a little cat, and then she runs.

I want to go after her, but what is the point? She will make a fuss and shout for the guards, show them her bruises. I turn and continue my search, running here and there, ducking my head into tents, feeling the panic rise.

At last, quite by chance, I come across an odd little makeshift shelter on the edge of the harem where a crone sits alone, a dark blanket draped over her head, hunched over a charcoal brazier on which she is cooking something for her lunch. 'Good day, lady,' I start, and she stiffens as if I have alarmed her. I am about to ask her if she knows where the English courtesan may be found, when something comes flying out of the shelter and hurtles towards me, chattering madly. I feel the scrape of cold claws tracking across my skin, and then suddenly there is Amadou on my shoulder, bending his monkey-face towards me, baring all his yellow, yellow teeth. 'Hello, my lad, have you missed me?' I ruffle the fur on the top of his head and he butts his skull against my hand and narrows his eyes in delight.

I turn to apologize to the old woman for the trouble my monkey has been causing her when she throws back the blanket and I realize it is no crone after all. Malik had told me I appeared older and thinner, but the effects of a hard winter in the mountains have taken a worse toll on the

White Swan. She is gaunt and sallow, with dark rings under her eyes, which seem twice their usual size. Her clothes are in a wretched state, filthy and worn; her body seems misshapen. She stares at me as if she has seen a wraith.

In some alarm, I set the monkey down and kneel beside her. 'Alys. My God, Alys, what has happened to you?'

I would deny it if I could, but the smell of her almost knocks me backwards. Is this the radiant beauty I left behind, a woman as ripe and fragrant as a pomegranate, of whom I dreamed every night? What in the world would stop someone as fastidious as Alys Swann from visiting the hammam with the other women? Only something appalling, only fear, or madness . . .

'I thought you were never coming back.'

Her voice is as harsh as a crow's croak, and she does look like a crow, all black and hunched over. Overcome by compassion, I forget that at any moment someone might walk behind the tents and spy us, and reach out for her and pull her to me. I hold her tightly, taint and all, bury my face in the matted tarnish of her once-gold hair. As I do so, something moves between us, and then begins to wail. When I look down, I realize that Alys has strapped the baby across her chest. It waves its fists peremptorily, and its face screws up into a ball of noisy demand. As she moves away from me to suckle the babe, a sharp pain shoots through me. Everything has been for this: servitude, humiliation, captivity, apostasy; and now even madness. And yet the child itself is gloriously, selfishly unaware of its mother's sacrifice. It is a greedy beast: it seems to feed for ever, as if it would suck the last human morsel of her away, leaving nothing but a hollow shell of flesh behind. Perhaps Makarim is right: perhaps Alys has been taken by djinns . . .

I bow my head over the pan of soup that is cooking over the brazier – a thin-looking mixture of vegetables and chicken bones innocent of any discernible seasoning and apply myself to stirring this grey gruel while my mind churns. Striving for some small degree of normality, I say, 'So, Alys, tell me: what have you called the baby?' I realize I have not even asked its sex.

She looks up, and her eyes are full of love: but not for me. 'He is Momo, short for Mohammed; Mohammed James, one name for his new family, one for his old. Is he not beautiful?'

All I can see is a tumble of yellow hair and an intent red mouth. I make a non-committal sound; it is a boy, then. Ismail will be pleased. 'Tell me what has happened that you are out here in this . . . condition,' I urge her. 'Was it Zidana that drove you away?' My ruse with the Targui woman must have failed.

She laughs, the sound like a rusty hinge. 'Zidana, ah, yes, it always comes back to her. But not only her: there has been an unholy conspiracy against me. You would not believe the things they have done . . .'

It is as if someone has unstoppered a leak in a bucket: the words pour out of her. She tells me, in a rush, how Momo was stolen from her, how she feared the baby would be killed. She tells me that for these last weeks she has lived in this terrible limbo – neither in the harem nor out of it – keeping herself out of everyone's view. At all times she has the child strapped to her: she sleeps fitfully, sitting upright, as I found her. 'That way if they surprise me, they cannot easily separate us,' she explains, as if it is the most natural thing in the world. At night she has walked the camp when everyone else is asleep, and gathered scraps for the cookpot and linens for the child. All the while she tells me these things, as if they are sane and normal behaviour, I stare at her, aghast.

'There was a time when I thought your ape would be the death of us,' she confides, 'but if it were not for Amadou's scavenging skills I don't know what would have become of us. He is a fine little thief! Heaven alone knows where he has managed to find figs and oranges at this time of year.' She smiles and her face is transformed and I see in a sudden flash the Alys I left behind and my heart tears all the more.

'I am back now.' I swallow. 'And so is Ismail. No one will dare do anything to harm you or the child now. All shall be well.'

She stares at me. 'I cannot stay here. You have to get us away! You and Ismail will go away again and then they will kill us.' Then she clutches my arm with such urgency I can feel her fingertips digging down to the bones. 'Get us out of here, Nus-Nus, I beg you.'

Can it be done? Insane schemes tumble through my mind: darkening the giveaway golden hair of both mother and child with ashes and water, making myself a beard of sheepskin, bribing a guard or two (or five, or ten . . .

but with what? I have no money) to get us into the soldiers' compound, and beyond, where the camp-followers lurk on the outskirts of the settlement. And from there, a mule, or two, and a long trek on back roads and through open country to Meknes to see if Daniel al-Ribati is still there and may help us leave the country . . . Almost I have persuaded myself that all this is possible, when I hear the high, brassy sound of Fassi trumpets blaring out, announcing the arrival of the sultan, and the chill of cowardice runs through my veins, extinguishing my hot thoughts. I turn my mind swiftly in a different direction.

'Go quickly to the hammam,' I tell Alys. 'Take your child and clean yourselves thoroughly. I will send someone to you, a trustworthy servant, with clean clothes for both of you. Then you must come out and present Momo to the sultan.'

Tears spark to her eyes; she begins to protest. I have to shake her. 'It is the only way, I promise you.'

I dash back to the kitchens. 'Malik, I must speak with you!'

He looks alarmed. 'You can't bring that monkey in here!'

Amadou chatters excitedly: there is food *everywhere*. I keep hold of him so tightly he becomes infuriated and tries to bite me. 'Malik, how old is your oldest girl?'

'Mamass? Twelve, coming up thirteen.'

'Perfect.' One-handed, I take off my belt-pouch and shake the contents on to the table. 'It's yours. All of it. Or put it away for her marriage chest.' I explain my plan and he stares at me. I know exactly what he is thinking, but in the end he just gives me a look and sighs, then tucks the coins swiftly into his money-belt, rattles off some orders to his kitchen team, wipes his hands on his apron and strides away.

Twenty minutes later Amadou is safely tied to a tent post and Mamass is trotting along beside me, looking by turns apprehensive and excited. It is an honour to work in the harem, especially serving those who have given birth to the sultan's sons, but she does not know what to expect; however, she is a bright girl and has learned much from having a father in such a position at court. 'Keep your eyes open and your mouth shut,' I warn her. 'Always be pleasant to the empress and her favourites; but if ever you sense a threat to the White Swan, come running for me as fast as you can.'

She peers at me, all eyes, over the top of the bundle of clothing her mother has given us: cotton, not silk, but as clean as snow, and nods solemnly, taking it all in.

I wait for them outside the hammam, trying to look as if I have business there. When Alys finally emerges, the breath rushes out of me: she looks like a goddess, all white and gold, the babe a cherub in her arms. We are just making our way towards the main pavilion when we meet the sultan's entourage coming the other way – hard to miss since it is preceded by four eunuch heralds bearing enormously long trumpets. The heralds and attendants (sweeping the ground before the sultan with gigantic ostrich feathers) part, and suddenly there is Ismail, with Zidana right beside him. Her eyes fix instantly, with chill fury, on Alys and Momo. She tugs her husband's arm. 'There are some new girls I have had brought in for you, my lord, from the corsairs' latest trawl of the Mediterranean. One of them is from China, a pale slip of a thing, breasts like apples and hair of black silk, destined for the harem of the Great Turk himself. You will like her, she is very exotic; but fiery too. I have had to cut her fingernails . . .'

But Ismail has eyes only for the child in Alys's arms. He strides forward, with barely a glance at Alys herself, takes Momo from her and holds him up wonderingly. 'My son?'

Zidana's face darkens murderously, but the child is in the sultan's arms now.

'Don't be taken in, O light of the world: what you see is foul sorcery,' she says as he unswaddles it. 'The child is a demon only pretending to be a boy. My women have seen the White Swan consorting with djinns, suckling them, lying with them, bargaining with them to gain the power to produce this illusion. Ask anyone: they have stolen her wits – she has been living amongst them in the filth and refuse of the camp. People hear her singing with them at twilight; she has been seen dancing with them naked. And the men! Always there are men sniffing around her. I have heard she leaves the harem secretly at night and spreads her legs for any man she takes a fancy to. She is a lewd creature, my love. With my own eyes I have seen her lying with the Hajib –' She makes a signal and Makarim comes sliding past her and casts herself on the ground before the sultan.

'My lord, it is true! I too saw this happen. I was the servant to the White Swan, but she sent me away when I tried to stop the grand vizier entering the tent. "Let him in, let him in!" she wheedled. And when I protested that it was not seemly, she struck me across the head in a great rage and drove me away, so I ran to find the empress and she came running to prevent such dishonour taking place in your majesty's harem, and so it was that she witnessed this evil scene!'

'You see?' Zidana's eyes gleam with triumph: two enemies struck down with a single blow. 'And there are others who can attest to the disgusting behaviour of this whore.' She bends to whisper something to Taroob, who bobs her head and runs.

Ismail's face is full of blood and flushing darker by the moment. He wraps the child hastily in its linen, pausing for a moment to examine the gold ring on the chain around its neck. 'My lord,' I find myself saying suddenly. 'You cannot believe this calumny?' My heart is beating wildly: and the sultan's visage darkens further. I can feel Zidana's gaze crawl over me: surely this will be my death warrant, by the hand of one or the other. But Alys is too bewildered to defend herself, and so I must speak for her. 'The White Swan has given you a son, a truly beautiful son,' I press on. But the sultan is staring at Momo now as if he is indeed an alien being: an evil succubus; a tricksy djinn. And it is true: there is no great similarity between father and son. Blue eyes, yellow hair: it is as if Momo has thrown off his Moroccan heritage in favour of his mother's.

Ismail turns to me a face that appears hacked out of wood: mad and ravaged. I doubt he has heard a word I said. He surges past me to glare at Alys. They stand eye to eye: the sultan is not a tall man. 'It is true?' he growls at her. 'You and the grand vizier?' She stares at him, then down at the baby. She makes to take the child back, but Ismail holds it closer, so tight that it starts to cry. 'Answer me!' He thrusts his face at her: spittle lands upon her chin.

Terror robs her of her wits. 'He . . . he . . . I do not know . . .'

I catch her before she hits the ground.

★

208

The faint saves her; but nothing can save Abdelaziz. One after another, Zidana's paid witnesses step forward to add their testimony to hers and Makarim's, saying how they have seen the grand vizier entering the harem at all hours of the day and night, particularly when the muezzin has sounded and all godly men are at prayer; and always he went straight to the English-woman's tent. Even the ma'alema testifies angrily that she found him alone with Alys, since he had sent her servant away. 'But no fault can be attributed to the lady, my lord: she did not encourage the grand vizier's visits and tolerated him only because he insisted he was your right hand.'

Ismail tells me to fetch Abdelaziz. He is controlled, stony. 'Tell him nothing. I would not have him prepare a series of pretty lies.'

The grand vizier takes some finding: eventually I track him down to the hammam, steam swirling around him so that he looks like Ala'ad-Din's djinn emerging from its lamp. The hammam attendant, who has been soaping his back, takes one look at me and scuttles out. The Hajib blinks as I stand over him, wipes the sweat out of his eyes. 'Well now,' he says, looking me up and down with a curious expression on his face. 'Here you are, back from the wars, and in one piece, give or take. Remove your clothes, Nus-Nus, and bend over, there's a good boy.'

'The sultan requests your presence.'

He purses his mouth, blows out a great huffing sigh. 'That's a shame.' He heaves himself to his feet, shameless in his nakedness. 'Surely whatever he wants can wait just a little while?'

'Get dressed,' I say shortly. 'I will wait for you outside.'

He takes an age to be dried and clothed. When I can bear it no longer, I storm back in, and of course find him gone. The hammam attendant lies in a pool of pale pink blood in the rapidly cooling chamber. There is no steam left in the place: it has escaped, along with the grand vizier, through a slit in the tent wall.

I fully expect to lose my head when I relay this news to Ismail, but he just smiles grimly. 'Only the guilty run before they are even accused.' He sends riders out from the camp in all directions.

It is two days later when they bring him back, bruised and dishevelled. 'He put up quite a fight.' The bukhari captain is almost admiring.

Two days is a long time in Ismail's memory: he could easily have forgotten all about his edict by now. But it seems his anger has been smouldering away steadily; or perhaps it is Zidana who has been stoking the fire, reminding him of her rival's many and various crimes. She presents herself today in a most oddly combative aspect, marrying the style of a Lobi warrior with . . . well, heaven knows what. She wears a leopardskin across her back, with its head resting upon her head and one of its great forearms draped over one shoulder, its paw tucked into her belt. She carries a sword at her hip and in her right hand is a great plumed lance. Her eyes are made up to look even more ferocious than usual. Clearly, her spies have got ahead of the riders bringing in the vizier to let her know the glad news and she has arrayed herself in this bizarre manner to crow over his downfall. Oblivious to the usual protocols, she now thumps the butt of the spear down perilously close to Abdelaziz, who covers his head with his hands and cries plaintively, 'Forgive me, forgive me, O Great One!'

For a moment, Ismail looks upon him almost kindly. Then he kicks him so hard in the midriff that his whole body quakes. 'You sack of filth! You abomination! You would dare to lay your foul hands on that which belongs to me, and only to me?'

Abdelaziz moans. 'O, Sun and Moon of Morocco, Lord of Mercy and Charity, forgive your humble servant for whatever you believe I may have done.'

'Do not try to wriggle out of it, you grub!' cries Zidana. 'I saw you lie with the White Swan with my own two eyes.'

The vizier's face recomposes itself: this was not the accusation he had expected. And now a calculating look comes into his eyes as he assesses the various odds for his survival. Making his choice, he says, 'But, my emperor, all who know me know that this accusation must be false. My appetites — for my sins, which I acknowledge to be manifold — lie not with women, no matter how lovely they may be. It will not please you, I know, sire, for me to say this, but you have only to ask your chief scribe and Keeper of the Book, dear Nus-Nus here.'

The sultan turns his opaque eyes upon me, his basilisk gaze so penetrating that I think I may be turned to stone by it. 'Speak, Nus-Nus.'

I feel myself begin to tremble. I want to kill my prone enemy, to silence for ever his smiling crocodile mouth; I want to be swallowed by the ground. What I do not want to do is to broadcast my shameful past for all to hear. I am a bukhari now, a warrior who has survived a mountain campaign: I have no wish to be seen as a catamite. But I have to save Alys. I swallow, then say quickly, 'To my knowledge, the grand vizier's taste is more for men than women.'

'For you?'

'He has shown his . . . interest, on occasion.'

This evasion does not satisfy Ismail. 'Speak plainly!'

'You are amongst friends,' Zidana encourages, her voice honeyed with anticipation. If the ruse with the White Swan does not work, she will happily accept another route to her goal. Then, with a wink, 'Senufo spirit, remember?'

I gather my resources. The shame is not mine, I remind myself. I summon my second face, the kponyungu. *I am not myself.* 'Abdelaziz ben Hafid forced himself upon me as we travelled from Gao to Fez, after buying me at the slave-market and having me gelded, raping me three times before I was fully recovered from the cutting. He has made other, unsuccessful, attempts since that time.'

Ismail's eyes narrow as he takes this in, but he does not look surprised. 'Other attempts, while you were under my protection?'

I nod. My mouth is dry, so dry I can hardly speak. 'The last time was the day we arrived at the River Melwiya and you had to . . . ah . . . discipline the slaves who pitched the tents incorrectly. He had me drugged and carried to his tent. The Kaid ben Hadou can vouch for this.'

The kaid is brought. He raises his eyebrows when the question is put to him, looks first at the Hajib, who glares back defiantly; then at me. Do I see pity in his eye, or just amusement? Whichever, he tells the emperor that indeed he was fetched by one of the vizier's own slaves and found me attempting to escape Abdelaziz's unwanted attentions. He phrases it nicely but exactly, adding the unpleasantly telling detail that the child who fetched him had also fallen victim to the Hajib's unnatural lust. Ismail's face darkens by the moment.

'You see!' Zidana crows triumphantly. 'Men, women, children: he is indiscriminate!'

'I never touched the White Swan, my lord, never! This is a plot by my enemies to be rid of me –'

Ismail takes the lance from his wife and deals the vizier a blow that knocks his head back. 'Do not speak unless I bid you speak!'

Zidana, to whom this rule seems not to apply, laughs. 'Such desperate lies. All who know the grand vizier know him to be obsessed with status and power. While you were away, he sat upon your throne, he strode around the encampment in your stead, proclaiming himself your "right-hand man". He even bestowed the gold ring given only to your trueborn sons to the White Swan's brat.'

Ismail prods the Hajib with the lance. 'Is this true?'

'Yes, but –'

The sultan smiles, and passes the lance back to his wife. It is a benevolent smile, almost warm. 'Stop grovelling and get to your feet, man. Come, take my hand –'

Abdelaziz catches hold of the extended hand and hauls himself inelegantly upright, standing there on quivering legs, looking suddenly hopeful that their long, brotherly association has reasserted itself, despite everything; after all, it always had done until now. Ismail, however, does not let go of him, but clutches his wrist ever more firmly, bringing it up close to his face. 'That's a very handsome ring you have there, Abdou, a fine stone. May I take a closer look?'

The vizier tries to wriggle his hand free of Ismail's grip, but the sultan's fingers are like iron. He hauls at the ring, getting it as far as the first knuckle, and there it sticks fast. An undignified struggle ensues, the vizier by turns yelping in pain and offering to remove the item himself, if his gracious lord will be so kind as to let him. A moment later there is a more piercing howl, and the Hajib clutches his hand, blood spurting between his fingers. Ismail wipes his dagger on his robe, pulls the ring free and throws the offending digit to the floor, where one of his cats noses at it curiously, then gives it an exploratory tap. When the finger refuses to play, it turns disdainfully away, sits and extends a leg skywards and proceeds to lick clean its nether regions.

'I believe I recognize this stone, Abdou. It is one of a number given to me by the Governor of Herat: lapis, shot through with gold, out of the Pamir Mountains of Afghanistan. But, before you offer me an excuse, let me say that this comes as no surprise to me.' He leans closer to the grand vizier. 'Do you not think I know everything there is to know about you, Abdou?' The diminutive is sounding ever more menacing. 'Do you really think I sent my men after you only because of my First Wife's accusations? All these years I have been aware of your unnatural proclivities, but I decided to ignore them while your usefulness outweighed your avarice and ambition. I think that balance has finally tilted, and not in your favour. I am perfectly well aware that you have been dipping your fingers into the Treasury these many years: it amused me to let you do it. But while I was away it seems you have given your greed full rein. Do not seek to deny it: I had the Tinker arrange a full inventory on our return. There were, shall we say, some considerable discrepancies . . .'

The Hajib begins to mew now, shocked beyond the ability to articulate.

'And we might have turned our eye even to this theft were it not for the vanity and ambition that has seen you overreach yourself so shockingly in my absence. There is only one emperor of Morocco and his name is Abul Nasir Moulay Ismail as-Samin ben Sharif.' With the jewelled dagger he prods the Hajib a little more forcefully with the iteration of each name. 'Only I may declare legitimate a child and bestow upon it my own seal. The succession of my realm is of no concern of yours, you worm! The Empress Zidana has already shown me evidence of the tampering with my couching book made at your orders by your nephew, so this punishment has been a long time coming.'

I stare at him; then at her. She told me she would not tell Ismail, pretending weakness: lies, all lies. She catches my eye and gives me the languorous smile of a satisfied snake. It is a long game that she has been playing, move by careful move, weighing the advantage of the moment, dripping her poison into her husband's ear drop by drop, tightening her coils inch by inch, till she was sure her adversary could not bite her.

He instructs ben Hadou and the chief of his bukhari to take the prisoner and bind his feet to the hindquarters of a mule, which is then to be driven hard across the rough ground to the west. 'I will not besmirch my kingdom by having him die facing the Holy City.'

The Hajib finds his voice: he pleads, but Ismail's face is of marble, cold and hard. He goes out to watch the execution of his orders and takes his personal staff with him: a lesson to any who might think to overstep their place. Zidana begs to come with us, and is told to stay in the harem. She goes meekly enough, knowing she has won, but it is the first time I have ever seen Ismail refuse her.

The fat man is taken to the western outskirts of the encampment and bound to the largest and feistiest mule in the stables by his heels, still squealing and begging for mercy. Not once does he pray: I sometimes think if he had, Ismail might have relented; but his thoughts remain fixed on the fate of his corporeal self rather than on his soul. The beast rolls its eyes wildly, disliking its treatment, and is driven off in a great lather by much whipping and shouting from the bukhari. I watch as my enemy's head bounces against stones and brushwood, the flesh being flayed from him till he is like an old piece of meat dragged for hunting dogs. I turn away, nauseated.

Ben Hadou glances sideways at me. 'You do not rejoice, Nus-Nus, to see the end of your foe?'

'I would not wish such an end on anyone.'

The Tinker shrugs. 'You can't afford to be choosy when it comes to righting life's balances.'

And maybe he has a point. But, rather than any sense of triumph or relief at the death of the man who took my manhood from me, all I feel is emptiness.

The Hajib's death casts a pall over the whole court. That one so powerful should fall so suddenly and so ignominiously – dragged behind a mule! – makes everyone recall the insecurity of their own positions. It makes people fear their mortality even more than they do in times of war or plague. Zidana is subdued: she dares not raise a complaint when Ismail declares Alys's son as his own, and thus an emir of the realm.

But wherever I go, people look at me knowingly and talk behind their hands. They smile, they snigger or, worse, they show pity. It takes every iota of spirit I can summon to look them in the eye and face them down. After two weeks of this, they have started to lose interest; in three it seems forgotten, but I am left with a growing resentment. I wanted to settle my own account with Abdelaziz, but now my vengeance has been stolen from me and I am sorry for it. In my land, if a man dishonours you, you can redeem the insult only by taking his blood with your own hand: if he dies by other means, the dishonour remains to haunt you, the ghost of your good name dogging you for the rest of your days.

As we make our way back to Meknes, I hear egrets call over the plain and am convinced I am hearing the Hajib's dying cries.

25

Ismail's thoughts soon turned to his capital. A Frenchman was captured, a merchant caught supplying the still defiant English garrison at Tangier with gunpowder. Normally this act in itself would be enough to guarantee the man a swift death, but the gunpowder had been diverted to Kaid Omar and his besieging force, and the kaid was so delighted that the merchant was spared and instead sent to the slave-pens with the prisoners of war. There, one of the guards heard him babbling about Versailles and knew this would interest the sultan. The man was brought in, along with a batch of new workers destined to end their days in Meknes. The merchant, when presented to the sultan, was in a pitiful state. In one of his odd moments of benevolence, Ismail ordered that the man be taken away and his wounds cared for, that he be clothed and dressed more fittingly. You could see the look on the merchant's face change from dread of his imminent violent demise to one of bemusement, but by the time he was brought back he had regained a certain jauntiness and at once launched into details of the works being carried out on Louis XIV's great palace.

Apparently, the Sun King's architect was in the process of planning a fabulous Hall of Mirrors at the heart of Versailles. It would consist of a vast open gallery with seventeen arched windows giving out on to opulent gardens; the opposite wall would be lined with seventeen arched mirrors to match. Thus the light entering the gallery would reflect the wonders of the gardeners' art in the mirrored glass and give the sensation of walking in verdant space whilst safely enclosed by marble and gold. The merchant went on at some length about the exorbitant cost of the Venetian glass that would be used in these mirrors; of the gilding of their frames and the capitals of the towering marble pilasters that frame them, until Ismail was sent into a froth of envy and ambition.

All of a sudden, we were returning to Meknes amidst wild schemes of parklands and mirrored galleries; bridleways, orchards and olive groves; even a lake full of golden fish, with a fleet of pleasure boats to sail over their heads.

But the Meknes to which we returned was not the same Meknes we left, being greatly depleted: here and in Fez the plague carried off upwards of eighty-five thousand souls; but even more than that number had fled in its wake to far-flung parts of the realm. The building works had ground to a halt, with many of the overseers and artisans dead or gone, though surprisingly the remaining slaves appeared remarkably hale: it seemed as if the matamores had been the safest place to be.

For the next two years Ismail set about his building project once more with the fervour of a driven man. He had palaces throughout the kingdom stripped of their finery: the gold that powdered their walls and ceilings; their exquisitely carved friezes and cedarwood doors. He sent out orders for shiploads of the best Carrara marble to be brought from Genoa to Salé. Then a team of surveyors was dispatched to the ruins to the west of the city, and commanded to make note of those parts that were of ornament or use for his palace at Meknes.

I am sent out to catalogue the site for Ismail, no doubt to ensure that others do not steal anything of value before he can himself take it.

'Bring me back a stone of your choosing,' he tells me, and gives me a fine piece of silk in which to wrap it. I go reluctantly, I will admit, for the sun beats down like a hammer on the head, and without great expectation. But the place is astonishing. It sits upon a prominence on the plain, a commanding position that can be seen from miles away, and the size of it becomes more astounding with every step we take towards it. In the shadow beneath its triumphal arch, I gaze up. This place must have been raised by a race of giants, for it towers higher even than the minaret of the Great Mosque, and its stones are so massive it is impossible to think of them moved by mortal men. For hours I wander amidst its roofless pillars, their capitals carved in fanciful flourishes that seem so sharp-edged they might have been completed only yesterday, hardly knowing whether to stare skywards to marvel at their height or at the ground beneath my feet, which is decorated with millions of tiny coloured shards of tile as intricate as the work of our very best zellij-masters, yet depicting not mere abstract patterns but entire living tableaux. I come across a mosaic of monstrous creatures swimming in the sea; then a man sitting backwards on a horse, performing some acrobatic gesture; long walkways bearing cartouches of dancing, drinking figures; a robustly naked woman climbing into or out of a great deep bath, attended upon by two other equally curvaceous servants. I think: this Volubilis must have been a lively place, and its king a great voluptuary, and I sketch them for my own interest as I go around cataloguing the number and quality of the pillars and pavements for Ismail.

So taken up with my studies am I that I almost forget to select a stone to take back to the sultan, and when the call goes out that the expedition is returning to Meknes, I have to scramble to find something uncommon and eventually have one of the men help me to take up a piece of fallen pillar, a fragment of carved capital showing something of the ancient stonemason's art. We wrap it carefully in a length of silk and place it in a pannier on one of the mules. The poor beast walks lopsidedly all the long way home.

Ismail is very pleased by my choice. He marvels over it, moving the tips of his fingers admiringly across the carving. The pattern suggests, rather than depicts, a tracery of leaves and flowers. 'This comes from the heart of the first African empire, Mauretania Tingitana, established by the Romans. Already my own domain here exceeds its extent.' He turns lambent eyes upon me. 'Imagine that, Nus-Nus: my power is already greater than that of the Romans with all their mighty armies. Now all I have to do is to expel the wretched English from Tangier and the infidel Spanish from Larache and Marmora and I shall restore the purity of the true faith through the length and breadth of our lands. It is my destiny to do this. It is my duty. Do you know why I sent you to Volubilis?'

I shake my head. Sometimes it is wiser not to speak.

'It was there that Moulay Idriss, great-grandson of the Prophet, first brought Islam to Morocco when he fled the assassins of the Abbasid caliph. And it was there that his son, the second Idriss, was born, who unified Morocco and established its firm allegiance to the words of the Prophet, bringing together in one faith and under one banner this great kingdom. There is magic in these stones, Nus-Nus – for they are imbued not only with the might of the ancient Romans, but also with the word of God. And that is why I must incorporate them into my city, for their power will aid me in my sacred task.'

All this time, punctuated by more uprisings in the Rif and reports from the siege of the English colony at Tangier, Ismail threw himself with fervour into the re-creation of his palace, often working stripped to the waist beside the slaves like a common labourer, his face and arms streaked with earth and lime. He worked like a man compelled, a man who simply could not rest because his dreams were eating him from the inside.

That second summer was fearsome, the heat unyielding. The wells ran dry and the few surviving crops were ravaged by a vast flight of locusts blowing in from the desert. By the end of the year the drought still had us in its grip. The fountains were turned off, and mosquitoes bred in the stagnant water and terrorized us at night with their whining flights and blood-sucking.

News that the English garrison defending their colony at Tangier had managed, after a long and bloody fight, to repulse the sultan's forces could hardly have arrived at a worse time. Ismail's general, Kaid Omar, rides in from the north one third day in Muharram 1091 to discuss a possible truce with the infidel, who will also, he reports, be sending a representative to the Meknes court.

The sultan commands the attendance of his judges and scholars to rule on the lawfulness of such an action. The conflict with the English is costly and sapping, especially when the country lies in the grip of this drought. He wants the enemy out of Morocco, but war with them has become more than an inconvenience, and the prospect of defeat is unacceptable. If force of arms has failed to drive them from our shores, perhaps there are other ways to persuade them to leave. Can some sort of truce be made without infringing the laws of the Qur'an? The atmosphere is fraught: many of the gathered chieftains argue that to make any kind of agreement with the Christians would be shameful; but ben Hadou counters that political expedience in our current circumstances would be sensible. This seems to inflame the most intransigent further still: they cry that Allah is on their side, that he will provide; that the infidel must be cut down and trodden into the ground they have defiled. The Tinker addresses himself through the din to the sultan. 'My lord, if you are seen to be patient and merciful with the English, the crowned heads of Europe will surely seek your friendship.'

Ismail cocks his head, interested. He lifts a hand and the din falls away. 'Do you remember what happened after the conquest of Mecca?' He looks around the room, a light in his eyes. I scribble the transcription, knowing where this is heading. 'As the huge army approached Mecca in triumph, Said ibn Ubada, to whom the Prophet had given his standard, called out to Abu Sufyan, leader of the Quraysh of Mecca, who had for so long violently resisted Islam, but knew that there was no chance of resisting this army: "Oh Abu Sufyan, this is the day of slaughter!" "Oh Messenger of God!" cried Abu Sufyan, "have you commanded the slaying of your people? By God I beg your mercy, on behalf of your people, for you are of all men the greatest in piety, the most merciful, the most beneficent." "This is the day of mercy," said the Prophet. "On this day God has exalted Quraysh." And so he granted amnesty to his enemies.'

Kaid Omar laughs. 'I hope we shall not be granting amnesty to all our enemies, or it will be seen as an invitation to the Christian hordes to trample over us.'

'Was Saladin weak, when he showed mercy after the conquest of Jerusalem? His beneficence surely increased his greatness.'

The tide is turning: you can feel it in the room.

'My lord, peace with the English would be most advantageous to us.' The well-modulated voice of ben Hadou rises again. 'In a time of peace, we can import arms and munitions more cheaply, the better to deal with those rebels within our own borders; and, in time, with the Spanish, and if necessary the English too.'

There is some discussion at this; some agreement too. I watch Ismail casting his eyes from one face to the next, judging his moment. Then he holds up his hand again. 'We shall show the infidel mercy: but we shall also be astute in our dealings with them: always we have the long view in our mind, and that is to see them expelled from our soil.'

The messenger from England comes riding proudly on his horse, dressed in the height of English court fashion – all ribbons, lace ruffs and slashed shoulder pads, with a retinue of equally foppish guardsmen and servants, half of whom are refused entry and told to go kick their heels. Water is so short, we cannot be wasting it on our enemies. The Englishman is brought in to the newly refurbished Ambassadors' Hall, its walls gleaming with the powdered gold stripped from the grand vizier's quarters, its ceiling painted azure blue with bright gold embellishments. Incense burns all around, giving off fragrant clouds of smoke; candles flicker in sconces. The sultan awaits in state, seated upon a low couch amidst a crowd of richly dressed kaids and pashas, his slave-boys fanning him with huge ostrich feather fans. The Englishman does not know where to look first: his eyes dart everywhere, evidently in awe of all this finery and opulence, which is exactly the impression Ismail wishes to convey: one of infinite wealth and resources. Show no weakness to the enemy and their bargaining will be made all the harder.

The man sweeps off his hat with a flourish and declares himself to be Colonel Percy Kirke, with a message from the English ambassador, Sir James Leslie, who is unavoidably detained (ben Hadou translates, and I record). The sultan smiles, a narrow, glittering smile: all this he knows from his spies. The ambassador himself is in Tangier: what is delayed is the ship of gifts sent to appease the sultan by the English king, for it is unthinkable for a foreign ambassador to appear at Ismail's court empty-handed. And the reason for the delay? The French are blockading Salé and the sea to the west of Tangier in protest at the large number of their compatriots taken captive by Sidi Qasem's corsairs. Ismail's drive to complete Meknes has required ever more slave-labour: the old corsair chief and his fleet have been kept very busy supplying the sultan's demands.

Ismail's gaze sweeps over the visitor assessingly; sums him up and dismisses him. His smile becomes capricious, his focus sharpens. He is charm personified, accepting the man's apologies with grace and indulgence. When the subject of redeeming English captives is nervously introduced, the sultan clicks his fingers and sends two of the bukhari to fetch out four or five of the feeblest and least useful as a gesture of goodwill. These poor wretches come blinking out of the matamores and are gifted to Kirke, who exclaims his gratitude and thanks the sultan fulsomely, calling him emperor and great one, as if he is born to fawn in true oriental fashion. He appears so taken aback at the ease with which he has gained the freedom of these men that he seems to forget his purpose is to attempt to redeem two hundred more. I catch ben Hadou's eye during this nauseating display and he twitches an eyebrow at me as if to say, Is this the best that England can offer?

For the next two days Ismail plays the gracious host. He takes the Englishman and some of his companions hunting in the hills outside Meknes for wild boar and antelope: the kills are roasted in spectacular feasts. While the infidels defile themselves with the consumption of wild pig, the sultan eats alone, his favoured couscous with chickpeas and just a little meat. The English sate themselves with meat and hippocras and kif-rich tobaccos in the *chicha* pipes that we assiduously pass amongst them. Even the following morning they remain befuddled and heavy-headed; and it is in this state that talks resume.

As they walk in the orange groves, Kirke raises the subject of a truce at Tangier, and I translate. Ismail smiles widely and promises that no shot shall be fired against Tangier while Kirke remains in it. It is the emptiest of promises: Ismail does not keep his word with unbelievers. But the Englishman does not know this: he puffs out his chest like a peacock, thinking his skill as a great diplomat has won over this most fearsome of enemies.

More refreshments are taken in the gardens: mint tea for the sultan; plenty of hippocras for the Englishman, the fruit and spices in the concoction masking the powerful brandy beneath. He knocks it back smilingly, no doubt to be polite to his host, though I have heard the English have a great appetite for alcohol. As they partake, my lord Ismail gestures widely. 'So, my dear Kirke, look around you. As an English aristocrat, used to the finest things in life, what do you think of this palace I am making here?'

Kirke, flattered to be taken as a noble and to have his opinion sought, is effusive in his praise. It is, apparently, finer than anything he has seen in London, although he hears that the French king's new palace at Versailles may rival it.

Ismail's face darkens and swiftly Kirke adds, 'But of course the French have no taste. Gadsbodikins, lud, no taste at all. 'Tis all frippery and furbelow, I have no doubt. Not like this.' He spreads his arms wide, indicates the huge vista of ongoing building works, the masons and artisans, gardeners and foreign labourers sweating their guts out on the walls. 'This is . . . the work of giants, indeed, sir. Mightily, massively . . . ambitious.'

Ismail inclines his head. His eyes are sharp and bright, like those of a hawk that has sighted prey and is preparing to stoop. 'Of course, such an undertaking attracts great jealousy and bitterness — I am sure you have noticed how others dislike to see your light shine more brightly than their own. I am forced to protect my works from enemies even in my own land, savages who do not enjoy your degree of discernment, who do not appreciate the art that goes on here, who look with envy upon my creation. I must arm myself against such barbarians if I am not to see my legacy destroyed.'

He beckons to me to take a note of the conversation from this point. It is barely the lift of a finger, this signal, but I am well attuned to such things. I mix my ink with a quick hand, dip the reed and hold it poised.

'I would beg your indulgence, my lord.' Ismail promotes the man shamelessly. 'What I need — what I cannot come by elsewhere in this splendid country of mine is something only you can help me with. We have the finest artisans in so many disciplines, but no one can match the English when it comes to one thing.'

'And what is that, sire?'

'Why, guns, man. Cannon. What I really need in order to defend myself from these wicked Berbers who would see all I have created reduced to rubble is ten of the best English guns. I need a steadfast man, a trustworthy man, to take this commission from me and place an order with the best manufacturers England can boast. You, Percy Kirke, you strike me as a trustworthy, steadfast fellow — as my good friend, can you aid me in this?'

The colonel sweeps an elaborate bow. 'I would be most honoured to, sire.' He signs my notes at Ismail's prompting, even though they are in Arabic and could say anything at all, and probably will before too long.

Having got what he wanted, and in writing to boot, the sultan cheerfully packs the man and his retinue off back to Tangier with goodwill gifts and many empty promises. I cannot imagine the true ambassador will be very pleased with the way in which his witless emissary has overstepped himself. I feel almost sorry for the man.

And still the drought continues. Prayers are redoubled: Ismail has become convinced that such severe weather must be a sign of Allah's wrath, though in response to what he does not say. The children of the city are sent out into the fields to dance and pray for rain, but not a drop falls. The sultan decides the responsibility must now lie with the marabouts and talebs, who tailor their prayers to suit the situation and make a barefoot pilgrimage of saints' shrines. Still no rain.

Ismail falls into a fury. His vast granaries, constructed at great expense, stretching for miles beneath the city like catacombs, are barely one tenth full. If, God forbid, any enemy (his errant brothers; the Berber tribes; the infidels) were to lay siege to Meknes now, we would starve like rats in a bucket. His ire turns to the Jews of the city: he banishes them out of the city to pray for rain, saying that if they really are God's chosen ones, as they claim, surely he will listen to their pleas. They are not to return, he decrees, until it rains.

The skies cloud over and for a while it looks as if God indeed favours the Meknassi Jewry; but then the sun breaks through once more and beats down as mercilessly as ever. There is a glut of meat in the market: in the villages outside Meknes the people are slaughtering their animals since there is no fodder with which to feed them. Some have left their homes and gone up into the mountains with what livestock remains to them, but many old folk have died of heatstroke.

Ismail has auguries cast, but the signs are hard to read. At last he declares that designated members of his court shall go out into the fields unshod, and in the oldest and grimiest garments we can lay hands on. Abid and I are sent into the poorest part of the city to buy dirty cast-offs, teeming with lice and ragged at hem and sleeve, the filthier the better. Old women selling off their husbands' clothing grab the proffered coins with fingers like talons and shut the door quickly before I can change my mind. Word soon goes round and soon I am surrounded by men gleefully stripping off their old robes in alleyways.

The next day we stand there in the morning sun, which is already burning hot even though it is just risen, having washed before first prayer, so at least our bodies are clean; but the clothes on our backs are rank and verminous, and the sultan's are the worst of all. He leads us out of the Bab al-Raïs, where the wolf's head gazes down upon us out of its empty white eyesockets. I would swear those bony jaws are smiling to see its tormentor, Emir Zidan, reduced to scratching himself like a flea-ridden dog and crying to be allowed to stay home with his mama. But Ismail is determined: all the royal emirs have been made to come, even little Momo, just gone two, whom I have had to wrest from the arms of his wailing mother. Alys cannot bear to be parted from the child even for a short while; I think it must have been nearly losing him to Zidana's wicked plotting that has made her this way.

We cross the Sahat al-Hedim and people come out of their houses to stare at us – a ragged band, led by a ragged man. Do they even know he is their emperor? It seems unlikely: they have never seen Ismail without his gold-caparisoned horses, his ostrich-fan-wielding slave-boys; his bukhari armed to the teeth. But no one says a word. Something of the solemn nature of our pilgrimage seems to touch the onlookers. Some of them must have joined the procession: by the time we are outside the citadel walls and into the hills beyond, our numbers have swelled. We go from shrine to shrine offering prayers, and all the time the skies remain cloudless and the sun beats down mercilessly. We eat and drink nothing: it is hard upon the children, but of them all Momo is the most stoic.

When we return at last to the palace, the emperor is in a towering temper and everyone is doing their best to avoid him. Some of us, unfortunately, do not have this luxury. He storms about the place, shrieking. Guards are dispatched to the matamores to remove any images of Christian saints that may be interfering with our prayers or drawing Allah's wrath down upon us. In the hammam, I manage to drop one of his slippers in a pool of water (there is, it seems, always enough water for the emperor's frequent steambaths) and stain its perfect lemon-yellow leather. He picks it up and belabours me with it most fiercely, raising welts on my neck and shoulders. I can only thank God he was not armed with anything more lethal.

That evening I follow him as he walks the harem, to decide on a partner for the night ahead. There are some European captives just brought in by Sidi Qasem's lieutenants, alongside a batch of new workers. He lingers over a pale-haired Russian, then turns sharply on his heel and goes straight to the White Swan's quarters.

Fourth 4th Day, Safar 1091
  Al ouez abiad, born Alys Swann. Converted English captive, mother of Emir Mohammed ben Ismail.

It rains the next day.

26

Alys

I remember the time when I thought I might just manage to endure my life here, those months almost three years ago when I was pregnant with my precious boy. I thought: I shall be a mother at last, and all will be wonderful. I thought it would transform everything in the world, having a baby. I was right about that; but not in any way I could have imagined.

I look from the hood of my skull out of my eyes; I look around at the other women of the harem devoting themselves to their daily round of prayer and gossip, henna and preening, as if they are benign beings, harmless and charming. But I know better now. I have seen what lurks beneath the kohl and the clay, the silks and satins, the perfume and the unguents. Beneath, all is rotting and poisonous, in thrall to evil.

And the name of that evil is Zidana.

The harem belongs to her: it is her realm and she rules it by terror. If any other than I see this they do not acknowledge the fact. They sing and chatter and fawn upon her, gather like bees around this queen: but it is not honey that is produced in this hive but vitriol. Any who cross her become her enemy, and thus the enemy of all the other women here. They mock, they bully, they ignore; they play petty tricks and spread malicious rumours; they leave only the spoiled fruit and the stale bread from the daily deliveries; they spit in the tea urns and spill scalding water on you in the hammam.

I am lucky, I suppose, that they dare do no more, though I am sure the bouts of sickness I have endured are no natural phenomena but have Zidana's collection of herbs and powders at their root. But how can I prove it? And who would listen to my complaint even if I should make it? It seems to me that Ismail is almost as much in her thrall as any other here. It is hard to countenance that such a fearsome man should go in fear of any other, but I have seen him start when he hears her voice; I have seen the look in his eyes when she touches him. Is it by magic that she holds his attention? A belief in sorcery used to run counter to everything I believed as a good Christian woman, but it is hard not to believe in it in a world that is soaked to the bone with superstition.

Magic imbues this country. It runs below the surface of things, like an underground river, bubbling up insidiously, rotting the foundations of life. People accept it as part of the everyday world: the women in the harem are forever appeasing demons, which they call djinns: leaving out food for them, using salt and kohl and iron to keep them away. They believe that Zidana can transport herself elsewhere in the blink of an eye, and Zidana encourages this belief. She boasts that she can transform herself into animals and birds, so that no one dares to plot against her for fear that she is eavesdropping upon them in the form of that lizard on the wall, that cat slinking by, that pigeon sitting overhead. It is true that she appears to know everything that is going on in all corners of this vast palace, but there is little mystery about this: Nus-Nus has told me she has spies everywhere, and pays them well.

And so I am vigilant, for myself and particularly for Momo. Zidana's sons stand well above him in the order of succession, but that does not stop her removing others out of sheer malice.

Do I make any outward show of my suspicions? No, I smile sweetly; I wish them God's peace. I look down at my hands knotted in my lap and they are the hands of an old woman: thin, veiny claws. I keep my nails long and sharp, in case they are the only weapon I have against my enemy. I read, and pray, and watch Momo like a hawk. It is not always easy: he is an active little boy, determined and big for his age. He soon kicked off his swaddling clothes and escaped his cot, and then our quarters. Turning my back for a moment, I would find him gone. I never knew a baby could crawl so fast! Sometimes I felt like attaching a string to him so that I could reel him back in from wherever mischief had taken him, and as soon as he started walking, and then of course running, it was so much worse. He is like a little djinn himself: he seems to vanish at will. Under supervision, he strides around like the emir he is, bearing his ring on its chain proudly, examining everything (though he has been sternly warned to eat nothing that does not come from my hand, or from Nus-Nus when he is with the sultan). Now that his hair has grown darker, Ismail likes him better, declares him a proper little Moroccan, despite his blue eyes. He likes to swoop down into the harem and gather him up on to his shoulders and bear him away.

To Zidana's evident annoyance, he heaps gifts upon Momo: my darling sports the gaudiest of costumes, which he adores, the brighter and shinier the better. He has retained his magpie's eye: I am always finding him in possession of some new gewgaw or another and whenever I ask him whence they come he fixes me with a guileless blue regard and tells me, 'From Dada.' But twice now I have found this not to be true. The empress made great moan a week ago about a missing pearl pendant and beat her maids most severely for its loss. I find it tucked beneath Momo's blankets; and that is not all. A great emerald-headed pin with a long, hollow shaft of silver is also hidden there, along with a bracelet of orange glass beads and cowrie shells, a miniature portrait of a dark-haired woman and a gold ring inscribed with the emperor's seal identical to the one Momo wears all the time. But it is not his own ring, this hidden treasure, for that hangs around his neck; and then I remember how yesterday Zidan's tantrum filled the harem courtyards with shouts and screams and Mamass telling me it was because he had lost something valuable. I cover the treasure-trove up with the blankets again. It seems I have been raising a talented sneak-thief.

When Nus-Nus next comes to the harem, I send Mamass away on an errand, beckon him to me and show him, wordless, Momo's little hoard.

His eyebrows shoot up; then he bursts out laughing. 'What a little Ali Baba you are harbouring!'

'What should I do?'

'Leave it with me,' he says.

He engages Momo with teasing compliments, but then exclaims that his garments — red satin trousers and a tunic of bright blue — are too dull for a true emir and require more decoration. At once the child runs away and returns some moments later laden with his treasures. One by one, Nus-Nus coaxes the stolen ones from him after discovering their provenance, and to make up for taking the jewels away, he gives my boy the great gold arm-band he wears. It is much too large for Momo's arm and he spends a long while trying to find a way to wear it: too small to put his head through, too heavy to wear on a neck-chain. At last he decides to wear it on his thigh, where it sits most oddly, and off he goes to play in the courtyard, where I can see him.

'He is a brigand!' Nus-Nus declares, almost admiringly. He promises to return the items to their rightful owners: the ring is indeed Zidan's, the miniature taken from the Venetian ambassador, as Momo was cradled in his father's arms right next to the man; the cowrie-shell bracelet belongs to one of the other wives; the hollow emerald and silver pin to Zidana's favourite eunuch, Black John. This last Nus-Nus handles gingerly, touching only the jewel at its head.

'What is it?'

He bites his lip, then explains as decorously as he can that not only does it embellish John's turban, but that it has another, less decorative purpose. He will not meet my eye. I find myself colouring from neck to crown, can feel the hot flush of embarrassment rising like a tide.

After a long, painful silence, he tucks the stolen treasures away in his robe, bids me farewell and walks quickly away. He is a kind man, Nus-Nus, and a good friend.

As Momo takes his afternoon nap, I apply myself to the copy of the Eng-lish Qur'an the corsair chief's wife gave to me when first I arrived in this country to divert my mind towards a more worthy purpose. But, as ill luck would have it, I open upon the story of Yusuf, a handsome man who is sold as a slave to an official of the Egyptian court called Al-Aziz. The mistress of the house is so struck by Yusuf's beauty that she falls in love with him and constantly bids him lie with her, one day becoming so angry at his steadfast refusal that she locks seven doors to prevent his escape and pleads for him to come to her. They race together for the door and Yusuf reaches it first, and as he does she tears at the back of his shirt. There comes into my mind sud-denly the sight of Nus-Nus toiling away at the camp in the mountains, shirtless, the sheen of sweat on his skin . . .

Concentrate, Alys, I tell myself, fiercely. But the text does not help me: 'With passion did she desire him, and he would have desired her, but for a sign from the Lord and he said, "I seek refuge in Allah! Truly, your husband is my master, who has made my stay agreeable so I will not betray him."'

I am pondering the uncomfortable parallels the tale presents when a shadow falls across me. So intent was I upon my thoughts that I am not alert to the arrival of a visitor. 'Oh!' I cry, and then, belatedly, throw myself down in prostration, for it is the emperor. The book tumbles from my lap on to the ground at his feet and he bends and picks it up. Through the hair that falls across my face, I glance upward and see him scan the text, face impassive; then the cover, turning it over in his hands. At last he tells me to rise and hands it back to me. 'What is it, this book?' he asks quietly.

And so I tell him that it is a copy of the Qur'an, but translated into my own language and printed in England, for, although I have been doing my best to master the Arabic tongue, I still find it challenging to read. All the time I watch his face darken, flushing to a florid purple, then to a forbidding black. And still I cannot seem to help myself rambling on, and start explaining that in the Bible the same story is told, though there Yusuf is Joseph and Al-Aziz is named Potiphar . . .

'Silence, woman!' he roars, and I wonder what I have said to make him so angry. Was it that I admitted to finding Arabic a difficult language to learn, or that I cleaved to my own tongue despite being at his court? Or perhaps he does not like a woman to read or, I think suddenly, maybe he does not do so himself. I seem to recall Nus-Nus saying –

'In English?' he thunders. 'The Holy Qur'an in *English*?' He rips it from my hands, drops it on the ground and stamps on it, which shocks me mightily, for Mahometans treat their sacred book with infinite respect, washing their hands before even touching it.

'I am sorry, I am so sorry!' I wail.

My cry must have woken my son, for suddenly there he is, watching in horror as his father rages and I weep. And then Momo bravely – foolishly – rushes at his father and beats at his legs with his little fists. 'Leave Mama alone!'

Ismail looks down. Then, almost casually, he swipes my boy away and

Momo goes flying across the floor, fetching up against a small carved table on the other side of my salon. Then he picks up the offending book and walks away without a backward look.

Later that evening a huge basket is delivered to my apartment. Inside are toys and jewels, cakes and pastries, a tabby kitten with a silver collar, a little suit of clothes made from cloth of gold. And on the top, a richly embellished volume of the Qur'an. In Arabic.

27

First 2nd Day, Rabī al-Awwal 1091 AH

I am returning from an errand for the empress when I round a corner in the harem and find Zidan straddled across Momo in an otherwise deserted courtyard, holding the child's head under the water of the fountain. Momo is kicking furiously, but Zidan at nine years of age overmatches him effortlessly. So occupied is the little monster in his murderous task that he does not hear my approach; and such the surge of fury that comes over me that I am able to pick him up by the back of his neck and hold him off the ground by one hand. For a moment my own strength scares me – how easily I might squeeze the life out of him there and then; and how much I wish to – but it scares Zidan even more.

Momo clambers out of the fountain and sits shivering on the tiled edge and I spy a terrible bruise on his forehead, which makes me even more furious. I shake Zidan as a lion might shake a puppy. 'I will tell your father,' I promise him fiercely. 'And if you ever touch Mohammed again I will kill you myself.' I put him down then and he just stares at me, eyes like ragged holes in his face, showing nothing but a void. Then he takes to his heels. I know exactly where he will go: straight to his mother. Well, that is something I will have to face later: for now I do not care. I put my arm around Momo's shoulders, then examine the bruise, which is a rich dark colour, like an overripe banana.

'Does it hurt?'

He shakes his head resolutely. Momo is such a sturdy lad for his age that it is easy to forget he is only three. 'You must never wander alone: the world is a dangerous place.'

He nods solemnly. 'It was only a game,' he says at last.

Such bravado! He has his mother's pride. I feel my heart swell as if he were my own. 'It was not a game, Momo, and we both know it. Now, I shall take you back to your mother and there you must stay.'

'You won't tell, will you?'

'I will not tell your mother: it would worry her too much.'

'No, I mean, you will not tell Dada?'

'Why should I not?'

'He will think me weak.'

For a long moment I just stare at him. Such wisdom in such a small boy is so terrifying it takes you aback. 'I cannot let Zidan escape unpunished for this.'

'If you do not tell, I promise I will be careful.'

'What, and if I do, you will not?'

His bottom lip thrusts out: blue fire sparks in his eyes. We hold each other's gaze and I think, this one will be quite a man, if he ever survives that long. At last, I promise.

The next day I am at the mosque with the sultan, helping him into his babouches after asr prayers, when a harem servant throws himself down in front of us, forehead to the floor.

'The empress demands your presence,' he gabbles.

Ismail grabs the boy by the shoulder and hauls him upright. 'She does what? No one *demands* anything of me!' He glares, a fearsome sight.

The child starts to cry and quite unexpectedly Ismail's gaze softens. 'For heaven's sake, Ali, don't be so feeble. Deliver your message properly.'

Ali hesitates, then looks at me. 'The Empress Zidana demands *your* presence,' he says pointedly.

The sultan raises his eyebrows at me. 'Has she forgotten you work for me?' The question is rhetorical: I keep silent. 'Well, you'd better go and see what she wants. Go on. I'll take Samir with me to inspect the works.'

Samir?

A figure emerges from the shadows of the Shoe Hall. Above a robe of white silk he wears a knitted red skullcap, and the bones of his face are sharply defined. His beard is so dainty as to appear drawn on in kohl with a fine brush. He carries inks and pens, a sheaf of paper. The look he gives me is one of undisguised triumph. The last time I saw him he was accompanied by three other thugs, intent on murdering me, and I dismantled his shoulder and sent him on his way. With sudden savagery, I hope it pains him still.

'Run along, Nus-Nus,' he sneers. 'I'll take care of his majesty.'

I want to run at him, batter those sneering features to a pulp; but of course I do not. I drag my eyes from him, bow deeply to the sultan and walk quickly out of the hall and into the late-afternoon sun.

All the way to the harem the question nags at me: how has the nephew of an executed traitor managed to worm his way back into the good graces of the sultan? And why is he here, my enemy? I cannot believe that revenge does not lie somewhere within his strategy, whatever it may be. I remember the falsified couching book, and how it has been set aright, and clench my fists against my sides.

All this at least serves to steer my mind away from Zidana's summons, the reason for which I know only too well. And indeed, when I am ushered into her presence, there is Zidan, red-eyed, at his mother's knee. He must have been at the onions, I think: even a brat like Zidan cannot cry for twenty-eight hours straight. I make my obeisance, trying to appear as calm and solemn as possible: the emperor's dignified servant.

But Zidana is having none of it. She is flanked by the other royal wives – Umelez and Lalla Bilqis – and the three stare at me like a bank of judges, as if I have committed some heinous crime upon which they are to pass sentence. Then all semblance of formality is shattered as the empress erupts from her seat, eyes bulging, spittle flying from her mouth. She shakes a tiny black figure in my face. 'See this? See this, Nus-Nus? This is your death!'

It is a fetish-doll, made of some sort of black moulded clay, its eyes small white beads with a black dot painted in the centre, its mouth nothing but a hole, as if emitting a silent scream. It wears a replica of exactly what I am wearing now: my daily uniform of a white cotton robe with gold embroidery at the neck and sleeves; yellow babouches, a white turban; even the absence of the gold bangle I gave to Mohammed a few days ago has been noted.

A reflexive shudder runs through me. Even though I have roamed the civilized streets and palaces of Europe, read the literature of a dozen other races, and given my soul to Allah, I cannot shake my Senufo beliefs, taught to me at my grandfather's knee.

Zidana lifts the doll's robe: cruelly, at the forked intersection of its lean torso and long legs, is a small male member, and no balls. She runs an orange-hennaed fingernail caressingly up its belly to its breastbone. There the fingertip hovers, then presses and a little door in the fetish's chest flies open to reveal . . .

Bile rises in my throat. What I am seeing is simply not possible. Inside the fetish beats a tiny red flesh heart. Even as I watch, horribly fascinated, it pulses rhythmically, quickening as my pulse quickens.

Zidana snaps the little door shut over this atrocity and smiles at me. 'All I have to do is to remove that, and you will fall down dead. Do not ever touch my boy again.'

She takes a sandalwood box, opens the carved lid, places my image inside. Before she can close it again, I glimpse other figures. One, unmistakable, has golden hair and is made of pale clay; beside it a small boy with blue beads for eyes . . .

I try to tell myself it is all nonsense: just Zidana's way of terrorizing people – manipulation, rather than magic. That the dolls have no power except to scare, that the organ I have seen beating within my effigy was only an illusion; but a primal fear has its claws in me and will not let go. My dreams are unnerving, and I cannot shake them.

My fears are not just for myself but also for Alys and Momo. I have always walked a perilously narrow path between the sultan and his First Wife, but I had thought matters settled between Zidana and the White Swan, if not amicably, then at least with some degree of acceptance. Now I see that is not the case. Zidana's hatred runs deep, and is implacable. One way or another she will bide her time and see her rival – and her son's rival – dead, just as she did the grand vizier: by poison, by assassination, by intrigue. Or by *vodoun*, her ritual magic. I shudder.

★

An audience is held for Sir James Leslie, the English ambassador, in the Ambassadors' Hall. The place is packed with dignitaries and functionaries in their most gorgeous dress; Ismail is attended on by a multitude of fan-waving servants. His current favourite cat – an elegantly striped madam he calls Eïda – has draped herself across his lap, utterly at ease, and surveys us all coolly through sea-green eyes. I seat myself at the sultan's feet with my writing desk and an official records book; but a moment later Samir Rafik appears, armed with a sheaf of paper and reeds, and positions himself on the other side. For a moment we glare at one another as if we would do each other to death with our pens, then I stare around at Ismail in outrage. He laughs at my expression and pats me on the head, as he might his pet cat. 'Two scribes are sometimes better than one.'

'But he cannot speak English, let alone write it!' I exclaim, sounding even to my own ears like a petulant child. 'What use is he in this task?'

'For all I care, Samir may transcribe the songs of courting pigeons,' Ismail laughs. 'If the English ambassador believes me to be surrounded by learned scholars, he will tread more carefully, and his king will treat us with the respect we deserve.'

Sir James Leslie is a tough-looking character, florid of face and stocky of body, dressed dully but properly in a blue justaucorps, ochre waistcoat and dark breeches. His wig, beneath a feathered hat, is dusty brown and reaches in untidy curls to the shoulders. He has not a ribbon in sight: a very different prospect to his feeble emissary. For some reason – or maybe because of the very contrast in appearance – Ismail takes an instant dislike to the man and beckons ben Hadou forward. 'Tell him he must remove not only his hat but also his wig, while in the royal presence, as a mark of proper respect!' The message is duly relayed. After a long and bad-tempered pause, the ambassador complies. Beneath the wig, Sir James's skull is patchily covered in a grey fuzz; he looks both uncomfortable and furious, but masters himself, and the pair exchange greetings and the necessary pleasantries required of a state visit.

Next, the ambassador's gifts, which have finally arrived, are presented; though he might have been better to have come unencumbered, for Ismail is most unimpressed by them. After the long delay – over two months – he has been anticipating all manner of fineries, the height of English luxury and manufacture. But here are bales of brocade and silk that have been spoiled by their voyage – mould-spotted and water-marked. The English muskets the ambassador has brought explode on being fired, all of which makes Ismail furious and puts poor Sir James in a not much better mood. He berates his lieutenant for not checking the muskets properly before handing them over: from the helpless look on the lieutenant's face I wonder if they thought Morocco such a backward place that modern weaponry was little known here (even though we have been bombarding the walls of their fortresses at Tangier with our cannon, and blowing up their culverts with our gunpowder for years now); or that the sultan was a play-king, rather than a warrior chieftain?

Next to be inspected are half a dozen Galway horses brought for the sultan's stable that have been selected for their fine bloodlines and the length and quality of their tails. At first glance they look handsome enough animals, and at least someone has taken the trouble to tend to them before they are presented, for their manes and tails have been combed, and their harness is polished. But they have not been tricked out in the gaudy accoutrements the sultan prefers; and anyway he is in a foul temper now, and at once declares them 'nags, fit only for the knacker's yard'.

I do not know if the slight he felt from the inadequate gifts made him change the terms he was minded to offer, but Ismail is brusque with Sir James now. The ambassador is given the choice between a half-year peace and a two-year truce. The English colonists may trade, graze their livestock, forage and quarry stone; in return for which the Moroccans are to receive vast quantities of cloth (unstained); muskets (which fire without blowing up); shot, powder and cannon. He refuses absolutely Leslie's insistence that the infidels be allowed to rebuild the old fortifications outside the town.

Sir James shakes his head. The terms are impossible, being disadvantageous to the English. He reminds the sultan that Tangier was not acquired by aggression but as part of Queen Catherine's dowry on her marriage to the English king.

This serves to heat Ismail's temper further: the Portuguese never had the right to the land in the first place, he tells the ambassador. It was never theirs to give away, along with their second-rate princess, to a pauper king.

Sir James purses his lips, but does not rise to this bait. At an impasse on the subject of Tangier, he now turns to the matter of the number of English captives held by the sultan. Ismail takes him on a tour of the building works, Samir and me running along behind him with the rest of his huge entourage, trying to take notes as he strides from site to site, pointing out the many foreign workers, all of them (it seems) French, Spanish, Italian, Greek, Portuguese. Not an Englishman amongst them. The ambassador does not believe this of course: he points to one man, then another, and they are fetched down. 'Say your name and country!' they are instructed. One by one they answer: Jean-Marie from Brittany; Benoit out of Marseilles; David of Cadiz; Giovanni from Naples.

'Where are the prisoners taken from Tangier?' Sir James demands, exasperated. 'Over two hundred members of the garrison have been taken captive.'

Ismail spreads his hands apologetically. 'Many have expired, I fear. From their battle wounds or other weaknesses. It seems the English are not as hardy as one might expect of such a warlike race. I gave those survivors I could spare to your messenger as a gesture of my goodwill and mercy.'

Sir James continues with characteristic bluntness: 'And there are at least fifteen hundred men taken from our merchant fleet and other vessels over the past few years. Scores of our ships have been seized, and their crews have disappeared without trace.'

'The seas around your coasts are known to be extremely stormy.' The sultan looks supremely uninterested. He is a good actor. I know full well where most of the English captives are: stashed away in the lightless matamore that runs beneath the Ambassadors' Hall. It is Ismail's idea of a joke. 'Some others have accepted the true faith and are now living lives pleasing to Allah. They have taken good Muslim wives and are raising good Muslim children, as freed men in my realm.'

He has one such renegade brought forth, who gives his original name as William Harvey of Hull. I recognize him, even in his Moroccan garb, as one of the captives who hurled insults at me from the palace walls on that fateful day on which Sidi Kabour was killed by the man in the red knit cap now standing three feet away from me. Harvey, without any shame, tells Sir James that he is content with his lot, that he has converted of his own free will, that he has married a beautiful black woman who is far more willing and cheerful than the wife he left at home, and that life here in Meknes is in a hundred ways better than his life as a member of his English majesty's navy.

You can see Sir James's face darkening throughout this eulogy, but he keeps his temper and eventually Ismail admits to having just one hundred and thirty English slaves, of whom seventy were taken from Tangier; and another sixty who are part of his retinue, servants to his functionaries, currently being trained in the ways of the court.

'Your majesty, I will offer fifty pieces of eight to redeem each of them.'

The sultan laughs in scorn. 'Two hundred for each man is the redemption price; more for my courtiers' slaves, if they choose to return.'

'Two hundred pieces of eight? That is preposterous!'

'I had thought England to be a rich country that valued its people highly.'

'Sir, a man's value is beyond price. But two hundred pieces of eight —'
Words fail the ambassador, who is now bright red in the face, and huffing.

Ismail is all charm. 'Think upon it more, dear sir. I shall send cakes and sherbets to your rooms so that you may refresh yourself and consider the matter with a cooler head.'

If Sir James had hoped to beard the sultan at that night's banquet, he is to be sorely disappointed: Ismail rarely eats in public — to be seen indulging in such base human matters diminishes his status, he believes. But after my duties as the emperor's food-taster I am sent to sit beside the ambassador to answer his questions about the court and generally to keep my ears and eyes open, especially with regard to ben Hadou, seated on Sir James's other side, for whom Ismail has an equivocal regard. A week ago he threw a valuable Isnik pot at the Tinker's head, shouting, 'Out of my sight, dog, son of a Christian woman!' The kaid ducked, the pot smashed, and it was I who had to clear up the shards. I forget what it was that put my master in such a temper — some days it does not take much — but the imputation that ben Hadou was the son of an infidel woman was fascinating to me. Perhaps it explains his ability with the English language. At any rate, he is seated on the ambassador's right, while I sit on the less favoured left. Of Samir Rafik, I am happy to say, there is no sign.

The table is spread most sumptuously: Malik has excelled himself. The centrepiece is an entire roasted sheep still on its spit, prepared with honey, coriander, almonds, pears and walnuts. In a dish of beaten silver there is a stew of goat's meat in a sauce of fresh green coriander and cumin; on platters of gold, chickens roasted with saffron; a fragrant couscous of pigeon and chicken studded with almonds and raisins; hot pies of soft white goat's cheese and dates; fritters and sweet pastries flavoured with cinnamon and dripping with honey; little almond cakes in the shape of a gazelle's horns and crescents, filled with crushed pine kernels and pistachio nuts and perfumed with rose water. Earlier I have eaten just a handful or two of Ismail's staple food – his favoured chickpea couscous – and so I am more than happy to apply myself to this feast with the rest: for a long time there is no sound but that of eating and praise, praise and eating.

I wait until ben Hadou leaves the table to relieve himself, then say quietly to Sir James, 'Please show no alarm at what I am about to tell you, sir: lives depend on our discretion.'

The ambassador is no stage-player: he stares at me in surprise. I bend my head to my food, as if engrossed by the task of separating meat from bone. I have noticed they have given Sir James and his retinue some newfangled eating implements, as if their two hands are not adequate. Still fiddling with the gristle, I say quietly, 'There is an Englishwoman in the sultan's harem. Her name is Alys Swann. Her people came to The Hague during your civil war, her father a staunch Royalist who fled for his life. Alys was taken captive by corsairs as she sailed from Holland on her way to be married to an English gentleman. The corsair divan made a gift of her to the sultan four years ago; she has been here ever since. She had made no effort to be redeemed: she says her widowed mother is elderly and near-penniless, and she has never met her fiancé.'

I risk a glance and find I have his attention. 'Why are you telling me this?'

'Her life is in danger here: can you help to get her out?'

'To pay her redemption price, you mean?'

'Yes.'

He laughs. 'Your sultan tried to charge me two hundred pieces of eight for a common slave: how much do you think he'd want for one of his harem-women?'

A fortune, I know. But I persevere. 'She is an English lady: is it not a shame to your country that she should be here?'

He purses his lips. 'Has she turned Turk?'

Such a coarse phrase. 'Sir, only by form of words; never in her heart. If she had not accepted Islam she would long since be dead.'

'Then I can do nothing for her, whether she turned renegado by duress or not.'

'If you do not help her, sir, I fear neither she nor her young son is likely to be alive before the year is out.'

'Well, I cannot help that. She is a Mahometan now, as is her brat. You must look to your own.'

'That is most unchristian of you. Sir.'

His eyes turn to gimlets. 'I am not used to having some bollockless nigger teach me manners!'

I try not to let my anger show. Instead, I reach across the table to a bowl of sweetmeats and offer it to him with a smile. 'Forgive me. I overstepped myself. Let me make amends: I am sure these will be to your taste, sir, they are a great delicacy.'

Mollified, he spears one on his fork, cuts it in half and pops a piece into his mouth. 'Mmm. Most delicious. What is it?'

'Sheep's testicles cooked in five-year-old grease,' I tell him with some satisfaction, and watch him blanch and dab his thick lips. As ben Hadou returns, I excuse myself and take my leave.

The next day negotiations do not start well: the ambassador has left his hat behind in his quarters but has had the gall to bring his wig with him. Ismail makes no immediate comment about this deliberate insolence, but then spitefully declares that he cannot possibly do business with an infidel who does not even have the grace to remove his boots when in civilized company. The ambassador protests that Englishmen do not do business in their stockinged feet; but Ismail is adamant. And when the boots come off we can well understand why he wished to keep them on: Sir James's stockings are in a parlous state of disrepair, having gone to holes at toe and heel. For the rest of the interview he is evidently greatly discomposed by this fact and keeps trying to hide his feet.

The discussions about the future of Tangier look as if they will be fruitless, for Ismail is in a truculent mood. At last Sir James, seeing that he is losing all chance of either peace or treaty, concedes the terms; but on one proviso. 'Sire, then I would ask you to send an ambassador of your own with me to England to meet King Charles and his advisers to discuss the matter further.'

After some consideration, Ismail agrees to this, which surprises me. It seems to surprise the ambassador as well, who clearly thinks he may have won a point and decides to press his case about the English slaves. But on the subject of the redemption price, Ismail is immovable. 'Two hundred pieces of eight for each man, or nothing.'

Sir James sighs heavily. 'And then there is the matter of the English-woman in your harem.'

'Englishwoman?' Ismail repeats, as if he is not sure he has heard aright.

'An Alys Swann, I believe.'

Sitting beside the sultan, taking notes, I bend my head and shut my eyes in despair. These Englishmen are so blunt! Do they not know it is hugely impolite to go straight at a delicate subject like this, like a bull charging through a rose garden? But Ismail appears much amused. 'In my palace's private quarters I have a thousand women, from every country in the world,' he boasts. 'There are women here from France, from Spain, from Italy, Greece and Turkey; ladies from Russia and China, from India and the coast of Newfoundland. From the jungles of Guinea and Brazil and the ports of Ireland and Iceland. And yet you would single out a lone Englishwoman?'

'She is my compatriot and I am told that her father was a staunch sup-porter of our king's late father. I am sure our sovereign would be most grateful to you if you would return her to us.'

Ismail does not even blink. 'Gratitude costs nothing. But the White Swan . . . ah, the White Swan is beyond price. But even were we to agree a sum (which of course will never happen, for she is most dear to me), the lady herself has converted to the true faith and would not wish to leave her little paradise here; nor indeed her child. Our son Mohammed stands in the line of succession in this, his country; he can go nowhere without my blessing.'

'I . . . see.' The ambassador is uncomfortable: he shoots me an accusing look. 'Well, we are back to the subject of the male captives, then . . .'

The sultan waves his hand: he is bored by all this. 'Come, Nus-Nus.' He turns his back on the Englishman, an unforgivable insult, and walks away without another word.

The next day Sir James Leslie and his retinue leave. I am one of those delegated to ride with them to the north road. As is Samir Rafik. It is hard to know who is spying on whom: even though the Tafraouti speaks little or no English, I see him watching me and ben Hadou and Kaid Omar and the ambassador whenever one of us utters a word. Sir James is curt with me and will not meet my eye. He blames me, I think, for yesterday's embarrassment. When I take my leave of him, English style, with a shake of the hand, I ask that he will pursue the matter further when he returns to England, but all he says in return is, 'The book is closed on that matter,' and wheels his horse away to take his formal leave of the kaid and the Tinker.

'What was that about?' asks Samir, his sharp face alight with curiosity.

I mask my disappointment. 'Nothing that concerns you,' I tell him shortly.

'He will never let you go, nor Momo either,' I tell the White Swan when next I have good reason to visit the harem. 'I am sorry, Alys. I tried.'

Her eyes well up. Water gathers in them, then trembles and spills, making a runnel in her kohl. She dashes the tears away angrily, as if her body is betraying her just like the rest of the world. A black streak mars her perfect face. My hand itches to reach out and cup her cheek, but she is in a temper now.

'Damn it! Damn them! Damn all men!' She looks up. 'Forgive me, Nus-Nus. I do not include you in that.'

I do not know which makes me feel worse: to be included or exempted from the general category of men.

28

Alys

For weeks now, Momo has been suffering terrible nightmares; twice I have found him walking in his sleep. Last night, I woke to find him standing in the courtyard.

I have heard that when the French king was a child a craftsman called Camus designed for him a miniature coach and horses, complete with footmen, page and a lady passenger, and that all these figures were capable of exhibiting the most life-like movements. When I called my son's name and he turned towards me with the moonlight in his eyes, he looked like one of those ingenious devices: a perfect replica of a human being, but soulless, dead and empty inside.

'Momo!' I called softly. 'What are you doing?'

He answered me like an automaton. 'I have to be ready.'

'Ready for what?'

'He is coming to kill me.'

'Who is coming?'

He did not answer me, just kept staring with his white moon-sheen.

'Darling, come with me, let me put you back to bed. You will be quite safe there.'

'No one is safe.'

I cannot help but shiver.

I got him back to bed eventually and he went straight to sleep again and did not stir till morning, but I lay awake all the rest of the night. This morning as I dress him I ask, 'How are you getting on with Zidan?'

He throws me a swift, dark look, his eyes almost black. 'He is my brother.'

'He has not done anything to you?'

His expression becomes guarded. 'No.'

'Are you quite sure?'

He nods but will not look at me.

'And he has not threatened you in any way?'

'Silly Mama. He is my friend.'

'If he does, you must tell me, Mohammed. Do you promise?'

'I promise, Mama.'

'And I am sure your father did not really mean to hurt you when he hit you that time. His mind was elsewhere. He was angry with me, you see, and when he loses his temper, well . . . he cannot help himself. But he loves you dearly, Mohammed, do not ever doubt it.'

Momo nods solemnly, though of course he is far too young to understand. He is such a brave little man, and barely more than a babe. I have to save him, no matter what it costs me, though the thought of being without him makes my heart clench like a fist.

I have a plan, a plan that came to me in my hours of staring at the ceiling these past nights. I have learned much here at the Moroccan court. I have learned craftiness and watchfulness and self-reliance. I have learned some Arabic, and not to show I know it: I have listened to Zidana as she gives instructions to her maids and tells them tales of poison. I have learned to don the second face, as Nus-Nus advised me to, to smile when I had rather spit and claw. I have learned to show pleasure when all I feel is pain and degradation: in short, I have learned to be so good an actress I could take to the stage alongside the best whores in London.

And in all this my little maid, the cook's daughter Mamass, aids me as an extra pair of eyes and ears. She has proved herself a clever spy. She looks so small and innocent, hardly more than a child herself, that tongues are left unguarded around her. She asks questions no other would dare. She has befriended the herbman's boy and, with her understanding of unusual ingredients, thanks to her upbringing in the palace kitchens, is able to chatter with him on all manner of subjects. She is a proper little treasure. And because her father is Malik, the sultan's cook, she has free run of the palace: all she ever has to say is that she is visiting her father. But she is rarely challenged: everyone knows little Mamass, with her great black eyes and enchanting, gap-toothed smile.

I send her to fetch Nus-Nus to me.

'I hear there is to be an embassy to London.'

I stare at Alys with some surprise.

'The harem may be walled and gated and guarded, but rumours do sometimes manage to penetrate these fortress-like defences,' she says.

'Yes: the Kaid Mohammed ben Hadou is to lead it. The English ambassador asked as a boon, having had no joy of the sultan over the redemption of slaves, nor the matter of Tangier, that a Moroccan embassy be sent to visit the king in London to negotiate terms further. I think he feared to be blamed for his own inability to press either discussion to a successful conclusion.'

'This, I had heard. Also, I gather that Kaid Mohammed Sharif will go, the English renegade Hamza and a dozen more.'

Sharif is a decent enough man, for all he is related to the sultan's family in some complicated way. But Hamza! The name jolts me with a sudden shock of memory: he was one of the three men who accompanied Samir Rafik in their failed attack upon me all those months back. Why has such a man been included in this prestigious embassy? A bitter taste fills the back of my throat.

'So, do you know if the dozen are chosen?'

I shrug. 'I am not privy to such information.'

'Who makes the choice?'

'Why, the sultan, of course.'

'You must ensure that he chooses you to go to England with ben Hadou.'

'Me? Ismail will not send me!'

'For my sake, Nus-Nus, can you not find a way?'

She wishes to send me away from her. At first, this is all I can think. But then I see the fire in her eyes: she is determined, driven.

'I will try, but you had better tell me why you wish this of me.'

'I want you to carry . . . a message for me.'

29

I am just about to leave the harem when Samira, one of Zidana's maids, comes running up to me. 'My mistress summons you.'

I follow her to the empress's private quarters and there find her seated in state, on a couch covered in leopardskin, crowned by a high headdress of gold with teardrops of crystal arrayed across her forehead and with a collar of cowrie shells and pearls reaching high up her neck. Her robe is of silver and purple, stiff with embroidery. In her right hand she holds a sceptre topped by the skull of some poor, fanged animal.

I make my obeisance but she bangs the staff impatiently against the floor by my head. 'Get up, get up, get up!'

When I scramble to my feet she strikes a theatrical pose, neck twisted to present her face to the sun so that all those crystals dance and flash. 'Am I still beautiful, Nus-Nus? Of all men, you of the Senufo can best judge a Lobi girl.'

Girl she is not, and complications following the last birth have slowed her down: her fat is spreading ever outward. When she moves the staff, ripples of flesh run down her arm. She has jowls now, and wattles: to be honest, she looks exhausted and age-slack. Of course, I cannot be honest. 'Madam, you are as lovely as I have ever seen you.'

'Don't lie to me, eunuch. I am old and tired and losing my charms. My husband does not call on me as often as he used to, my joints pain me and the women of the harem are becoming unruly. They sense my power is waning; they jostle for position amongst themselves, waiting for any opportunity to take my place.'

'Your sublime majesty, I am quite sure they walk in fear of you.'

She waves a ring-laden hand at me. 'I did not summon you here to seek empty compliments. I have a mission for you.'

I incline my head. 'I am at your command, madam, as ever.'

'There is something I need. From London. You must fetch it for me.'

I almost fall down. Why is it that suddenly everyone wants me to go to London? 'But, sublime majesty, I am not going to London.'

'Yes, you are. I shall talk to Ismail and ensure that you are chosen to go to England with Al-Attar's embassy. When you are there I need you to seek out that country's finest alchemists. I hear they have discovered some miraculous substance that will ensure everlasting life and youth. Pay them whatever price they demand and bring it back with you. Or, if they will not sell it, bring, by whatever means, the man who made it so he may come here to make it for me.'

'Everlasting?' I cannot keep the note of scepticism out of my voice.

'If it only gives me another ten, fifteen years of influence I shall be happy – enough to see Zidan safely to his majority and his succession secured.'

'You could ensure his succession for yourself, I am sure. You've managed to do so these past nine years.'

'He dotes upon the Swan's pale worm! Heaping the little beast with gifts and compliments. Have you seen the size of that gold cuff he has given him?'

Time to play the dangerous game. 'His father loves to spoil him. Only last week he sent a great basket of jewels and treats for the boy. He is forever carrying the child about the court with him, showing him off to visitors, saying what a fine little emir he is. I am surprised you have not removed this obstacle to your Zidan before now.'

She looks at me oddly. 'Why do you say this now? I thought you had a certain . . . tenderness for the White Swan and her brat.'

I force a laugh. 'She is a little strange, don't you think? Cold, I have always thought, and after we came back from the southern campaign, quite mad.'

Zidana laughs. 'Ah, yes, you mean when she was living like a wild sow, grubbing up the earth for her food. How Ismail can bear to rut with her any more I cannot imagine, but men can be such odd creatures when it comes to what provokes their desire.'

'I have heard there's a merchant visiting from Florence who deals in . . . medicines. They are, I believe, a most subtle race in their use of' – I lower my voice – 'poisons.'

She thinks about this for a moment. Then her eyes narrow. 'You have travelled in Italy, haven't you? And you speak the language, don't you?'

I acknowledge that this is true.

'Well, well, Nus-Nus. I think you know the sort of . . . medicine I might require. Do this thing for me and I will lift the curse I have put on you.'

Such largesse. 'Your majesty deserves only the best.' I bow my head.

Zidana is as good as her word: the next day, as I am helping Ismail robe himself after his visit to the hammam, he says to me, almost casually, 'So, Nus-Nus, how would you like to visit London?'

I do my best to pretend shock. 'London, sire?'

'Ben Hadou needs a secretary for his embassy. My lady Zidana believes that you would be best suited to that position, and I must say I think it an astute choice. Besides there is another matter that needs to be addressed.'

He thrusts an object at me. It is a book. I open the cover: the flyleaf reads: 'The Alcoran of Mahomet, Translated out of *Arabick*' – my eye skips onward – 'and Newly Englished, for the satisfaction of all that desire to look into the *Turkish* Vanities. London Printed, Anno. Dom. 1649.'

Turkish Vanities? It is as well Ismail does not read English . . .

He cuts into my thoughts. 'I want you to find the man who printed this abomination. Do you hear me?'

I nod, nonplussed. 'Of course, sire.'

'Search London and when you find him, kill him and bring me his head.'

'Kill him?' My head shoots up in shock. 'I . . . I am no assassin, my lord –'

He looks at me coolly, head on one side. 'Are you not, Nus-Nus?'

I feel my knees begin to tremble under his regard. Retract the denial, for heaven's sake, I tell myself, but cannot summon the words.

'How can any good Muslim abide an infidel defiling the holy book so? The only language in which the Qur'an can be read is Arabic, the language in which Allah dictated his final revelation: to make a translation is to make a travesty, an atrocity: a blasphemy.'

'Of course, sire, I understand that.'

He sighs, shakes his head wistfully. 'You cannot truly understand: you are not of our people. Though that is not your fault.' He takes the book back from me. 'Go in peace, Nus-Nus. I will not ask you to act against your nature.'

I stand there for a full second, not believing what I have heard. Someone, somewhere, must have worked some strange magic, to render him so amiable.

Second 5th Day, Shawwal
Lalla Zidana, born Aisha M'barka in Guinea, now Empress of Morocco, First Wife to his sublime majesty the Sultan Moulay Ismail.

The next day, just after dawn, there is a knock at the door of my chamber. I open it to find little Mamass standing outside. Wordless, she takes a roll of fabric out of her sleeve and hands it to me. 'My lady has made something for you to take on the embassy.'

'I see word travels fast.'

She beams. 'We are all so proud of you.'

I look down at the object. It appears to be an embroidered scroll, but when I try to open it out, I find it has been sewn shut.

'It is for the eyes of the English king only: a gift from the White Swan.'

I smile. 'I doubt very much I shall be in a position to give him a gift from my own hands, Mamass, but tell your mistress I shall do my utmost to carry out her wishes.'

When I seek ben Hadou a few days later, I pass a crowd of petitioners outside his official quarters and inside find the Tinker embroiled in a merchants' dispute that has clearly become very heated: some shipment of expensive French soap has apparently been stolen. The aggrieved merchant whose stock has gone missing brandishes a bill of lading that shows that his goods sailed from Marseilles the previous month and were unloaded at Salé. 'It is a nest of vipers and crooks!' he cries, beating his chest. 'And this . . . this . . . *thief*' – he points an accusing finger at the other man, long-bearded and grinning at his opponent's growing fury – 'has many friends amongst those vipers.' Spittle is flying everywhere. 'He has greased their palms –'

Ben Hadou laughs. 'I don't believe that serpents are blessed with hands, Si Hamed.'

Undeterred, the merchant continues to rant: his caravan was set upon in the Forest of Marmora by brigands, and somehow – strangely – his soap has now turned up in the souq in Meknes, where it is being sold by the Jews at premium prices. He digs in the pocket of his robe and pulls out a wrapped cake of the stuff, waves it under ben Hadou's nose. 'Pure olive oil soap, fragranced with lavender from the fields of Provence! I hold the monopoly with the Marseilles Company – so where has this come from?'

Ben Hadou takes the cake from him and unfolds the paper around it, holds it to his nose. 'Lavender? This smells to me of almonds, good Moroccan almonds.'

After a long peroration, he finds in favour of the bearded man and Si Hamed goes away swearing horribly. 'I will overlook your blasphemy,' the Tinker calls after him. Then he turns to the other man and shakes him by the hand. 'Have a box of the soap delivered to my residence, won't you?'

They exchange conspiratorial grins, and the bearded merchant leaves well satisfied. Ben Hadou turns to me, one eyebrow raised. I had always wondered where his income came from: his official salary is not insignificant, but it would never support the upkeep of two houses in Meknes and the one in Fez he is rumoured to keep, let alone the desert caravans he runs. I say nothing of course: discretion is crucial in my position. 'The sultan has asked for you, to discuss the particulars of the embassy, I believe, sidi.'

'We leave at the end of the week: have you packed?' he asks as we walk. His expression is sardonic. He knows I own practically nothing.

'I am ready, if that is what you mean.'

'Inks, reeds, a good supply of Egyptian paper.'

'Of course.'

'I hope you have suitable clothing?'

I shrug. 'I am a slave: does it matter?'

'Appearance always matters. You will be in the presence of the English king and his nobles. It is important that you are well arrayed: they will judge Morocco, and the emperor's power, by such details. If even the lowest member of our embassy is richly turned out, they will see our strength: it will bolster our negotiating position.'

The lowest member . . . I had almost come to think of ben Hadou as a friend. Foolish Nus-Nus: a eunuch slave has no friends.

We are rounding the corner into the shady colonnaded walk leading to the emperor's quarters, when we become aware of a great racket issuing from the harem: moaning and shouting, and, over the top of all the background noise, a woman's screams, on and on and on. We both stop dead and look at one another: the sound is unnerving. 'A stillbirth?' the Tinker suggests.

'Or a death.' I turn to him, my heart beginning to pick up speed. 'You go to Ismail – I'll go and see what's happened.'

He nods and strides off, glad enough no doubt not to be involved in the messy world of women that lies beyond the iron gate. I present myself to the harem guard. 'What is going on here?'

The guard – a big Asante man with a face that looks as if it has been etched out of stone – regards me coolly. 'Do you have a pass?'

'The emperor has sent me to find out what the noise is all about,' I lie.

He holds my gaze for a long moment, then stands aside to let me pass. I hurry along the walkways towards the storm of noise, knowing as I do so that I am nearing Alys's quarters, and a cold gripping of the gut assails me.

In the courtyard outside the White Swan's suite of rooms, women are weeping. I grab hold of Alys's maid, Mamass. Her eyes are swollen almost shut: snot drips from her nose. She buries her face in my robe, her entire frame shaking with sobs. I hold her from me: 'What is it, Mamass, what has happened?'

Her mouth begins to frame a shape, then wobbles. 'It . . . it . . . it's Mo . . . mo.'

'What, what about him?' But I know already. Putting the girl aside, I run into Alys's apartment. Inside, it is almost dark. The contrast between the bright winter light outside and the gloom within has me blinking for several seconds. Then, as my eyes start to adjust, I make out a tiny figure on the divan, an arm hanging limply, and Alys beside him, screaming and screaming. Her veil is torn into strips, the blonde hair beneath unbraided, disordered into a pale straw rat's nest. The face she turns to me is a mask of blood and smeared kohl out of which her eyes stare madly. For a second the keening wavers, then she takes another breath and the volume redoubles.

I kneel beside the divan and take Momo's tiny hand in mine. It is still warm. He looks as if he is asleep, lying with his head thrown back, his mouth open as if he is breathing through it. Except that he is not breathing at all. I shake him. 'Momo! Momo!'

There is no response: of course there isn't.

I run out into the courtyard, straight into Zidana. 'Has someone sent for the doctor?'

'There is no need.' She looks grave but there is a certain gratified sheen in her eyes that gives her away. 'It's far too late for that.'

'I will go. Has the sultan been notified?'

Now she smiles widely. 'Perhaps you would like that honour.'

I would not, but it's a task I have to shoulder. I run from the harem.

Doctor Friedrich's sanatorium is on the way to the sultan's apartments. I knock loudly on the door and enter without waiting for a response. A small, flayed creature lies spread-eagled on his workbench, all red and glistening. The doctor stands over it with a scalpel in his hand. He looks alarmed when I appear. For an instant I remember the beating heart in the fetish doll, then I say in a rush: 'You're needed in the harem: the little prince Mohammed is dead and his mother is likely to kill herself with grieving. I am going to find his majesty.'

Before he can ask me anything more, I am away again, running down the corridor, the slap of my feet echoing off the marble pillars.

The emperor is in deep discussion with ben Hadou. The only words I catch are 'transportable twelve-inch mortars', which mean nothing to me. They look startled when I run in, though their faces relax as soon as they see it is only me. I cast myself headlong on to the floor, hoping Ismail will not kill the messenger. 'Most sublime majesty, I bring terrible news. The Emir Mohammed, son of the White Swan, is dead.'

The stunned silence that follows this pronouncement fills the room. I can feel my overworked heart beating against the cold tiles, thud, thud,

thud. Then the sultan lets out a great cry and I see his feet go past me, a flash of gold and green, and he is out of the door. I raise my head, to find ben Hadou watching me intently.

'Not an easy message to have to deliver.'

'Indeed no, sidi,' I say, getting to my feet. 'Poor little lad.'

'His father dotes upon him.'

'As do we all.'

'Maybe someone does not dote quite as much as the rest.'

We look at one another steadily. Then I say, 'I do not know the cause of the child's death, but I saw no mark upon him.'

'Some . . . substances leave no trace, I believe.'

'Doctor Friedrich is examining the body now.'

He makes a dismissive sound. 'Doctor Friedrich is in the empress's pocket.'

I keep my face motionless. 'I know nothing about that. Look, I must go and attend upon his majesty.'

I can feel his eyes on my back until I am out of his sight.

The boy is dead: Doctor Friedrich finds no pulse, and by the time Ismail arrives Momo's body is cold. Superstition prevents him from approaching the corpse; he just stares at it as if he cannot believe the child he was carrying around the palace on his shoulders yesterday, laughing and shouting, lies there silent and immobile and will never laugh or shout again. The body is duly washed, perfumed and wrapped in a pure white shroud, then carried to the mosque and placed before the imam. I have never seen the sultan weep before, but he is inconsolable, and when the time comes for the child to be interred he declares that he cannot bear to see such beauty consigned to the earth, and so I am sent with the kaids and court officials to oversee the burial. Momo's little body is laid to rest in its narrow strip of ground facing east, towards a holy city he will never see.

Prayers have also been said at the women's mosque, though I later hear that Alys was so overcome by grief, and behaving so wildly, that it was thought best she remain in her quarters, where she roars like a beast, tears her clothes to rags and her cheeks to ribbons. The next day when I visit the harem there are still traces of her mad passage wherever I go: a shred of cloth here, a drop of blood there, as if she is such a cursed being that no one even wants to clean up after her.

My heart yearns to visit her, but when I inquire after her I am told that she has shut herself up in her apartments and refuses to see anyone – that she has quite lost her mind and reverted to her previous animal state, one that is shaming to any good Muslim, indicative of her infidel soul.

The day before the embassy is due to depart I am summoned by Zidana. She is full of good humour: it radiates from her like sunshine. The White Swan's son's death has been attributed to natural causes, a crisis of the heart from a defect he must have carried since birth, so no suspicion has fallen upon her. Indeed, Ismail spent the previous night in her company (though I have not been asked to make an entry in the couching book), and has not even asked to see Alys, she tells me with some satisfaction. It seems the boy was more dear to him than the mother.

She hands over a calfskin bag full of coin and jewels for use in my quest for the elixir she seeks; or to persuade its maker to come to the Meknes court. Her hand closes over mine as I take it. 'Thank you, Nus-Nus: for all our difficulties over the years, you have proved yourself a true friend and a steadfast servant.'

I feel quite sick as I walk away.

I have one more task before I leave with ben Hadou, which is the handing over of my court duties and the couching book. I have been dreading this: there is bad blood between me and Samir Rafik. I do not want to go anywhere near him and it is with a heavy heart that I return to my little room. But the man waiting for me there is not Samir, nor even a man, but a slight, ill-favoured boy with a pale, Fassi look to him. He introduces himself as Aziz ben Faoud, and he has had the foresight to bring with him his own writing kit: inks, reeds and portable desk. When I take him through his duties he surprises me with his deference and his quick mind. His handwriting is elegant, his ways neat and precise. He listens to every word I say with rapt attention and carries out the exercises I set him accurately and without fuss.

He watches as I find the entry marking Momo's birth and, in the space that is always left for such eventualities, add: 'Emir Mohammed ben Ismail is pronounced dead Third 5th Day, Dhū al-Qada 1091, may God's blessing be upon him.'

'Poor little boy,' Aziz says softly. I am surprised to see tears in his eyes.

When I entrust the couching book to him, he takes it in his hands with awe, strokes the cover as if it is alive, and stows it reverentially in its cerecloth. 'I will guard it with my life, sir,' he breathes. 'You will have no need to chide me when you return: I shall do my utmost to maintain your high standards.'

I do not remember the last time I was treated with such respect; but I do not feel as if I deserve it.

I said I had one more task to fulfil: in fact, the handing over of the book was my last official duty. There is one more unofficial task to perform, though the most crucial of all.

The sultan does not leave his quarters that day. So, after last prayer, instead of turning left out of the mosque to return to the imperial apartments, I am free to turn right and head out into the city.

It is eerie in the medina at night. My footsteps echo off the narrow alley walls, so that it sounds as if I am constantly being followed and I am forever looking over my shoulder. When a cat shoots out from a doorway, my heart leaps like a frightened hare. The sound of my knuckles on the door of my destination is so loud I half expect guards to come running.

Daniel al-Ribati opens the door and for a long moment we stand staring at one another. I am sure this day has taken its toll on both of us: certainly, he appears haggard, and I am sure I look no better. 'Come in, Nus-Nus,' he says, and ushers me inside. We embrace: more than friends now, we are co-conspirators, brought close by shared danger.

I do not even have to frame the question that beats to escape, for he smiles and nods towards the ceiling. Upstairs, we enter a tiny back room lit by a small candle. In the circle of its golden light lies a small shape covered by a striped blanket. I kneel beside it and take the hand that is visible on top of the covering in my own.

'Momo?'

For a tense pause there is no response, then the boy stirs, wrinkles his nose, screws up his eyes, squirms; pulls away his hand as if he would turn over and retreat back into oblivion.

'Momo!' This time he opens his eyes. For a moment they are so black and blank that I feel sure he has lost his mind in the toils of our mad scheme; then personality surges up through the darkness and infuses them with life. He focuses and, seeing me, smiles.

I have never felt such relief in all my life. I hug him tightly. Over his head I see Daniel grinning at me. 'You see, he is fine. I gave him something to counteract the datura and when he came round this afternoon he ate half a loaf of bread and a leg of chicken as fast as a starving dog. After which he slept soundly– a proper, healing sleep.'

Momo is sitting up now. His skin is so translucent he looks like a ghost of himself, which in a sense he is. 'Where is Mama?' he asks slowly, as if it is an effort.

'In the palace, still. She's . . .' I pause. 'Well enough . . .' What else can I say? He's not four yet, how could he understand what is happening here, what his mother will be going through? I must go back, I think. Somehow I must get word to her that he lives or she really will go mad with worry.

'When will she come?'

'She cannot come, yet. Don't fret, Momo. You are going on a journey with me, on a long journey, at your mama's request.'

His face, alight one moment, now falls. Tears gather, but he is too proud to let them fall. 'Very well, then,' he chokes out. 'When do we leave?'

'Tomorrow. For a few days we travel by mule train to Tangier, and then by ship to England, where your mama's family come from. It will not be comfortable, Momo, and you will need to be quiet and brave. Can you do that, for your mother's sake?'

He nods solemnly.

'Let me show you the chest,' Daniel says softly, touching my shoulder. 'Let the boy sleep: he'll be more himself tomorrow.'

I tuck Momo back in his blankets and press the tips of my fingers against his forehead as my mother used to do to me, to keep bad spirits and bad thoughts at bay. 'Rest now. I will come for you in the morning, *insh'allah*.'

'*Insh'allah*,' he echoes sleepily, and turns away.

The great wooden travelling chest is a marvellous thing. The shallow concealed compartment in its base, in which poor Momo will lie, is lined with padded fabric punctuated with discreet breathing holes in the bottom and sides. No one searching the contents of the box is, I hope, likely to suspect the existence of the hidden drawer. I have a gentle soporific for him that may ease the worst of it, but, even so, it is hard to imagine how he will prevail, poor little lad: to lie prone and unmoving for hours, jolted by mules and porters, would be a trial to even the most desperate fugitive, let alone a lively child who cannot usually sit still for a moment, and who cannot fully grasp the necessity for such secrecy. Above him will be piled the cones of salt and sugar, the bags of saffron and spices we are taking to the English king as a gift of the sultan. Fine treasures, but not so rich or rare that they will attract casual thievery or undue attention, I hope.

There is still so much that could go wrong with this venture that I have to stop my mind from running headlong down all manner of dark alleys. But for now, at least, Momo is alive and shows no great ill effect from the dangerous potion with which he was drugged this morning by Zidana's own hand, thinking she sent him to his death. The potion with which I supplied her. It is an audacious double-game I have played, forced into such daring ingenuity by Alys's growing terror for her son and the slim chance of escape afforded by the English embassy. But I could have done none of this without the good merchant. He has risked his life to help us, and for no reward other than that of friendship. For it was Daniel – rather than any untrustworthy herbman – who procured for me the potion, a decoction in large part of desert thorn-apple, that I gave to Zidana, which put Momo into a death-like state; Daniel who assured me that his friend Doctor Friedrich would certify the boy's demise; Friedrich who for the past few weeks had tested the substance on all manner of creatures of increasing size to determine the correct dosage. It was Daniel who, with his son-in-law, Isaac, shadowed the funeral procession to the burial field, lingered till all had left, removed the body of the infant from his shroud within the soft earth as the light failed, replacing it with the bones of another, nameless child, dead of the plague, and brought Momo to his own home to await me. It was Daniel who had the travelling box made by a trusted carpenter; who has supplied the salt and other goods within – these being my alibi in visiting his house, since this commission at least was official and, for once, remunerated by the Treasury.

When I leave, he presses a note into my hand. On it, in his firm hand, is written a name and an address in London.

'Whether he will help you, I know not. I did not much care for him myself when we did business together, but that may have been a cultural misunderstanding, and we must trust to his better nature.' He folds my fingers over the note, then embraces me warmly. 'Go with God, Nus-Nus. I will see to it that the box and its precious contents are delivered to the palace gate first thing in the morning, to join the rest of the embassy's cargo. I will pray for your success, and, God willing, we shall meet again.'

I never did get to say farewell to Alys.

Deciding against involving little Mamass in our dangerous plot, I sought out Doctor Friedrich and asked him to get word to the White Swan that her son was well and on his way to England. He grimaced. 'I have already risked my neck once in this affair,' he said unhappily. 'I think I have ridden my luck in this place as far as it will go.' I cajoled him, but he just shook his head and paced out into the corridor, leaving me standing in his grisly laboratory, surrounded by jars of organs, racks of flayed skins and the boiled bones of a myriad unidentifiable creatures.

On the long ride to Tangier, I think of her, tearing her hair and her clothes, acting mad with grief, not knowing whether her charade may not yet turn out to be a cruel mirror of the truth.

As we make our way across the Gharb, we are set upon by optimistic bandits, who have underestimated our firepower. They are soon made aware of their error of judgement, but even so manage to make off with four of the mules at the back of the baggage train, and that is when I see the wagon bearing my travelling box is missing and spur my horse after them, yelling like the King of Djinns. Poor Amadou, who has accompanied me, and whose leash is wrapped securely around the pommel of my saddle, screeches with outrage at this unexpected change of pace. He turns his head to me, all gnashing teeth and rolling eyes. He gets in the way of my first attempt to level my gun at our attackers and I have to push him to one side. Terror concentrates the mind and adds steel to the arm: it also makes me a better shot with a musket than I have ever been before. One man goes down with a bullet through the back of his head that clean tears his face off: I see the red ruin of it as he cartwheels off his mount in front of me. My lance takes another through the thigh and pins him, wailing, to his saddle. Amadou echoes his unearthly howl and chatters like a demon. Seeing that I am merely the vanguard of a battalion of imperial troops, the rest of the bandits ride off at speed, abandoning the stolen wagons.

Ben Hadou surveys the scene with a raised eyebrow. 'Good work, Nus-Nus. Such fervour to guard the sultan's gifts to the English king! I don't ever recall you going after the Berbers with such a vengeance.'

I hang my head and mumble something about duty, and he laughs.

'You're an example to the rest. I'm going to promote you to deputy ambassador for the course of the visit – though you'll still be called on in the role of secretary. Agreed?'

Words fail me; I simply nod. Amadou capers on the horse's withers as if it is all his doing and ben Hadou laughs. He reaches across and claps me on the back. 'Good man. I need someone I can trust. They've already saddled me with some wretched English renegade, a man well known as a trouble-maker, and there are other vipers amongst the embassy too. Watch and listen and report anything suspicious back to me. If anyone else makes you an offer, tell me at once. I shall make it worth your while.'

The Tinker is not universally liked, I know, so none of this much surprises me. He has an imperious manner that can offend, a certain impatience with the slow-witted that he allows to show a little too readily. And there are tribal feuds as well – there are always tribal feuds amongst the Moroccans. I agree to be his eyes and ears: it is always better to be ranged with ben Hadou than against him. But I am not fool enough to vouchsafe my own secret to him, because, for all his trickiness, he is loyal to the sultan and, for all his apparent amity, I know he would have no compunction in sending the little prince back to Meknes, under guard and with my head in a sack.

The city of Tangier lies in a state of uneasy truce: you can tell as soon as you see its high white walls pitted by shot and blackened by fire. All around lie ruined forts, testament to the long bombardment the colony has been under these past years. There are peasant women foraging amid the churned earth for feed for the animals that they will overwinter; as our motley cavalcade passes they straighten up and ululate a greeting from behind the veils they draw across their faces. Riders come out from the city gates to see who we are, and when ben Hadou announces himself word is sent swiftly back and soon there are English troops everywhere standing to attention in their smartest uniforms, and cannons are booming out a welcome. Relations seem so cordial you would hardly think we were at war over this port, this finger of land sticking out into the sea, almost touching the coast of Spain, dividing Mediterranean from Atlantic. Sir James Leslie comes out to welcome us. Despite his difficult reception with the emperor, he is most cordial: we are treated to a great feast and volleys of musketfire, then fireworks, which explode in great bursts of colour, fizzing over the sea. I wish Momo could see them. When festivities are at their height, I slip away and go to check on him. He has been in the box for four days with nothing but bread and dates and a little flask of water to sustain him. But the cargo is under heavy guard, and I have no authority to exert here: I am turned away firmly but politely. It is impossible to sleep that night in my comfortable quarters knowing that the little boy lies cramped and filthy in his prison. The enormity of what we undertake overwhelms me again: to separate a child from his mother, perhaps forever, to risk everything . . .

Stop it, Nus-Nus, I tell myself fiercely. Be a man.

PART FOUR

30

The ship that will carry us to England rides at anchor in the blue embrace of the bay. The vessel's sails are furled and it bobs gently on the tidal swell. a functional-looking craft. Ben Hadou is disappointed. 'Two decks and no more than fifty guns. I was expecting better from the English, who think themselves such masters of the seas. At best that's a third-rate ship of the line. We shall look like beggars, arriving in such a thing. Already, I have a far smaller retinue than I could wish.' He frets over the poor impression we are likely to make all the way through the city and out through the gate that leads down to the water. On the dock, he says grimly, 'We are of the nation which raised the Koutoubia Mosque and Hassan's Tower, the descendants of Al-Mansour, the richest man in the world; courtiers of the most power-ful ruler in Africa. It reflects badly on the sultan if we arrive without more of a flourish.'

What he means, I know, is that it reflects badly on him. Ben Hadou's pride is legendary. But at least the ship looks stout and seaworthy. When I start to say this, the Tinker waves the explanation away impatiently, and rides off to shout at one of his lieutenants.

He is still in a poor temper as we load the cargo on board. At last, exas-perated, he turns to me. 'Oversee the rest, Nus-Nus: make sure nothing is spoiled or spilled. I'll be back before sundown.' He runs across the strand, grabs his horse's reins from the hands of the boy to whom he had entrusted it but moments before, vaults athletically into the saddle (impressive for a man over forty) and makes off at speed back towards the city.

One by one, the crates or cargo are stowed in the hold, and I ensure that Momo's box is stowed in such a position that air can circulate well and it can be easily accessed once we are under way.

The sun has started to redden the clouds low on the horizon by the time ben Hadou returns, at the head of a bizarre procession. A dozen men stagger beneath the weight of two huge crates, through the bars of which fraught movement can be glimpsed. Behind them come a host of men leading . . . I frown. Surely not? But as they come closer my suspicions are confirmed: it seems that somewhere amongst the merchants who ship their goods out of Tangier ben Hadou has managed to locate and buy a pair of Barbary lions and a great flock of ostriches. The lions stare out morosely from their prisons as the ostriches (thirty! I count them) pick their way past them down to the shore, lifting their large-jointed knees high, placing clawed feet with care, their bald heads weaving comically on their long necks, ostentatious tail feathers furling and unfurling neurotically. On the savannahs the relationship between cat and bird would be as predator and prey, but here they are reduced to mere cargo – cargo that we are ill equipped to carry.

'Where on earth are we to put them all?' My question comes out almost as a wail.

'I'm sure you'll find somewhere suitable.' He is inordinately pleased with his purchases. 'The English king will never have seen anything like them,' he declares, all good humour now that he has augmented the ambassadorial gifts to his satisfaction.

The Kaid Mohammed Sharif and I exchange glances, which obviates the need for words, while ben Hadou heads off to make his cabin comfortable.

The tide turns with the rise of the full moon. I stand on deck as the crew weighs anchor and we sail out past the white walls of the kasbah, into the prowling seas beyond. I watch the moon's serene face glow palely between the clouds, silvering their edges and the inrushing waters, and think of Alys.

Soon we are out on the open sea, and ben Hadou and the embassy staff seek their beds. I linger, feigning an unsettled stomach, then go below decks to release Momo from his captivity. My plan is to stow him in my small cabin, barely more than a cupboard in the officers' quarters, but a blessing that has come with my fortuitously elevated status. There, I have made a space beneath the bunk wherein a small boy may conceal himself with rather greater comfort, and in it I have placed not only some bedding but also some toys with which he may distract himself. And of course there is Amadou to keep him company, whose chattering should mask any sound the child may make while I am elsewhere on the ship, and whose presence will enable me to explain the need for me to bring food to my cabin.

I am congratulating myself on my fortune and forward thinking as I make my way back below; until, in the cramped companionway above the orlop-hatch, I am forced to step aside to let another pass. In the golden light of my little candle-lantern, his eyes gleam, then narrow. For a second we stare at one another, then he is gone.

I watch him depart, bemused and alarmed, until the darkness swallows him. What business had Samir Rafik in the hold? He cannot know anything about Momo, so he must have been spying, or in search of treasure.

My pulse racing now, I go down the ladder hand over hand with the lantern in my teeth, fearing what I may find. One of the lions, disturbed by the light, raises a half-hearted growl and thrusts a paw through the bars as I pass (and I note that someone has pared its claws, and wonder which poor wretch was given that task). The ostriches, meanwhile, have been stowed in the gun deck, the only space large enough to accommodate them, despite the displeasure of the crew, whose berths are near by; they complain bitterly of the noise and smell and snapping beaks.

It is decided that if we are stopped by corsairs, ben Hadou will show his colours, and if by the English navy, then Sir James will see them off, and there will be no need for guns.

I locate my travelling box and peer at the lock. Has it been tampered with? There are bright scratches on the brass, but that could be down to rough handling. Inside, though, it looks as if the contents have been rummaged through by determined hands, for they appear untidy and disordered. Seized by terror, I pull the bags of spices out convulsively, cast the cones of salt and sugar down upon them with no care as to whether or not they break, gifts for King Charles or no. 'Momo!' My urgent whisper sounds as loud as a shout in the confined space.

There is no response. At the bottom of the trunk, above its false base, one of the bags of turmeric has split. Golden powder spills everywhere. Cursing, I sweep it up and set it down with the rest, then lever the base up and out of the box with as much care as my shaking hands can manage. 'Momo?' I raise the candle-lantern, terrified of what I may find.

For a moment I am sure he is dead and that the valerian on top of the datura has been fatal, for his eyes stare unblinking at me out of his gaunt and shadowed little face. Then he sneezes violently and turmeric flies everywhere.

'Nus-Nus!' He raises his arms to me.

Bending double over the box's sides, I lift him gently from his cramped and stinking hiding place. 'What a brave boy you are. How your mother would be proud if she could see you now!' I hug him to me, for he is all I have of her; and he hugs me back, for I am all he has in the world now.

Only then does he start to cry, this stoic child. I feel his sobs as a shuddering of his tiny frame and tears start in my own eyes. What are we doing? But it is too late to turn back: there is nothing for it but to grit our teeth and carry on.

At last I set him down and pile everything back into the trunk. Turning the key in the violated lock, I feel how it moves raggedly, rather than with the precision it once had, and my mind slides back to the shifty, narrow gaze of Samir Rafik. What was he searching for? What does he know? I had thought the task of getting Momo safely on to the ship was our greatest challenge, but now I see our trials have just begun.

The next day I seek out ben Hadou and discover him confined to his cabin suffering from seasickness. Usually the Tinker is a dapper man who pays a great deal of attention to his appearance; but today his hair, released from its swathes of turban silk, lies lank on his shoulders and his skin is grey and sweaty. A sour-smelling bucket sits beside his bed; a plate of uneaten food congeals on the low table. His eyes flick over me with complete uninterest. 'Go away, Nus-Nus, you look far too healthy.'

'Apologies, sidi.' I bow my head but remain where I am.

'Well, what do you want?'

'I wondered why Abdelaziz's nephew, Samir Rafik, and the renegade Hamza have come with us?'

He raises a brow at the presumption of my question. 'The sultan has given them the task of bringing back the head of some infidel responsible for printing copies of the holy Qur'an translated into English. It seems that Rafik will stop at nothing to win back the favour lost by his uncle; as for Hamza – he'll do anything for a bit of gold. I told Ismail the printer was almost certainly dead and buried, given that the book was printed thirty years ago, but he was having none of it, and Rafik was keen to show his mettle, begged for the chance to prove his loyalty, vicious little quean.' He catches my eye. 'Sorry, Nus-Nus, no offence meant.'

'None taken.'

'He's no friend to either you or me, so keep an eye on him.'

I laugh bitterly, but inwardly I groan. So it is my own fault that my enemy is on the ship, watching my every move. Had I but accepted the sultan's task . . . 'Perhaps I should put him over the side, see how well he swims.'

Ben Hadou retches, spits some thin liquid into the bucket and sits back, wiping his mouth. 'If it were that simple, it would already be done. Ismail felt guilty over the punishment meted out to the grand vizier and by showing his interest has been trying to make it up to the boy: he'll want a full report if anything happens to him. As it is, I'm probably going to have to make sure we have a suitable head to take back: the sultan doesn't stand for failure.'

'Even if the printer's long gone?'

'Even if we have to drag him back from Hell.' He manages a thin smile. 'Perhaps we can tell Ismail we traded Rafik's soul for the printer's.'

As luck would have it, ben Hadou is not the only member of our embassy struck down by seasickness. When I have not seen him for four days of the voyage, I ask casually of the renegade Hamza the whereabouts of Samir Rafik. He stares coldly at me, then shrugs. 'Haven't the faintest idea.'

As I make my way back down from the forecastle, I see Rafik, staggering across the main deck below, his legs at odds with the rhythm of the ship. He makes it to the side and hangs on to the gunwale, looking wan. I give him a cheery good day and settle myself beside him, making sure I am well to windward. 'Magnificent, isn't it, the mighty ocean?'

He shoots me a look filled with loathing and does not reply.

'The way it runs and lurches like a living creature. Up and down, wave after wave . . .'

'Shut up!'

'And our little ship bobbing upon it like a cork in a bath, tossed and pitched, up and down. We are so tiny, and it is so vast. It's a wonder we survive, any of us.'

He closes his eyes, groans.

'Seasickness is a bane, is it not? I could give you something for your nausea. I have a case of fine spices and condiments below. Cumin is said to be good, especially when mixed with mutton fat –'

'Get away from me, you black bastard!' He bends over the rail and vomits a pathetic quantity of bile out into the thrashing tide.

'Just trying to be helpful,' I say, making a good fist at sounding affronted.

The last three days of the voyage pass without incident. I spend much of my time telling quiet stories to Momo behind the locked door of our small cabin: his favourite is always Ali Baba and his thieves, and he makes me tell it again and again till I am quite sick of it. Our crossing has been blessed by fine weather and fair winds, which are rare for this time of year. I take this as a good omen and am beginning to feel almost sanguine about our venture.

When we sail towards the shadow of distant land my heart grips suddenly in my chest. England! The land of Alys's ancestry, of which Doctor Lewis had spoken so often. He had described the southern parts outside the city as a veritable garden, lush with flowers and greenery cut through by rivers and streams and bosky woods basking beneath a gentle sun, bathed by soft rain. A dream of England has filled my head these many years. I am eager to compare that dream with the reality. But the low-lying, largely featureless coastline along which we sail is uninspiring, its colours muted and dull. We drift past a great bank of shingle over which surf runs in rills, then turn our bow in towards a wide anchorage. The English sailors tell me this is the Downs, below the port-town of Deal. We put in at the dock amid a hundred or more other vessels of all shapes and sizes – merchantmen, fishing boats, a few larger ships like our own – overlooked by a forbidding fortification bristling with gun emplacements.

The ship is unloaded by a band of raucous dockers, who run away at the sight of the ostriches and have to be whipped back to work by their foremen, a scene that reminds me of Meknes. I watch as Momo's box, which I have cleaned, reprovisioned and secured with a new lock, is put up on to a cart and remember how solemn he was last night when I explained to him that he would have to re-enter his prison. I could see he wanted to cry at the very thought, but was manfully holding back the tears. 'It is just for a short time. And then we will be in London, and you will be safe.' Such an empty promise: the Lord should have struck me dead.

Sir James Leslie takes ben Hadou and his officers, including myself, to eat at an establishment close to the seafront. The meal begins with an altercation with an innkeeper who negligently offers us salted pig meat and is sent packing by a furious Sir James Leslie, who berates the man for his ignorance. 'These good gentlemen are Mahometans, fool, and do not eat pork. Go bring them your best venison pasties and be quick about it!'

The innkeeper orders his serving girl to run to the kitchens, and then takes his displeasure out on his pot-boy, whom he treats as if he were his slave, though he wears no slave-bond and is as white as he is. The lad goes about us nervous and round-eyed, bearing a great pitcher with a foaming head, taking in the unfamiliar turbans and brown skins. When he gets to me his eyes get rounder still and he keeps his distance, pouring into my flagon at arm's length, as if he is afraid that although I do not eat pig, I may well eat him. I take a sip and find that the drink is a dark, bitter-tasting stuff. 'Stop!' ben Hadou cries, having just taken a sip of the liquid himself: 'If you are a good Muslim, you will take not a drop of this: it is alcohol, and forbidden.'

In response to this, the renegade Hamza downs his flagon with several loud gulps. 'In this country it is considered ill mannered to turn your nose up at their beer.'

The Tinker gives him a long, flat-lidded stare. 'You are a turncoat and an apostate: we do not expect the same level of good behaviour from such a one.' He reminds the rest of the members of the embassy that we are to uphold the best values of Islam while we are in this country: that we are the examples by whom our sultan will be judged by these unenlightened infidels, and we must at all times behave with modesty, moderation and good manners. 'You will not eat or drink the things that are forbidden by the Qur'an; you will keep a civil tongue, honour the name of Allah and lay no hands, nor even lascivious eyes, on the women.'

Several of the men exchange disappointed glances at this pronouncement.

Two days later we arrive at our destination. Night is falling and it is glacially cold. As we approach the wide River Thames, I can feel the hairs freezing in my nose. There is a brisk north wind blowing, and the grass over which we ride is crisp with frost: it is like being in the High Atlas in winter. We come in to London from the east through the marshes and, when we strike the main highway into the city, are passed by many horse-drawn carriages, the like of which I have never seen. All the Moroccans are staring about them in frank wonder as we pass beneath the archway of the Ald Gate between its two crenellated towers into the city proper. Ben Hadou catches us gawping and declares crisply, 'The Bab al-Raïs is far superior in its craftsmanship: this gate is very plain and poorly made by comparison.'

We cross the great river over a long bridge lined by tall buildings that narrow the roadway to only ten feet or so, thus herding us all together and making the sounds of our horses' hooves and the rumble of the cartwheels loud in our ears, whilst affording only brief glimpses of the dark ribbon of water to either side. In the middle of the bridge there rises a fantastic structure replete with turrets and cupolas, its intricately carved façade gleaming with gilt. Upon sight of it, ben Hadou declares, 'This must be the king's palace!'; at which the man riding beside me – a solid fellow in his middle years with as much grey as colour in his hair, who has told me his name is John Armitage, and that he is happy to be home after five years of being stationed in Tangier – guffaws and, raising his voice, explains it is just Nonsuch House, over a hundred years old, and no more than a fancy gatehouse, which effectively silences our ambassador.

The city into which we pass on the northern side of the bridge appears very alien to me, with its wide thoroughfares, and towering stonework grey-white beneath the rising moon: very different to the dark, dank, smoky hell Doctor Lewis had once described to me. And everywhere, this being, I gather, a Sunday and therefore the English holy day, there is the sonorous clang and peal of bells, a sound never to be found in any Muslim city, since Mohammed deemed bells to be the Devil's pipes. In general, London bears little relationship to my past experiences of European cities – Venice or Marseilles, with their winding canals and alleyways and smart merchants' houses; though here and there I catch a glimpse of Florence or Bologna in the porticoes and columns of the great buildings. But after a while it strikes me that there are similarities with our own Meknes here, for a great deal of demolition and building work appears to have been going on. I ask John Armitage the cause of so much activity.

'There was a fire,' he explains. 'Fifteen, sixteen years back. It destroyed whole swathes of the city – hundreds of streets and churches, thousands of homes. I remember how it was before, dark and teeming, rank with sewage and rats. They have worked wonders, Mr Wren and Mr Hooke, under his majesty's guidance.'

In comparison with the dark labyrinth of Fez and the busy passages of the Meknes medina, this is a very different world: spacious and unfussy. I find myself wondering what sort of king he must be, who rules over this great modern metropolis. Well, soon, I imagine, I shall find out.

31

10th January 1682

We are quartered in the royal palace of White Hall, an immense maze of a building containing, we are told, nigh on two thousand rooms. While we await the formal reception with the English king, which is to occur the next day, ben Hadou bids us all to keep to our chambers in case we embarrass him by succumbing to foreign temptations or misbehaving ourselves in ignorance of the customs of the court here.

The view from our window is fascinating to Momo: he climbs up beside me on the chair with a compliant Amadou in his arms, and I point out to him the people and animals in the park beyond the Tilt Yard and the horse guards' exercise square. There are lots of people out there parading up and down amidst the pretty trees and flowerbeds, and all manner of beasts wandering the grassy meadow beside the lake – sheep and dogs, cows and goats.

'Can we go and see them?' Momo pleads.

'Soon,' I promise, and hope I do not lie.

I wash him using a bowl of fire-warmed water (last night I had foolishly asked a servant whether there was a hammam at the palace I might use, explaining that I wished to bathe, and was stared at in amazement. 'There is a bath in the queen's chambers, but no other may use it. You might arrange a visit to the Streatham Spa or to Bagnigge Wells, I suppose; and the king in summer swims in the Thames, but . . .' He faltered, then bobbed his head, made an excuse and went running off down the corridor as if he had encountered a madman). Then I put Momo to bed, tuck the coverings around him and wait till he sleeps. Only then do I take out my leather satchel and check through the contents. Sewn into the lining for safekeeping is the embroidered scroll made by the White Swan that I was given by little Mamass. Taking my dagger, I slip the point carefully through the stitching and remove it, then turn the roll of fabric over and over in my hands.

The temptation to keep on with my clever dagger and unpick the stitching that sews it closed is high: now that we are safe in London what harm could it do to peep inside? I can feel my fingers itching to cut through those neat silk locks; I am, I reason, a fair hand with a needle myself, and have with me the small repair kit I always carry — I can sew it up again after looking. The lady has, after all, entrusted me with her son: what secrets can there be between us? After long seconds of indecision, I chide myself that if Alys has not seen fit to vouchsafe its contents to me, I must attempt to deliver it unmolested, since the information within is not for my eyes. Others, I am sure, would not be so scrupulous. Now, where to hide it, as much from Amadou's wicked little fingers as from any other threat? I could carry it on my person, but that would mean changing my robe for one bearing a pocket, or tucking it next my skin or inside my shoe, which would seem a churlish and disrespectful way to treat an object destined for the king's hand. At last I slip it back inside the satchel and sew up the lining once more with long, careless stitches. Perhaps it is safest always to carry the bag with me.

To this end, I remove all those items which will weigh it down unnecessarily: spare clothing for Momo, my copy of the suras, a cake of French soap that ben Hadou had kindly given me and that I cannot bring myself to use, it is such a luxury, a spare headcloth, a rolled pair of linen breeches, some leather socks. A little bag of dates and nuts with which to keep Amadou quiet. In the bottom of the satchel, beneath my pouch of money and Momo's little stash of jewels, I come across the scrip of paper Daniel gave to me and look at it long and hard, deciphering the unfamiliar hand. Might I risk the ambassador's wrath by leaving the palace to seek out the man whose name and address are written here? Golden Square, a rich and royal address indeed, which must surely lie close by: how hard could it be? Even so, dread gnaws at me, and I tuck the scrip away again in the bag.

Amadou, sighting the treats, chatters at me and paws my robe. Rather than have him wake the boy, I take out some dates and peanuts and put them on the windowsill. He capers after them and leaps up to squat upon the sill, and applies all his concentration to shelling the nuts. This reminds me that I have not eaten since dawn. Locking the door, I go to find something to eat.

Downstairs, the public rooms are much grander than our apartments, with high corniced ceilings, and walls covered with colourful tapestries and paintings of great men and women and scenes from stories – another strangeness to the members of our embassy, since the depiction of the world in any terms other than abstract ones is forbidden under Islam. Distracted from my purpose, I find myself drawn to an immense portrait, Italian Renaissance, vivid with colour. I am standing rapt beneath its ornate golden frame, taking in the glorious hues, the face of the Virgin translucently pale, gentle in repose, her blue eyes fixed adoringly on the child in her lap, and thinking of Alys and the child sleeping in my locked chamber upstairs, when a voice behind me says, 'Beautiful, isn't it?'

Without thinking, my thought pours out, 'She is so sad: she knows already she is destined to lose her son.'

'Od's fish, sir: that's a distinctly gloomy interpretation of such a pretty scene.'

I turn to find a tall, saturnine man behind me regarding the painting with a lugubrious expression on his heavy face. He is well advanced into his middle years, but his hair is as black as night, his moustache too. Too dark to be an Englishman, I think: Spanish, perhaps, or Italian? He is dressed in a simple suit of burgundy cloth with a plain linen shirt beneath and is attended by two small red-and-white dogs and three young ladies garbed in a most becoming, if immodest, fashion, the swell of their round white breasts provocatively displayed.

Tearing my eyes away from this distraction, I return to the painting. 'See the downward turn of her mouth,' I find myself saying. 'And look at the angle of her eye, gazing away past the child into the distance. She's looking into the future and seeing his death.'

He laughs, a deep baritone, rich and warm. 'You mean, unlike any usual new mother, who has eyes only for the babe in her arms and gives not a fig for the rest of the world, let alone her poor man?'

One of the women raps him lightly on the arm with her fan. 'Oh, Rowley, I never turned you away once, and you know it.' She comes closer to look up at the portrait. 'Don't she look sad? I never really looked close up before. Perhaps Mr Cross should have painted me as the Blessed Virgin, rather than as silly Cupid. My poor little Charlie, he was only twenty-seven when he passed on last year; even Christ got six more years than that.'

Scandalized, the other women tut and shush her, but all this seems to achieve is to goad her further, for she turns to me and peers at me lasciviously. 'Od's fish, but you're a big 'un!' she declares, mimicking the man's deep tones. Her gaze is as sly as a cat's, and she is clearly not as young as I had first thought. 'And as black as ink. Tell me, sir, are you that same colour all over?'

Her companions titter loudly and flutter their fans.

'Now, then, Nelly,' the man chides her. 'Leave the poor chap alone: he is here to spend a quiet, appreciative moment in the company of the sacred Madonna, not to be the butt of your profane and teasing ways.'

She drops a mocking curtsey. 'Begging pardon, my lord.'

My lord? The man raises a sardonic eyebrow. His eyes – large and liquid and as dark as onyx – take me in from my white turban to my yellow Fassi slippers, and whatever he sees seems to amuse him mightily.

'Forgive me, Lord . . . Rowley.' As I would in the Moroccan court when in the presence of one far more exalted than this slave, I prostrate myself with as much grace as I can muster, and at once one of the dogs comes and snuffles at me curiously, its bulbous brown eyes slick with light, its nose wet against my face. It has been eating something so pungently unpleasant that I am forced to hold my breath.

The women break out into peals of laughter now, and I wonder if it is because of the dog, or me, or some other unrelated thing.

'Come away, Rufus!' the man calls, and the beast retreats. There follows a long, profound silence in which all I can hear is my own blood beating in my ears, then the sound of heels clacking away over a stone floor. I raise my head, just an inch, and turn enough to see the company walking away on the other side of the room. I push myself slowly up on to my knees and watch them disappear, chattering merrily. How rude, I think. But maybe I have given offence in some way: it is true, as ben Hadou said, that we do not understand the customs of the court here.

Feeling rather cross, I go in search of food and resolve to keep to my room until I know better how to comport myself in this strange place.

The next day the embassy is to be formally introduced to the king at a reception at the Banqueting-house. Ben Hadou frets when informed that he cannot bring the lions and ostriches and other gifts with him; these may be presented at a private audience only, since today is a day of formal cere-mony. And so, it seems, all his plans for a grand entrance are thwarted; again, he is thrown into a black humour and keeps us all waiting as he pays extra attention to his costume for the event, and certainly when he eventu-ally makes his appearance – heralded by a fragrant cloud of frankincense – he does look most splendid, in a robe of rich crimson silk, embroidered in gold at sleeves and hem and neck, with a white woollen burnous thrown over the top, and a red turban wound around with pearls. At his side he wears his scimitar of damascened steel in a scabbard of leather and gold thread; on his feet kidskin babouches glittering with jewels. We have all done the best we can with our djellabas and whatever jewellery and per-fumes we own, but he puts the rest of us to shame. Which, I am sure, knowing the Tinker's pride, is his intent.

Carriages arrive to deliver us there in style, but we have no sooner boarded them and travelled a short distance than they come to a halt and we are at our destination. As we arrive, I understand why it would have been impossible to walk the short distance up the King's Street from our palace apartments to the impressive, pillared façade of the Banqueting-house. Huge crowds have gathered, filling the wide thoroughfare to the Holbein Gate and beyond, all craning their necks and surging forward, curious to see the exotic foreigners from far Barbary, the monsters who have all these years been abducting their countrymen to use as slaves, who have had the temerity to bombard the Tangier colony and kill their soldiers by the hun-dreds. When the carriages draw up, the mob presses forward, threatening to overwhelm the scarlet-coated ceremonial guards with their gleaming hal-berds. The smell of the mob – which permeates even the Tinker's strong frankincense – impresses itself on me almost as much as the imprecations they cry. Does no one wash in this city? The combination of the stench and the noise is overpowering, frightening.

'Black bastards!' I hear, and 'Heathen savages!'

'Murderers!'

'Rapists!'

'Barbary devils!'

I turn to Hamza and shout over the tumult, 'They are baying like hounds! I believe they would tear us to pieces if they were able. Do they really hate us so? And can you imagine Ismail standing for such behaviour?'

He grins wolfishly. 'As well that Ismail does not rule here. The English cut the head off their last king – outside this very building.'

He pushes past me and I am left staring after him in shock, wondering what a sort of country we have come to that could enact such popular savagery. It must be a most unstable place indeed. And then I think of Ismail's own words: 'My subjects are like rats in a basket, and if I do not keep shaking the basket they will gnaw their way through.'

Protected by the yeomen guards, we are led into a vast hall teeming with people dressed in flamboyant clothing: men in the main chamber, women leaning down over the galleried balconies to peer at us with no less curiosity, but rather more manners, than the populace outside. I had thought the Ambassadors' Hall at Meknes a grand venue, but this outdoes it a dozen times over. I gaze around at opulent tapestries adorning the walls; the dozens of tall, fluted pillars; the blaze thrown off by thousands of sconces and candles, the glitter of jewels on hands and ears and throats. The ceiling is divided into lozenges of riotous colour wherein some giant has painted vast scenes of heroic figures girded with flowing draperies, crowned kings and naked cherubs, all garlanded about with gilt flourishes and festoons. I look down again, feeling giddy, just as a hush falls across the chamber. The doors to either side of a great canopied dais now open, and out of them issue from one side a small, mousy woman whose teeth stick out at a most unfortunate angle and from the other a tall, magnificent gentleman. The man walks to the front of the dais and, taking the little woman by the hand, leads her to the two thrones set there, beneath a crimson canopy. She sits down in one and he in the other, and I begin to feel a little sick, a little faint, as I take in those lugubrious dark features, the black hair and moustaches of the man I encountered the previous day. It cannot be, surely? The man I saw yesterday was most plainly dressed, rather than in this extraordinary effusion of silks and frills, and without doubt this kind-faced lady with the rabbit teeth was not amongst the women who were with him, chattering so gaily and flaunting their soft white bosoms. I stare and stare, but there can be no mistake. The man with whom I traded words yesterday as with an equal is the king of England himself. And there, by his side, the queen, his wife, once Infanta of Portugal, Catarina of Braganza, by whose dowry Tangier came to be in English hands.

I am torn out of my appalled reverie by the sudden appearance of a court official in front of me. 'Who is the translator here?' he demands.

Hamza and I both claim the role at the same moment, then glare at one another. Ben Hadou raises his voice. 'I am the ambassador: I speak good enough English.'

'Excellent. Then you may inform your retinue that for the insult shown to Sir James Leslie in Morocco by your king, they are to divest themselves of their hats and footwear and approach the throne bare-headed and shoeless.' And with that terse instruction, he turns on his heel and marches back into the chamber.

I look at the bands of pearls threaded with such care through the crimson folds of ben Hadou's turban before my gaze drops to his darkening face. Suppressed fury emanates off him in waves as he unwinds his elaborate headwrap; when we are ushered through into the receiving chamber, he stalks all the way to the throne straight-backed and haughty, and neither bows nor makes any sort of reverence, which causes the English king to raise a thick black brow.

To be truthful, I can hardly remember what passes during the ceremony, so overcome am I not only by my horrible misstep of the day before, but also by a nagging terror that, having squandered the perfect opportunity to pass Alys's message into the sovereign's hands, I will probably never be afforded another chance. All I know is that during the Kaid Mohammed ben Hadou's extremely long peroration – greetings from His Majesty Sultan Abul Nasir

Moulay Ismail as-Samin ben Sharif, Emperor of Morocco and the ancient kingdoms of the Tafilalt, Fez, the Sus and Taroudant, to the exalted King of England; wishes for the extended good health of his body and his soul (including a detailed comparison by the sultan himself of those points in the Muslim religion and that of the Protestant English in which the two faiths share some correlation, thus making them superior to the beliefs of our shared enemy, the Catholics) . . . and on and on – King Charles's bored gaze slides past ben Hadou and connects with my own and I feel as if a small lightning bolt has passed right through my eye socket and is rooting me to the ground. His lips quirk, then one of those heavy lids droops in what might have been seen by others as no more than a twitch, but which looks remarkably to me like a wink.

Days pass in which we see neither skin nor hair of the English king, but only a succession of dull court officials, sent to take statements of intent regarding the matter of the Tangier garrison and its proposed rights and safeguards; then others to discuss the fate and possible redemption of certain named prisoners they claim are held by the sultan, none of whom either ben Hadou or I have encountered and are likely either to be dead or gone missing, or perhaps to have apostasized and adopted Muslim names.

When we do next see King Charles it will be at a private audience in his own state apartments. Is this to be my chance, I wonder? I tuck the embroidered scroll into the pocket of my robe in case a quiet moment presents itself. Ben Hadou preens anxiously in front of the mirror, concerned to make the best impression. He is a well-looking man, I will admit: fine-boned and fair of complexion (compared to me), with a good carriage and bright, intelligent eyes. He has trimmed his beard and moustache very close, the better to show his long jaw and full mouth; already I have noticed the ladies of the court paying attention to him, and I doubt not that he has noticed them too. This is his moment to present the gifts we have brought. These sundry items have been assembled in the vestibule below and are being brought up the long flights of stairs with great difficulty and, in the case of the livestock, with no little mess. The lions, at least, are safely left outside in a garden for the monarch to peruse at his leisure, otherwise I suspect there might be carnage.

'Private' turns out to mean a vast chamber stuffed with courtiers, including dozens of ladies crammed around the edges to watch the Moroccan contingent with avid eyes. First, we present the traditional gifts of spices, salt and sugar; the silks and brass sconces, perforated iron lanterns and hand-woven rugs from the Middle Atlas rendered up to the sultan as tribute by the Berber tribes. The king accepts all these with genuine gratitude and compliments the fine handiwork of the tribeswomen. I can see the Tinker's chest swelling with pride but I cannot help but feel a niggling worry. Other than the king's own little dogs, I have seen no animals wandering this elegant palace with its liveried servants, gilded chairs and expensive carpets . . .

'And now,' he intones, 'a special gift.' He claps his hands and in come the ostriches, bustling past their handlers, necks weaving, beaks snapping wickedly. One woman in a green silk gown is standing just a little too close, and the shriek she gives out as she gets nipped sets the entire flock booming and whooping, their hairy throats inflating alarmingly. Then they are beating their wings and stamping those great clawed feet, and pandemonium ensues. Courtiers flee through whichever door they can access: I even see one man fling back a drape and climb out of the window.

I look for the king, and find him roaring with laughter. He rescues one poor woman and shoos away the bird that is attacking her. At last guards are called for and the ostriches are corralled in an antechamber and thence removed to one of the royal parks, leaving behind them bespattered carpets, bitten limbs and a miasma of floating down. The reception is brought to an abrupt end.

Returning rather sooner than might have been expected to my room, I disturb a furtive figure outside the door. The figure turns, sees me and runs the opposite way down the corridor. But not before I have made out the sharp, unfriendly features of Samir Rafik. Heart thumping, I examine the lock: scratched but not otherwise damaged. When I fit the iron key into it, it opens smoothly. Inside the room, there is an eerie quiet. 'Momo?' I call quietly. 'Amadou?'

A screech: then something launches itself at me from the top of the bed canopy and the monkey lands on my shoulder. A face appears over the top of the canopy, eyes solemn.

'We were just playing.' Momo swings himself over the edge of the bed-frame and climbs as nimbly as a monkey himself down the post. 'It's boring being stuck in here, having to be quiet all the time. Why can't I go outside? You said things would be different when we got to England. You lied!'

I sit down on the bed and stare at him unhappily. 'I know. I'm sorry, Momo. It's just for a little while longer. But you mustn't make any noise, and you mustn't open the door to anyone but me. You do understand that, don't you?'

'Someone knocked on it earlier.'

'It was probably a servant, come to clean the room. I told them I would do it myself and that it was best left closed, since my monkey can bite.'

'I can bite too.' Momo reveals his teeth, then giggles. 'We can both bite, can't we, Amadou?'

The pair show each other their teeth in a display of mock-challenge, gums bared, heads shaking, presenting a disturbing mirror image. I begin to fear that if I leave the boy here much longer with the ape it will be hard to tell them apart.

'Open the door to no one,' I reiterate. 'Even if they pretend to be me.'

'Why would anyone do that?'

'I don't know,' I admit. 'But just don't open the door.'

'But what if there's a fire, or a flood or something?'

'There won't be.'

'There might be. It's not impossible.'

I sigh. 'There might be. But it's very unlikely. And if there is, I will save you.'

'Do you promise?'

'I promise.'

'You promised we'd be safe when we got to England,' he reminds me with impeccable logic.

'Momo, I'm doing my best.'

But I must do better: he is right to prick my conscience so. With a sigh, I reluctantly retrieve the scrip of paper and peruse once more the address

283

which Daniel found for me. It is not a task I relish, but it must be done.

With new resolve, that afternoon I seek out one of the servants and ask how I may send a letter. He looks at me sceptically, curls his lip. 'For your master?'

I give him a hard look: clearly he thinks such a one as I cannot write. But maybe if he thinks it is for the ambassador it would be better. 'Yes. To Golden Square.'

'For a few coin I can send a runner with it; or you could take a sedan chair and deliver it yourself. It's not far, only a mile or so.'

We are forbidden to leave the palace, but a mile — that would take no time to walk, ten minutes or so, and quicker with my stride than in one of those silly boxes. I could be back within a half hour, go during the time when ben Hadou and the others take their siesta. No one will know. I obtain directions from the serving man, then return to my room and change my court slippers for my old babouches and fling a dark burnous around my shoulders. With the hood up the mirror shows me a relatively nondescript figure, apart from the darkness of my skin, about which I can do nothing.

I walk quickly up the broad thoroughfare of King's Street, and before reaching the Holbein Gate cut leftwards into St James's Park, keeping my head down and my hands inside my cloak. Even so, I draw inquisitive looks from the people I pass; perhaps for the very speed of my progress, since they are all dawdling along, enjoying the elegant vistas, laughing at the birds slipping as they cross the ice on the lake to find open water. Gods, but it is cold! My breath issues out in great puffs of steam as my path leads me into a deer park. The animals, which have been bending their heads to the frost-crisp grass, raise them now and eye me warily. I imagine bowmen approaching quietly as I have done, to take one for the king's table: it is no wonder they are cautious. If I make a sudden move, they will be off across the park like gazelles, I am sure of it. Walking slowly, I skirt the area, sensing a certain fellow feeling with the beasts: such perceived freedom is in reality no freedom at all. We both belong to powerful men, the deer and I, and our time may come to an abrupt end whenever they will it.

I come out on to a paved path that takes me through some pretty parterre gardens and thence on to a wide road thronged with carriages and other traffic. Dodging amongst the pedestrians, horses, sedan chairs and coaches, I reach the other side and continue north through narrower streets, as instructed. The area becomes dirtier and meaner, strewn with rubbish and stinking of ordure. Pungent liquids flow in the gutters: the acrid stench is unmistakable. The tanneries in Fez smell better than this, I think to myself; I must surely have missed my way. A groom is inspecting a horse for a thrown shoe at the junction. 'Excuse me, sir,' I say, and he straightens up, startled. 'Can you tell me the way to Golden Square?'

He points towards an area of waste land much littered with rubble. 'It is just to the north of So Hoe: keep going up James's Street, past the old windmill and through Dog Fields, till you see much new building work, and you will find yourself there.'

A number of tall dwelling houses rise proudly amidst others half built and still others with barely the foundations laid. You can see that when the work is finished it will be an impressive sight; but for now it is neither golden nor truly a square but more like our Sahat al-Hedim. I find the address on the scrip and approach the door of Number 24. A brass bell hangs outside – a bad omen for a good Muslim – and this I ring. For a long time there is no response, then the door opens a crack and a face peers out. 'Coal deliveries around the back,' a woman says sharply, and shuts the door hard in my face. When her misunderstanding finally dawns on me, I rap loudly on the wood. This time the door opens wide and fast. 'I told you once –'

Now I have my foot in the gap. She stares at me, confused, then looks down and sees my foot. 'Get away, you black beggar!' she shrieks in outrage.

'Look, I have business with this gentleman.' I show her the paper, which she stares at uncomprehending.

Then: 'Help! Thief! Murder!' she cries. Arms grab me from behind, am I am wrestled to the ground. My attacker tries to set a knee on my chest to keep me there, but I twist and roll away, catching his standing leg as I do and bringing him down heavily; then he swears and labours to his feet. We stand there, huffing in the chill air, regarding one another warily. He is barely more than a boy, though built like a bull. 'I am no thief, nor any murderer. I am just seeking a Mr Andrew Burke.'

The woman comes out on to the step. 'Well, why didn't you say so?' She is red-faced and frowsty in a stained apron over a sturdy fustian gown. 'This is Mr Burke's house.' She frowns, waves the boy away. 'Off you go, Tom, there's a good lad.'

Tom looks disappointed, as if he had been hoping for more fisticuffs.

'And is the gentleman at home?' I press.

'Tell me what your business is.'

'I'm afraid I can share that information only with Mr Burke himself.'

Her mouth folds in upon itself. 'Wait here.'

Long minutes pass after she closes the door but at last a man comes out. He is not as I had pictured, being almost as fat as the grand vizier, and sporting a large black beard.

When he sees me, he too looks bemused. 'What can I do for you?' he asks, then sudden comprehension strikes him. 'Ah, you must be from the duchess.'

I shake my head. 'I know no duchess.'

'The esteemed Duchesse Mazarin?'

Again, I shake my head. I start to speak, but he cuts me off.

'Extraordinary: you're the spitting image of her blackamoor. You must be here for Mr Qallaah's serge, then?'

'No, I'm here –'

'Not the Syrian merchant's man come for his livery cloth either?'

I speak forcefully, before there can be further inquiries. 'No, sir. I have come from Morocco on a more delicate matter. Perhaps we might speak inside?'

'Morocco?' He looks alarmed. 'What business could some negard from Morocco have with me?'

'I come on behalf of Miss Alys Swann.'

'Who?'

This is not going quite as I had thought. 'Your . . . ah . . . fiancée.'

Now he looks appalled. 'Fiancée? Sir, I have no such thing, you are quite mistaken.' A pause. Then: 'Oh, the Dutchwoman. Of course, I never met her, and I believe the lady concerned was lost at sea.'

'Actually, sir, she was not.' I explain the bare facts, watch his mouth drop open.

'How the hell did you find me? And what in God's name do you expect me to do about it?'

'The merchant Daniel al-Ribati gave me your address,' I inform him stiffly.

His face changes. 'Oh, the Jew, of course: we have done a certain amount of business over the years. A decent man, despite . . . Well, no matter, I am sorry for the poor woman, but when I thought her dead I sought and found another bride and we have been married now these past three years. We have two boys already.' He spreads his hands. 'So, as you see, Miss Swann's affairs are no longer any business of mine.'

'And her son?'

'What would my new wife want with the bastard of some heathen king under her roof? This is no charity home for foundlings! Good day, sir.'

This time the door is shut for good.

I have to admit that my heart is unaccountably lighter as I retrace my steps to White Hall. Is it selfish of me to be glad that the graceless draper plays no part in Momo's future? And as for the idea of Alys married to such a brute . . . Well, perhaps her life would have been easier than in the Moroccan court. But she would only have been a different kind of prisoner in this place.

Now what is to become of Momo? I am at a loss.

32

Days pass filled with ever more frustrating meetings with civil servants and politicians about Tangier. They are half-hearted and ben Hadou is evasive: it is clearly a waste of everyone's time and it is all I can do neither to fidget nor to fall stone asleep: there is precious little of use to minute. One councillor even goes so far as to say that for all he cares we should keep the wretched place. 'The king may insist it is the brightest jewel in his crown, but we cannot keep on fortifying such a far-flung outpost; it is a hotbed of Popery and a terrible drain on the country's resources when the Exchequer is already overstretched. As it is, we are taking austerity measures: even the king is cutting down at his own table, and his wife and . . . ah . . . lady acquaintances.'

If I had hoped to see the king at one of these meetings, I was to be disappointed. After my initial chance meeting, I have spied him only at a distance, and now he has gone hunting, we are told. Ben Hadou is disappointed not to have been invited. When after several days of being confined to the palace he talks longingly of riding, one of the courtiers suggests that we might arrange to take mounts for the day from the king's stable and ride in Hyde Park. The Tinker immediately sees an opportunity to make an impression. He invites the courtier and any others who might wish to accompany us to view a Moroccan 'fantasia'. 'We shall show them what real riding is all about,' he says to me with relish, and sends me off to change into appropriate clothing.

I return wearing a white robe and cotton qamis and babouches, with my burnous over my shoulder. Ben Hadou comes down arrayed all in orange and red, a tight tunic worn over a huge-sleeved cambric shirt, an extravagant scarlet cloak, red leather boots, a jewelled turban. He looks magnificent, like a prince out of the *Thousand and One Nights*; and when he sees me he tuts. 'For heaven's sake, Nus-Nus, is that the best you can do?'

'It's all I have.'

'Well, it's not good enough. This is our chance to give the English a true taste of Morocco.' He stands beside me: there is a good three inches difference in our height, but that does not seem to deter him and he sends a servant to fetch some other clothing. Soon I am turned out in blues and greens with a mass of gold embroidery, and looking most resplendent, though the trousers are uncomfortably tight.

For each of the six the Tinker regards as the best riders – himself, Sharif, two cousins of the sultan, Samir Rafik and myself – mounts are led out from the king's stables. The horses are beauties: King Charles is clearly a man who knows his bloodstock. Hamza, dressed in more ordinary array, brings the lances, which ben Hadou must have packed and transported for this very purpose. It is discomfiting to see Rafik here: for a moment my stomach gives a lurch. At least, I tell myself, he is not left behind at the court to snoop about in my absence.

Hyde Park is a wonder: a vast expanse of green space in the midst of the city, filled with people walking and riding. By the time an area has been made ready for us, a hundred or more have gathered to watch, and we must put on a show. Back and forth we gallop, pushing the horses till they sweat, casting our lances at a target set up for archery practice, piercing it through the heart so often that the crowd cheers and cheers. Then we ride against one another in pairs, throwing and catching each other's spears to great huzzahs from the spectators. It is good to do something physical after all the time cooped up in White Hall and I find myself riding with euphoric abandon, standing high in the stirrups, controlling the horse with my knees only as I brandish my lance with savage delight. When I turn to cast it, I find the formation has changed and that I am now facing Rafik, who bares his teeth at me and casts his lance a deliberate split second too early. The spear arrows towards my face and suddenly everything around me seems to slow and all I can think is what more perfect opportunity could there be for an accidental-seeming assassination, far from home in the course of an innocent fantasia?

Abruptly, all is chaos and the next conscious sensation I have is of hitting the ground with immense impact, and everything dark around me.

I struggle to move and cannot, and everything hurts, and I think: is this how death comes – at play, in front of a foreign audience? There is a hubbub of voices: women screaming, men shouting, horses thudding and blowing. Then there is a ripping sound close by my ear and light blooms again. Ben Hadou stands over me, lance in one hand and my cloak in the other, torn through where the spear has pierced it, taking me off the horse and pinning me to the ground. 'You're a lucky man, Nus-Nus!'

I sit up slowly. My head is ringing: it is hard to think straight. I look down, see no blood. I move each leg, each arm: nothing broken. Gingerly, I get to my feet and stand there, swaying slightly, my turban cloth unravelling around my face.

'Lud, what a monster!' one woman cries.

'Is it a snake?'

''Tis a very Leviathan!'

They howl like a pack of hyenas, and then they are crowding in towards me, all laughing and shouting at once.

Ben Hadou thrusts the burnous at me. 'Cover yourself, man!'

Shamefaced, I gather the cloak to me and hide the nakedness the split breeches have revealed.

Suddenly, the Moroccan embassy is the talk of the town. Women giggle into their fans when they see us, men seize us by the hand and congratulate us on our performance. We are bombarded with invitations – to luncheon, to dinner, to the theatre, to card parties, all of which ben Hadou turns down with cool politeness. He shows me a handbill someone has left lying around: a bawdily rendered cartoon of the fantasia, showing us exotically arrayed in robes and turbans, five with lances at the ready, the sixth armed only with his enormous black prick . . . 'What do you think Sultan Moulay Ismail would say to this?'

I stare at it glumly. Such a question requires no answer.

I have already told the Tinker of my suspicion that Rafik tried to kill me and he scoffed. 'In plain sight of the English court? You simply weren't paying attention and now you have made laughing stocks of us all. The only blessing is that the king was not here to see such a vulgar display.'

I open my mouth to argue that his own vanity led, indirectly at least, to the predicament: had I not been forced to wear clothes too small for me . . . But there is no point in pursuing the argument.

Later that afternoon there comes another invitation. 'The Duchess of Portsmouth invites us to dinner,' he declares with satisfaction. 'This is what I have been waiting for. Louise de Kéroualle is the king's chief mistress and has great influence not only here but in the French court too. Without doubt, the king will attend.'

So the refusal of the ever-escalating invitations appears to have been a ploy, after all; and now we are like to dine with the King of England.

We gather the next evening at the duchess's extravagant apartments within the palace. Left in the antechamber to await our introduction, we gaze around at walls papered with hand-coloured flowers; at the swags of gilt-laden plaster and the elaborately painted ceiling; at the Chinese lacquer cabinets, intricately fretted screens, Venetian glass mirrors and vases of wrought plate, the tall French clocks and statues of naked figures clutching scant morsels of drapery to their loins. 'Not much sign of austerity here,' I say to ben Hadou and the corner of his lips tilt upward.

But if the antechamber is richly appointed, the huge dining room into which we are shown by the liveried slaves is breathtaking in its opulence. Damask-covered chairs, arms and legs brightly gilded; tapestries glowing upon the walls; a dozen massive branching candlesticks in solid silver; gold-framed paintings; thick Turkey carpets; crystal goblets and decanters; gold platters; mirrors, sconces, crystal chandeliers bearing a hundred blazing candles. And the women . . . Jewels sparkle in their high-piled, powdered hair, at their ears and throats and wrists, between their fabulously plumped-up breasts.

It is hard to know where to look without impropriety, so I turn my attention to the men, sporting more sober plumage – dark crimson suits with white openwork collars and cuffs – but these turn out to be the musicians: French, just come from Louis XIV's court at Versailles to play, they explain, the latest creations by M. Marin Marais, court musician to the Sun King, not yet published and quite the newest thing.

Ben Hadou works his way around the room, ever at the side of a fair

woman with melancholy eyes and a substantial figure decked out in diamonds and pearls and the entire contents of a draper's shop, whom I take to
be our hostess, the Duchess of Portsmouth. I watch as the musicians settle
in the alcove with their oboes and a number of seven-stringed wooden
instruments somewhere between a large Spanish guitar and a Moroccan
rabab. Their leader draws a melancholy note from his instrument with a
languid sweep of his bow, and they strike up a powerful melody whose
deep bass notes resonate in the bone. The oboes and a harpsichord swell the
sound, and I find myself quite transported, it is such a rousing noise. I am
almost shocked out of my skin when a hand is placed upon my forearm and
fingers gently squeeze the muscle.

'You shall sit with me, sir.'

I turn to find the woman who had accompanied the king in the great
salon where I had been admiring the painting of the Virgin on the first day
of our visit. She grins up at me impishly and steers me towards the end of
the table furthest from the hostess.

'No, no!' this lady calls. 'He is to sit here, between myself and Lady Lich-
field.'

'God's truth, Louise, you can't sit the fellow next to little Charlotte: the
poor love won't know what to do with him. But I shall take great good care
of him.' She puts her arm through mine, squeezing it close against her.

The Duchess of Portsmouth pouts. 'You will spoil my table setting,
Eleanor!'

'Oh, figs for that!'

Over Eleanor's shoulder I see our hostess's plump face crumple before
she summons her social reserves and with forced gaiety calls her guests to
table.

I bow to my companion. 'It will be a pleasure to sit with you, Eleanor.'

'You bet your life it will be. But for God's sake call me Nelly: *I'm* not one
for pretension.' She regards me inquiringly.

'Oh, Nus-Nus, court eu— ah . . . courtier to Sultan Moulay Ismail of
Morocco.' I drop my voice. 'I do hope we haven't given offence to our
hostess.'

'Don't worry about Squintabella.'

'Squintabella?'

'The Venetian ambassador fawned all over Louise when they first met, called her *bella, bella. More like Squintabella*, I said, maybe a bit too loudly. She and I don't see eye to eye.' She giggles at her own witticism and leans in close. 'I'm afraid it's stuck, and serves her right, snobby cow. She's over here as a spy for the French king, you know. Still, Charlie likes a bit of French, if you know what I mean.' When I stare at her uncomprehending, she rattles on. 'And she gets well paid for it too, as you can see.' She waves a hand airily. 'As far as Madame la Duchesse is concerned you're just a passing curiosity: we don't get to see too many blackamoors all dressed up fine and invited to supper, but I've never been one to judge others by appearance. As my Mam always used to say, *At doomsday we shall see whose arse is blackest! I* say a touch of the tarbrush makes a man more handsome: you've only got to see Charlie for proof of that. Now, Hortense (that's the Duchess Mazarin to you) has got a big chap like you — but Mustapha's so far beyond the pale he rarely gets to sit with us, more's the pity. As for Hortense, she's a bit of a character shall we say? She's already had two of the people in this room (and neither of them men!) as well as the king, and I'm pretty sure she has Mustapha too from time to time (Lord knows I would), even though it's said he's a eunuch.' She makes a snipping scissors of her fingers, in case I have not taken her meaning.

'A eunuch? How can that be possible?' I say faintly.

Nelly gives a throaty chuckle. 'Blimey, you don't know much, do you? It ain't balls as makes a man, and there's more ways to skin a cat than the bleeding obvious. 'Sides, you can get remedies for everything nowadays, if you know the right quack.'

'Quack?'

'Well, they're all the same, ain't they? Doctors, chirurgeons, charlatans, mountebanks, quacks: name depends on how much you're paying them, I reckon.'

'And there are doctors in London who profess themselves able to cure . . . ah, impotence?'

'Course there are, luvvie, though I can't imagine why you need to ask, big man like you. Word's all around London about your endowment.'

Her peal of laughter draws the attention of ben Hadou, who stares at her, then at me, disapprovingly.

'My, ah, queen has charged me with seeking various remedies for her while I am in London, so if there is anyone whom you might recommend?'

'What sort of remedies?'

'Well, she is concerned about ageing too quickly . . .'

Nelly scoffs. 'Best cure I know is a good laugh and a lively romp: it's them as turns their nose up at such things as gets to look like wrinkled old apples.'

I can't help but grin; her bluntness is refreshing. 'I think the empress would not be happy with me were I to return to Morocco armed only with *that* piece of advice.'

'You better get in with the scientist fellows. Go and talk to Mr Evelyn there.' She points out the long-nosed gentleman who suggested riding in Hyde Park to ben Hadou. 'Or my good friend, Mr Pepys, now he knows how to enjoy himself.' A jolly fellow, roaring with laughter at something the woman beside him has just said.

She points around the table telling me the names of the others present, and a tit-bit of information about each of them to root them in my memory. The lady seated on the other side of the ambassador is Mrs Aphra Behn, a writer for the theatre and one-time spy for the Dutch; the little boy is Louise's son, Charles, Duke of Richmond; the pretty young woman in the emeralds is Anne, Lady Sussex, daughter to the king and the Duchess of Cleveland, who had an affair with the Duchess Mazarin and is now embroiled with some diplomat in Paris; the next man is the French ambassador, Paul Barillon d'Amancourt – 'a great charmer with the ladies'; and so on, till my head is spinning. There appear to be a number of the monarch's children present, and I presume to ask my companion about the nature of his harem, which amuses her considerably.

'What, you think Charlie needs to coop 'em up like hens? They're queuing up on the Privy Stairs for the King's Touch: it's all Mr Chiffinch can do to keep 'em out!'

'Then how does anyone keep track of his issue?' I explain some of my duties regarding the couching book, which sends her off into trills of delight.

'How many wives do you say he has, this sultan?'

'Well, concubines rather than wives: I believe at last count a thousand or so.'

She claps her hands in delight at such excess. 'Whoo! He keeps you busy, then. And these ladies: what are they like? Are they all dusky beauties?'

'Many are; but there are some Europeans too. And one English lady.'

Now she is agog. 'An Englishwoman? How does she come to be in the harem?'

I tell her about the corsairs' trade in captives, about the palace works at Meknes driving the need for slaves; and about the high value of white women in our markets, though I do not choose to share with her the emperor's dream of breeding a vast army to take back Muslim lands from Christendom.

'There's some as'd be shocked that women should be bought and sold thus, but I ain't one of 'em,' Nelly avers. 'We're all trade goods in this life, one way or another: you trade up or, if your luck's bad, you trade down, and fate's a fickle master. Still, poor lady: does she not want to return to these shores?'

The temptation to blurt out my mission to her is strong, but I manage to hold my tongue since her own is so free. But perhaps there is a chance to advance part of my goal. 'The lady sewed a gift for his majesty,' I tell her. 'A pretty thing that I have promised to put directly into his hand, had I the opportunity.'

'Well, he said he'd drop in: I'll make sure you get the chance.'

'I had rather it were in private.'

'I hope you ain't planning on doing any harm to my Charlie.'

I assure her not and rather wish I had not mentioned it at all.

Sometime later, ben Hadou stands and blesses our hostess for her kind invitation, and says he prays for God's favour to her little son, and gives thanks on our behalf for such a fine dinner, and then we are away. In the antechamber the ambassador rounds upon me angrily. 'Whatever were you thinking, carrying on in such a shameful fashion with the king's mistress?'

'Shameful? I have done nothing wrong,' I bluster, thinking back over the past two hours with some mortification.

'I saw her pour wine for you and you drain the glass!'

Ah, the wine. I had rather hoped he had not noticed. 'I protested that I drank no alcohol, but she insisted and I did not wish to cause a scene.'

'You are a disgrace to Islam and to your emperor!'

'A disgrace, is he?' a voice booms, and we turn to find his majesty the English king bearing down upon us, face gleaming with perspiration, wig askew.

Ben Hadou at once bows low. 'My humble apologies, sire.'

'Why, what have you done?' King Charles claps him on the back and turns to me. 'Your ambassador doesn't sound too happy with you, sir: been flirting with the ladies have you? Can't blame you for that! Heard about your little escapade in the park. Well, you must repeat the show – perhaps this time without the trouser incident – for I dearly love to see brave horse-manship.'

The Tinker assures him we would be most delighted to stage another fantasia and turns to accompany the king back into the duchess's dining room, but Charles sends us all off with a cheery good night: 'Such lateness of the evening is a time only for rakes and card-sharps, and I am sure you are neither of those.' And so we are dismissed.

When I return to my room, it is to find Momo peering, white-faced, over the bed canopy. 'A man came in,' he informs me shakily.

'What man?' Dread clutches at my belly.

He describes Rafik perfectly, right down to his round-toed slippers.

'Did he see you?'

Momo shakes his head. 'I climbed up here. Amadou bit his hand and he said a lot of bad words and kicked out at him, but Amadou made a lot of noise, so he looked around for a bit and then he left.'

'But how did he get in? The door was locked.'

'He had a key.'

So Rafik must have befriended the servants here and got hold of a copy; the original was tucked into my sash. Relief that Momo is well and not discovered by my enemy is tempered by the fear that Rafik will return the next time I leave the lad unattended. Then another thought dawns on me. My bag . . .

I search frantically but it is, of course, gone. Along with all my money and that entrusted to me by the empress for the purpose of securing the elixir. And hidden in the lining, Alys's embroidered scroll. There is nothing for it: I must confront the man at once. The money, well, there is nothing I can do about that, but the scroll . . . I take the stairs two at a time, up to the garret where the rest of the embassy staff have been accommodated, and enter without announcement. They have moved the unfamiliar high wooden beds to the far end of the long room and, apart from three playing cards quietly in a corner, lie on the floor wrapped in their blankets and cloaks like giant grubs. A candle gutters, casting grotesque shadows.

'Samir Rafik!'

My voice fills the low roof-space, until one by one the sleepers groan and stir. Rafik peers out of his cloak balefully and when he sees me gets at once to his feet. There is a knife at his waist: what honest man would sleep with a knife at the ready?

'What do you want?'

'I want what has been taken from me.'

Rafik turns to play the crowd. 'What would I want with your balls, cat-amite?'

Some whistle and click their teeth; one man laughs out loud. He is in shadow, but I know the sound of that bray: Hamza, the renegade. I grit my teeth against the insult. 'You came to my room and stole my bag, and in it are items given me by the Empress Zidana.'

His eyes narrow. 'Are you calling me a thief?'

'You are a thief. You were seen.'

'And who is the liar who says this?'

'Someone whose word I trust.'

He bends and flings his blanket aside. 'As you can see, nothing here.' He turns again to the onlookers, makes an obscene gesture. 'He dreams that I came to his room!'

Now the laughter is louder, and general. Hamza strolls across the room, his movement as deceptively lazy as a cat. 'I think you had better apologize for disturbing our peace, and for calling Samir here a thief.'

I look contemptuously down on him, then slide my gaze past him to

Rafik. 'You seem to have hurt yourself.' There is a piece of cloth wrapped around his right hand. 'I believe the bandage hides a bite given you by my ape.'

Rafik curls his lip. 'This? I got this in that travesty of a fantasia the other day, where you played the fool and brought shame on us all.'

'Your hand wasn't bandaged yesterday. If it is not a bite, show me the wound.'

'It is a clean lance-cut,' Hamza says. 'I bound it for him myself.' He has his hand on the hilt of his dagger and is making sure that I see it.

So that is how it is, I think to myself. Without another word, I turn on my heel and walk quickly away, thinking, if they come after me now it will be two armed men against one still in his dinner robes, in a dark corridor, high up in the servants' quarters of a rambling foreign palace. It would perhaps have been wiser to have gone to ben Hadou and sought his authority for a search, but he has not forgiven me the debacle in the park; besides, having to explain the existence of such a large sum of money, let alone Alys's piece of embroidery, would be problematic. My heart beats fast all the way back to my room, but no one follows.

Even with a chair wedged between the armoire and the door, I hardly sleep at all.

33

25th January 1682

The next day the Duchess of Portsmouth sends a page to invite us to take tea in her chambers. Ben Hadou sighs heavily. 'It would be rude to disappoint her after her kindness last night, but I have promised the king that we will demonstrate our horsemanship to him.'

'Surely it cannot take all day to take tea with the lady?'

Returning to my room to change, I show Momo how to wedge the chair up against the door and give him my dagger, which pleases him mightily. He flourishes it with great gusto, making feints and thrusts, till I catch him by the wrist. 'This is serious, Mohammed. Rafik is a dangerous man, and he wishes us harm. Do not open the door, and if he tries to force his way in, stab him and run, do you hear me? Make as much noise as you can.'

He laughs. 'Amadou and I will see him off. We are great warriors, aren't we, Amadou?' The little monkey bares his gums and capers. It is an unholy alliance the pair have formed.

I may have reckoned without the slow rituals of the English court. First, we are kept waiting for the best part of an hour, while the duchess rises, despite the fact that it is well past eleven; then, when we are shown in, we find her still *en déshabillé*, with three ladies curling her long light brown hair and applying Venetian ceruse, not only to whiten her face, but also her neck, arms and very considerable *décolletage*. I see such sights in the harem all the time; but ben Hadou becomes very still in that manner he has when concentrating very hard on not giving himself away and is clearly finding it difficult not to stare at her bosom. He gathers himself and bows very properly to the duchess, who seems unfazed to have two foreign men intrude upon her intimate toilette, and introduces me as his deputy ambassador. She smiles graciously and extends her hand. '*So* delightful to meet you, Mr Nus-Nus: do call me Louise. I *am* sorry Eleanor monopolized you for the entirety of the dinner last night but I hope you will accept an apology on her behalf: she has not, I fear, *le bon ton*. Not her fault, of course: she was not bred to the court.'

Mr Nus-Nus. Given the English honorific, the name sounds more ridiculous than ever before, especially in such a pretty French accent. I bend over her hand, as I have seen others do, and brush one of the many rings with my lips.

'I know I invited you for tea,' she smiles, 'but I have taken the liberty of ordering coffee: I know you Moors love your coffee. It may not be as strong as you like it – I must plead my delicate constitution – but I fear otherwise my soul will be tainted by it.'

Her ladies shriek with laughter. Ben Hadou and I exchange a mystified glance, then settle in the chairs brought for us as the screen is brought around in front of our hostess, and, as we discuss the weather, how we find London, comparisons with the Meknes and Versailles courts, the styles of Moroccan ladies' dress and the like, we try not to be distracted by the unmistakable rustling of silks and the drawing of corset-strings. The coffee is weak and tasteless compared to what we drink at home: unlikely to taint anyone's soul. I can see from the way the Tinker's feet keep tapping that he is keen to be gone from this place of women. His answers become shorter as time wears on: the time for lunch will soon have come and gone.

At long last, she reappears, laced into a dress of figured yellow silk with billowing blue sleeves slashed to show the fine cambric beneath, against which the unnatural whiteness of her skin almost merges. Ben Hadou leaps to his feet and abruptly announces he must be away: an appointment with the king. As I make to leave as well, she cries, 'Ah, to deprive me *so* utterly of *such* charming company would be *most* cruel!' I notice that the white ceruse has cracked where the corners of her mouth turn down. Ceruse is made from white lead, designated a poison even in Galen's time: why would any woman imperil her health in the quest for the arbitrary goal of beauty?

Louise's exclamation is probably little more than court politeness, but the ambassador says at once, 'Nus-Nus, you shall stay with the lady — we shall do very well without you,' and off he goes.

The duchess sniffs. 'Well, I suppose I shall have to be content with the *deputy* ambassador, and not take the slight to heart.' Before I can muster a suitable response, she turns and calls out, '*Jacob, viens!*' and a boy emerges from behind a fretted oriental screen, white teeth flashing in his dark face. Black curls have been cropped back hard against the unmistakable round-ness of an African skull. He pulls a velvet doublet down over the white ruffles of his shirt and parades in front of her. '*Ça va, madame?*' He twirls around, sees me and almost falls over.

'*Ici petit, laisses-moi voir.*' His mistress beckons him and he goes to her, though he keeps his gaze trained on me all the way as if I might beat him, or eat him, or worse. The duchess tugs the little doublet straight, pats it down, arranges the ruffles, lays an affectionate hand on his head. '*Très joli.* This is my boy, Jacob: *Jacob, ici Monsieur Nus-Nus, de la court du Maroc.*'

Big eyes fix upon me. Then he says, in clear Senufo, 'You look a lot like my uncle Ayew.'

While I am wondering at this, Louise snaps her fingers. '*Les bijoux, Marie.*'

One of her attendants fetches an elaborate jewel-box and the duchess upturns it in her lap, discarding diamonds and rubies the size of sparrow's eggs, gold chains and brooches, diadems and bracelets. She sorts through string after string of pearls, till she finds the precise necklace she seeks and fastens it around the boy's neck, then shows him his image in a tortoiseshell hand-mirror. Suddenly I find myself thinking of Momo, how he would relish the sight of all these bright baubles . . .

'Do you have children of your own, sir?'

'I have never married.'

'That is not quite what I asked. *Mais quel dommage.* You would make handsome sons, I think. Like Jacob here.'

One of the women brings a yellow sash and there is much fuss over plac-ing it correctly. They lead her away to a chair beside a window that overlooks the courtyard garden outside and arrange the folds of her dress. Keeping my eyes trained on the duchess, I ask Jacob where he is from. He names the neighbouring village to my own, which is less of a surprise than it might be. 'Your uncle was Ayew Diara?'

His nod stirs the air between us.

'He was my good friend.' When we stood shoulder to shoulder we were the same height, the same build. People often mistook us for one another, from a distance at least: he liked to say he was better looking than me; certainly he was more sure of himself, especially with the girls. We went hunting together, shared our manhood ceremony; but he laughed at me for my love of music, and we grew apart.

'He is a great warrior!' Jacob cries. 'But he left the village and never returned.'

The lad must have been no more than Momo's age when Ayew and I were taken. He has a good memory. So do I, unfortunately: I remember how the enemy tribe who took us staked Ayew out in the full sun, having cut off his eyelids, his lips, nose, ears and penis. They left him his tongue, more's the pity. His cries followed us for a day.

'A great warrior, yes. And how came you here?'

'The tribe to the south wanted our land, so we fought them. They won. I survived in the ship of those they sold us to; my mother and brother did not.' His expression becomes closed.

Beaten and bought and sold, and by our own people too: the old, old story.

I watch as a painter comes marching in, followed by two assistants carrying easel and paints and canvas. He kisses Louise's hand, compliments her matchless beauty, walks back and forth between subject and half-finished painting, adjusting this and that, chattering in French. From a distance he sounds much like Amadou.

Suddenly he turns towards us. 'Where is the blackamoor?'

Jacob slouches over to take his place at the lady's side. The artist complains: too much sleeve showing, the pearls all wrong. He takes the boy's head and roughly moves it into position as if Jacob is inanimate. '*Prends ça et ne bouges pas!*' A great shell is placed in his hands, overflowing with loose pearls.

Jacob rolls his eyes. 'I am a symbol of the bounty of the colonies.'

'No more talking!'

I take this as my cue to depart, sweep a bow to the duchess, grin at Jacob and move towards the door. As I leave I snatch a look at the half-finished portrait. The artist has captured Jacob well enough, though for some reason he has omitted the boy's slave-brand; but the woman in the picture looks nothing like the duchess, being slimmer and blander of face. Thin and expressionless, is that what is regarded as desirable here? I shake my head, recalling Zidana's irrational terror at her diminishing shadow. Women are never content with their lot: if they are fat, they want to be thin, if thin, fat. I will never understand them.

Back in the embassy's quarters, I find my fellows long gone with ben Hadou to show off their horsemanship. Since those who were not riding must have gone as spectators, even the garret is empty. I take the opportunity to search it thoroughly, but an hour later come away empty-handed. They will have hidden the money somewhere else; the jewels too. The satchel is no doubt long gone, burned or otherwise disposed of, Alys's embroidered scroll along with it. Mastering my despair, I make an effort to concentrate on the practicalities of the present. In the kitchens I charm a maid into giving me bread and cooked meat, and repair to my room. 'Amadou, it is only me!' I call out, in case anyone is spying, and a moment later I hear the sound of the chair being dragged away from the door. Inside, Momo and the monkey fall upon the victuals with the appetite of those oblivious to fear, while I turn over and over in my mind what to do.

When the knock comes I leap up in surprise. I put a finger to my lips, then lift Momo up on to the bed's canopy. Flinging the door open, I find Jacob outside, his arms full of fruit and cakes, no doubt looted from the duchess's apartments. Amadou at once elbows past me, more interested in the food than the visitor. He pulls himself up on to my shoulder, the better to peruse the treasures, then quick as a blink snatches an apple and an iced cake and makes a vast leap up on to the canopy, to consume them before I can snatch them back, chattering in self-congratulation. With a great ripping sound, the canopy tears clear across at the force of his landing and down plunge monkey, boy, treasures and all. Gold spills across the floor: Momo looks guilty, for a short moment, then begins to giggle at the expression on my face. It must be the gold Zidana gave me to effect her purchases: Rafik and Hamza will surely be disappointed in their theft of the bag.

'Oh, Maleeo!' I pull Jacob inside and slam the door before any curious passer-by can see in. Then I take the tray from him, set it on the table and, going down on a knee, look the lad in the eye. 'Jacob, did you love your uncle Ayew?'

He drags his gaze from the sight of Momo and Amadou sprawled in the wreckage, and nods.

'Then you must not breathe a word of what you have seen here. Swear by Maleeo and Kolotyolo and the spirits of your ancestors.'

His eyes grow wide. 'I swear.' He touches his forehead, then his breast.

'Good. Come here, Momo, meet my cousin Jacob.'

Momo solemnly wipes cake icing off his shirt and extends his hand. 'Pleased to meet you.' They regard each other in delight, forming an immediate bond as children often will, while I collect up the gold with some relief. It is not all here, but maybe that is to the good, or Rafik will be wondering why I should be making such a fuss about an old leather bag. 'Is there any more, Momo?'

He shakes his head emphatically. 'I was just playing with it. I was a king and Amadou was my slave.'

We clean the room and reattach the canopy as best we can, and I explain some of our situation to Jacob, whose eyes shine to be a party to our conspiracy. He proves to be a resourceful lad.

An hour later, we admire our handiwork.

'We can't do anything about your eyes,' Jacob says critically, 'and your hair is very fine despite its new colour.'

I find a spare headcloth and show Momo how to wind a turban from it. After the third attempt he has the knack perfectly. Not yet four, I think wonderingly: it took me months, and I was nineteen . . .

Momo is thrilled by the game. He admires his reflection in the mirror, posing this way and that, compares the new darkness of his skin first with mine, then with Jacob's, and proclaims himself well satisfied. 'No bathing, though!' I say fiercely. 'Or the walnut stain will come off.'

He laughs happily. 'I *hate* bathing!'

'Look at the floor rather than at people: a black page with blue eyes stands out.'

'It would be better not to speak,' Jacob adds. 'Your English is too good.'

Momo casts longing eyes upon Amadou, eating the last of the scraps from the corner I have swept them into. 'Can I take him with me?'

I shake my head. 'I'm sorry: he's too well known and we can't risk your being connected with me. It's not for long, I hope, this disguise.'

For a moment his lip trembles, then he squares his shoulders. 'It is a good game,' he declares, as if trying to persuade himself of the fact. 'I shall pretend I am mute. Like Old Ibrahim.'

'Perhaps you would like me to cut out your tongue for best effect?' I say gravely, and make to snatch it as it protrudes from his mouth.

He shrieks in mock-terror, and after some rough and tumble is in better spirits.

Jacob has his own cabinet in the Duchess of Portsmouth's apartments, which extend to over twenty rooms. 'Momo will be safe here. I will tell madame he is my cousin, sent to work in the palace. I doubt she will ask too many questions: to have a black boy on either side of her will set off the whiteness of her skin; she is always looking for advantage against her rivals for the king's affections.'

It is not a perfect solution, but it will have to do for now. Momo takes his leave of me manfully enough: I hug him fiercely, tell him to behave himself, and have to walk quickly away before he sees the water welling in my eyes.

Amadou scolds me furiously when I return alone, mightily annoyed to have his playmate taken away.

Ben Hadou and the rest of the embassy staff return in late afternoon in high spirits. The fantasia has been a great success, the king most admiring of their feats. 'He asked after you – "the fellow with the split breeches" – and I told him you were unwell,' the Tinker says breezily. 'So I'm afraid you can't attend the dinner tonight.'

I cannot say I am greatly disappointed: the artifices of the day have proved wearing and I had little sleep last night. I find a manservant in the corridor and ask whether food might be sent to my room. He looks me up and down and tells me, 'In this country slaves are not waited on by honest men', and stalks off, muttering, 'Fucking negard.' A maid is passing, a homely-looking girl with a mass of honey curls escaping her cap. 'He's like that with everyone, Thomas,' she says. 'Pay no heed to his rudeness, I beg you. I'll fetch you something myself, if you like.' She turns to leave, then turns back. 'You'd better say what you eat – I'm not sure what your people like.'

'What, black people?'

She colours. 'No, sir, Mahometans.'

It is my turn to be ashamed.

'It's just that there's a pig roasting downstairs, and I wasn't sure you'd want that.'

I find out her name is Kate, apologize for my rudeness, and gratefully accept an offer of roasted chicken, bread and strong cheese.

'But no ale?'

I grin. 'I'd love some ale, Kate.'

She is as good as her word: shortly after, there is a knock at the door and she is there with a japanned tray laden with food and a large earthenware jug. When I thank her for her generosity, she blushes prettily. 'Big man like you, I'm sure you have quite an appetite.' She holds my gaze for a moment too long, her colour deepening all the while. I am not so foolish as to mistake her meaning, but for both our sakes I pretend to, and merely take the tray and bid her farewell.

It is not the tranquil dinner I had hoped for, for Amadou is out of sorts and keeps stealing morsels of food and then casting them on the floor and demanding more until I could cheerfully throttle him, and am contemplating doing just that when another knock comes at the door. Keeping the jug of ale to one side, I gather the rest of the dinner things on to the tray, dig out a small coin for the girl and open the door with a smile.

The next thing I know I am flat on my back with Rafik's foot on my chest and a knife at my throat. 'Close the door,' he hisses, and in comes Hamza too.

From his perch on top of the bed, Amadou screeches wildly.

'Shut that bloody monkey up!'

Hamza lashes out, and Amadou goes flying across the chamber and hits the wall with a dull thud. I hear his little body drop like a stone.

'Where is he, then?' the Tafraouti demands.

'Who?'

'The boy. The sultan's son.'

Shock slows my brain. How can they possibly know? 'The sultan's son? He has so many, I don't know which one you mean.'

'Don't play the innocent.' Hamza kicks me in the ribs. He is wearing shoes of hard English leather and it hurts. 'The one everyone thought was dead and buried: the Englishwoman's boy. We know you've got him, just didn't know why – but now we know that too.' He leers down at me, makes a gesture with his fingers. 'Thought you'd make yourself a fortune in London, did you?'

This time the blankness of my expression is unfeigned. 'Let me up: I don't have a clue what you're talking about.'

He kicks me again and the air huffs out of me. I can taste the ale coming back up my gullet in a rather less pleasant fashion to the way it went down.

'Stop kicking the bastard and search the room!' Rafik says angrily. He drops to one knee. 'It's your fault my uncle was lashed to those mules and driven through the wilds till the flesh was stripped from his body and his bones snapped like twigs. So I'll not hesitate to slit your black throat if I have to: call it an honour killing. Now where's the brat? I know he's in here some-where: there was no one else could have seen me take the bag – I made damned sure of that. Apart from the wretched monkey, and it's not talking.'

Well, that clears up one part of the mystery, but how did he know the observer was Momo? With a sudden dull sensation, it strikes me: Alys's scroll – she must have written of her son in the scroll, and Rafik must have been more thorough in his search of my satchel than I had thought. He must have found it and had Hamza read it for him. I go hot, then cold: what a fool I have been.

'There's no one here.' Hamza sits heavily on the bed. 'So what have you done with him, eh?' A crafty expression settles in his eye. 'Tell us and we'll keep the secret, split the redemption money three ways: the sultan will never know a thing.'

Rafik rounds on him angrily. 'That's right: add treason to your greed and apostasy, infidel! The sultan is my lord: we have to find the boy and take him back. But we'll cut this bastard's throat first.'

'Calm down, man. This fucking palace is massive: he could've stashed the brat anywhere – even smuggled him into the city. I told you, he's already been out making inquiries. You're going to have to keep him alive or we'll never find the kid.'

In answer, Rafik presses his little knife deeper into my neck. I feel the skin tighten there, then give with a scarlet, rushing agony. Like alchemy, the pain transmutes into blind fury, and with a bellow I throw Rafik off me and lumber to my feet, ready to make a fight of it. He falls back against the table and the japanned tray and everything on it goes crashing to the floor, making a terrible din. The thought pounds through my head: I will have to kill them both, for if they send word back to Morocco, Alys is a dead woman. The terror this idea generates lends me even greater strength. I clutch Rafik's throat with one hand, his knife hand with the other. Bang! We stumble against the armoire, a huge and solid piece of furniture. Under the force of our bodies, one of its great doors flies open and hits the onrushing Hamza full in the face. Swear words pour in a torrent from his bubbling mouth. What with the noise of that and Rafik's defiant threats I am hardly aware when the door to the chamber breaks open and armed guards run in. Two of them drag me off the Tafraouti, whom they disarm; another secures the renegade. Behind them, in the corridor outside, I see the maid, Kate, clutching her hands. Then I remember Amadou.

His head lolls when I pick him up. His neck is broken, and I cannot help but wail.

The girl is beside me at once. 'You're bleeding!' she cries, which is rather a statement of the obvious. Then she looks down. 'Oh.' She backs away. 'Ugh.'

I cannot blame her for her disgust: poor Amadou looks as if he has been savaged by eagles, for I have bled all over him.

Ben Hadou is fetched and after a long delay he arrives, looking flushed and hectic. He glares first at Rafik, then at me, as if he would like to stab us both on the spot for having him dragged unwilling from dinner at the king's table, and explains to the guard captain that there has long been bad blood between Rafik and me and that he will personally vouch for our good behaviour from now on. 'As for Hamza: the man is an apostate, but as an Englishman he is subject to your laws. Take him away and do with him as you will.'

When we are alone again, ben Hadou demands: 'What's all this about?'

There is a long, strained silence. Surely now is the time for Rafik to revenge himself on me for good and all? I wait for him to accuse me: to wave the scroll in front of the Tinker and demand the palace be searched for the sultan's son, but the Tafraouti surprises me by keeping his mouth shut. He is well aware of ben Hadou's loathing for him and must consider me greatly preferred in the ambassador's eyes, and there has already been the incident in Hyde Park . . . But maybe, I realize, he does not have the scroll, and without that he would appear to have made a lunatic charge. Is it burned, along with my bag, or does Hamza still have it? In any case, I cannot accuse him of the theft.

With both of us mute we are at an impasse, and eventually ben Hadou vents his spleen on the pair of us, telling us that if there is further trouble we will be dispatched back to Morocco on the next ship, with orders for severe punishment at the other end. He marches Rafik outside. At the door, he turns back. 'You'd better get that seen to,' he says, indicating the wound on my neck. 'Ask one of the servants for a chirurgeon.' He digs in his pouch, takes out some coins and hands them to me. 'That should cover it.'

He is gone before I look down. In my hands are three gold pieces. Enough to buy a chirurgeon. And his daughter, and the family dog as well. Well, maybe I exaggerate. But he must be feeling guilty: perhaps it was the sight of the poor monkey that did it.

I wash the blood from Amadou and wrap him in a piece of cloth. Momo will be heartbroken when he finds out. Then I sew up the wound on my neck myself – wincing and yelping – and cover the untidy repair with a bandage of my own making. At last I go down to the kitchens, where I find the maid, Kate, warming her feet by the stove. I thank her profusely for bringing the guards and give her one of the gold coins. She stares at it silently for a long time, then hands it back. 'I can't take it, really I can't.'

'It would please me if you did.'

But she shakes her head. 'I was only doing what was right. How is your neck?'

'It was a scratch, no more.'

'A scratch? It was gushing. Let me look.'

She tuts over my handiwork, touches the place gingerly. 'It'll scar.'

'And mar my beauty?' I laugh. 'I'll add it to my collection.'

'Where are the others?'

'There are too many to recount,' I say, a bit too brusquely. 'I have another favour to ask.' For a moment her eyes brighten and I realize too late she was hoping I might have changed my mind about her unspoken offer: so now I have insulted her with money and spurned her twice. Truly, I have no gift with women. Blundering on, I ask, 'Where would the guards have taken the Englishman who was in my room, the renegade named Hamza?'

She tells me and I make her a solemn bow and leave before I can entangle either of us further. The cells are down in the undercroft. I bribe the man on guard with a piece of gold to allow me ten minutes with the prisoner.

'Just don't mark his face, is all I ask,' he says, and wheezes with laughter.

Hamza looks up hopefully when he hears our footsteps, but his expression darkens when I come into view. His nose is a clot of black blood: the armoire door must have broken it. 'What do you want, eunuch?'

The insult comes out as 'you duck' and the guard doubles up. 'Let me know if you want any more help roughing him up,' he offers once the hilarity has passed. He lets me in to the cell. I wait till his steps retreat, then turn to the renegade. 'So, where is it, then?'

'Where's what?'

'The satchel you took from my room.'

'Wasn't me took it.'

'You've seen it, then?'

He looks crafty, scratches a mole on his cheek. 'Why're you asking, exactly?'

'I need it back.'

He smiles: a chilly sight. 'Sorry about your monkey.'

I can see he is not. I show him a coin. 'Tell me where it is.'

He looks puzzled. 'That old bag? Piece a rubbish: you can buy another hundred of them from the Fez tannery for that. What, you got a never-ending stream of gold you can't wait to give away or something?' He leans forward. 'Look, we can cut Rafik out of this – I know the two of you don't see eye to eye. You could use me, you know; I know my way round London and am quick on my feet – enough to follow you to the merchant's house without you seeing me. Heard every word you said. We'd make a good team, I reckon. Shake hands on it and we'll ransom the boy and split the dividends and I'll make sure Rafik meets a nasty end in an alley, all right?'

So that was how they knew. The relief I feel is fleeting: I must still make sure there is no evidence. 'You have an easy choice, Hamza: tell me where the bag is and take the gold for your trouble, or I walk away now and leave you the poorer.'

He shrugs, and tells me. I should have kept my end of the bargain and walked away, but I am afraid I give in to baser instincts, and kick him hard in the balls.

'That's for the monkey!' I tell him with savage glee.

Twenty minutes later the satchel is in my hands, none the worse for wear other than for a strong smell of horse shit: not surprising, since it has been buried in the stables' midden. The bright moonlight illumines my poor stitching, undisturbed: the scroll is where I left it, sewn into the lining. I rip it out of its hiding place and stash it inside my robe, against my beating heart.

I will probably have to kill the renegade now, and Rafik as well; but at least while the boy is safe they have no proof. Now I must get Alys's message to the king; or destroy it and take Alys's and Momo's fate into my own hands.

I bury Amadou beneath some rose bushes in one of the courtyard gardens. It is a tranquil spot. When next I see roses bloom, I will think of him.

34

On Candlemas Day the embassy is invited to visit the great abbey at West-minster and watch a candlelight procession to symbolize the entry of Christ, the Light of the World, into the Temple for the first time, forty days after his birth. Ben Hadou declines politely. He is a devout Muslim, he explains, and for Mahometans Christ is no more than a prophet: revered as a bringer of God's word, but a mortal man nonetheless.

'I hear it is an architectural wonder, this abbey,' Sharif says. 'And I am sure that it does no harm to bear witness in this house of God if we do not take part in their rituals. Besides, if we all refuse their invitation it will appear rude.'

'Very well, Nus-Nus will go with you.'

I open my mouth to remonstrate – I had been hoping to visit Momo in the Duchess of Portsmouth's apartments – but then I think, the king will be at the abbey, and who knows what opportunity may present itself? So I shut it again. The scroll is with me at all times: I even took it with me into the baths at Charing Cross when I finally got fed up with washing in a bowl of lukewarm water carried up three flights of stairs from the kitchens, and was greatly stared at, even though I kept my qamis on; but a conjunction of king and scroll has not presented itself in over a week, and I am beginning to despair.

The procession would be a spectacle anywhere in the world; but the abbey itself is a wonder, with its towering pillars and fabulously vaulted ceiling, though the effigies of the dead wherever you look, gilded and lifelike, lurking in their alcoves, are eerie indeed, for sometimes in the flickering light of a thousand candles it seems as if they move.

If ben Hadou had hoped that Sharif and I would be inconspicuous, he is likely to be disappointed, for within moments of our taking our places amongst the press of folk a court official bustles his way through to us and tells us space has been made for us where we shall have a better view of the proceedings, and, after much pushing and shoving and treading on people's toes, we are finally seated in the pews set aside for the sovereign's guests, within sight of the king himself.

Of the ceremony itself I shall say nothing save that it is as fine and solemn as theatre, but when the music begins, I am lost in awe, for the notes of the vast organ fill the space, even to the soaring roof, and at times it is like the roar of a lion, at others like the trill of a bird; and when the sweet notes of the choir meet it, it is as if angels speak, or as if the abbey channels the voice of God himself. I am transfixed, not even aware of the tears that roll down my face, until Sharif jogs my arm and mimes with some alarm that I should wipe my cheeks.

'If our sultan comes to hear that you have been moved by this heathen display, we will all be in trouble,' he whispers fiercely in a lull.

There is, of course, no chance to approach the king. I watch him swept along in the adulation of his people, who press forward hoping for a word or touch, to which they seem to accord an almost magical quality. I cannot help but muse that our sovereign emperor's contact with his subjects is generally somewhat less beneficial to their health.

As we turn to leave, a voice beside me says, 'Good day to you, gentlemen,' and I turn to see one of our fellow guests at the Duchess of Portsmouth's fine dinner. When he smiles I remember Nelly's description of him and just in time his name pops into my head. 'Good day, Mr Pepys, a pleasure to see you again.' I introduce him to the kaid, whose English is basic: Sharif inclines his head and bares his sugar-rotted teeth.

'Are you heading straight back to White Hall, or could I perhaps escort you to the Candlemas market at Westminster Hall, which is quite a sight to behold?'

I translate for Sharif. 'An English souq? That I would very much like to see.'

Mr Pepys leads us through the cloisters and into the monastery garden behind the abbey to avoid the crowds. It is a pretty, tranquil spot lit by pale February sunlight, filled with herbs and vegetables and the bare trunks of fruit trees. I crouch to examine the silver-green fronds of a plant by the pathside. 'We grow this in Meknes,' I tell our guide. 'We call it *sheeba*, but I think you may better know it as artemisia, or wormwood.'

Our guide bends to peruse the herb better, and as he does so something swings clear of his collar. He tucks it back in quickly, but not before I have glimpsed fur and claws. He catches my eye, looks embarrassed. 'A hare's foot, to ward off the colic. I have a tendency to overindulge.'

I smile. 'You would do better to take some of this in a tisane: the emperor enjoys a pot of wormwood tea from time to time. It is a known stomachic.'

'Are you a medical man, sir?'

'I served for a while with a doctor from Aberdeen and learned a little of the human anatomy and its failings.'

'I cannot imagine a strapping fellow like you' – he indicates my general size – 'should know much of physical fallibility.'

Sharif, when I translate, laughs. 'He is eunuch,' he says loudly.

Mr Pepys is visibly taken aback. 'Good God, really?'

I nod unhappily.

'Is it for the singing? There are some wonderful castrati. I have often wondered whether the famous treble, Mr Abell, is in full possession of his . . . ah, faculties.'

I assure him it has nothing to do with singing, and he regards me with a sort of appalled wonder. 'I can't think of anything worse.'

We walk in silence for the few minutes it takes us to reach the great hall, a massive lump of architecture bolstered by huge buttresses of stone. Already the hubbub from the as-yet-unseen market is such that our guide must raise his voice. He asks if there is anything in particular we might wish to purchase, and the kaid admits he would dearly love some confectionery, and I say that if there is good writing ink to be had it would be most useful, at which Mr Pepys smiles. 'Ah, the Tangier discussions: all those minutes.' He shakes his head. 'I was on the committee for years: a wretched business, always one step forward, three back. I should imagine you're fully at log-gerheads over it, for I can see no easy solution. You must remember it is not a simple matter of logic: there is much emotion and irrationality involved.'

I smile. 'On both sides, I am sure.'

'As in all human dealings. The colony costs us a fortune to support, more than we can in all honesty afford, but the king feels he would be letting his wife down to let it go – it came as part of her dowry, you know – and as he has failed her in much else, he stays firm on this. Then of course there is the matter of the poor Earl of Plymouth.'

I raise a questioning eyebrow.

'Charles's son – illegitimate of course, but a son nonetheless. Gave him the command of the King's Own Regiment, made him up to colonel. Off he went to Morocco in the summer of '80, died of the flux four months later. Only twenty-three, poor lad: Charles took it hard.'

'How many children has king?' Sharif asks.

Mr Pepys laughs. 'At last count a baker's dozen, but only ten extant, though none to his good wife, more's the pity. He likes the ladies – and who can blame him? What think you of our English women, Nus-Nus: they're a saucy lot, aren't they?' He stops suddenly, recalling my condition. 'I am sorry, sir, I meant no offence.'

'None taken. I am still able to appreciate the aesthetics of a painting, even if I cannot wield a brush, and the ladies of your court are most delight-ful.'

'Our king have five hundred child!' Sharif says loudly, interrupting.

Our guide grins, evidently not believing a word of it.

'And thousand wife!'

I nod. 'Ismail boasts he has a woman from every country known to man.'

'La, that's quite the collection! I have to say one's quite enough for me. Now, here we are, stay close: there are pickpockets everywhere these days.'

The interior of the hall is impressive: I am surprised such a magnificent space should be used for a mere market and say so. 'The Law Courts operate here the rest of the time,' Mr Pepys bellows back. 'See those grim baubles above?' He points to where three black, unidentifiable objects hang from one of the huge hammer beams. 'Those are the heads of the traitors who sentenced the king's father to death in this very chamber – Cromwell and his generals, Ireton and Bradshaw. They're left there as a reminder of what happens to those who rise against the Crown.'

I grin. 'Our sovereign does the very same thing.'

'Eight hundred head on walls of Meknes,' Sharif expounds gleefully.

'Eight hundred?' Mr Pepys catches my eye. 'Five hundred children, eight hundred heads and a thousand wives: what a bountiful country is Morocco!'

Stalls are set up throughout the hall selling all manner of goods. Vendors pass through the throng of customers bearing trays of sweetmeats, combs, oranges, knives. I spy a man selling notebooks and inkhorns and make a purchase; after much deliberation, the kaid avails himself of a large bag of gingerbread. A man selling domestic fowl scores points against the competition by displaying a sorry-looking peacock on a string; another vendor offers hot ass's milk. Mr Pepys makes a beeline for a stall selling ladies' accoutrements and spends as much time eyeing the pretty clients as they pore over the goods as he does the goods. I watch as he exchanges words with one, and see the way she colours and walks quickly away from him. He shrugs, then returns to us. 'Come, see the mountebanks: they're always amusing.'

At the back of the hall there are vendors mounted on the steps, the better to shout their wares, and gathered around each of them is a great press of onlookers, for the most part men. The first is offering a tincture of herbs 'from the dark African continent, guaranteed to earn the gratitude of your wives! One dose a day and you'll be going all night.' He taps his nose and leans forward in mock-confidential pose. 'She'll never keep up with you: you'll need to take a mistress or two on the side!' He does brisk business. 'Your king must have a good stock of such herbs,' Mr Pepys laughs.

'He have no need,' Sharif says hotly, catching the imputation.

The next mountebank is waving around something that looks remarkably like a bull's pizzle, which is, it transpires, exactly what it is. He also has for sale the virile members of a lion, a tiger and a whale: and more mysterious African herbs, which look to me like common feverfew, betony and rue.

A third offers 'a universal pharmacopoeia' including bezoar-stones, moss from the skull of an executed criminal, the saliva of a fasting man and the urine of 'a pure boy'.

The last mountebank has attracted a crowd of women. He holds up a glass jar containing a clear liquid that is, he claims, 'pure May dew, collected beneath a mighty oak at dawn; nothing short of miraculous in restoring a perfect complexion even to those marked by the pox'. I cannot help but laugh aloud. Even in Marrakech, where we have our fair share of charlatans, you would not get away with selling plain water. He also has 'health peas, for the losing of excess weight'. When I explain this to Sharif, he scratches his head. 'You wouldn't make much selling *that* in Morocco.'

'In our country,' I explain to our guide, 'the women seek to be voluptuous. They eat a paste of bitter melon seeds and honey every day in order to gain weight.'

Mr Pepys rolls his eyes. 'Women. I adore them, but I don't understand them now in my forty-ninth year any better than I did in my nineteenth.'

'What those for?' Sharif asks curiously, pointing at a cage of puppies beside the mountebank, tiny beasts, barely more than a few days old.

Mr Pepys guides us away. 'People will go to the most extraordinary lengths in the pursuit of a cure for their perceived defects and ills. I fear the poor fellows are destined to be boiled with wine, then pressed to extract their essential juices, which apparently whitens the skin.'

We are turning to leave when I hear, quite clearly, the words 'magical elixir' and 'return the patient to a perfect state'. I catch hold of our guide's sleeve. 'Wait!'

'What is it, dear fellow?'

'An elixir, someone said, but I cannot tell who.' I scan the crowd, to no avail.

He laughs. 'You won't find the Elixir of Life here! But if it's scientific miracles you're after, you should come along to one of our meetings.'

'Meetings?'

'The Royal Society, my good sir: the Invisible College, as was. There are fellows there performing all sorts of wonders.'

The next day a page comes with another invitation. I find myself foolishly hoping it may be to one of Mr Pepys's meetings, but no: it is a grander invitation by far, to a musical performance that afternoon in the royal apartments.

I am alarmed, as soon as we set foot in the chamber, to see Momo on one side of the Duchess of Portsmouth with Jacob on the other, all tricked out in a suit of gold lace, between whom Louise – in creamy white and pearls, her hair powdered with gold – fairly shines. They make a striking tableau, one that draws the eye. In some terror, I snatch a glance at Rafik, but his gaze is wandering over the rich trappings of the room, and when Momo looks up and sees me and grins like a loon, it goes blessedly unremarked.

The king enters late, with Nelly on one arm and a statuesque, strong-faced woman on the other. Behind her, a tall black man with wide cheekbones and tribal scars: so this, I surmise, must be Mustapha and the Duchess Mazarin. Her eyes sweep languidly over me and her mouth hitches up in a half-smile as she sweeps past.

The music is sublime, combining as it does a stirring collection of stringed instruments and a harpsichord thumping out a powerful bass line that I can feel thrumming in my breastbone. When the castrati join their voices to the work, I feel as I did in the abbey the previous day, as if my spirit were soaring out of my body. Beyond my control, tears gather in my eyes. But when I look around to share the moment I see that the rest of the Moroccan contingent are sitting stiffly to attention in their best clothes, trying not to look too uncomfortable or bored; and that several of the courtiers, worse than unmoved, are talking amongst themselves. Such behaviour would be unthinkable at Ismail's court: there would be blood, and screams, and heads rolling.

At last the recital comes to an end and polite applause ensues. The harpsi-chordist stands and bows, evidently the author of the work, though a young man, solemn of aspect.

'Bravo, Henry!' Mr Pepys cries. 'Another triumph!'

As we all begin to file out, a page tugs at my sleeve. 'The king wishes to speak with you.'

Ben Hadou turns, eyes glittering. 'I think you must mean me. I am the ambassador; this is only my secretary.'

'No, sir, it is the big black fellow the king wants.'

The Tinker glares at me. 'I can't imagine why he should wish to talk to you, but I shall make it my business to find out.'

We are brought into the royal presence and I manage not to throw myself headlong in obeisance, having learned by now that the English court is a somewhat more casual place than the court at Meknes. The king's regard sweeps over ben Hadou with little interest, then comes to rest on me, 'Did you enjoy the music, sir?'

Even though the question is not meant for him, the ambassador answers quickly. 'Superb, your majesty, quite superb.' He lies, I know: for he has no interest whatever in music. All the time the king's dark eyes measure me: he seems amused. Then he steps between us and takes me by the elbow. 'Do you play?'

I freeze. The Tinker will skin me for this snub, I think. But what can I do? 'I play a little guitar, sire, and the oud – an Arabic type of lute.'

'Then we shall have a capital time of it.' He gestures to the harpsichordist to attend him. 'Mr Purcell, come with me. And you, Mr Pepys. Mr James, select your best violinists and bring them to the music room!' He turns back to me, grinning like a boy. 'Come, sir, we shall make some fine noise! I noticed you in the abbey: I swear I've never seen another mortal soul so moved by music.'

The king is a man of prodigious energy: it fairly radiates off him. In that he reminds me of Ismail: they share a similar restlessness of spirit and a quickness of foot. I have been told that Charles rises early each day to walk or play tennis; that he swims and rides, and hunts and dances (and no doubt beds his concubines) with the prowess of a man half his age. Certainly, I find it hard to keep up with him as he makes his way out of the audience room and down corridor after corridor, and yet my stride is as long as any man's. Glancing back, I see the musicians lagging after us, hampered by their instruments, Mr Pepys and the young harpsichordist, closely followed by a suspicious ben Hadou. Is this my moment? I have been strictly schooled never to speak to the sovereign unless addressed, but this may be my only chance. 'Sire,' I begin, girding my courage, 'I would speak with you on an important matter.'

He darts a curious look at me. 'Go on, sir.'

'There is a lady, sire –'

That makes him laugh. 'Ah, there is always a lady. I see you have not wasted your time here.'

'The lady concerned is in Morocco, at the sultan's court. Indeed, within his harem. She is an Englishwoman of good family.'

'I do believe Nelly mentioned such a thing to me. Continue.'

I explain, concisely, the circumstances of Alys's captivity.

'And the name of this paragon?'

'Alys, sire. Alys Swann.'

'And where did you say she was from?'

'The Hague, sire: her father was a supporter of the Royalist cause and fled to Holland during the war.'

His face goes very still; his pace slows and finally he comes to a halt. 'I wish to hear no more.'

Reckless now, I plough on regardless. 'Sire, hear me out, I beg you. She asked me to give you this, sire, if ever I had the chance. She sewed it herself and closed it to keep it secret.' I dig the scroll out and present it to him, shielding the action from the swiftly approaching on-comers with my body. When he hesitates to take it, I press it rudely into his hand. 'Please read it, your majesty: three lives depend on your doing so.'

For a moment we stand there with the rest of the music party bearing down on us and I think, 'It is all over, and I have failed.' Perhaps he sees my despair, for at last he takes it from me and thrusts it into his waistcoat. 'I mislike intrigue, young man,' he says shortly, before striding on. 'But a man who loves music as you do must have an honest heart, so I have decided to trust you.'

I can hardly recall the details of what passed during the hour that followed, such an ecstatic mood took me with the accomplishment of my task. I do vaguely remember I played a duet with the king on the Spanish guitar, and that he was a far better hand with the instrument than I. And Mr Pepys played the flageolet, and I the lute, backed by a dozen stirring violins and Mr Purcell on the spinet; and the latter told me with shining eyes that North Africa was proving a great inspiration to him at the moment, in that he was writing a piece based on the love story of a Greek hero and a tragic

Carthaginian queen, and he was really very delighted to have made my acquaintance.

My exultant mood is soon chased away by ben Hadou, however. Taking me firmly by the arm as the party breaks up, he hustles me back towards our accommodation. 'Are you determined to sabotage our mission? First you play the fool in the park; and now you attempt to hobnob with our host as if you are equals, rather than slave and king. I am the leader of this embassy, and if the king is to address anyone amongst us, it should be me. Now what did you speak about?'

'Just music,' I lie.

He grunts. 'And that is all?'

I nod, not trusting myself to say more.

Just after midnight there is a quiet knock at my door. Bleary with sleep, I open it to find a page outside with a silver salver and upon it a note sealed with a lump of red wax bearing the royal seal. I take it and retire to my room, heart thudding. The letter, dashed off at an untidy slant, is somewhat difficult to decipher: I am not used to reading an English hand. It says:

Birdcage-Walk, St. James's park
Tomorrow at dawn
C. R.

35

4th February 1682

I am up before dawn: for once, not for prayers, though I make God a great number of promises as I hood myself with my burnous and slip out into the dark mist of the morning. By the time I reach the place I believe to be Birdcage-Walk – for there is quite an aviary collected here, in and out of cages, mostly blessedly asleep still with their heads tucked beneath their wings – a rosy light is limning the clouds to the east and painting the still waters of the pleasure lake. I hunker down beneath the trees and wait, and before long a tall, lean figure wrapped in a cloak approaches at a fast clip. The gait is more than a clue, despite the tricorn hat: I step out into his path and am on the point of making my obeisance when the king's deep voice commands me, 'Od's fish, man, don't bow!' He strides into the shelter of the trees where I had been crouched. 'The boy she mentions, you brought him to London with you?'

He regards me with incredulity as I explain the contrivances I have been forced to make to bring Momo safely out of Morocco and into the palace. When I come to the part about transforming him into a blackamoor, he chuckles loudly. 'Well, I must say you are a resourceful fellow, Nus-Nus. Hiding the boy in plain sight shows great audacity; and placing him with Louise is a stroke of genius! I want you to bring him to me, tomorrow, after the couchée. Come up the Privy Stairs: Mr Chiffinch will have instructions to let you pass. Can you do that?'

I nod. 'Of course, your majesty. Thank you.' I cannot help but fall to my knees and reach to kiss his hand in gratitude and relief, but he just laughs and walks away.

As the sun comes up over the roofs of White Hall, I feel as if it is shining just for me and I thank every god I have ever prayed to. Tomorrow Momo will be safe in the king's protection, and the ground will be laid for Alys to join him. I have done all that was asked of me: now I have only Zidana's task to complete. Ah, Nus-Nus, you are a fortunate and capital fellow, I congratulate myself: audacious and resourceful, as the king said; and who am I to gainsay a king? I feel like crowing like a cockerel, so full of pride am I.

I should have remembered that pride goes before a fall. The omens were all there for me to see. On the horizon, dark clouds gathering; a black cat that crosses my path as I enter the palace; the salt I spill as I procure a little breakfast from the small kitchen. There I ask the cook, a bad-tempered old woman, 'Is Kate here?' and she barks back, 'No she isn't, the lazy bitch, though it's no business of a damned blackamoor where she might be!' In disdain for my skin and the slave-bond in my ear, she gives me bread so stale to accompany my coddled egg that I crack a tooth on it, and am immediately transported back to the prison cell at Meknes all those years ago. That should have warned me too: danger lies around every corner, and death lurks on the edge of every pretty vista.

As I slip up the stairs back to my quarters, I round a banister and am so distracted by my heady combination of elation and pain that I almost run into the back of ben Hadou, creeping barefoot up the stairs. I stop and let him continue ahead of me, blithely ignorant of my presence, and wonder where he has been at this hour, and without his shoes, when he is always so proper? Perhaps to bathe and then pray, I chide myself; or, like me, to seek an early breakfast. But it nags at me.

The day brings a new invitation: for Mr Pepys has been as good as his word and arranged for the ambassador and myself to attend a meeting at the Royal Society.

'It is members only, usually,' he confides, as we take a carriage through the crowded streets later that morning, 'but I have had a word with Sir Christopher and he will allow you to enter for the day as a special favour to me. Perhaps if you stay longer in London and would like it, we will be able to make you honorary members?'

Ben Hadou is much taken with this notion and evinces a passion for science I have never suspected in him. He questions Mr Pepys thoroughly on the history of the society and its better-known members, and our host is happy to oblige. The unfamiliar names wash over me, leaving no trace. My mind is as serene as beach sand washed smooth by the ebb of a wave. I feel blessed by the world: apart from my wretched tooth. Even the city we pass through – with its grime and mud, its beggars and street-criers, its stink of fish and horse shit – seems a more benign place than it ever did before, even though the sky is visibly greying and a fine rain is starting to fall. I smile indulgently at a knot of men engaged in conversation on a street corner; but my quietude is soon shattered as they break into a brawl and abruptly there are knives flashing and a sudden spray of blood. Mr Pepys at once leans out of the carriage window and calls something to the coachman, who blows three loud blasts on a whistle. 'That'll bring the charleys running,' he promises. 'Please don't concern yourselves overly, my friends: the constables will sort it out.'

Gresham College, on the wide Holborn thoroughfare, is a tranquil place by comparison. We reach the meeting room via a colonnaded walkway bordering a lovely inner courtyard planted in an orderly fashion with grass and trees, and are greeted by twenty or thirty bewigged and solemn gentlemen, of whom I recognize five or six as court regulars. The president, Sir Christopher Wren, a supercilious-looking man in his middle years, bids us welcome, though his smile does not reach his eyes. 'I hear your embassy is quite the social sensation of the year,' he sneers, and turns away to talk to Mr Evelyn.

At this snub the Tinker looks much deflated, but rallies when he is introduced to Mr Deane, who compliments him on his riding and has observations to make about the shortness of the stirrup leather used with regards to torsion and speed.

There is displayed a live scorpion found in an oil shop in London. Ben Hadou and I exchange glances: if this is the standard of wonders to be found here, we are going to have a dull day indeed. Several large pieces of amber containing insects are displayed: these, again, are nothing new to us. Zidana has a necklace in which a vast spider crouches, preserved for ever in the fragrant resin: it often sits at her throat.

There follows a long discourse in Latin of which neither the ambassador nor I can understand a word, though it appears to involve the relative qualities of a number of different substances and objects, including gold and silver, water and fur, a bee and a leaf, which are then examined most thoroughly by means of an odd-looking instrument comprising a long, decorated tube and a round glass lens to which one places one's eye. Ben Hadou is invited to look down the tube at the mouthpart of a bee, and at once leaps back, exclaiming in some horror at the monstrosity he has perceived, which causes considerable mirth. I choose rather to examine the leaf, which sits better with my mood, and am rewarded by a beautiful pattern of lustrous greens and yellows cut through with translucent veins. The experience is almost hallucinogenic; when eventually I come upright again I feel dizzy and overwhelmed, as if I have somehow been allowed a glimpsed into a secret world hitherto unseen.

By now recovered from his encounter with the suddenly-giant fly, Ben Hadou insists on examining everything else on the table, including his own finger, and as the meeting wears on I allow my mind to drift off into pleasant fantasies of the future that awaits: Momo dressed in a fine blue silk suit beside his lovely mother in creamy satin. No need for powdered gold or poisonous ceruse to heighten the natural beauties of Alys's porcelain skin or sunlit hair; no drops of belladonna required to widen that perfect regard. And I, in a fine coat and waistcoat of figured velvet, standing proudly behind them, with silver buckles on my shoes and a long black periwig to replace my turban, posing for the artist who paints the portrait that will adorn our new home. In one of these delicious fancies, I imagine Alys cradling a little girl – our daughter! my wayward imagination supplies – wrapped in a froth of lace, showing her off to a circle of court ladies. Such foolish nonsense! I catch myself up and chide myself silently. I am a eunuch: I can have no children of my own. More than that, I am a slave and she is a gentlewoman; I am as black as night and she as white as day; and never the twain shall meet.

Ah, but you may be the night and she the moon, a little voice encourages coaxingly, and who knows what possibilities may be offered by that conjunction?

I am brought out of this reverie rather sharply by a sudden twinge of the damaged molar, and, although I think I have successfully stifled the groan it elicits, a gentleman in a tumbling brown wig leans over and asks after my well-being. 'Just a little toothache,' I explain. 'I cracked one this morning on some rather hard bread.'

'Goodness me: austerity measures at the palace must be rather more severe than I thought!' He introduces himself to us as a Mr Ashmole, up from Oxford for the meeting, and questions me most genially about my origins and the Tinker about Moorish customs, explaining that he is something of a collector of antiquities and unusual items, and is indeed in the process of setting up a museum to share his collections with the world at large. He sighs. 'How I would love to travel more. It seems the world is enlarging day by day – Africa, America, China . . . Imagine the wonderful treasures that might be gleaned on such trips, the artefacts from so many different cultures . . . We have the most remarkable flayed skin of a native Indian king to display, and the saddle used by Genghis Khan himself.'

Ben Hadou grimaces. 'I'm afraid I can't offer you anything so grand, but I have a pair of fine Moorish spurs you might like for your collection.'

Ashmole looks thrilled. 'That would be most splendid. But I can't possibly take them without offering something in exchange.' He thinks for a moment, then declares, 'Maybe a magnifying glass you could take back to your country with you; and in the same house I have a friend who can mend this gentleman's tooth.'

Ben Hadou's eyes gleam. 'I'm sure Nus-Nus does not need to bother your friend, but I must say I would dearly love one of these magical glasses.'

'I cannot promise you it will be as strong as Mr Hooke's microscope, but I think you will be pleased to have it. Come with me after the meeting to Mr Draycott's house and I'll see what we can do. It is not far from here, just to the south of Fleet Street.'

I can see the Tinker is greatly torn, but in the end he declines politely, explaining that he has duties back at the palace. It is arranged that I am to go with Mr Ashmole to fetch the glass and am dismissed from my duties for the rest of the day.

Mr Ashmole proves to be excellent company. He insists on walking from the college, rather than taking a chair or carriage, pointing out curiosities as we go. 'At my age you have to keep moving, you know, for fear of what will happen if you stop.'

I raise my eyebrows, but say nothing. He cannot be more than fifty, and moves with as much speed as the king, his walking stick no more than a stylish accessory: yet he speaks as if he is an old man. We are making our way down Chancery Lane at a trot when the heavens open.

'Goodness,' says my companion, looking up from under the dripping brim of his hat. 'I fear your headcloth will be quite ruined. I never thought to bring an umbrella.'

'Can't stand the things,' I assure him cheerfully.

We duck into the Black Spread Eagle tavern and wait for the worst of the deluge to pass. The inn is noisy with custom and full of smoke and smells, but the sight of me seems to attract considerable attention and an uneasy quiet falls.

Then someone bursts out with, 'By Gad, what a monster!' and there is general laughter, and more catcalls.

'Is it real, or paint, do you think?'

'We don't want no negards in here!'

'Hoi, Othello, get back on the stage!'

Mr Ashmole looks appalled. 'By my soul, Mr Nus-Nus, I do apologize for the rudeness of my countrymen. Better we brave the rain, I think.'

We are just making our way out again when a man grabs me by the arm. 'Oi there, Mustapha, remind your mistress she still owes me eighty quid from the tables!'

I turn and look down at the speaker, a richly dressed but dissolute-looking young man with a sparse beard, badly trimmed. 'I am not Mustapha.'

He screws his face up, perplexed. 'Can't be two of you such a size and hue. You just tell her, you hear? Tell her Mr Jakes sends his compliments and reminds her of her debt. I'll see her at the opening of *The City Heiress*, right?'

Out in the street, the rain is still falling like spears. Mr Ashmole takes me by the arm and walks me quickly away, tutting. 'Theatre folk, quite dreadful. This used to be such a nice area.'

We make a right on to Fleet Street, then cross it and enter a road flanked on either side by tall houses, at the bottom of which the river can be glimpsed slinking by like a great serpent. A few yards further down he turns right into a narrow alleyway, and we mount steps to a door with a brass knocker in the form of a lion's head and are ushered inside by a pink-faced man with a pair of spectacles strapped to his head, the glass of which makes his eyes look vast and aquatic, like fishes in a bowl of water. 'Elias!' he cries. 'Back so soon?'

'I hope we have not interrupted some essential process.'

'I am in the middle of transmuting water and dried leaves into a potable libation,' Mr Draycott says, smiling. 'Perhaps you and your guest would join me for a cup of tea?' He leads us into a dark parlour, where a kettle hangs from a hook over a small fire. The entire room is grimy with soot and littered with papers and books: it is hard to know where to sit, especially in a white robe, so I hunker down African-style.

As we drink this English tea (a bitter, execrable brew), my companion explains that I have a cracked tooth that needs mending and our host rubs his hands in glee. 'A patient? How excellent.'

'Not paying, I fear, Nathaniel. As a favour to me, if you would be so kind.'

I watch Mr Draycott's face fall. 'I have money,' I say quickly, but he shakes his head. 'No, no. I cannot take money from a friend of Mr Ashmole: everything I have I owe to him, including this house.'

'Nonsense, my dear Nathaniel: it is our shared venture, this laboratory: where else would I practise my experiments?'

We go down a flight of rickety wooden stairs into a long, low-ceilinged cellar lined with shelves on two sides. Upon the shelves are piles of books and papers, and as many labelled bottles and pots as in an apothecary's shop. Leaning towards them I read: 'viper's flesh', 'goa stones', 'hiera picra'; 'spider silk' and half expect to come upon a jar containing mouse eyelashes or dragon's teeth: it reminds me of Sidi Kabour's stock. Against one wall sits a large cylindrical furnace, the coals within glowing red and around its base heaps of dark matter, metal tailings, powders and ashes. The room is gloomy and smells sulphurous; there are dishes and crucibles on the tables, retorts and melting-pots, mortars and pestles, all stained with a variety of substances. On one of the tables a collection of vials containing larvae and foetuses of animal origin; and a rodent is pinned to a board, displaying its vital organs and skeleton. I think of Zidana's secret chamber and the hairs prickle on the back of my neck.

'Perhaps I should see a chirurgeon with this tooth, have it taken out by the root.'

'Nonsense, dear fellow: no need to give yourself over to barbarians with pincers and levers. Nathaniel has perfected a wonderful amalgam that permeates every hole and crack and sets as hard as stone.'

Giving words to my thoughts, I ask, 'Are you are an alchemist, sir?'

'I'd rather be called a natural philosopher,' Nathaniel says cheerfully. 'Making rigorous inquiry into the hidden laws of the universe.'

'Though the word "alchemist" is by no means an insult to men of vision such as ourselves, seeking evidence of the pure essence of the Lord's creation.' Mr Ashmole pats my shoulder. 'Now, sit down here and let's take a look. Hand me that candle, Nathaniel.'

They peer curiously into the cave of my mouth. 'Remarkable teeth,' says Ashmole. 'They'd take some drawing: the roots will have a powerful hold.'

'A cracked grinder on each side: couldn't be simpler!' exclaims Mr Draycott. 'A swift coating with my patented mixture and they'll be as good as new.'

'It really isn't hurting much any more,' I lie. 'I'm sure I can live with it.'

But Mr Draycott is already mixing up his ingredients with a terrible briskness of purpose. 'A little tin and zinc,' he murmurs, 'a touch of copper, and a drop of vitriol —' The crucible gives off a violent hiss and the flames of the spirit-burner flare green, then blue, and a horrible stink fills the air. Mixing frenetically, he moves it off the heat and reaches for a heavy flask. 'And now to let it cool a moment before we add the quicksilver . . .'

The fumes are disquieting: I leap to my feet and the flask goes flying, and suddenly there are globules of metallic silver everywhere. The sight of what should surely have been a liquid, now bouncing and rolling in balls of bright argent down my robe and across the floor, has me staring in wonder.

Mr Draycott laughs at my surprise. 'Ah, sir: mercury is the most remarkable element, neither a liquid nor yet fully a solid: it is the First Matter, from which all other metals derive. But, more than that, it is the transcending principal of transmutation, like Hermes himself, moving between heaven and earth, bringing life, and death. As calomel, it is the most powerful medicine, able to cure even our most debauched rakes; but expose it to sunlight and it becomes a fatal poison.'

'By the Ancient One, I do not wish to have such a deadly element in my mouth,' I declare firmly.

Mr Ashmole brings the candle close to his face and shows me a set of metal-covered back teeth. 'Fifteen years I've had these: I was Nathaniel's first patient, and by God he's been a life-saver. Not just the teeth either: he's mended a broken bone in my writing hand and warded off the tertian ague with his necklace of spiders.'

Necklace of spiders? I can see that Mr Draycott and Zidana would get along well.

Seeing my hesitation, Mr Ashmole smiles indulgently. 'What age would you say I have, sir? Do not be afraid to insult me: I shall not take it badly.'

'Fifty, maybe fifty-two?' I hazard.

'Sixty-five!' he crows exultantly and slaps Mr Draycott on the back. 'All down to his tonic mixture, which I take every day: if you had seen me fifteen years ago you would not have recognized me, for I was dwindling fast, but his spagyrical tincture has put flesh on my bones and kept my muscles supple; and as for my hair: well, pull on that, sir. Do not be afraid to give it a good yank.'

Tentatively I tug on his wig, and am amazed to find the luxuriant locks are sturdily anchored.

'You see? Why he is not a celebrated man, I cannot imagine.'

Mr Draycott blushes. 'Now, now Elias, I am no miracle worker, all I have done is to refine the recipe. It has long been recognized that the Primum Ens Melissae is a most powerful tonic, as much for women as for men.'

'He gave it to his servant, Agnes,' Mr Ashmole confides, 'a woman of gone sixty, and all her hair fell out till she was as bald as an egg —'

'About which she was not happy!'

'But then it grew back as black and lustrous as it had been in her youth, and she started to menstruate again for the first time in two decades. Last year she gave birth to a fine lad: and if that is not a miracle, then I don't know what is!'

The prickling feeling now runs from my neck down the length of my spine. Have I found Zidana's elixir? It seems too fortuitous to be true, and yet moment by moment as the pair of them talk on, I find belief taking root. The long and short of it is, I let the alchemist treat my teeth, which is by no means as unpleasant an experience as I have feared, and am even able to chew my way painlessly through a meagre supper of bean soup, cold lamb and bread with the gentlemen as I ponder my next step. By the time I come to leave it is full dark. Over my shoulder I carry a cloth bag containing the promised magnifying glass and a small cork-stoppered flask of a yellow liquid as bright as sunlight. Mr Ashmole insists on accompanying me to White Hall: 'It is on my way back to Lambeth; and perhaps I might collect the Moorish spurs the ambassador so generously offered this morning in exchange for the glass.'

As we walk in the Temple Gardens, the moon shines on the river through a gap in the clouds, silvering it with a mercury glow and, caught up in the triumph of my run of good luck, I am just thinking I have never seen a lovelier sight, when we are set upon by footpads. There are two of them, big fellows with their faces muffled for disguise.

'Give me that bag, you black bastard!' one shouts at me.

The other faces off Mr Ashmole. 'And you: jewellery, money, whatever you have.'

They come at us, swinging clubs and one knocks Mr Ashmole down. As I move to defend him, the other thumps me hard in the midriff with his weapon, stealing my wind. He tries to snatch the cloth bag from me, but I hold on grimly. It is a mistake: another blow takes my legs out from under me and I land with an ominous crash on the bag. The unmistakable sound of broken glass greets me as I move, and so enraged am I at the loss of the valuable magnifying glass that I catapult myself to my feet. As my attacker comes at me again, I catch hold of a club and wrench it out of his grasp with such force that he spins off-balance. A well-placed foot sends him cartwheeling across the grass, to smash up against a tree. Turning, I find Mr Ashmole is laying about the second man with his stick: seeing me coming with the club raised, the footpad makes off, swearing; and after a moment the other scrambles up and follows him, limping heavily.

'Are you all right, sir?'

Mr Ashmole examines a rip in his coat. 'One of my better suits, damn them. But other than that, no great damage. And yourself?'

I shake the bag, demonstrating the telltale tinkle of broken glass. On further investigation it turns out that the magnifying glass is in pieces.

★

We part at Westminster, Mr Ashmole apologizing over and over for his foolish choice of route, the gardens being well known for robberies after dark. He hails a boatman to carry him across the river to Lambeth, and I walk the remaining few hundred yards alone, feeling much deflated after my earlier euphoria. The palace guards stare at me curiously, and one says something to his companion that I do not catch; they both laugh. Up in the embassy's accommodation all is quiet. I decide I had better report the matter to ben Hadou and get that unpleasantness out of the way, and am about to knock at his door when it opens and a woman tumbles out, giggling and trying to stuff her honey-coloured hair back into her cap. She has her stockings over her arm: there can be little doubt what has been going on.

'Hello, Kate.'

Her hand flies to her mouth and she goes a deep red, then grabs up her skirts and flees towards the stairs leading down to the small kitchen.

Ben Hadou tries, and fails, to stare me down. 'It is all quite innocent,' he protests.

'It is none of my business, sidi, what you do.' Despite everything, I cannot help but grin.

He looks pale. 'You must say nothing of this to anyone, do you understand? It is not what it seems: we are going to be married.'

'Married?'

He nods. 'Yes, but not a word: if it gets out there will be trouble.' We lock eyes, then his gaze travels downward. 'Good God, Nus-Nus, have you pissed yourself?'

I look down. Where the flask broke my white robe is stained a lurid, incriminating yellow. The excitements and discoveries of the day have been excessive: I decide there is no point in explaining the circumstances after all. My room feels unnaturally silent without the presence of either Momo or Amadou. I sit on the edge of the bed for a long while, thoughts tumbling wildly. Then I try my best to wash the stain from my robe, but, as if determined to prove its transforming prowess, the tincture resists all my efforts.

36

5th February 1682

I wake early the next day, filled with an unaccountable optimism and energy. Today I shall present Alys's son to the king, and once that is achieved all will be well.

After enduring a tedious meeting between the ambassador and his majesty's ministers about the proposed treaty, more long-winded and even less decisive than the last one, I am finally dismissed by ben Hadou and it is nearing midday. So much the better, I think: there will be less time during which I have to keep Momo hidden. I make my way via the maze of corridors and galleries towards the Duchess of Portsmouth's apartments, and am just rounding the final corner when I meet Jacob coming the other way. When he sees me, his face takes on an almost comically tragic expression.

'I was coming to find you.'

'I was coming to see *you*,' I return brightly. 'I am to present Momo to the king tonight, privately, in his chambers.'

'Oh. He is gone. That's what I was coming to say.'

'Gone?'

'I asked madame where he was and she waved her hand at me and said, "*Il n'est plus à moi.*"'

'What?' The pit of my stomach feels as if I have swallowed a cannonball.

'She will not tell me. Perhaps she will tell you.'

Louise is sitting in her dressing room, flicking through the pages of a gazette, surrounded by fussing attendants. When she sees me, she offers a dazzling smile. 'Monsieur Nus-Nus! How charming. Come, sit with me. What do you think of this new style of fontange? Is it too high for me, do you think? Will it make my face look too long?' She turns the magazine – *Le Mercure Galant* – towards me and I am greeted by the sight of a woman wearing a lacy headdress that makes her look like some ridiculous crested parrot.

'It's hideous,' I say shortly, forgetting my manners.

She trills with laughter, hits me mockingly with the magazine. 'Men, what do you know of fashion?'

'I've come to ask about your little page boy.'

'Jacob?' she looks surprised. 'He was here a moment ago.'

'Not Jacob, the other one, the small boy.'

Her face clouds. 'Oh, Miette? Jacob's little cousin? He was such a dear but I'm afraid I have had to let him go.' She leans towards me confidentially. 'He has – how you say? Magpie tendencies.'

I stare at her, uncomprehending.

'*Un voleur!* A terrible little thief. *Mes pauvres bijoux!* I found three ropes of pearls and my best emerald brooch hidden away amongst his things yesterday afternoon. And so when I lost heavily at basset last night I decided the best thing all round was to sell him, finances being what they are. The agent, he give me a very good price.'

'Whatever he has offered I will double it!' I cry. 'Treble it!'

'For that much, *cheri*, you can have Jacob!' Louise pats me on the arm. 'What is it coming to when a blackamoor wishes a blackamoor for a servant? La, the world's turned upside-down!'

Five minutes later I am running through the Tilt Yard and out into St James's Park with a name and address in my pocket.

The turn for the worse in my luck continues: the agent, Mr Lane, is not at his home in Pall Mall, but at his offices in Cornhill. I do not even know where Cornhill is – it sounds disturbingly rural and distant – but I take note of the address from his servant and hail a hackney carriage. The driver agrees to a vastly inflated fare, but only if I ride up on the box alongside him. 'Can't be seen to take you inside the carriage,' he says. 'It'll spoil my business with persons of quality.'

I am tempted to walk, but swallow my pride, and there is, as it turns out, a benefit to the man's prejudice, for the view from the top of the carriage is exhilarating, as we bowl through the busy streets of the capital, and soon I am even recognizing landmarks and streets: there is the river, and there where I walked with Mr Ashmole to visit Mr Draycott; there the junction with Chancery Lane, leading north towards the Royal Society's meeting place. It is reassuring to gain some understanding of the geography of the city, its being smaller than I had at first thought: by the time we fetch up in Cornhill, I console myself with the knowledge that I could, if I have to, retrace the route on foot, without the need to prostrate my pride to London's hackney-coachmen. Then I remember that I will have Momo with me, and that a small child's legs may be a different matter. Well, I will climb that tree when I come to it, I tell myself, still full of optimism, paying the coachman his two-shilling fare.

Nothing is simple. I scrutinize the address more closely. 'Jonathan's, Change Lane, Cornhill' is what I have written, which seemed simple enough as I took it down; but the lane turns out to be a little kingdom in its own right, spawning alleys and bifurcations, all gloomy and canyon-like, for the sun does not penetrate their narrow compass. I walk along, dwarfed by the tall buildings that channel the loud conversations of the young men who pass me, too pleased with themselves and their discussions to take any notice of a lost foreigner seeking directions. I pass wig shops, pawnbrokers and taverns, but the overwhelming smell of the place is of coffee. I stop a lad carrying a sack across his shoulders. 'I am looking for Jonathan,' I tell him. 'Jonathan Lane.'

He makes a puzzled face at me. 'Eh?'

'An agent in slaves.'

'I don't know no Jonathan Lane, but Jonathan's is there, across the alley.' He indicated a large, colonnaded coffee shop. 'That's where the traders do business.'

Jonathan's is a huge and noisy cave full of earnest men in tricorn hats talking urgently at one another over close-crammed tables. I catch stray words as I stare around the room – 'yield' and 'commodities', 'stocks' and 'margins'. It is the language of trading, but the only money changing hands appears to be for the food and drink being served in the establishment. I ask a lad in an apron carrying a tray of coffee-jugs where I may find Mr Lane, and have to shout over the hubbub. 'Over there,' he points to a far corner. 'He's with Mr Hyde, the Duke of York's agent from the Royal African Company.'

I make my way over to them with some difficulty and have to hover for several moments before either of the men takes notice of me, so intent are they on their business. At last, the one in a light brown periwig glances up. 'No more coffee, thank you.' He looks away again.

His partner, a man in a blue velvet coat laden with expensive frogging, is regarding me now curiously. 'He don't work here, Thomas, not in that oriental get-up, not unless it's some gimmick to sell a new brand of Turkish coffee. Perhaps he's one of yours?'

Thomas turns back, looks me up and down; frowns. 'You're not one of mine. What do you want?'

I explain that I am looking for the child who till this morning was in the employ of the Duchess of Portsmouth.

'Oh, Louise's little blackamoor. What about him?'

'I wish to buy him.'

This has both of them laughing. 'Are you setting up in competition, then? Selling your relatives?'

'I'm with the Moroccan embassy. There has been an unfortunate misunderstanding: the child was sold by mistake.'

Thomas Lane bridles. 'There was certainly no misunderstanding; it was a very fair deal I gave her!'

The other man, Mr Hyde, looks at me askance. 'You're not from Morocco, are you? Originally, I mean. Where do you come from?'

I tell him and he smiles knowingly. 'Ah, I was worried the Africa Company had missed out on a bit of a goldmine, with fellows your size to be come by. But no, we've got that region covered. Good to know.'

I do not fully understand what is meant by this, but it smacks of slaving, which makes him a devil, and renders the agent doing business with him another trader in misery. The idea of giving either of them money is repellent, but I must save Momo.

I turn back to Mr Lane. 'Whatever the duchess gave you for him, I will give you more: you will make your profit.'

He spreads his hands. 'Too late, I'm afraid. I had a customer already waiting: I sold him this morning, to Mrs Herbert. She wanted something a bit special to show off at the premiere of *The City Heiress* this afternoon.'

An hour later I have managed to make my way back across London to the Dorset Garden Theatre, down on the riverbank to the south of Fleet Street. My poor luck holding, it started to spit with rain almost as soon as I stalked out of the coffee-house; by the time I arrive at my destination, my robes are plastered against my skin and my turban has doubled in weight. Under the shelter of some trees, I wring the wretched turban out and rewind it upon my head, watching the carriages roll up to discharge their passengers. Although it is only four in the afternoon, the flambeaux have been lit, for the gloom of the day is profound: by their leaping light I have a good view of the theatre-goers. I ignore the ordinary hackneys, reasoning that a woman who would buy a black child as an accessory for the occasion is likely to turn up in osten-tatious style. Despite the bad weather, the crowds have turned out for the play: soon the square outside the theatre is heaving with coaches, and I watch them all like a hawk, but there is no sign of Momo, just women in masks and gallants in powdered wigs. Then three golden carriages arrive at once, dis-gorging a collection of richly dressed passengers – all ostrich feathers and tabby silk – who head swiftly up the steps out of the rain and into the theatre. There is such a mêlée that I cannot see between all the wheels, and the horses and have to dodge out from my shelter. I think I catch a glimpse of the woman who sat next to ben Hadou at the duchess's dinner: yes, there she is, and beside her the Duchess Mazarin, her striking face framed by the masses of black wavy hair that escape her hood, with her servant Mustapha, his crimson brocade vivid beneath a long black cloak. So struck am I by their appearance that I almost miss the arrival of a particularly opulent coach-and-four, out of which issue two splendidly dressed servants wielding vast umbrellas, and three women, one in a dress as wide as a sofa. I am afforded a brief view of Momo, all done up in his gold lace suit; then he is ushered away by the women, and they all disappear swiftly into the building.

Swearing to myself, I dash across the carriage yard and up the steps after them, but am stopped at the door and asked for my entrance fee. More sec-onds are lost as I sort through the unfamiliar currency, then lose patience and drop a handful of coins into the man's palm. Inside, all is chaos: the lobby is pell-mell with people, and although I am a head taller than most, the ridiculous wigs, feathers and headdresses obscure my view. At last I spot Mustapha and push my way through to him. We look one another in the eye. 'Senufo?' he asks, head tilted assessingly.

I nod. 'Asante?'

'Dogomba,' he specifies. His tribal marks are little vertical lines that run down his cheeks, like tears.

'Can you help me? I am looking for a woman called Mrs Herbert, she has a little boy with her.'

An expression of contempt flickers over his face. 'She has a box upstairs.'

I thank him and turn towards the stairs, but he catches my arm. 'Come up with us. Follow close behind when we go up with my lady in a minute. There'll be quite a crowd: Mrs Behn is with us.'

Mrs Behn is surrounded by a large group of folk come to pass on their congratulations and to be seen with the playwright; the Duchess Mazarin sweeps in like a galleon in sail and bears her away; and then we are moving up the narrow stairs into the gallery, and no one stops me as we make our way into the enclosed box. From this eyrie-like viewpoint, I can see the entire theatre — right across the gallery and the private boxes, down into the pit, where women in vizards mingle with the hoi polloi. The upper gallery is magnificently appointed, with plush seating and gilded cherubs everywhere; but all of this is taken in in a flash, for suddenly I spy Momo two boxes away with a vastly ornamented woman who must be Mrs Herbert, two thinner, younger versions of herself who must surely be her daughters and a pair of liveried servants. All Momo's attention is on a little lapdog in his arms: the two wear matching diamond-studded collars.

There is a fanfare from the musicians down below. As inconspicuously as I can, I detach myself from the duchess's retinue and ease myself into the narrow corridor that gives access to the other boxes. I open the door of the second box and thrust my head in. At once a servant puts himself in my path, looking much alarmed. 'I warn you, I am armed.'

'I have some business with Mrs Herbert. It won't take a moment.'

'I tell you, sir, begone: the play is starting.'

And so it is, I realize: four gentlemen in coloured clothing have come out upon the stage and struck attitudes; a footman lingers behind them, carrying a cloak. As they start to speak, Mrs Herbert's servant cannot help but snatch a look, and, as he does so, I push past him. 'Mrs Herbert –'

One of the daughters gives a little yelp at the sight of me; but the general noise of the place carries it away, for already people are catcalling the players, booing the strict uncle, cheering the feckless nephew. The other daughter hides behind her fan.

'Go away, you ruffian!' cries Mrs Herbert. Her hands go to the jewels at her throat. 'You shan't rob me, not in full sight of all!'

'Madam, I am no robber: I have come for the boy. The Duchess of Portsmouth sold him in error, and I have come to take him back.' At the sound of my voice, Momo turns, his eyes and grin gleaming out of a face still as black as my own.

'Lud, I only bought him this morning, and for a lot of money!'

'I am instructed to pay you double what you paid for him.' I show her the gold, but she shakes her head. 'I couldn't possibly: dear Fanny has taken such a liking to him!'

'I will give more, to ease dear Fanny's pain,' I say desperately. Whoever Fanny may be. While Mrs Herbert deliberates, my eyes stray past Momo, towards the lit stage and the crowded populace below. Something has snagged my eye, perhaps a sixth sense at work: for down in the pit, amidst the mass of dark hats and cloaks, a single face is turned away from the stage, staring upwards, scanning the gallery.

It is the English renegade Hamza. So he has escaped from prison, or, more likely bribed his way out thanks to Rafik.

The moment my gaze lands upon him he sees me and our eyes lock. At once he starts pushing his way through the crowd.

I dump the gold in Mrs Herbert's lap, grab Momo by the hand and drag him away.

'Fanny!' one of the daughters wails, and 'Thief!' cries Mrs Herbert, and now the two servants rather unwillingly give chase.

Wrenching the lapdog out of Momo's grasp, I hurl it towards them. In their efforts to catch dear Fanny the servants fall over one another, and in doing so take down one of the girls, who in turn collapses into her mother, while the dog runs around and around barking delightedly, as if this is the best fun it has had in its life. I propel Momo through the door and into the corridor and then we are careering down the narrow stairs, into the lobby and out into the pouring rain, which at once begins to wash Momo's dye from him, turning his face into a streaky horror.

'Hoi, eunuch: stop!' Hamza comes bowling out of the theatre. At the sight of Momo's dissolving disguise his eyes flash in triumph. 'I knew you were up to something!'

Unceremoniously, I throw Momo over my shoulder and run, my feet slapping against the wet cobbles, desperation powering my muscles. Dodging parked carriages and stamping horses, I zigzag right, then left, into a maze of small streets behind the theatre, with no goal in mind other than to avoid our pursuer. My lungs are soon burning, but still I run, right, then left again, and straight on down a narrow alley littered with stinking refuse. By the time I realize this alley is a dead end, it is too late.

Footsteps echo in the distance, and then suddenly there he is, the renegade, silhouetted in the entrance to the alley. I stare around, but there is no way out. Hamza comes on at a half-run now, a knife glinting in his hand. 'You've led me a damned chase these past days, you fucker! But I'm feeling magnanimous, so put the boy down and walk away, if you know what's good for you.' Now he is just a few feet away, grinning demonically.

'You'll have to kill me,' I tell him grimly.

He just laughs. 'Did they remove your wit as well as your balls? There's no need for heroics. No one's going to hurt the child: we're just going to take him home to his papa, score ourselves a reward for bringing him back from the dead, since the fucking draper couldn't be arsed to pay for him, and who can blame him? Look, what do you have to lose: just hand over the boy and walk away. Take ship for America or some such: I hear there's plenty of work there for a big negard like you!'

I transfer Momo from across my shoulders to cradle him in my arms and he looks up at me, round-eyed. 'Is the game over, Nus-Nus?'

'I fear so, my dear.' I put him down carefully, and as soon as his feet touch the ground I yell, 'Run, Momo, run! Back to the theatre. Go!'

I give him a shove and he takes off running, dodging neatly past the renegade, who swears foully and turns to go after him, his blade bright in the gloom. I launch myself at Hamza's back and we both go down in the filth. He twists and rolls and grabs me, and somehow forces the knife to my throat and we struggle mightily down on the ground, amid the turds and vegetable waste. As we do, my turban unwinds itself and tangles his knife hand and he curses as he tries to free it. I reel the turban in and I butt him hard in the face, deliberately aiming for his broken nose. He howls and blood bubbles out, smearing us both, but still he does not let go of the weapon. Whipping my head back and sideways, I manage to escape the folds of cotton that are obscuring my sight and land a satisfyingly vicious blow on his arm. He cries out and the knife falls, spinning away in the gloom. I go after it, feeling a surge of joy as my hand closes on it; then Hamza's fist smashes me in the ear so that the world is roaring and red and I fall sideways and lose my grip on the hilt.

In that unguarded moment his boot catches me in the guts, making me retch and gasp for air. Maleeo, that hurt! The pain is immense, but, as his foot comes at me again, I manage by luck to catch it and wrench and he comes crashing down beside me. But he is a tough man, and used to street brawling; and luck seems to be with him, for at once he is up, and again he has the knife in his hand. We scrabble to our feet and circle one another like fighting dogs, snarling, in our own languages, heaving for breath, covered in filth and wet through; and still the rain beats down.

He casts the blade negligently from one hand to the other. 'Throat or belly, eunuch?' he rasps at me. 'Fast or slow? I can't deci—'

Without finishing the word, he lunges at me and as I duck away from the blade I slip on some wet vegetable or worse and the knife catches me in the shoulder. I spin away, howling, but with an almighty leap he pins me up against the wall, the knife pressed against my ribs.

His eyes bulge and blink at me through his mask of blood. 'You stupid negard! Now I'm going to have to kill you, and all you had to do was walk away . . .'

The knife slides through the fabric of my robe and I writhe and feel it slip chill, then searing, across my skin, a taste of death. A poor way to go, ignominiously, in a filthy London alley, far from home and help. He gets the blade square to me again and then lets out a shout and looks down, shaking his leg. Something darts away, a little demon with blood around its mouth. It grins, and its teeth are red, and for a moment I think it is Amadou, back from the dead to revenge himself on his murderer, but as it capers away in its gold lace suit I realize it is Momo. The next thing I know, a great shadow detaches itself from the gloom and sends the renegade and his knife flying in different directions. Hamza hits the wall hard and slides down it, his legs sticking out in front of him. He coughs and swears, tries to get up; but the shadow puts a foot on his chest, then bends and very neatly and deliberately slits his throat, stepping quickly sideways to avoid the sudden jet of blood. Then he wipes his knife clean on the renegade's cloak, stows it in his belt and turns around.

I always knew I was going to have to kill Hamza, but to see him dispatched so efficiently before my eyes shocks me silent. At last I manage to blurt out, 'Why?'

Mustapha regards me inscrutably for a long moment, then he shrugs. 'I'd already left the theatre to come after you: I met the boy running back. He said there was a bad man trying to kill you.'

Momo hugs me hard around the legs. 'I bit him, Nus-Nus, did you see?'

'I saw.' I hug him back, then look up again. 'I don't know what to say. Thank you seems very inadequate. But I give you thanks, Mustapha, from my heart.'

'Please, call me Addo. It is my tribal name.'

'King of the Road.' I nod. It is exactly what he looks like standing there in the gathering gloom in his cloak and turban with his eyes gleaming. 'My true name is Akuji.'

'Dead, Yet Awake. Very apt. Certainly better than Nus-Nus.' He gives me a crooked smile, his teeth very white in the shadow of his face. Then he becomes serious. 'They'll be looking for you. Or, rather, they'll be looking for two blackamoors. But I think three of us are likely to cause a riot, and I should get back to Hortense before I'm missed.'

'Don't worry about us, I know where we can go. Thank you, Addo.' We clasp arms briefly, and then he strides away into the darkness.

★

I take Momo to Nathaniel Draycott's house, which, I realize belatedly, is but two streets away. The rain is still coming down hard; there is no one around, which is as well. By the time we reach his door, Momo is half white again.

Nathaniel, to give him credit, merely raises an eyebrow at our appearance and waves us inside. He stares at Momo. 'Great heavens, nigredo becomes albedo! What strange alchemy is this?' Momo giggles delightedly.

'Mr Draycott, I fear I must ask for your help,' Quickly, I sketch the situation for him 'I am very sorry to involve you in such an unsavoury business, and I will not blame you at all if you want to call out the constables. However, hear me out, for I have a proposition for you.' An hour later, clean, with my wounds bound and with a handshake on my proposition, I climb into the sedan chair that Mr Draycott has summoned for us, enveloped in a borrowed cloak, with a tricorn hat pulled down low over my face. The sedan-bearers huff and puff their way back to White Hall. 'Lord lumme,' one of them says as I emerge at the other end with Momo riding my hip beneath the cloak. 'Beg pardon, sir, but you weigh as much as an 'orse.' I apologize and give him my last remaining gold piece, which shuts him up.

That evening, after the king's couchée, I run with Momo down unlit corridors, along rarely used galleries and back stairs: all those unfrequented parts of the huge palace that will gradually lead us, unchallenged, to the Privy Stairs. There, the doorkeeper, Mr Chiffinch, ushers us in to the royal presence.

We find the king tucking into a private supper, and upon the sight of food Momo falls upon the leavings like a wild beast. The king, having been divested of his daily garb, lounges in an Indian robe, like an oriental potentate; perhaps (I am being generous) this is why Momo feels so at home as to fall to eating without a word of entreaty or permission. More likely, he is simply famished; and that is my fault. I rebuke him sharply and apologize for his lack of manners, but his majesty pays me no attention. Instead, a curious, soft expression steals over his face as he watches the boy cramming pie into his maw. After a while he looks up at me. 'Did you know they called me Black Boy when I was his age? My complexion was a good deal darker than this little chap's, and my eyes were never blue. His mother must be very fair.'

'Her skin is very white, her hair like spun gold.' It has been nearly four months since last I saw her: I am beginning to forget the precise configuration of Alys's face, just hypnotic details: the shadow cast by her fair lashes upon her cheek in bright sunlight; the nest of fine lines around her mouth as she raises her lips to mine . . .

The king nods thoughtfully, then beckons to Momo. 'Come here, young fellow.'

Momo, having finished the pie, except for what is left crumbled and smeared about his face, obeys. 'You must bow,' I prompt. 'This is the King of England.'

But Momo is too fascinated for bowing. Instead he asks, 'Where are your jewels?', which makes the king roar with laughter. Composing himself, he replies, 'Kings do not need jewels to make them royal, young man.'

Momo considers this for a long moment, then takes off Mrs Herbert's diamond collar, which in my agitation to get him here unscathed I have quite forgot about, and solemnly hands it over to the sovereign. 'I don't need this, then,' he pronounces regally. He then proceeds to empty the pockets of his lace suit, extracting from them a pearl brooch, a pair of diamond earrings and a fine gold chain bearing a crucifix.

I am mortified. 'Oh, Momo . . .'

Charles raises a heavy black brow. 'Well now, this is quite a haul. Do you know what we do with robbers in my kingdom?'

Momo shakes his head, perplexed. 'Oh, I did not rob them,' he says airily. 'I am just taking care of them. But I don't need to any more because you are the king and so they must belong to you. In Morocco, the sultan owns everything in the kingdom.'

'Does he now?'

'Yes, papa was always telling me: "Everything you see, Momo belongs to me: every person and everything they have is mine." That is how it is when you are king.'

The king smiles wryly. 'Od's fish, your great-grandfather would have loved you dearly.'

I frown. 'His great-grandfather?'

'My father, King Charles the First.'

Still I am stumbling stupidly. 'The boy's great-grandfather is, I fear, long dead in The Hague, in Holland.'

'My father never, to my knowledge, visited that city, and it has been a long time since I was in exile there. Over thirty years: time's wingèd chariot, and all that.' Charles regards me curiously before understanding dawns on him. 'You did not know?'

'I am afraid, sire, that I am quite lost.'

He gets up and crosses the room to an enamelled chest and from it extracts Alys's embroidered scroll. This, he unfurls in front of me and on it I read:

Sire, forgive the presumption of your unfortunate subject.
I ask nothing for myself but beg only that you will provide for my son, your little
grandson Charles, known also as Mohammed, son of Ismail, Sultan of Morocco,
who keeps me as a wife here in the city of Meknes.
In shame and desperation, your daughter Alys
(born to Mary Swann in The Hague, October 1649)

The world spins. I collapse into a chair and close my eyes, and it is some moments before I am myself again. When I open my eyes, it is to see that the king, now bald as an egg, is draping Momo in his vast black periwig.

'See, how do you think you will like having to wear such a monstrosity, young man? You will have to if you grow to be a man here, you know, even though the wretched things are most damnably hot and itchy.'

'I will start a new fashion,' Momo declares, shaking off the offending wig. 'Everyone shall shave their heads like you and Nus-Nus and wear a hat when it is cold.'

'What a sensible little fellow you are.' The king looks across at me. 'I will reward you, of course, for bringing him to me. I shall take him to Nelly's house: she will love him dearly, and I will visit often. He will have a capital time there.'

'I want no reward,' I say hoarsely. Alys has asked nothing for herself, not even to be ransomed. She has given up her son for ever. I curse myself for not slitting open the damned scroll and stitching in the addition myself. Well, too late for that. 'And what is to be done about his mother, sire? She is held captive through no fault of her own, taken by corsairs from a ship bound for England.'

I watch his face cloud over. 'Well, now, that is rather a different matter: the lady now belongs to the sultan and by all accounts he is a very contrary man. As it is, I gather the Tangier discussions are not going well.'

I have to bite my tongue. The Tangier discussions have not been progressing not only because of the king's ministers' own intransigence and because Ismail has clearly instructed ben Hadou to be evasive, but also, I now realize, because our esteemed ambassador has taken up with the maid (no longer), Kate, and is spinning out our time here for his own pleasure. 'But, sire, if the request were to come from you direct, from one monarch to another, perhaps a ransom could be arranged?'

The king holds up a hand. 'My dear chap, the kingdom is almost bankrupt as it is, and ransoms are an expensive business. If we cannot come to terms even on the matter of a ransom for the poor fellows taken at Tangier, I cannot see much hope of arranging the release of so expensive a person as the sultan's wife.'

'But Alys is your own daughter!' The idea of it still seems impossible to me.

'If I were to go around interfering in the marriages of all my offspring, my life would be difficult indeed. And I cannot officially recognize her as my own: it would be much too complicated. Besides, I imagine the lady must have turned Turk, since she has borne the sultan a child?'

I nod unhappily. 'But under the greatest duress, sire.' Duress; and, oh Nus-Nus, persuasion.

'Well, there is no hope for it, then. I cannot intervene. But if the sultan will release her willingly, I swear I will do what I can for her. There now, that is the best I can say. But, as for you, Nus-Nus, you are always welcome to return here. I hope you know that.'

And then he makes me a kind offer, but since it is unlikely anything will ever come of this, I just thank him gravely and shortly after take painful leave of Momo, who does not appear to have grasped the enormity of what has transpired. Indeed, at such a tender age how could he? I make my slow way back to my room, my heart, which mere hours ago had been as hot and light as pure alchemical gold, returned abruptly to dead, cold lead.

37

The Tangier treaty is eventually signed at the end of March, neither side having much satisfaction in the terms. But still ben Hadou delays our return to Morocco, first on the pretext of investigating the disappearance of the renegade Hamza, whose death is eventually put down, due to lack of any evidence, to random cut-throats; then there is the order for the cannon Ismail charged him with bringing back, a commission that will take at least two months. In the midst of all this, he interests himself in the matter of aiding Samir Rafik in tracking down the printer of the English translation of the Qur'an, in order to carry out the sultan's fatwa on the man. This, to his great annoyance, proves to be easily resolved: the corpse of Alexander Ross has been rotting away these past twenty-eight years in a churchyard in Hampshire, but even so Rafik is dispatched to disinter the body: the sultan has demanded the man's head, and his head he shall have. This nonsensical quest buys yet more time in which the Tinker may dally with his pretty kitchen-maid. And so we continue to accept invitations from the great and good of London, to travel beyond the capital: to the Oxford colleges, where we are much fêted and presented with a number of valuable books in Arabic to take back to Morocco; to the university at Cambridge; to the king's residence at Windsor; and to the races at Newmarket. We are in London for the anniversary of the coronation and for the king's birthday celebrations at the end of May. And to ben Hadou's great delight, he has his portrait painted not once but twice; is elected an honorary member of the Royal Society, and at last presented with a replacement magnifying glass. Mr Ashmole takes the Moorish spurs to install in his new museum in Oxford.

At least the delay enables me to visit Momo often at Eleanor Gwynne's house on Pall Mall and see him settled there. He has a little dog of his own – a spaniel puppy from one of the royal litters – and he and Nelly have formed a happy bond. It has been decided, for Momo's safety, and that of his mother, that his identity is to be obscured. He has been presented as a by-blow of Nelly's own dead son, and no one appears any the wiser. I have to admit that the sight of him has become bittersweet: a painful reminder that Alys remains a lonely prisoner in the Meknes palace. Every time I see the lad he seems to have grown up a little more, to have become a little more English, a little more like his mother and less like his father, though he retains his father's magpie eye. (I warn Nelly to keep an eye on her jewels, but she just laughs: 'Ah, bless him: let him have his fun. I'm a better pickpocket than Charlie will ever be: I just steal 'em back again when he's not looking.')

My heart yearns for Morocco – for Alys – even though it means returning to my servitude.

At last, in July, and laden with gifts for Ismail – including a fine French coach and six horses, twelve hundred barrels of the best gunpowder and two thousand muskets – we take ship from Deal.

We return to a country in triumph: the Spanish have at last been driven from their foothold, the port of Mamora. Kaid Omar is much praised, for it was by his wiles that the enemy were finally removed. Having overrun a small garrison post on the outskirts of the Spanish colony, he granted unexpected mercy to the defeated men, who went straightway to the Governor of Mamora to report that a huge Moroccan force was on its way to storm the town, but led by a man of utmost chivalry, and it would be best to surrender, their own safe passage bearing testament to Kaid Omar's benevolence. After much deliberation, the Spanish governor decided it was probably the wisest course and sued for peace, negotiating freedom for himself and half a dozen of the highest-ranking families. Of course, the citizenry were all taken captive, and even now are probably festering in the matamores of Salé and Meknes, awaiting their unlikely redemption. Always it is the small folk who suffer in war.

As a result of this glorious victory, Ismail is rather less intent on discussing the terms of the treaty we have agreed with the English concerning Tangier, and we find ourselves able to undertake the journey from Salé at a more leisurely pace than expected, even allowing for a brief stop in the city of Fez, for ben Hadou to settle some outstanding business affairs. There, he settles the alchemist, Mr Draycott, into one of his many houses, while we continue on to Meknes. I want to make sure Nathaniel will be well received by the empress before introducing him to her. As I have explained to him, there are immense rewards to be won in her service; but there are also immense dangers. He did not seem overly disconcerted by this dichotomy, being too delighted by the concept of becoming Morocco's Alchemist Royal; but then he has yet to meet Zidana. The kaïd, in the meantime, seems most delighted to have a man of science dependent on his generosity; it enhances his sense of his standing in the world. It is curious to note, however, that he has not brought his new wife, Kate, back to Morocco with him, perhaps treading as carefully with the sultan as I must tread with Zidana; but he has installed new servants at the house in Fez where Mr Draycott currently resides, and there is a great deal of coming and going from the haberdasher's and the furniture-makers, which suggests to me he means to send for her as soon as he feels the time to be right. Seeing all this nesting makes my heart burn for Alys. I am so close to her here in Fez, and yet so far away I might as well still be in England. Having stoically borne these past months of delay to our return, since there was nothing I could do to influence the decision, I am now reduced to a furious impatience in which I can find satisfaction in nothing, and my days in the world's greatest city drag by in a cloud of barely suppressed loathing for everything and everyone.

We enter Meknes a week later, and find the palace and grounds in their usual disarray; indeed we get lost on our way to the imperial quarters, since a number of pavilions and courtyards have been demolished and rebuilt elsewhere to make way for a new set of barracks. After sending word of our return, we receive the message that the sultan will see us later, but is currently drilling the troops. Ben Hadou raises an eyebrow. 'So, Nus-Nus, it seems we will have a few hours' grace before we make our report.' He looks me in the eye. 'You have been an excellent deputy during this embassy: I shall be sure to make that clear to the emperor.' He holds my regard for a long moment, and in his expression I read a certain nervousness.

'Be assured I shall speak of nothing that might reflect badly on our visit.'

He grins and claps me on the back, then walks quickly away. And at last I am free to visit the harem, on the pretext of an appointment with Zidana, to present to her a flask of the precious elixir she ordered from England. The harem quarters alone seem entirely unchanged, as if hardly a day has passed since I was last here, and I am assailed by a sudden terror that I will round a corner and find Alys in her courtyard, with Momo playing at her feet. But, though I scrutinize every pavilion and garden I pass, there is no sign of her, and after a while a cold dread begins to seize me.

I do find Zidana, however. She looks me up and down. 'London agrees with you, Nus-Nus. I have never seen you looking so well.'

I cannot say the same for the empress. These seven months have not been kind to her: there are shadows beneath her eyes, the whites of which are yellowed and bloodshot, and she moves more slowly than she used to, the skull-headed staff appearing more of a necessity now than an adornment. She takes the flask of Primum Ens Melissae and sniffs it suspiciously. 'All I can smell is lemon balm and alcohol,' she accuses.

'The alchemist who perfected the recipe makes considerable claims for its efficacy.' I proceed to reiterate all that Nathaniel and Elias have told me of the stuff.

'Makarim!' The maid slinks into view a moment later, looking curiously between me and her mistress. 'Take some of this,' Zidana orders the girl, holding out the flask. Makarim goes pale. As well she might, knowing the sort of medicines that the empress usually dispenses. Her hand is shaking as she pours a measure of the golden fluid, and, though she hesitates, at last gulps it down, no doubt reasoning that the mere possibility of poisoning is a better prospect than having her head caved in by the staff. Zidana watches her swallow, her black eyes reduced to slits in the folds of her face. Of course, nothing happens, immediately or outwardly.

'Did you take me for such a fool I would accept the first charlatan's potion you chanced upon? I should have your head for this, eunuch! And perhaps I shall. Now give me back the gold and jewels I vouchsafed to you as payment for my elixir and I will let you live. At least for another day.'

Ah. After an awkward pause, I promise I will return them to her the next day, though of course they are long spent.

'Now!' she screeches.

'I am afraid our baggage has yet to be unpacked from the mule-train,' I hazard, trying desperately to buy some time.

She whacks me with the staff, but luckily there is little strength behind the blow. 'Do you think I am as much of an idiot as you? Who would leave gold and jewels behind in the mule-train? Go and fetch them at once! Makarim will go with you. If you are not back here by noon, I shall send the guards for you.'

We are both subdued, Makarim and I, as we leave by the iron gate and walk along palace corridors. I wonder briefly whether ben Hadou might lend me the money to pay Zidana; then decide that he probably would not. Who, then? My mind is a perfect blank. At last the silence is broken by Makarim, who asks, her face full of dread, 'What is in the potion? Will I die?'

'I expect so,' I say gravely.

She stops and stares at me, round-eyed. 'It was poison?'

I almost laugh aloud at her terror. Let her think just that, I think, remembering her malicious plotting, the hurt she did Alys. I say nothing.

Makarim hugs herself and shivers. 'There has been so much death already these past months.' Her face twists and tears fill her eyes. 'Oh, I don't want to die . . .'

'So much death?' A cold hand grips deep inside my chest. 'What do you mean?'

'The bloody flux: it has carried off so many.'

'Alys?' My voice is so hoarse I can hardly get the word out.

She gives me a slit-eyed look, then nods. 'Oh yes, she was one of the first.'

I go hot then cold and start to shake as if gripped by a fever. The blood beats so loudly in my ears I do not catch the rest of her sentence, but stagger back against the wall and slide down it, till I find myself sitting on the ground.

Makarim watches me curiously. 'Are you unwell, Nus-Nus?' A small smile flickers across her lips: despite the possibility that death has spread his wings over her, she is enjoying this.

I have no words, just look at her dumbly, frozen to the spot despite the intense heat of the day. It seems there is nothing to be said; nothing to be done. Zidana will take my head, and it will not matter one whit. I have played my part. I have got Momo away to a new life, out of the perilous toils of this place. I bow my head.

You would think that nothing could impinge upon my hopelessness, but I cannot help but notice a trail of ants winding their way across the corridor, from a crack between the intricate zellij tiles on towards the distant courtyard, each bearing a grain of rice or a crumb of bread. I watch them marching on, tiny creatures carrying on their little lives despite being dwarfed by the monumental architecture of a mad sultan's dream. I watch them in a sort of trance, from which I am abruptly interrupted.

'Nus-Nus: you have to come with me!'

It is Abid, the sultan's body-slave.

'I have been looking everywhere for you,' he puffs, out of breath.

'He cannot go anywhere,' Makarim pronounces, glaring at the boy. 'He is on the business of the empress.'

Abid glares back. 'Moulay Ismail demands his presence at once in the assembly rooms.'

And that is that: even Zidana dare not gainsay the emperor. Makarim pulls at my sleeve as I drag myself to my feet. 'Was it poison? Tell me truly.'

I stare at her dumbly. Then I shake my head. 'Quite the opposite.'

'I will live?'

'I am sure you will outlive us all.'

Restored, she at once recalls her task. 'Quickly, then, give me the money now and I will take it back to Zidana and save both our skins.'

I stare at her as if she is mouthing gibberish. 'I have no money. No jewels. I have nothing. If she must have my head as payment, then so be it. What do I care? You can go back and tell your mistress that.' Then I follow Abid down the corridor to my cabinet to collect my notes, and then on towards the assembly rooms.

A great group of ministers and qadis has been convened, including a new vizier: a spare, pockmarked man with an obsequious manner, he wears a plain robe and no jewels, and appears to be Abdelaziz's opposite in every visible fashion. The sultan is seated in state, two servants wafting cool air over him with huge ostrich-feather fans. If he recognizes me when I rise from my prostration, he makes no sign of it: his eyes slide across me without interest. At his feet sits Aziz, reed pen poised over the paper on his lap-desk to take note of the proceedings. Ben Hadou enters a moment later and, having given my notes a cursory glance, launches into a very full account of our time in London. The first business of the day is of course the treaty; but Ismail waves an irritated hand at the ambassador as he begins to outline the terms agreed. 'Circumstances have changed since you left to negotiate this matter, in case you had not heard. We have expelled the infidel from Mamora, so now we have another port at our command. The Spanish left behind some excellent cannon, so with those and the English guns you have brought back, as well as the excellent muskets and powder the English king has gifted us, I think we are in a somewhat stronger position to renegotiate terms. I shall insist King Charles sends me another ambassador.' And he rubs his hands in some glee at the prospect.

The dismay on ben Hadou's face would have been comical, had I the heart to find it so. Instead I watch without interest as he bows his head and rolls up my copious notes into a tight scroll, his movements suggesting he would like to tear them into pieces and throw them in his sovereign's face. But he is much too careful a man for such a gesture, the Tinker. When he raises his head again his expression is bland. He answers the sultan's questions about court life – about the king, his palace and estates – concisely, always careful to play down their magnificence. White Hall, he tells Ismail, is a labyrinth of passageways full of moth-eaten wall-hangings, spiders and their webs, linking great empty chambers in which Charles's meagre courtiers rattle around like seeds in a gourd. 'Parts of the palace date back many centuries and newer sections have been added on over the years in an arbitrary fashion. It lacks the grandeur and epic proportions of your own great achievement here, your sublime majesty.'

Ismail is gratified to hear this: he leans forward. 'And what of his wives?'

'Under Christian law, sire, he may take only one, and Queen Catherine is a mousy creature, with teeth like a buck rabbit's. Unlike a rabbit, unfortunately, she has failed to breed.'

'Then who will succeed him? He is well over fifty now: he should be wasting no time in putting the Portuguese infanta aside and getting himself an heir on another!'

As ben Hadou explains the great difficulties surrounding the English succession, my attention wanders back to the White Swan. I wonder whether she was alone when she died, whether anyone could have saved her; whether Zidana helped her on her way. I wonder when, exactly, it happened. Was it when I was availing myself of a glass of good French wine at the Duchess of Portsmouth's table? Or perhaps when I walked in the rose garden about a month ago, and dreamed of sitting there with Alys, breathing in the fragrance of the flowers in the gentle English sun? Maybe she died of a broken heart not long after I took Momo away with me.

I torture myself with these thoughts, every so often catching a phrase here or there of ben Hadou's descriptions of the English court. Now, they are discussing the women . . .

'Are they all as pale as the White Swan was?' the emperor asks with interest, and my heart clenches tight.

'For the most part they are a dull lot,' the Tinker opines, 'brown of hair and covered in paint and patches to cover their pox scars.'

This pleases the emperor mightily and he prompts his ambassador for more and more detail on the subject, especially of the king's mistresses.

'You should ask Nus-Nus about those,' a voice says nastily. 'He spent a great deal of time with the English king's whores.' My head shoots up. I turn to find Samir Rafik watching me, his lips curved into a scornful smile. 'You see how he mourns them?'

The emperor is sitting forward on his divan, regarding me with a curious expression. 'Nus-Nus, come here.'

I take a step forward, another.

'Kneel.'

I do so, and Ismail reaches out a hand and touches my face. 'You are weeping?'

I am? My hand rises to my cheek and comes away wet.

'Why do you weep?'

I find I cannot answer.

'Perhaps he weeps in shame!' Rafik says into the silence. 'He and the Kaid ben Hadou took English concubines while we were in London, and when the Kaid Sharif and I complained at their debauchery, they sent us off into the countryside on some wild goose chase that would keep us out of their way while they carried on defiling the good name of Islam, of Morocco and of your sublime majesty's embassy.' And now he takes from beneath his robe a great scroll that he unrolls and proceeds to read, a long list of precise notes detailing every instance in which any member of the embassy has strayed from the straight path, and much invention besides, reserving always the worst lapses for his enemies: myself and ben Hadou.

Ismail's face has darkened ominously, but I find I simply do not care: and anyway most of the charges are plainly absurd. A wild peal of laughter escapes me, enraging the sultan still further. 'You laugh?' he roars; and that just makes me laugh more. I can see ben Hadou gazing at me aghast: if it is not bad enough that Samir Rafik has made his desperate gambit before we even get to the chancy matter of the long-dead printer and what little is left of his bony old head, which he knows will not satisfy our bloodthirsty sultan, now his deputy has gone quite mad. He gives me an urgent stare, as if he can will me back to rationality, but it's too late for that now.

The sultan is on his feet. 'Sharif!' he yells, and the kaid practically crawls forward. Ismail kicks him upright. 'Is it true?' he screams. 'Have these men brought shame on their religion, their country and on ME?'

Sharif looks despairingly from the Tinker to me and back again, at a loss as to what to say that will not make matters worse. I become aware of the assembled ministers' rapt attention: they are like hyenas, waiting nervously for the lions to finish their business before nipping in for the scraps. Because as long as it's someone else's blood that is spilled, that means they're safe — for the time being.

Ismail thrusts his face into Sharif's. 'Did they cut out your tongue in London?'

'N-no, sublime majesty,' he stutters.

'Well, answer the question, then. Did these men consort with women and betray the faith I placed in them?'

'S-sire, your s-servant Nus-Nus is . . . is . . . a eunuch.'

Ismail regards him as if he is a cockroach. One that he is about to stamp on. Then he begins to wrestle his dagger out of its sheath, and the thing gets caught in his sash, which sends him into apoplexy. 'I will kill you all, every one of you!' He gets the blade free at last, puts it to Sharif's scrawny throat. 'Now tell me the truth!' Spittle flies, showering the kaid's upturned face.

'I . . . ah . . . did see Nus-Nus drink a g-glass of wine,' he manages to get out, rolling his eyes like an Eid sheep. 'And . . . ah . . .' He tries to recall some other peccadillo against the precepts of Islam, something incriminatory but not too serious. 'And . . . ah, the Kaid Mohammed b-ben Hadou . . . ah . . . had his p-portrait p-painted.'

'Twice,' Rafik adds spitefully.

'Twice,' Sharif concurs.

'Son of a dog!' He pushes the kaid aside and launches himself at ben Hadou, who puts up his hands to ward off the sultan's frenzy. 'The word of Allah forbids the making of images! You shall die for bringing this shame down upon me, the Champion of Islam, the Defender of the Faith!' He stabs the Tinker in the leg, and ben Hadou falls to the floor with a shriek. For a moment there is a lull, as if Ismail's sudden bloodlust may have been satisfied, then he shouts for his guards. 'Take them all to the lion enclosure!'

I had thought I did not care whether I lived or died. But when you are trapped in a pit with seven hungry lions circling and the prospect of being torn apart and eaten alive, it is rather a different matter.

'Keep together!' ben Hadou tells us. I have bound my turban around his thigh, but he is already weak from blood loss. 'If we get separated it will make it easy for them to take us one by one. Throw sand at them, rocks, pebbles – anything you can find.'

'Throw *him* at the lions!' Samir Rafik cries, gesturing at Sharif, who is clearly going to be of no use in repulsing giant predators, the sight of them having rendered him immobile, huge-eyed and practically dead of terror. 'That'll keep them busy for a while.'

For a heartbeat it seems as if the Tinker is actually considering this cruel option; then I realize his wound is slowing his thoughts almost to a standstill.

'Wave your arms at them and yell,' I suggest, remembering what we were told as children, growing up in a region in which lions hunted prey; but that was a tactic designed to scare off a lone animal, not seven starving beasts. Still, this keeps the lions at bay for a few frantic minutes, but before too long they decide the noise poses no threat to them and begin to circle in again.

The lions of Barbary are reputed to be the heaviest and most powerful of all lions, and certainly these are monstrous-looking beasts. One might even call them handsome or even noble in different circumstances, with their massy bulk and vast black manes, their wide faces and intelligent amber eyes. It's just that for now, maddened by the smell of the kaid's blood, and no doubt deprived of food for several days, all that crafty intelligence is bent on weighing up how to worry large chunks of flesh out of us with their truly massive teeth.

It is the females who take the lead: huge tawny creatures, smooth of coat and sharp of eye. They are smaller than the two males, but what they lack in bulk and mane they more than make up for in ferocity and guile. Two feint an attack, dodging in and back out of reach, distracting us while another prowls silently behind us and, correctly assessing the victim least likely to do damage, snatches Sharif by the arm. The poor kaid howls in agony and digs his heels into the sand: but the lioness is by far the stronger. With a wrench of her great head, she drags him away, and there is nothing the rest of us can do to save him. The noise is horrible – the tearing and crunching; the screams . . .

Now the male lions move in and try to muscle the female out of the way, and a moment later a vicious fight breaks out. The roars of the great beasts reverberate in my breastbone as I stare about me, weighing our few options. At the edge of the enclosure is a wide ditch, full of water – too wide for the lions to leap across – and after this a tall iron fence. After discovering the ability of lions to dig after the incident in the slave matamores, and some other less successful methods, it has been determined that this is the best way to keep the beasts from getting out and ravaging the palace population, though it mars the spectators' view of proceedings. Usually, it is just some poor, anonymous slave who gets thrown to the lions; that it should be four prominent members of the returning English embassy means that the event has drawn quite a crowd. They are all crammed up against the fence – people I have known for years: palace functionaries, guards, stablemen, potboys and slaves; lords, merchants; as well, of course, as the blessed sultan himself and even the Empress Zidana and her sons – waiting for us to die. Watching poor Sharif being torn limb from limb with expressions of rapt avidity that make me feel quite sick.

'Quickly, make for the ditch!' I say to ben Hadou, calculating that our chances against lions on solid ground are likely to be significantly smaller than they may be in the chancy waters of the moat.

Desperation lends him strength: together we race across the pit, the Tinker's arm draped across my shoulders for support. We make it to the ditch before the lions give up their tussle over what is left of the kaid, and Rafik and I both thrash our way across the ditch to the fence. With my hand wrapped around an iron post, I hazard a look back, to see ben Hadou splashing and yelling wildly at a determined lioness, who has also braved the water. 'I cannot swim!' he cries.

Rafik sneers. 'Bad luck for you.' Then he shins his way up the iron railings and levers himself over the spikes at the top, falling to the other side scraped and bloody, but intact.

For a long moment I hesitate. I could save myself as easily as Samir Rafik has done; but seeing Kaid Sharif ripped apart by the lions has imprinted itself horribly in my memory, and I hardly knew the man; with the Tinker I have shared a great deal more, though I have not always liked him. How could I live with myself if I left him to perish in the jaws of the lioness? Besides, only an hour ago, I was wishing death would take me. Now, strangely, it comes to me that I would prefer to live, even without the White Swan in the world. Drawing deep, I summon up Senufo spirit; my mask, the kponyungu.

I failed to complete my initiation into the Poro, the secret male society that teaches the young men of the Senufo wisdom, strength and responsibility, for I was taken by the slavers in the year in which I began to learn our rituals. But I had made the kponyungu dance, and I knew its power. In our culture the purpose of the mask is for the battling of evil, whether of this world or the next; natural or supernatural. Sometimes a mask is a passive shield, a smooth carapace to turn aside evil; but it can be an expression of utmost aggression. I conjure into my mind the powerful jaws of the crocodile, the teeth of the hyena, against which nothing can resist; I add the tusks of a warthog and the horns of the musk-ox; and between them I set the chameleon, the creature of change. As an afterthought I imagine a troop of ants marching up and over the mask with the determination of the unstoppable. With a snarl, I plunge back into the water, and unleash all the anger and fury and grief I have ever felt through the mask. This is no longer my second face; it is my own. And I am no longer Nus-Nus, half-and-half, eunuch, slave; my name is Akuji. And I am Dead, Yet Awake.

The lioness stares at me uncertainly. Then she wrinkles her muzzle, showing the full extent of her vast incisors: but it is a gesture more of fear than of hostility. After a few seconds charged with violent potential she wheels away, throwing up a great wash of water, and lumbers back on to solid ground to join the others in their feast.

Ben Hadou stares at me, wordless. I cannot imagine what he sees, and for once I no longer care. I do not think, I simply act, and there is such purity in the simplicity of the deed that it sears through me, a bolt of elation and power, as if I am channelling every ancestor I have ever had. I grab a handful of his robe and haul the Tinker unceremoniously behind me, out of the water and up to the iron fence. Then, suddenly, there are guards swarming over the fence – four, five of them, armed with spears and swords. So this is it, I think: if the lions do not kill us, the bukhari are here to make sure we do not escape our punishment, to prod us back into the pit. But they pick up ben Hadou and carry him out of the pit; and then they come back for me.

They treat us as carefully, as if we are valued guests of the sultan who have by some terrible misfortune managed to tumble amongst lions.

38

Rajab, 1092 AH

Samir Rafik's freedom did not last long. The sultan, ever contrary, took against him for his selfish escape from the lion-pit and sent him to be tortured. Under Faroukh's ministrations he admitted that the charges against the Kaid Mohammed ben Hadou and against me, as his deputy, were false.

Although of course the Tinker did have his portrait painted in London. Twice.

And took a palace servant to wife.

And I had indeed tasted both wine and ale during our stay in England.

And, of course, most heinous of all, I stole the sultan's son away and gave him up to the English king. But without any evidence, it seems that Rafik decided against mentioning this last and greatest offence.

But there was no whoring or drunken revelry, as he testified after our arrest, and other members of the embassy, seeing the lie of the land, now decide to throw in their lot with ben Hadou, rather than with the man on the rack.

By the time Faroukh carried out his most exquisite procedures, the grand vizier's nephew would have sworn to anything, and indeed does. I hear that he has admitted to all manner of bizarre crimes, including the murder of the herbman, Sidi Kabour, which he claimed was part of Abdelaziz's plot to oust Zidana and her poisonous offspring, itself partly inspired by his uncle's desire to imprison me in his house as his catamite. But since none of this has anything to do with the sultan's orders regarding information relating to the London embassy, it is dismissed as empty babbling, and the man who tells me of it apologizes profusely for repeating such defamatory nonsense.

Rafik expires not long after.

Ben Hadou is reinstated as Ismail's first minister. I am granted my freedom. (When I remove at last the silver slave-bond from my ear, my head feels oddly light, lopsided. I throw the bond into the moat: it seems a fitting resting place for it.) I think in the moment in which the kponyungu took me, the sultan saw something in me that made him decide he did not wish to have me as his scribe, or his Keeper of the Couching Book, or even as his Servant of the Slippers any longer. He appoints me a high officer of the bukhari instead, and sends me to Fez.

It is there, four months later, that I receive a message from the Empress Zidana. The courier shifts from one foot to the other, awaiting my response. He has dust all over his clothes; he has not even had time to wash.

'Tell your mistress that I shall come to her in three days,' I say. The delay does not please him, but now that I am a free man Zidana does not exercise the same power over me she once did. I watch him go with misgiving: if I never see Meknes again it will be too soon. Even the thought of the harem fills me with a furious, burning anger at the waste of Alys's dear life, and I have no wish to see the woman who wished her ill for so long, and may well have hastened her on her way. But I have made a promise to a friend, and that promise must be honoured.

And so the next day I go to visit the alchemist, Nathaniel Draycott. I find him in the garden room bordering on the courtyard of ben Hadou's house, distilling some sort of viscous orange liquid. When I greet him, he beams at me through his thick spectacles, taking in my unaccustomed uniform and no doubt changed demeanour. 'My dear Nus-Nus –'

'Please, call me Akuji. I have dispensed with my former name.'

He blinks at that. 'Akuji,' he says slowly, then repeats it to himself. 'Most unusual. I must remember to tell Elias when next I write. Here, try some of this.' He offers me a spoonful of the liquid. 'It's an oil pressed from the fruit of ancient trees that are native only to the south-west of this realm, or so they tell me.'

The oil is slick on my tongue and tastes sweet and slightly nutty. As I savour it, the call to prayer sounds from the Qarawiyyin Mosque and trembles across the whole walled city, to be followed moments later by the muezzins of a hundred others. It is an unearthly sound: even after several months here, I have not got used to hearing it. Is it this that lends such an extraordinary sensation to my swallow of the oil?

Nathaniel smiles, and when the final notes have died away he says, 'The common folk called this substance "argan", or perhaps that's the tree. My Arabic is improving all the time, but I believe it's a Berber word. The peasants collect the undigested kernels once their goats have eaten the fruit and subject them to a complex and extremely time-consuming process of roasting and pressing. Then they use the oil thus produced sparingly in their cooking, and it is indeed delicious; but I have reason to believe that once further distilled and refined it may have near-magical properties – for the complexion and the digestion, and also to combat ageing – it may perhaps prove to be even more miraculous than the Primum Ens Melissae.'

'It's about the elixir that I've come.' And I relay to him Zidana's message.

For a moment he looks disappointed. But he brightens when I assure him he may return to his refining process within the week. He goes to change – into a red turban and a long black gown. With this costume and the beard he has grown these past weeks, he could pass easily for a scholar, a taleb at the Qarawiyyin.

I take his bag and sling it over my shoulder, and together we wind our way through the dusty, narrow streets of the medina down towards the river and the funduqs, where horses await us. We have just crossed the bridge beneath the university's walls when a hand reaches up and tugs at my burnous. I look down.

A dreadfully deformed wretch of a beggar is sitting there on the ground, his pitiful collection of alms laid on a square of coarse cloth beside him. Leprosy, or some other ravaging disease, has eaten away his extremities – his nose and lips, and most of his fingers and toes. It has also taken one of his eyes, and left vicious furrows in whatever other skin is visible. I cannot recall ever seeing a more hideous sight. '*Salaam aleikum*,' I say softly, and dig reflexively in my money-pouch for a few coins for the poor soul, but he pulls yet more insistently at my cloak.

'Nss-Nss . . .'

'He appears to know you,' Nathaniel says, gazing at the beggar some-what appalled. Even London offers nothing as viscerally repulsive as this poor creature.

Recognition comes over me as slowly as sunrise in winter. It is the grand vizier. Or, rather, it is what is left of him after being dragged for miles across stony waste land, tied to the strongest mule in the sultan's stables.

'By Maleeo . . . Abdelaziz.'

The remnant of the man who had me gelded gives a ghastly smile: teeth gone, tongue a stump, and tries to haul himself to the ruins of his feet, before subsiding, defeated.

I should enjoy a moment of bitter triumph at the sight of my enemy thus reduced, but all I feel is pity. From the bag over my shoulder I take one of the smaller flasks of Nathaniel's elixir, and cast it into the beggar's lap. 'You deserve everything that has happened to you,' I tell him grimly. 'But I know what it is like to be mutilated.' I leave him staring in bemusement at the golden liquid, no doubt thinking it a cruel trick. He'll probably just throw it away. Well, if he does, it's his choice.

Zidana and I eye one another warily through the clouds of incense rising from her burning brazier. It is fiendishly hot in the room, even without the fire.

'You've changed,' she says.

'So have you.' It is true: she looks greatly different to the last time I saw her: no less vast, indeed perhaps more so, but somehow rather than giving the impression of being consumed by her bulk, she now appears abundant, full of life. Ironically, it transpires, that is exactly what she is. Full of life. Despite her age, for she must be nearing fifty. Doctor Friedrich tells her he believes she is pregnant with twins, which is regarded as the greatest of good luck in this country. When she gleefully announces this, I feel like sighing: more monsters to be brought into the world. But I congratulate her nevertheless.

She walks around me. 'No slave-bond?'

'No.'

'Nor slave-name either?'

'People call me Akuji now.'

'Dead, Yet Awake.' She grins. 'Not very Islamic.'

I shrug. 'It's my name.'

'So, have you brought me the alchemist?'

'He is here in Meknes.'

'You are a good boy to have found him for me. His elixir is wondrous. Though unfortunately I had to get rid of Makarim: after she drank the stuff Zidan became infatuated with her, a situation that was absolutely unacceptable, given that she was my maid.' Her eyes gleam. 'We are going to do great things, he and I.'

I had heard Makarim's body was found with strangle-marks on the neck, but of course no one is likely to accuse Zidana. 'He will work for you only on two conditions. First, that he will not live in the palace, but will maintain a house of his own in Fez; and second that you will not use his work to harm others.'

I expect her to explode in fury, but she just pouts, the gesture of an unnervingly younger woman. 'Now, where's the fun in that?'

'Did you kill the White Swan?' I had not meant to ask so baldly, but suddenly I have to know.

She looks at me strangely. 'The mad Englishwoman? Are you confused in your head, Nus-Nus-No-More? The White Swan is not dead, she is just mad, and put away.'

'But Makarim told me . . .'

I force myself back to that terrible moment in the colonnaded walkway, with the sunlight slanting between the pillars and the long train of ants heading for the courtyard.

What exactly had Makarim told me? There had been a long list of victims of 'the bloody flux' and that Alys had been 'one of the first'. She had not actually said she was dead, but, expecting the worst, I had heard the worst. Dead, Yet Awake? More like Alive, But an Idiot. I am too stupid to live.

'She is in the Little Palace, on the edge of the city. After the little boy was so cruelly taken from her, she went quite mad, poor thing, and Ismail couldn't stand to have her around any more, so he sent her there.' Zidana

speaks as if she had no part in Momo's 'death': perhaps by now she had persuaded herself of it.

I feel a rough, wild joy swelling inside me, a seed of unbearable hope, and
have to turn away before Zidana can see it; but her black eyes are fixed on
me, unblinking.

'I saw you amid the lions,' she says almost admiringly. 'I saw the warrior
within.' When she smiles, you catch a glimpse of the Lobi girl she once was,
such a very long time ago.

But the illusion is soon dispelled. She crosses the room to a carved
wooden box and brings it back to the brazier. From it she takes a fat little
fetish doll twinkling with jewels and another, tiny, with blue beads for
eyes: both go on the brazier, where they sizzle and smoke. 'Both dead,'
she declares with satisfaction. She holds up the third, all white with a floss
of blonde hair. 'As good as,' she says carelessly, and on to the brazier that
goes too. At last she draws out the figure of black clay, its white eyes
bulging, as no doubt my own are right now, remembering the hellish
trapdoor in its chest and what I had seen in there. 'Shall we see if they've
regrown?' she asks mockingly, twitching the hem of its robe. She sees the
look on my face and bursts out laughing. 'Ah, poor Akuji: still as easy to
tease as the slave who was Nus-Nus.' Then this figure too she casts on to
the fire.

The Little Palace is a tranquil place surrounded by a garden full of citrus
and olive trees, with bougainvillea tumbling over its walls. Cats lounge in
the shadows, slit-eyed, at ease. All the way there, walking fast, I keep thinking, perhaps she played her part too well. Perhaps she really has gone mad.
But then the wild joy rises up again to swallow these black thoughts. After
all that we have been through, I cannot believe that what is written in Fate's
Book could be so cruel.

It is Mamass who opens the door to me, in a plain cotton robe and hijab,
looking very grown up: she stares at me blankly, confused by the uniform.
When I grin at her, she shrieks with delight and hugs me like a child, then
remembers herself and solemnly asks after my health and well-being.

The shriek has attracted attention: there is a movement in the shadowed

corridor behind her, and suddenly a voice says, 'You look so different . . .
and yet, and yet . . . it is you!'

Mamass bobs her head and slips away grinning, leaving Alys and me to
stand face to face for a long, charged moment, gazing each at the other as if
we would eat one another. When I take her in my arms I can feel how thin
she is, fragile as a bird. But I can also feel the strength in her: an extraordinary, steely strength.

'Momo is safe, and well, and waiting for you,' I say at last, into her hair.

She lifts her face. It is wet with tears. Nus-Nus would have hesitated, but
Akuji's hand rises and touches her cheek, gently wipes them away. She lays
her hand over mine and presses it to her mouth. Her lips are hot on my
palm: I can feel her breath on my skin. 'I thought you were never coming
back,' she says, and I remember the last time she said those words to me, and
all that has changed in that time.

'Come to London with me,' I say, and then I cover her mouth with my
own and we do not speak for a long time.

Epilogue

A week later Alys and I take ship on one of Daniel al-Ribati's merchant vessels, slipping swiftly and anonymously away with a very few possessions, with letters from Mr Draycott to the Royal Society, and with a number of flasks containing his mysterious elixirs. Ben Hadou, cognizant that I had saved his life, gives me a good sum of money, in return for which I undertake to ensure that his new wife, Kate, is safely dispatched to him on the ship's return voyage, along with a list of items as long as my arm for the house in Fez, to be ordered from the London markets.

What life will be like for us in London it is hard to imagine. England is not like Morocco, where black men take white women to wife on the sultan's orders and no one thinks twice about it. Perhaps we shall have to marry in secret and live outwardly as mistress and servant, like the Duchess Mazarin and Addo, a King of the Road under the adopted guise of the slave Mustapha. But we shall have Momo, and Momo has been the key to all of this. And just as well, since it is highly doubtful that we shall make children together. We make an unlikely family, but neither Alys nor I care greatly about the approbation of the world: we have survived worse than hard words and hard looks, and whatever future we can forge together will surely be better than the pasts we have suffered.

Besides, the king made me two promises before I left: that he would do his best for Alys if ever the sultan were to release her from his harem; and that if I were to return and would wish it, I should have the position of a royal musician at White Hall, and I hope that, given these circumstances and our own fortitude and determination, we shall prevail against the odds.

Is it so much to ask that men and women be no longer slaves and are free to make their lives together?

We can but hope: after all, other miracles have been known to occur.

Historical Note

Moulay Ismail was the Sultan of Morocco from 1672 to 1727: a remarkably long time to rule over his 'basketful of rats'. One clue to his success lies in the name by which he was often known: 'Safaq Adimaa', or 'The Blood-thirsty'. Another can be derived from his policy of exerting authority via display, by generating awe in the populace through the pomp and grandeur that surrounded him. In this, as in the extent and application of his power, he was the last sultan who can genuinely be said to have been on a par with his European counterparts.

In his fifty-five years as absolute monarch he humbled the wild mountain tribes of the Rif and Atlas, recaptured the coastal towns of Tangier and Mamora, Asilah and Larache from foreign powers, maintained Moroccan sovereignty by defending it against the Ottoman Turks; rebuilt mosques, shrines, bridges, kasbahs and of course the extraordinary palace complex at Meknes, the remains of which are now a UNESCO World Heritage Site.

In 1703 a visiting ambassador asked one of Ismail's sons how many brothers and sisters he had. After three days he was presented with a list of 525 boys and 342 girls. In 1721 he was reputed to have '700 Sons able to mount Horse'. (The last of Ismail's sons is said to have been born to him eighteen months after the sultan's death, which is quite a feat.) His wives and harem members are even harder to keep track of, since even in official records most are noted by a single Arabic name, often bestowed upon them only on their conversion to Islam, whether by choice or duress. Amongst them all there is only one constant: Lalla Zidana, bought as a slave from the sultan's brother for the sum of sixty ducats. By all accounts in her later years she was a huge and monstrous presence, vastly fat, strangely dressed and dreaded by all as 'the witch Zidana'. Despite this – or maybe because of it – she maintained a thirty-year ascendancy over Ismail's affections and exercised absolute power over his harem. Her eldest son, Zidan, was proclaimed as

Ismail's heir, despite not being his first son. However, he was disinherited by his father in 1700 in favour of Zidana's equally worthless second son, Ahmed al-Dhahebi, 'the Golden'.

After Ismail's death in 1727 there was an almighty succession battle amongst his surviving sons, and in a very short time the unified kingdom of Morocco fell apart in a stew of civil war and moral dissipation.

Meknes has been called a second Versailles. Moulay Ismail and Louis XIV shared a fervour for building as well as for power, and both were passionately involved in the construction of their respective palaces. Versailles may not have been built with slave-labour, but Louis was heedless of the lives and safety of his workmen. In the bitter winter of 1685 there were almost forty thousand men working on the site, despite the terrible cold and the ravages of disease, and many of them died. Of course, the fate of the thousands of slaves at Meknes was even more terrible. But where Versailles was symmetrical, ordered, elegant, the palace complex at Meknes, with its fifty connected palaces, mosques, courtyards, barracks and parks, was vast and rambling in its ever-shifting design, as walls and pavilions were constructed, then demolished, at the arbitrary whim of its creator.

His successors continued with his building programme, but in 1755 the shocks of the huge Lisbon earthquake, which is believed to have reached a magnitude of 9.0 on the Richter scale, severely damaged the site, reducing to rubble in minutes what had taken many decades and thousands of lives to create. Of Ismail's madly ambitious project, only his extraordinary mausoleum, parts of the Dar Kbira, the vast granary, some of the outer walls and the city gates remain. Despite this, the ruins are well worth visiting to gain a sense of the sheer scale of the sultan's megalomania.

Charles II had no legitimate children. But records show he engendered somewhere between a dozen and fourteen illegitimate offspring, and very likely there were others who did not survive or who were not recognized. Wherever he was billeted during the long years of his exile before the Restoration in 1660, he sowed his seed: from Jersey in 1646, to The Hague in 1649, from Paris in 1650 to Bruges in 1656. Alys Swann is a fictional character; but Moulay Ismail is reputed to have had at least one and maybe two English wives with whom he was much enamoured, one of whom died (or disappeared) and another, later than my Alys, who gave birth to a son who was designated an accredited heir, also by the name of Moham-med (although it must be said that Mohammed is the preferred name of first sons in Morocco).

The Moroccan embassy of 1682 arrived in London in January under the command of Mohammed ben Hadou Ottur, sometimes known as 'the Tinker'. The almost-seven-month visit is well documented in the records of the day, and is particularly colourfully described in the diary of John Evelyn, who writes that ben Hadou was 'the fashion of the season'. The ambassador had his portrait painted twice, both by anonymous artists. One of these handsome portraits can be found in the archives of the National Portrait Gallery in London.

Nus-Nus – or Akuji, to give him his true name – is my own creation.

Glossary

abid	slave
afrit	devil
alhemdullillah	thanks be to God
bab	gate
babouches	leather slippers
baksheesh	literally 'charity', though usually cynically used to mean 'bribe'
baraka	good luck
bukhari	the Black Guard
burnous	cloak
charaf	honour; also a term of affection
chicha	hookah pipe
Dar Kbira	Great Palace
djellaba	hooded robe
djinn	spirit of smokeless fire
Eid	feast
Fassi	from Fez
fkih	sir
funduq	guest house
hajib	vizier
hammam	steam bath
haram	forbidden
harem	women's private quarters
hijab	Islamic headscarf
insh'allah	if God wills it
kaid	senior civil servant, administrator
kasbah	fortress
khanjar	ceremonial dagger

kif	marijuana
koubba	domed, four-sided building, often a shrine
lalla	madam, honorative
ma'alema	teacher
marabout	holy man
matamore	slave pit
marhaban	welcome
mechoui	spit-roasted lamb
medina	old, walled part of city
Meknassi	from Meknes
mellah	'place of salt', Jewish quarter
mezian	good
nus-nus	half-and-half
oud	Arabic lute
qadi	judge
qamis	loose leggings
qibla	direction of Mecca
rabab	Moroccan instrument
raïs	captain
ras al hanout	mixture of spices
Ribati	from Rabat
salaam aleikum	peace be upon you
shahada	profession of Islamic faith
Shaitan	Satan
sherif	descendant of the Prophet
sidi	sir, lord: honorative
smen	preserved butter
souq	market
sura	chapter of the Qur'an
tadelakt	specialist plaster
Tafraouti	from Tafraout
tajine	earthenware cooking vessel, and the casserole made in it

taleb	scholar
tarboush	a 'fez': hard red hat
zellij	mosaic tile-work
zelliji	master tiler
zumeta	rich paste of nuts and seeds

Acknowledgements

With thanks to my wonderful agents, Danny and Heather Baror, for all that they do; to Emma and Philippa for feedback and support; to Venetia and Will at Viking Penguin for their passion and care, to Donna for her exacting standards. And to Eugène Delacroix, whose 'Portrait of a Turk in a Turban', glimpsed across a Moroccan restaurant, started a lively discussion and inspired the character of Nus-Nus.

Bibliography

Aouchar, Amina, Jean-Michel Ruiz and Cécile Tréal, *Fès, Meknès* (Paris, Flammarion, 2005)

Bejjit, Karim, *Encountering the Infidels: Restoration Images of the Moors* (essay, University Hassan II, Casablanca)

Blunt, Wilfrid, *Black Sunrise* (London, Methuen, 1951)

de Beer, E. S. (ed.), *Diary of John Evelyn* (London, Everyman's Library, 2006)

Daileader, Celia, *Racism, Mysogny and the Othello Myth* (Cambridge, Cambridge University Press, 2005)

Doutté, Edmond, *Magie et religion dans l'Afrique du Nord* (Algiers, Société Musulmane du Maghrib, 1909)

Forneron, Henri, *The Court of King Charles II* (London, Swan Sonnenschein & Co., 1892)

Frasier, Antonia, *King Charles II* (London, Weidenfeld, 1979)

Harris, Tim, *Restoration* (London, Allen Lane, 2005)

Lithgow, William, *The Totall Discourse, of the Rare Adventures, and Painefull Peregrinations . . . to the Most Famous Kingdomes in Europe, Asia, and Africa . . .* (London, N. Okes, 1632)

Mafi, Maryam and Kolin, Azima Melita, *Rumi: Hidden Music* (London, Thorsons, 2001)

Matar, Nabil, *Islam in Britain* (Cambridge, Cambridge University Press, 1998)

Mernissi, Fatema, *Dreams of Trespass: Tales of a Harem Girlhood* (New York, Perseus, 1995)

Milton, Giles, *White Gold* (London, Hodder & Stoughton, 2004)

Ogg, David, *Europe in the Seventeenth Century* (London, A & C Black, 1943)

Pearson, Hesketh, *Charles II* (London, Heinemann, 1960)

Picard, Liza, *Restoration London* (London, Weidenfeld, 1997)

Tames, Richard, *City of London Past* (London, Historical Publications, 1995)

Vitkus, Daniel J. (ed.), *Piracy, Slavery, and Redemption* (New York, Columbia University Press, 2001)

Pierre Mignard's portrait of Louise de Kéroualle, Duchess of Portsmouth (painted in 1682 during the Moroccan embassy visit), is held at the National Portrait Gallery, as are the two anonymous, but very handsome, portraits of Mohammed ben Hadou. The latter two are not on general view, but arrangements can be made with the curators to see them.